SECRETS OF SILVER & STEAM

VOLUME I | THE NEW AWAKENING

RICKY HAYES

Secrets of Silver & Steam: The New Awakening by Ricky Hayes
Volume I
Published By Ricky Hayes – DBA Publisher's Brew

ISBN-13: 978-0-578-27834-6
PAPERBACK
EDITION NO. I

CREDITS:
Editor: Ricky Hayes
Cover Design: Ricky Hayes

PERMISSION REQUESTS:
Website: publishersbrew.com
Author Page & Portfolio: publishersbrew.com/rhayes

SOCIAL:
Facebook: facebook.com/publishersbrew
Instagram: instagram.com/publishersbrew/
Author's Tik Tok: @rickyhayes_author

Kingdom of Westmain
Solice
Langdon
Prag
Nium
Harvenger
Triune
Starvel
Folesk
Botel
Reave
Slavin
Resk
Kingdom of Nod
Northern
Territory
Deadlakes
Orye
Quodon
Southern
Nodtides
Territory

Kingdom of Eastguard
Kirshan Outpost
Pure Bone Clan Estate
Havensire
Ugnis Ro
Vlok
Raven Caste Estate
Poe
Drac
(Holy City of the Fallen)
Ye
Isle of Secrets

CONTENTS

PREFACE AND ACKNOWLEDGMENTS

The prestigious Council of Antiquities and Curators of Abstruse Chronicles (CACAC) holds in the highest esteem the esoteric records presented into publication for the purpose of informing, educating, and advocating the enlightenment of such historical events concerning individuals known as Master Keepers (MKRs). The documentation presented in this volume as well as others to follow, has eluded scholars and public catalogs for some time, over two hundred years to be precise. In the past, only a handful of records mentioned MKRs. Never has such extensive documentation been released surrounding what many scholars and acolytes dismissed as myth. However, the view of the council's perspective was transformed during our annual convocation in 478 RB with the presentation of the first accurate translated volume cross-referencing many other documentations of MKRs once thought of as hysterical tripe.

None thought the wiser when the volumes were received all those years ago by an unknown benefactor who passed along a hefty sum to our organization in exchange for keeping the volumes in our archives. They were never studied extensively due to the enigma language in which they were written, and never would have, had it not been for a young graduate student, Ann-Conley Delfied, who has later become one of our finest members and at the time was searching for a unique area of study to invoke her interests as well as those of her professors. Her exceeding accolades in Expiry Linguistics & Manuscript Revitalization allowed the CACAC to piece together the puzzle that has stumped scholars since the volumes came into our possession.

Delfied began translating with the assistance of one of her superiors, Prof. Holbrook Bedelstein, who by his own admission could hardly keep up with her yet was able to track her scrupulousness of the translations to be astonishingly accurate. At his request, he recruited professor and wife, Prof. Kaldeen Bedelstein, who accommodated the pace and assisted adamantly in solidifying the accuracy of Delfied's translations. All three now hold significant reputable renown in the council and continue to prove their prowess. As a result, Delfied was honored to name the volumes of her works "Secrets of Silver & Steam." She continues to translate and format the volumes for publications to the pleasure of historical advocates, scholars, and individuals interested in evidence of what remained dismissed as impossible.

Unanimously, the seven members of the Board of the CACAC Elder Council have deemed Delfied's work superb and concise with all other historical documents surrounding the subject. Upon witnessing the evidence, they swiftly signed the affidavit of proceeds to publish the works as historical facts. They sought other members of the council to comment on the results themselves.

"Delfied has academically unlocked the unbelievable, interpreting events of a forgotten era. While many other scholars may remain skeptical of her works, Secrets of Silver & Steam is an impressive achievement for historians to 'take another look' at the past" - (Neilan Foyles, Geographical Engineering & Civil Anthropology, Ph.D., and best-selling author of "Bygone Civilizations & Their Mothers").

"Secrets of Silver & Steam is not only essential to the growth in our understanding of history but mapping an opportunity in the development of our humanity" - (Selurd Gates, Documentation Extraction & Psychological-Analytics, Ph.D., and best-selling author of "Humanity: What Good Is It?").

The CACAC, as the public should be aware, places great faith in the abilities of its members, and no one joins the council lightly. We scrutinize candidates' intellect and character on several formidable merits in every measure, enabling the council to weed out any fabricated or fraudulent entries. Among the thousands of candidates who apply each year, the average number of candidates accepted is two, with one exception of a single year in the council's history where six became admitted.

Each one remains an invaluable resource. Cadlin Jonz was one of these candidates and has become one of Delfied's greatest advocates.

"I admit I was one of Delfied's greatest cynics until I began compiling the evidence for myself. I had taken an interest in her progress, suspecting a fictitious portrayal of the text. Delfied was able to prove otherwise," Cadlin Jonz, Commerce Science and Investigative Public Strategies, Ph.D., and best-selling author of "Exposing the Cover-Up of Criminal Trade").

Interpreting the volumes' text remains the highest priority of Delfied's career. Her second is taking on students with the same passionate fervor for linguistic knowledge. One of her graduate students and Keepers in the council's employ, Markus Goldmeier, wished to also comment on her works.

"Keepers are a well-known fact in our world. They adhere to specific laws and regulations that oversee their enchanting abilities. Mystic Silver is another well-known commodity in our world. Until now, the origins of enchanting were lost in the annals of time because one puzzle piece was thought irrelevant. Yet Secrets of Silver & Steam brings to the light the knowledge needed in defining their origins, thus giving Keepers an understanding of our own." (Markus Goldmeier, Keeper and Curator of CACAC Central Archives).

Secrets of Silver & Steam carries a percentile accuracy rating of ninety-six, which only a few other works claim such authoritative verisimilitude. It is the privilege of the CACAC to release this translated and formatted first-volume manuscript, "Secrets of Silver & Steam, The New Awakening," now to the public (480 RB).

COMMENCEMENT

I am Aagneya Nym, daughter of Lester and Joselane Nym from the Kingdom of Westmain. Though I do not know what the future holds, I have charged myself to give this account as I wish to create a historical record of what has transpired that reveals the hidden knowledge of our existence and coincides with the documented events of my ventures. As a recent graduate student of Langdon University, a new explorer, and an educated scholar intrigued by chronicles of magic, which fascinated me as a little girl, I believe it is crucial to provide contextual history and perhaps some impractical social norms should this account survive to reach a new generation if the culture and understanding of magic are perhaps dramatically transformed by what is taking place in these present times. I apologize if I am thorough. I believe it is necessary to understand our current era.

The current year is 263 RB from when I began this chronicle. Re-Birth (RB) represents the beginning of the world anew after The End War, time-stamping historical events in what is known as The Last Age. Three civilizations were victorious in their alliance at the war's conclusion: the Kingdom of Eastguard, the Kingdom of Westmain, and lastly, the Kingdom of Nod. Ceasefire in the world returned when the war ended in 135 RB. Each alliance has remained strong between the three victors, swearing an oath to maintain peace with one another.

Once, the earth was separated into various land masses known as continents, spread out with unique civilizations, with great distances of water between their expanse. We know there were at least seven main masses. Our historical records show that the continents collided, forming one enormous landmass, "The Great Collide," a catastrophic earthquake period that nearly caused every civilization's extinction. It occurred approximately six hundred years ago—a year being calculated by our current standards as three hundred and twenty-four days, a cycle of twenty-four hours, one thousand four hundred and forty minutes, and eighty-six thousand four hundred seconds. There are twelve-month cycles, with each month cycle calculating twenty-seven days.

People who survived the Great Collide's one hundred years of tremors and the appearance of sudden rifts swallowing cities whole began to rebuild. Several encased their cities into mountainsides created by the collision of the continents, erecting outer walls, many too steep and treacherous to scale for other growing civilizations to forego an invasion. Yet conquering walled cities became more accessible once the ability to fly was invented. Thus, the race for Steam Tech and building the best airships began. During The End War, battles mainly occurred on airships known as wairships (military airships) rather than on the ground. But before the first airship took flight, various people groups began to disappear into what is identified now as the Deadlands.

Scholars who recorded the land's rapid transformation during the war described the region as "thriving and breathing," to quote one famous explorer and scholar, Sandulf Collins. Therefore, airships are often used today to travel from region to region, keeping passengers and cargo from being lost. Even within their own kingdoms, people have whispered of the land changing before their very eyes as if possessed by magic. For this reason, it is uncommon for civilized folk to leave the safety of their city's walls. Although there are other means of travel, such as madmen sailing machines across treacherous seas or explorers who dare to trek the Deadlands on foot.

The End War would last eighty years, three months, and twenty-two days, with numerous clans conjoining into factions during that time. And while others surrendered to the supremacy's rule due to their inability to possess the resource that allows the enchanting of machinery, Steam Tech continued being researched, yet enchanting the auto navigation for airships was practically impossible until Mystic Silver became introduced as a fuel source.

The mysteries of magic are very elusive in its workings or how to wield it. It is commonly known that when someone encounters the rare metal, something is awakened within them. There are, in fact, rituals in Eastguard of mothers and fathers taking their children into temples that house the priceless metal on a pilgrimage to have their offspring touch it and see if they are awakened as Keepers. Incredibly, they could be anyone within or outside the civilized world, beyond the Dwelling Gates, pertaining to *anything not within walled cities*.

The discovery of Mystic Silver awakening a Keeper was revolutionary. When Keepers began using Mystic Silver to power machines, they were sought out and even targeted for assassination by other civilizations. Some of these eliminations succeeded, hindering promising developments of specific Steam Tech, and assisted in developing mistrust between rival civilizations and sparked many short skirmishes between neighboring lands. By 55 RB, the entire landmass was in conflict, and racing to take control of the skies with the new fuel source.

While Keepers can only perform the sole task of enchanting machines to create new Steam Tech, a Master Keeper (MKR) is an entirely different mystery, as no one knows how to become one. Elior Lystander is the only MKR indeed known—until now. Also, no other mind has come close to achieving what he has done. To his credit, he invented the essential navigation tools referred to as bio-engineered Steam Tech, and each of his inventions has momentously assisted us explorers and scholars in finding new artifacts and propelled Steam Tech advancements of the three kingdoms.

Nanomites (119 RB), also known as Living Silver is a widely known for patented, type of sentient enchantment made directly from Mystic Silver that lives without food, water, or even oxygen. Nanomites are housed inside several items and are enchanted to send signals to one another, even allowing audio signals to travel great distances. The disadvantage of Nanomites is the exposure to oxygen, and rapidly perish when subjected, rendering any enchanted item they are in sync with entirely useless. Nanomites are created within a vacuum-sealed environment and encased in an enchanted item. The amount of Mystic Silver to create the Nanomites necessary for most Steam Tech is less than 1/1000th of a mass unit. Thanks to Elior's knowledge, Keepers can scrape a few flakes off the core of the metal to enchant machinery.

The second of Elior's patented inventions are Single Hand Clocks (SHCs) (120 RB), specific navigation devices for airships and explorers. Navigators of airships today use Nanomites housed in the navigation deck. The captain charts a course, and the navigator turns the SHC hand to any direction desired, making the airship automatically fly along the specified route. This does not keep the airship from being manually controlled. Yet if an airship battle ensues, captains can grab hold of the helm to fly the airship during its engagement manually. Once the battle is over, and if the airship has survived, it will instinctively turn back to the course it was plotted by the SHC. Due to the invention of the SHC, airships are being built more prominent and able to go higher into the skies without ever needing to see the ground.

A smaller model of SHCs is a wrist-worn fashion statement used by explorers and citizens to navigate throughout a city, syncing to Nanomites kept in a specific tower. This tower is known as the "North" tower, a historical directional term once used before the Great Collide. Other directional terms such as "South," "East," and "West" are still used today but are only terms used when referring to a region or place in relation to one another on a map or a clearly defined area such as within a city. The Deadlands is never a clearly defined area, and neither are the skies.

Each city has a "North" tower, allowing an airship to gauge the direction of the city they are flying into. These North towers house a third unique bio-engineered invention of Elior's known as "Magic Beacons" (159 RB). Cities use Magic Beacons in their North towers and other specific markers to communicate with airships or citizens about the city's layout. For example, if an airship is looking for a precise landing platform, it may be directed to an exact location in the city using North, South, East, or West. These terms are applied to city walls as well. Two of these terms also remain within the names of two of the three kingdom territories, Westmain and Eastguard.

The society of explorers and scholars has so aptly renamed the Magic Beacon invention "Magic Beans." For that is what it is, a bean grown from the soil. Nanomites in Magic Beans remain protected in airtight pods, but over time, the rubbery pod deteriorates, making it impossible for the survival of the nanomites. It makes things hopeless for explorers to revisit discovered places in the Deadlands without reconnoitering. However, it is one of their most helpful devices, designed explicitly to help them navigate when roaming around in caves, especially as navigation goes when venturing into the Unlight.

"If an explorer survives the Unlight, they usually go become professors," I heard one of my lecturers at Langdon University say. But for the sake of finding lost artifacts, and let us be honest, the money, explorers risk their lives going under the surface, where ancient cities fell, to find treasures worth more than Mystic Silver—books of long ago, making knowledge one of the highest-earning commodities.

I was to accompany my fellow explorers and recent graduate classmates with armed military personnel into the Unlight, a large cave opening that suddenly appeared outside the city. Soldiers do not always accompany explorers on their explorations. So, I understood this was a special mission, perhaps to harvest a large sum of Mystic Silver. You might be asking yourself, why not just get on an airship and fly there? I would prefer it. However, Westmain does not see anything under a week's journey on foot as necessary to fly to it—the very reason why explorers are educated and made, after all. An airship usually drops Magic Beans the day before the journey, giving explorers ample time to track the signal through the Deadlands. Yet I felt something was exceptional about this undertaking, as I believe we had all assembled, apart from awaiting the arrival of one more.

It indeed was arduous as I anxiously waited to set out, much like other explorers who travel only with the necessities of life and carrying a modest means of defending themselves—a drill gun, a single-hand, bolt-action weapon that can weigh between two to three mass units, depending on the design. Some drill guns are designed to be loaded with single drill bits pushed into a rotation chamber. Others have loading clips that house ten to twelve drill bits at a time. Each drill bit can be between 1/4 to 1/2 a unit in length (depending on the design), and each drill bit is 1/8 of a unit in diameter. It is the sidearm of choice by most, including military personnel. When fired, the bit's velocity travels in the blink of an eye and with immense rotation. The sharp end of the bit can pierce and drill deep through flesh, light armor, and even tough animal hide.

Military infantry's primary weapon of choice is the buzzsaw rifle, a pneumatic-powered weapon with a pressurized tank located in the butt of the rifle and attached to the trigger mechanism. The barrel is flat and fastened to a smooth, wooden frame, and a grip handle is attached to the front, allowing soldiers to stabilize their aim. The buzzsaw rifle fires small steel sawblades approximately half a unit in diameter, with each clip holding thirty to forty sawblades. The front of the barrel has a snap-down bayonet attachment, where soldiers can attach their military-grade bayonet, termed the drill grip. The drill grip is a narrow, sharpened, and threaded piece of metal that can be powered by the rifle's air tank pressure in a high-speed circular motion. A small switch just above the trigger can divert pressure to the bayonet. Only models without this attachment are available to be possessed by civilians (legally).

My eyes remained keen that morning as I waited, staring at who would accompany me and watching Westmain's wairships fly off in the distance. I carry another fascination for military Steam Tech, stemming from traveling with my father as a youth. Thus, seeing wairships remind me of home, though I am not often fond of my parents. I usually prefer my own company.

My family and I have lived in Westmain my whole life, yet I have a couple of fond memories of traveling with my father to Eastguard. As a former top military academy graduate, my father's intellect made him a brilliant high-class officer and a businessman when he left Westmain's reserves. In the days when he was on active duty, we traveled to Eastguard together. I was about eight years old then. What I remember most is my father's wonderment of wairships, an awe I share with him. He and I specifically toured the most famous wairship during our visit—Skyhaven, The Savior of Eastguard.

The massive wairship is approximately 43,200 units long, 30,240 units wide, and has a hull depth of 21,600 units, harnessing ten giant balloon lifts and expanding fifty wings that hold two giant propellers each. It has twenty-five levels, including the main deck, each one approximately 864 units high. The lowest level of the hull is the thickest part of the wairship and houses Exploding Death Orbs (EDOs) that drop from two hundred different EDO bays dispensing one hundred EDOs at a time.

Along Skyhaven's deck and down to the twenty-third level are mounted cannons evenly spaced apart. There are two hundred and twenty-five cannons on each level, bringing the total number of cannons to five thousand, one hundred and seventy-five. Like on most wairships and some merchant airships, pressure pipes are connected to each cannon's breech that shoots steam up through the cannon's muzzle when the cannon valve(s) open. Pressure continues to shoot out until the cannon valve(s) are closed. The cannon pipe(s) pressure is controlled by an automatic steam release valve or "SR valve." When built up to a certain amount of pressure, the SR valve allows only enough pressure to be released to prevent the cannon pipes from expanding or exploding. When ready to fire, a loaded cannonball is inserted into the muzzle, keeping constant pressure flowing up to the cannons.

I turned my attention back to the six other newly recruited explorers, all boys and fresh from the University, waiting by the Dwelling Gates, along with seven well-seasoned veteran explorers and thirty-one military personnel. I gripped the drill gun my father bought me for the expedition, latched to my hip in its polished holster. He bought me the clip design (loaded with twelve) because he said I needed to learn how to shoot, and the more bits I had, the better. The boys bragged amongst themselves, like a grunting and haughty sort of Sus that displays its dominance toward the butcher before being seized, cut open, and hanged upside-down by its hindquarters to be bled out. The deafening sounds are what my father refers to as "squealing profit."

Squealing profit is how my family retains its wealth. My father became a third-generation tailor supplier after his military service, producing the largest supply of Sus hides in Westmain. The meat of the Sus is sold to local meat markets, of course, while the hides remain preserved to become the latest fashion. The hides are usually dyed and made into all types of clothing. Leather is also made from Bos Taurus, Equus Caballus, or Ovis Aries, combined with either Gossypium or Cannabis fibers to create immaculate apparel.

One should know a bit of historical context here about how dyes distinguish the characteristics of one's societal position today. There are eight primary dye colors, four made by Tailors for the upper-middle-class who can afford the credit rates and wear either royal crimson, dark cocoa, royal cocoa, or gold. The colors of dull, stone, muck, and tan hide are worn more by the lower-class societal members. Thus, my closet growing up was filled with a hanging bloodbath draped down in the shapes of skirts and dresses, sometimes mixed in with dark cocoa or gold trim.

If it is at all beneficial to distinguish clothing color to depict the treatment of social class, then I best mention peoples' ethos descriptors as well. As I am sure ethos descriptors have changed much since the Great Collide, I would have historical records reveal the current knowledge of this present age. Though I am not a historian of how these terms came to be, I know that Eastguard pressed for such standings to be applied to describe the skin tone features and bone structure of a person's ethos makeup. Nationality is used in combination when describing a person's genetic markers that make up their appearance and personhood.

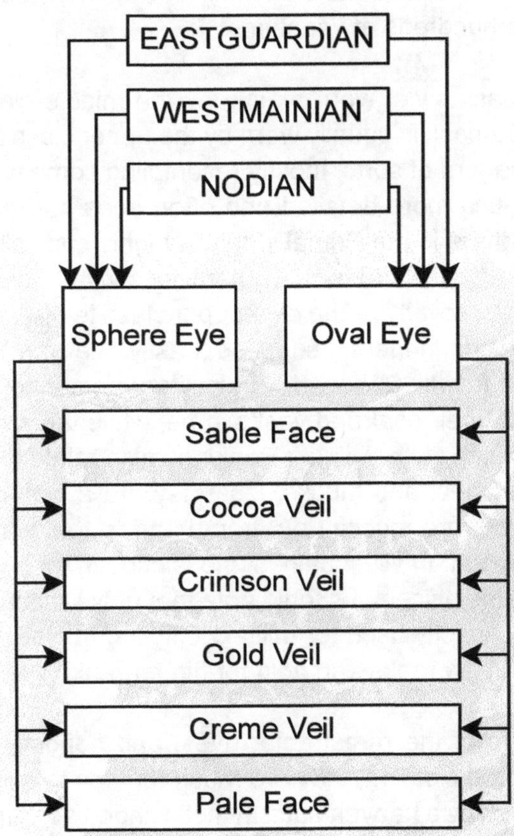

I am what you would call a Westmainian Sphere Eye Pale Face.

An expected social norm is to use Ethos Descriptors for classifying lineage. Still, even those of the same lineage can be subject to discrimination if they are of lower class, depicted by their clothing color. However, one exception to the rule is the Sable Faces from the Southern region of Nod are quite unwelcoming to any Eastguardian or North Nodian, no matter the color of their clothing. The discrimination mostly comes from their refusal to trade, as the Kingdom of Nod remains in discord between the North and South and has been lengthier than Westmain's civil conflict. Eastguard has continued trade solely to the North of both kingdoms, allowing the regions to fend off the onslaught from Southern rebels.

But let us return to speak of clothing. I find Tailors fascinating individuals, highly regarded artisans no matter what ethos or region they dwell in, and jealously guard the names for the rarest dyes and styles. Clothing styles and unique colors have their place, as we are all taught early in our lives, no matter what kingdom we hail from. Tailors stick to four main styles in their weaving, but each can have hundreds of variations.

The first is a Damask style, worn mainly by the middle class, while what is known as a Leaf Damask is usually worn by the upper class and beyond. Both are a variegated pattern of sorts, mostly resembling some type of foliage. The Leaf Damask is much more detailed and often does not resemble simplicity of any kind. Then there is the PrimaDonna, a highly specialized embroidered weave into formal attire. It intrinsically intertwines with Leaf Damask patterns and is worn chiefly by royalty or the elite upper class to distinguish themselves from the rest of the commoners, I suppose. Lastly, Slavyanski is considered a military design and is only to be worn by military personnel. The embroidery is usually sewn into their coat and vest's arms, while the rest of their uniform is free from any civilian style. Military Rankings also relate to color, but mostly stay in the dulls, stones, and mucks, less they are a high-ranking officer. In Eastguard, low ranks are mucked out from head to toe, while high positions remain in royal crimson. In Westmain, stone is chosen for low ranks and royal azure for high-ranking officers. I should note that only Westmain Tailors create azure dye, and it is strictly used for military officers. In Nod, they are a mix of dull and tan hide for low ranks and gold for higher ranks.

This leaves the two of the rarest color dyes, and honestly, if a person can afford heaven-colored clothing, they are much too rich to exist, in my opinion. High-end Tailors display a heaven outfit in their windows to passing customers, showcasing such fabric decadence to advertise their shop and skills, but only one outfit in a single size. As for mystic midnight, its development is for one specific person. Every tailor I have known who carries the dye reserves it expressly for MKRs. I had never seen mystic midnight clothing worn until that day by the Dwelling Gates.

Prior to Elior's arrival, I was having trouble not overhearing the constant boasting of my classmates, hormone-driven boys also dressed in royal crimson except for one in dark cocoa. I stepped away from them to give myself peace of mind, only to spot his entrance from the crowd. It startled me initially because the air around him seemed to bring a strange calm. He was undoubtedly a sphere eye with a creme veil complexion. I can only describe his features as young yet seasoned, flowing into the jawline of his beard that was slightly streaking heaven. His beard and hair held a gold hue, but his eyes caught me and drew me into the peaceful demeanor of his constant smirk. As he walked closer, I saw that his sphere eyes swirled and interchanged between sunny day azure skies, golden starlight, and a bright hue of viridescent meadow fields, something one might find in an art gallery of sorts.

He wore a fit & flare frock, as is the norm for men's overcoats, that swayed down to the back of his thighs like a sleek, mystic midnight drape. It had copper-coated buttons down the front and along the wrists. I could barely see his stone-colored long sleeve through his frock, also covered by a mystic midnight Sus hide gentleman's vest with a unique Leaf Damask design infused with what appeared to be azure in the thread. It was snap-buttoned up except for the top, revealing more of his stone undershirt. His trousers were sleek skinny denim, solid mystic midnight with stained dark cocoa outlays. His jaunty Sus waist harness was stained to a glossy mystic midnight shine. His Ovis Aries wristband wrapped around his left wrist, in-laid with an SHC, and his hands were covered in polished Sus mystic midnight gloves. His steel plate-toed, leather-strapped boots were stained dark cocoa, as was the shoulder harness holding two copper-plated rotator drill guns just peeking out of his frock.

He reached up to take off his top hat as he approached me. It was a pleasantly crafted mystic midnight hat with a dark cocoa band around the rim. He brought the hat over his chest and slightly bowed as is customary to a lady. With one soft breath, he spoke to me. "Greetings Miss. Might I inquire if this is the explorer party to set out today?"

At first, I did not say anything as I could not stop my gaze toward his unusual yet fitting hairstyle—a close side trim and high fade into a wavy and lengthy slicked-back tail. The expense of such a cut is well worth taking the time to describe it. Suddenly, I realized I was gawking. He was still waiting for my answer and sustaining a polite grin. I pushed out a kind smirk of my own and replied, "Why yes, it is good, Sir."

FIRST STEPS

"My name is Elior Lystander." His grin grew slightly and he placed his top hat back upon his head, tipping it toward me again. His tall frame cast a shadow over me as he slipped by and greeted the captain in charge of our expedition. His voice remained an echo inside my mind, sprouting tranquility beyond reasoning.

"Quiet!" A bulky brute boomed to grab our attention. I recognized the man as Bartus Picaren, a veteran explorer who often taught at Langdon University in "whipping students into shape." The man was born with a hardened, cut muscle frame and raspy vocal cords from too much grunting during his wild exercises within his mother's womb. The fact he was never dry simply made me wonder if he was more amphibious than human. The sweat dripping off his face seeped through his clothing made him frightfully unattractive, but apparently only to me. Every girl in school ogled him as a fantastic specimen. I would not be surprised if most of them followed him into his bachelor's lair.

"We have a pressing assignment," Bartus continued. "I look around here today and see some who will not make it back." I do not know why his eyes shot back at me when he said that. Yet I turned about and kept my gaze upon the man in mystic midnight, speaking with the captain. The two of them appeared as if they knew one another and carried on with their private conversation. Suddenly, I heard the brute exclaim, "Let's move out!"

Elior and the captain slowly turned from their conversation and began making their way to follow the rest of us. Bartus stepped quickly in front of the MKR, his face breaking all barriers of proximity to one's respectable distance.

"We have an MKR accompanying us." Bartus scoffed. "Let us hope that your sorcery does not attract the dangers of the wilds while bumping around down there."

"If danger rears its face to harm us, I am sure your breath is more than adequate to keep it at bay," Elior calmly replied, receiving a bit of a chuckle from the captain who stood just behind him.

I covered my mouth to keep any squeals of laughter from escaping. Bartus sneered at the comment but did not budge. Something strange happened, though, when I blinked. Elior was suddenly standing behind Bartus. Yet he had no time to side-step around the bulky man. Bartus appeared baffled as I did. I observed the captain, who chuckled again and then caught up to Elior, moving away from us. Just the brute and I remained. I did not care for that at all, and I scurried to catch the rest of the pack.

Realizing I had just taken my first step outside the Dwelling Gates and into the wilds of the Deadlands, my heartbeat began reverberating. Even the boasting brats who were puffed up before we left were lockjawed—not even a peep. I kept behind them, but not too far. A woman, who I could tell was a veteran explorer, slicked back her stony hair with streaks of heaven. I thought she held an extraordinary elegance, even with the slight wrinkles beneath her eyes and lines tiptoeing into her face. She smiled at me and then moved in close to whisper in my ear.

"My name is Cenobia." Her voice came across as somewhat gruff but remained pleasant. That is when I noticed the large scar on her throat, somewhat covered by a tan hide cloth she had wrapped around her neck. "You must be Aagneya Nym."

I could not recall whether I had met Cenobia before or not. Something about her felt familiar, but I could not place it. I shook away the thoughts racing through my mind, realizing my rudeness in not answering her.

"Yes," I replied softly. "How do you know me?"

She clarified that I was a small girl when my father brought me to ride my first wairship. Cenobia was the captain of that ship at the time—the Cloudguard of Westmain, now a retired vessel in the fortified city of Harvenger.

"I do." I almost burst out too loudly. "That was the day I fell in love with airships. But my apologies if I do not remember you."

Cenobia smiled, letting me know that my memory was not crucial. After leaving the military, she clarified that she had sustained her friendship with my father. And she had joined the expedition to see me home safely as a favor to him personally. I do not consider myself a crier, but my eyes swelled up with tears. My father has always found it challenging to show he loves me. So, in his own way, he finds a means to communicate it occasionally.

The group stopped and stared at what I had heard so many times about, the Deadlands. We had trekked not more than an hour or so from the Dwelling Gates, yet we had ceased for the moment at a ledge displaying a wide-open view of flora in lush hues I could only dream about wearing, and diverse landscapes—forests, a marsh, and a desert all within our gaze. I had only surveyed such things from above, high in the clouds.

A chill made its way up my spine, and the sweat on my brow became cool. My hands began to tremble uncontrollably, and then I felt someone clasp one of them. I thought it was Cenobia, but I peered down to see a mystic midnight glove. I peered upward at Elior's grin, which brought a great calm over me. I reached up with my other hand, wiped the sweat from my brow, and heard him quietly tell me not to be afraid.

The MKR moved away but motioned me to follow him. The captain and a few of the soldiers accompanied our footsteps. The others remained stationary, still talking and staring out over the horizon. I saw Elior halt at a tree, not much taller than him. The sun was gleaming down through the rest of the tall Quercus foliage surrounding us. I had never seen a spectacle such as sunlight dancing amid the branches of what is known as a glade. The books I had read about such sights were not even close to what I had fathomed. The moment tore my imagination apart. And I realized I was about to venture further into the dangers of the wilds, and my mother always taught me that beauty always leads to a beast.

Speaking of beasts—Bartus grunted as he approached the gathering in the glade with the rest of the group in tow. The captain, with us, motioned for him to be silent. Elior stood very still, his eyes closed, and I could feel his strange peace bubble up inside me again. But I could see something, light coming out from his eyelids. Even with his eyes closed, it could not be hidden. The light went away almost just as quickly as it had appeared. Then Elior opened his eyes. The captain stared at him for a moment. Elior playfully shouted, "There lies our course," and pointed. Bartus nearly fell over and quickly retorted for Elior to keep his voice down.

"He would not put us in danger," the captain calmly reprimanded him. "We can all save our hushed tones until otherwise instructed."

The second in command to the captain announced to the new explorers as Elior, the captain, and the others began trekking in the direction the MKR had pointed out. We were told to stick close to the veteran explorers and the soldiers and not to leave the safety of the party. "We cannot protect you if we do not know where you are."

I rushed to be by Elior's side as I had several questions twirling through me. I had never seen an MKR use magic, and my curiosity erupted from all corners of my mind. However, my mother's voice kept my mouth from flapping, hearing her tell me how improper it was to blurt out questions without first getting to know someone.

"Are you really going to remain silent, Miss?" I heard Elior's voice reach me when I had just managed to pace my stride with his. "I will not be offended by your questions. I promise."

"Please, good sir, you may call me Aagneya," I replied.

"Well, Aagneya. I thank you for permission to be informal." Elior's eyes spiraled to a new coloration with his pleasant smile. "And if I may be so bold, please—you may call me Elior."

I did not hesitate to ask my questions after the pleasantry of our permission to be informal. I was intrigued by the spectacle of what Elior had performed back in the glade that it probably came off rude and prying by firing off so many inquiries. Yet he indulged my curiosities with great patience and a handful of chuckles that made me believe he enjoyed my company.

The first thing I inquired of, in almost a demanding tone, was his abilities in the use of magic, beginning with what he had performed in the glade. He stunned me with his explanation of what he called his "Mystic Memory," referencing his ability as "Light Touching Knowledge," where he acquired memories of objects, time, and places that allowed him to recall certain things the light of sun touched, including landscapes in the now forever changing Deadlands. This ability revealed to him what was and what now was, allowing him to find the correct navigable path no matter what had changed within the environment. I felt my eyes widen as I could not fathom what I heard.

"What about people?" I asked. "Can you remember people? Do you spy on them, observe them all the time?"

"I do not wish to know anyone, less I wish to know them," the MKR replied. "You cannot truly get to know someone by observation alone. Perceiving gives us an angle, often filled with follies due to our inadequacies. To truly know someone, one must talk and interact."

Taken in by his philosophical tenor, I did not realize I had whipped out my notepad to jot down his words. After five years of university education, I was apparently still taking notes for an examination later.

"Will you tell me more about what you can do?" I swiftly responded. I knew it came across as impolite, but I could also see Cenobia beside me, nudging me to continue my interrogation. She must have found it fascinating as well.

Elior just beamed and began explaining some of the other abilities he could perform with certainty and ease—all of which kept me enthralled. By nightfall, I had my face in my journal next to the fire. I did my best to remember and write down what Elior had described about his power—precisely what he called "Bright Bending," referring to his ability to project his frame in one place, then to another before an additional moment had passed. I could only imagine he did this when Bartus invaded his personal space at the Dwelling Gates in Langdon.

Another described to me was something that worked in tune with his Mystic Memory, where Elior could feel light. By feeling light in a specific place, he could get to know the region without being physically present. I had asked him if he could feel people when using this ability, to which he replied, "No, just the light touching them." I was unsure what that meant, but I recorded it nonetheless.

We sat around the campfire, all the young graduates huddled together. The explorers made an inner circle, and the soldiers surrounded us along the outer rim. That night I learned the names of my fellow post-graduates as they engaged me with negligible curiosity.

Garvish, the loudest of the six, made known his boyish conquests during his days at the University. His slender frame was not weak but fitly cut like many boys I met at Langdon trying to have a good time. I admit his sphere eye, creme veil appearance remained not bad to look upon. Yet, he was highly boastful, constantly running his fingers through his gold hair and bringing up his specialty in studying Strategic Marksmanship & Survival Tactics that convinced the others of his prowess. However, I remained convinced he would not "conqueror" the wilds so virile.

Pramyan held a very high intellect, I shall admit. Yet I pinned him as the type who would raise his hand in a classroom and bluntly announce to the professor they forgot to assign studies for the class to take home. I could relate to him in my love for learning, but not on that level. He constantly debated with the others, trying to outmatch them with his wit. His specialty was Documentation Extraction & Knowledge Preservation—another way to say one belongs indoors reading books. The fact his eye spectacles were neatly tied around his head told me he would be blind without them. He was a scrawny oval eye pale face, but oddly enough, there was strength in his hands.

Jish and Ferid were unmistakable athletes, with creme veil skin, sphere eyes, and dark cocoa hair—constantly sizing one another up in a competitive yet playful demeanor. I soon learned they were teammates for all five years of their studies at Langdon. They had both studied to specifically become explorers, specializing in Medicinal Assiduity & Applied Kinesiology Practices. It was comforting to have two individuals capable of patching me up if some monster in the wilds or the Unlight took a bite out of me.

Bikarma had incredible oval eyes with a light touch of gold in his cocoa skin. He had straight, shoulder-length, sable hair, elegantly brushed and tied behind his head. But he jawed off like the rest. He had participated in several campus organizations to become an explorer specializing in Authoritative Communication, Bio-Navigation, & Weaponry Engineering. His accolade symbols tattooed down his arms are what pompous Langdon graduates do when they cannot show off the hunk of metal stashed somewhere in a glass case. Bikarma had an entire showroom of his awards displayed like artifacts in a museum-like fashion at his family's estate.

These boys were all born of Westmain.

Nirnasha, though, was much different from the rest. He was slenderly fit like Garvish but a bit shorter. He was a Nodian oval eye sable face, with short, curly sable hair, who had ventured to study in a foreign land. His eyes seized a bright cocoa shimmer, smooth like his sable skin. Apparently, he was not as comfortable speaking about his accomplishments as the other boys due to his thick accent. Yet he communicated his specialties—Musculoskeletal Therapies & Botany Biology—when they asked him.

"What did you study?" Pramyan's voice reached me across the campfire as I remained jotting in my journal.

"Psychological Premonition & Secret Arts," I replied, peering up from the pages.

The entire gathering of boys suddenly went utterly silent. I knew the reason why. But I refused to be ashamed of my curiosities of enchanting and magic. Most people think studying the Secret Arts is a waste of time if you are not already a Keeper, but a massive part of our world is typically ignored regarding the MKR. I had studied several articles interviewing Elior—none revealed much other than praising his accomplishments.

"Are you a Keeper?" Pramyan asked.

I shook my head.

"Am I to gather that you spent all your time studying how to read emotions and magic, yet you are not even a Keeper?" Garvish scoffed with a snicker or two, pulling back his overpriced, textured golden locks. Jish and Ferid joined in the laughter while Bikarma added in his scorn.

"What are you doing out here?" Bikarma interjected. "Why would you study magic if you are not a Keeper? Your parents must be proud."

"Trap it, you nit!" I spat, feeling my anger rush to my head as I stood up. I did not realize my hand had grasped the grip of my drill gun.

"Looks like someone studied emotions but didn't learn how to control them," Garvish continued his mockery.

I turned quickly away from the group and marched off toward my tent. Tears enveloped and streamed down my face. But I was hidden by the shadows, hopefully. Cenobia joined me in the tent when I set foot inside and dropped into a huddled mess on the ground. She said nothing. She walked over to me and slowly sat down where I lay on my wilderness bedding, hearing me sobbing as softly as possible. I felt her arms, and then she ran her fingers through my hair. However, all I could think about was putting a bit between the eyes of Bikarma and the other three.

I awoke late that night, assuming I had cried myself to sleep. Cenobia lay resting soundly, no more than an arm's length away. The strangest sounds were coming from outside my tent. I have never been a heavy sleeper, and the noise maintained a faint yet frighteningly crackling as if someone was breaking wood apart. I stepped outside my tent and into the moonlight. A shadowy figure stood just on the edge of the campsite with a dim glow protruding from his face. I knew it to be Elior. He appeared wide awake, and I wondered where his gaze fixated. I did my best to make my footsteps as silent as possible to avoid disturbing the others. Elior turned slightly as I came to stand next to him. I did not realize the chill the night in the wilds held until my teeth began to chatter. Before he said a word, Elior threw his fit & flare frock around me. The warmth of the overcoat settled my chattering, but my face could still feel the briskness of the incoming breeze.

"They are on the move," Elior whispered to me. He pointed down the cliff-side where, to my disbelief, I saw trees stirring and shifting from one place to another.

"The land is changing," I uttered, scarcely believing my eyes. "Are they alive, or is it magic that stirs them?"

"They are mysterious creatures," Elior answered. "Mystery is an element of our existence. The source of this clandestine can only be found in exploring beyond what one is willing to believe. Even then, the more we know, the more questions are presented to us."

"You, yourself, are something of an obscurity," I stated. Elior's response was nothing more than a smirk at first. But he responded, keeping the pleasantry of the conversation.

"I could say the same for you, Miss Aagneya," Elior sighed. "I have been around long enough to know that magic is nothing more than a part of the story waiting to be played out. There is a reason for the unknown in this world just as much as there is a reason to draw breath and to dream. The trees move because magic is part of the story, despite what things may have or not have been before."

"I have always been fascinated by magic," I blurted out, much louder than what would be considered polite in a crowd full of sleepers.

"Everyone has a story in them," Elior turned to me, his eyes lighting up like the noonday sky. "But not everyone is brave enough to explore their narrative and allow it to manifest."

I sprang up from my wilderness bedding, wondering if my encounter with Elior that night was real, but I heard several perturbed voices outside my tent. Cenobia was not beside me. I jumped up and quickly put my boots on. When I emerged from my tent, the boisterous lot became dumbfounded by the sight

I had witnessed with Elior. Although the trees were still on the move, the MKR was nowhere I could see. The captain and Cenobia were entirely composed, standing next to them early in the morning.

"Pipe down," Bartus barked to the younger explorers.

I thoroughly enjoyed watching them whimper like younglings about to be spanked. It made them less intimidating than the tongue-lashing I received from the elite intellects the night before. Only Nirnasha was not scared. At least he did not show it. While the others were still cringing at the trees moving and murmuring amongst each other, Nirnasha separated from the pack about six or seven paces. I decided to approach him gradually.

Staring with the same awe and wonder I had in my heart when I first saw the trees move during the night down the cliff. The trees had all but scattered away from the landscape, migrating to another location. When I peered down the hillside again, standing next to Nirnasha, I saw Elior in the distance, his silhouette outlined in the rising sun and his feet planted on the bare ground where the forest once stood.

"You study this kind of thing?" I heard Nirnasha break the silence.

"I have, but only in theory," I replied. "I had yet to see it with my own eyes."

"What do your studies tell you about trees moving around as we do?" Nirnasha pressed.

"Stay away from them if you can," I said. I saw a smile spread across Nirnasha's face, almost as if I had drawn a laugh. Yet he did not make a sound. We both turned to see the others were breaking camp, and somehow Elior was back in our midst.

We were ready for another day's journey, and Elior pointed the way. We followed tracks where the trees had traveled for a time. Then our course took us away from their prints. The ground remained barren for many hours, with only grassland and a few colorful flowers in sight. The skies overhead soon crowded with dark, fluffy clouds swiftly forming to block the sun. All of us knew what was coming. And within a few hours, the massive downpour split over us—an unusual rain, a sweetly scented aroma lulling us to drowsiness, and a stickiness that made us feel like honey pouring over our skin.

"We need to find shelter," I heard Elior's urgency over the noise of plummeting rain crashing and soaking the ground. "Stay awake!"

No sooner did he say this did Pramyan collapse into slumber. The soldiers and veteran explorer next to him swiftly caught his body before he fell to his face.

A howling began to echo in the distance. I speedily reached and held tight to the grip of my drill gun as we hurried to find shelter underneath the cliffs. The once faint howls began to grow louder. Bartus kept shouting at everyone to pick up their feet, and anyone who stumbled would be left behind, while Elior persisted in ensuring no one was straggling. Whatever was chasing us in the storm, none of us wanted to learn its appearance. Yet we did not have much of a choice.

THE UNLIGHT

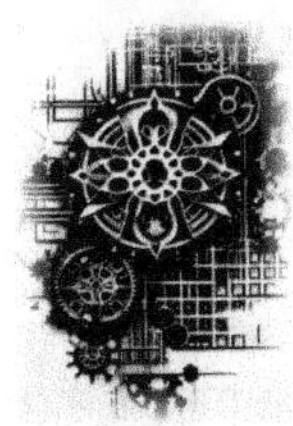

We huddled, pressed against the cliffs. Soldiers formed two lines with their buzzsaw rifles ready to fire—one line kneeling, the other standing just behind. All the veteran explorers had their drill guns aimed, guarding the flanks of the soldiers. The newcomers, including myself, held a more frightened position, kneeling on the ground beneath the rockface with our drill guns pulled from their holsters but too afraid to point them at anything. Pramyan lay snoring behind us, and soon we all waited in drenched clothing. A stillness grasped the winds until a sudden howling broke the silence again.

One by one, the creatures came into our sight out of the mists of the storm, well over twenty or so. Elior plopped down on the small boulder beside me. He had told the captain to hold fire unless the creatures came within 20 footsteps.

"Are you not an explorer?" I heard Elior chuckle. "This is your first moment of danger. Should you not be excited?"

I had no answer, only a question as I fumbled through my pack to dry my hands and grab my leather-bound notebook. I began to inquire about the beasts when Garvish interjected a snotty retort to what Elior had said. The MKR told him that we would have to feed him to the beasts if he was not quiet. Elior's comment made me giggle, but only momentarily, as he did not appear to jest.

"The beasts are known as Reverie Hounds. You might say they are a hybrid of the Canis Lupus variety," Elior uttered to me. "They are drawn to loud noises like thunder or shouting, and they especially love the scent of a particular rain that falls in the Deadlands."

One beast drew closer, just in the line of my sight. The Reverie Hound's appearance was dullish and stone-colored, coupled with splattered hues of dark cocoa. Its musculature was broad, with razor-edged claws and a peculiarity—an exposed spine resembling armor along its backside.

"See that hardened extra layer of bone along its back?" Elior continued to explain. "Keeps the creature from standing on its hind legs and raising its head too high."

"You mentioned they follow the scent of this rain," I responded. "Why is that?"

"Makes things smell and taste sweet," Elior clarified. "The scent can send other creatures into a full ecstatic trance, like Pramyan over there, that heightens the senses to the point of passing out. Reverie Hounds find these victims and easily make a meal of them."

"Reverie Hounds are cowardly in nature," I heard Cenobia quietly chime in a reminder. "But they will attack if provoked by loud noises or on the verge of starvation. They are also known to be cannibalistic."

I jotted these notes down in my journal. They had taught us about such an animal at Langdon. The difference from book to experience was uncanny, and I felt I had forgotten every lesson I studied in my Wilderness and Beasts course. One by one, the Reverie Hounds faded back into the mist whence they came. I overheard Elior tell the captain to ensure we remained close once the storm passed. The Reverie Hounds were surely going to follow us at a distance.

Nirnasha inquired more about the rain with the specific scent. I interjected my pleads for elaboration as well. I had not heard of such a thing. Elior only smiled and let us know that it was one of the mysteries of the Deadlands. We could not press the MKR further despite our skepticism of his answer.

Our pace doubled once the rain let up. Pramyan had awoken in a keen panic and remained close to the front as we traveled. We trekked for at least another half day without incident. All we heard were a few howls in the distance. Then as darkness retook the land, we were near our destination and close to the mouth of earth that would take us into the Unlight. We paused for one more night to sleep just inside the entrance to the cave before going any farther. As we set up camp, we heard the howls draw dreadfully closer to us. Elior's head slowly perked up. He urged everyone to be silent. Again, the howling grew louder and doubled in numbers.

"Captain," Elior cried out. "Get everyone into the cave. Now!"

His urgent tone did not leave the captain much time for hesitation. He and his soldiers grabbed what supplies they could and practically shoved us all into the throat of the cavern, fumbling for our lanterns.

"We need guards at the entrance to keep them from following us in," Elior insisted.

The captain nodded and shouted for fifteen soldiers to take up arms while the rest of us stood behind them.

"Hold this ground!" he commanded. "Do not let any of them through!"

"I will remain here for now and catch up once the sun rises," Elior explained as soon as the soldiers were in place. The captain nodded. "Keep a steady pace. Ensure everyone stays together and not go near dark pools of water."

I watched as the captain led the rest of the soldiers ahead of everyone else, down into the dark, with lanterns held high to guide our feet. I glanced at Elior as he reached into his fit and flare frock to reveal the dark cocoa holsters clasping his drill guns coated in copper. He pulled them swiftly from their nest and pointed them toward the howling that now thundered in echoes inside the cavern.

A sudden tug pulled me away, a grasp that reminded me of my mother when she was angry with me. Cenobia yanked me away to keep up with the others. When my head turned, and my feet began to shuffle along the rocky floor swiftly, I heard sawblades resound, the snarls of hounds turning to silence, and shouts of men mustering courage against a foe I had never truly fathomed. The echoes of violence followed us as we marched deeper into the tunnel and began to fade as we ventured further into the Unlight.

For three hours we journeyed downward. We heard nothing to hear except the sound of the wind in our lungs and the shuffling of feet, though we did our best to step lightly. I could hear whispers from the young men who had scoffed at me days earlier. I had resisted joining their company for some time. Now, we clustered together to remain safe, and I could sense their fear held the potential to endanger us all.

Roaming in the Unlight is strenuous on the mind. Even after a few more hours, I swore I could feel vile hands lurking in the dark to drag me off to meet my doom. I am sure many of the others felt the same. At times, I thought I would see glowing eyes staring back at me from the gloom. But then I would blink only to see my lantern flickering before me. The veteran explorers appeared nervous as well. I have never seen so much sweat drip from middle-aged men. Cenobia remained by my side. Her darting gaze kept my thoughts uneased.

"I hope we reach the Mystic Silver soon," she whispered. "I have never gone into a cave such as this, where shadows so swiftly abduct the light away."

"Perhaps we are not only here for the precious metal," I reasoned to her. "What else would be worth searching for to risk our lives so frivolously?"

"It is not frivolity," a man's voice reached me. Cenobia and I jumped. We turned to see Elior standing just behind us. The others must have heard us jump, and all the footsteps stopped. The captain made his way back to where Elior stood. The two began to converse, where Elior reassured them he had not lost any soldiers and that they would have caught up with us sooner should one of the soldiers not twisted his ankle coming down the mouth. The captain thanked Elior for keeping his soldiers safe. He then commanded us to rest and stepped forward to address us.

"I want you all to listen very closely," he began. "You may already know that this is not just a normal expedition. No expedition is normal out here in the wilds. But this one is essential. We are not seeking Mystic Silver to extract. We are journeying to ruins that fell long ago to find ancient artifacts, one we hope to bring home with us. Should we find Mystic Silver along the way, we shall do our best to extract as much as we can carry."

The captain elucidated that once we had secured any artifacts, we would bring them to the surface. From there, a wairship would find our signal from the Magic Beans he carried. We were all given a couple in case some did not make it out alive.

I began to analyze further the risk we were taking for what could be the only possible artifact more valuable than Mystic Silver—books. I could feel my adrenaline pump fiercely as our march resumed, and I heard the others murmur about the creatures we might face. The Reverie Hounds already staunched my mind with fear, realizing they were beyond what I imagined. Yet the monster leaping around from the boys beside me was about Gloom Gnawers, a disgusting species and a prominent threat when exploring the Unlight. Their breed is classified as "Humanoid Rattus." We know they keep in clans and can breed into the thousands with extreme cannibalistic tendencies. They often breed out of the necessity for food and wage war against one another, carrying off the dead to feed their clan. Gloom Gnawers also feed on arthropods, glowing mushrooms, and anything else they can sink their teeth into. The discovery of their species came from the famous explorer I mentioned before, Sandulf Collins from Eastguard, as I recall.

Collins is much accredited for discovering other organisms while roaming the Unlight. Some have said he was more interested in the thrill of discovery than the actual lining of his pockets from his ventures. During one of his excursions, he discovered what we have come to know as "Lurkers." Lurkers are classified as 'undead,' corrupted by magical properties, and are found solely in the Unlight. Mystic Silver is, of course, the assumed property for why they are walking around. Lurkers are usually found near large amounts of Mystic Silver. Collins led several expeditions, allowing him to study the behavior and movements of Lurkers. Much like Gloom Gnawers, Lurkers can gather in great numbers and become overwhelming. My heart had no desire to see such atrocities, but I had prepared myself to face them, hoping I would not vomit at my first gaze upon them.

My spiraling worry became disrupted as the lanterns ceased moving just ahead of Nirnasha and me as we entered another large cavern. For what felt like a day or so, as tracking the time of day in pure darkness is difficult, we walked in hushed tones as Elior led the way. Now he stopped just inside the cavern entrance, appearing to be listening for something. Our breath could not even be heard as we all held our exhales until Elior finally turned back and smiled with a nod. His dim-lit grin told us to proceed, and we entered the cavern, preparing to rest.

I assumed Cenobia heard me shivering while I tried to sleep. I felt her gently stir me. She whispered that I was more than welcome to bed with her. My slim frame does not retain heat like her adorable chubby dimples. Usually, I do not care to talk about my frame. Though I am slim, I do not care so much for my bulky hips, untamable crimson locks, and boyish chin—a ruthless raillery expressed to me by my mother. I do not care much for skirts or dresses either. Growing up and being forced to wear such things has tainted my taste. Though for social graces, I will wear a bustle with a corset now and then. My preference, however, is exactly what was making me freeze while I slept—my lucky royal crimson and gold pin-striped ruffle shorts. Before snuggling into my wilderness bedding, I should have dawned my specially made skinny denim trousers.

Cenobia's hands felt like frost when they touched my bare legs. I opened my eyes to see a tiny man with sable slithering hair in the dimness of my lantern, kneeling next to me with a frightening hue. His eyes shimmered like heaven, his fingers bony and long, with sharp fingernails like the claws of a predator wrapped around my thigh. He wore a neatly kept, formal style of attire, frills, and all, yet with a poor-looking gent's top hat full of rips and tears. His skin appeared paved with death and scars but carried light brushstrokes of a daylit azure sky. I could not make a sound, sensing my throat dry with dread. I was dreaming to the best of my knowledge, but his hands were soft and carried a chill that made me struggle to regain the life in my lungs. His wicked smile, revealing his pointed dentitions, made me jerk my drill gun to meet his face and pull the trigger. The tiny man instantly vanished without any success of my bit piercing his terrifying features.

Cenobia jumped up, bearing a blade. She screamed at me, demanding to know why I had fired a shot. Elior, not far behind her demands, appeared in front of us, taking us both off guard. He lit up the gloom just enough to put us at ease. And when he looked into my eyes, I felt he knew what I saw.

"There was a man here," I blurted out. "He was very short but did not look alive."

"He appeared dead," Elior interjected. I nodded, and the MKR continued. "He knows we are here."

We heard more footsteps approaching us. From the echo, it must have been the entire camp. Elior quickly turned and stepped swiftly toward the others.

"Captain," Elior said. "It is no longer safe to rest here. We must move out immediately."

Everyone hurried to pack up the campsite without question when I noticed Jish and Feris were missing. I swiftly mentioned it to Elior, and he grabbed my arm tightly. He shoved me toward the far exit of the cavern with almost a panic in his tone but assured me that we would look for them. We did not need to search for long as we heard blood-curdling screeching from the next corridor, where everyone headed. The MKR did not waste any time finding the source.

Pramyan had resounded the alarm overlooking a bloody carcass sitting up against a rocky slope just outside the cavern leading further into the Unlight. Elior saw the trousers and proclaimed Jish had fallen. Every soldier with us unstrapped their buzzsaw rifle and held them close, ready to fire. The captain bellowed an order for them to watch the shadows.

I could not believe my eyes. Seeing what was left of Jish nauseatingly horrified us. In the dark, he appeared to have been bitten in half from the waist up. Elior clarified, though, telling us Jish had been torn.

"What could have done this?" I asked Elior.

"There are many things down here with us that should not exist," he replied. "But if I were to venture a guess, I would say it was a type of Lurker. According to the tracks, I would say it was of abnormal size. And it appears poor Jish wandered off to urinate as I can smell a hint of ammonia from the wall. Whatever killed him did it quickly, and likely Ferid went with him."

"Why is Ferid's body not here then?" I inquired.

"Likely due to the monster taking him away," Elior deduced. "Not sure why a Lurker would drag off an explorer's body without creating a blood trail to follow."

It was our first encounter with the dangers of the Unlight. We had one dead explorer and one missing and likely dead. We also had more than one enormous problem than a Lurker to deal with. In the next few moments, Bartus hysterically tried to take charge. He began screaming in the captain's face about our foolishness to follow the leadership of an MKR. The captain did not take Bartus' insubordination for long, though. As Bartus continued blabbering to the rest of us about how we should all turn back, he found a drill gun in his face and fifteen buzzsaw rifles pointing at him when he turned back around to face the captain again.

"You will be silent," the captain gritted his teeth. "Otherwise, I shall have you executed for sabotage and insubordination."

"We should make him bait for the Lurker," one soldier chimed in but was quickly reprimanded by the captain.

"Not a bad idea." Elior stepped into the circle of troops now gathered around the captain and Bartus. "This beast needs to be destroyed; otherwise, it will continue to hunt us."

"How does a Lurker know how to hunt?" Pramyan stammered out.

That is when we all learned more about Lurkers than we truly wished to know. Elior enlightened us that Lurkers can often change into something other than an "undead" thing. Sometimes, they become more robust and agile, like a sophisticated predator. Some even grow a sense of intellect that could possibly communicate their thoughts. Undoubtedly, their thoughts would only be to eat the living. Bartus appeared to wet his trousers when he heard Elior's words.

"Lurkers can often smell terror," Elior continued, closing the gap between him and Bartus. "It is the nectar of their appetites. They will track it until they can bite into it."

From that point forward, Bartus walked ahead of us, unarmed, in the company of the captain and five other soldiers. The rest of the soldiers spread amongst us, watching the shadows. Elior's eyes glowed somewhat dimmer now, much less than before, barely matching the light of our lanterns. Even though I felt terrible for Bartus, I could not help but feel the MKR knew we would not see the Lurker again, at least for some time.

"What do you think happened to Feris?" I heard Nirnasha whisper to Elior.

"As I said, lost and gone into the dark," Elior replied after a moment had passed. "I remember his light. If I could see it, I would find him."

My heart thumped with a vast majority of fear, even shedding a couple of tears for the fallen. I could see it in the faces of the others in the dim light. Garvish, Pramyan, and Bikarma began walking well in front of us. I could not see their faces, but I could only imagine they were just as terrified. Nirnasha seemed well composed, considering Elior's fatalistic response to his question. I ventured a question to the MKR about whether we would run into the Lurker again or more. He did not respond. He looked at me, and I watched his eyes turn from azure to their golden hue and then to viridescent meadow fields. His head turned from me once his eyes became azure again, and he stepped away from Nirnasha and me. I suspect Elior did not wish to frighten me further.

We did not speak until we came to a much vaster cavern than we had traveled previously, with ruins from a lost civilization. We all knew what had caused the structures to collapse where they now lay sprawled out in the shadows. The city's remains appeared to command high significance to the civilization that once dwelt there in its day.

Elior led us to a sizable broken structure that had stood aesthetically with tall pillars in its frame and perhaps grand archways to depict its significance. It was much unlike the structures built in cities of our current day and age. Westmain architecture is more box-shaped, rectangular, and even carved out from the side of mountains. Our significant buildings always have some sort of thick plates of metal wedged inside the walls and foundations of concrete and iron. The building that Elior had led us to did not have thick metal plates from the walls anywhere, just broken iron bars embedded in the destruction. It gave me pause to theorize that people did not think of war at one point.

I noticed Elior gazing at it as if searching for something of import. I did not mean to pry, but I asked him about the significance of such a place. He looked at me as if holding back tears from falling. Yet still, he said nothing. He turned back from the ruins and remained silent. After a few moments, Elior told the captain the soldiers should create a perimeter. He would scout the inside to ensure no Lurkers or other beasts were inside.

Elior walked up the steep rubble and found his way inside the broken structure. While he was away, I began investigating the outside further. Cenobia stayed close to me as we remained within the perimeter of the guard. Suddenly, I heard Cenobia whisper to me. I turned around, and she motioned toward a large metal plaque resting beneath the soil. Though cracked, the pieces had remained together. It read:

Library of Congress, Thomas Jefferson Building.

I was so excited that we were standing on the ruins of an ancient library that I almost did not take notice. Cenobia had also pulled something else from the dust. She began shaking off the debris from the large piece of fabric.

"I think I know what that is," I told Cenobia with the enthusiasm of a little girl gorging on sweets. "It must be the banner of the civilization."

"I believe you are right," Cenobia concurred. She quickly whipped me around to reach my pack. "You carry it, Aagneya. I left my pouch where the others are resting.

"We can also etch this plaque," I said. "That way, we can describe where we found this artifact."

"While you do that," Cenobia sounded just as excited as me, "I shall start writing up the descriptive notes for the finding, then we can both sign them!"

If you are unaware, explorers who discover things together sign off on descriptive notes should something be too heavy to carry back with them. In this case, the ruins of a building from a past civilization do not fit into a pack. Instead, explorers who write descriptive notes and sign them receive much higher validation and accolades for their findings. The banner and the etching would also contribute to proof of the findings.

I finished the etching just as Elior reappeared outside. He motioned to the captain. All of us followed Elior back inside the ruins of the library, except for the captain and fifteen soldiers who stood guard at the entrance. Surprisingly, the rubble had a clear path, despite a few awkward, winding, and twisting turns. A large, dark pool of water spread in the center of the foyer, approximately twenty arm lengths in diameter. Elior led us well away from it and went to the other side.

"Take whatever books you can carry," Elior said. "But stay quiet. We do not need to advertise our presence."

All the explorers fanned out and began flipping through dusty covers and pages, each one choosy in their findings, estimating what books would bring a higher price. All became first found, first served—as the soldiers began packing up books that held any decent condition. I had gathered that Elior was looking for a specific book but had difficulty finding it. However, it appeared as if he knew the foundations of the ruins well.

We scoured the musty collapsed shelves and torn manuscripts, seeing plenty worth scavenging. The MKR did not take notice of any of the ones I found, though I believe they were an excellent treasure and somehow remained in remarkable condition. One such discovery of mine was a book entitled *The Legend of Sleepy Hollow* by an author named Washington Irving. By the artistry of its illustrations and skimming through its text, I conceived there must have been a time in ancient history when a phantom of sorts preyed upon a small town.

The second of my findings was a book titled *Moby-Dick* by Herman Melville. The artwork depicted a monstrous sea creature. I can only assume it to be a historical documentary of a monster of the deep, which is not uncommon from what I have learned growing up. No one ventures the vast oceans, no one of sanity anyway.

Nirnasha almost picked up my third find, but his hands moved past it, proceeding to grasp a different book from a pile of manuscripts we found. I believe I chose it because the title intrigued me—*The Scarlet Letter* by an author named Nathaniel Hawthorne.

Its title appeared somewhat romantic, and I figured that it would be a delightful read once we returned home. I will not keep you in suspense—the documentation is outlandishly horrid that I scarcely believed it is a part of humanity's ancient history. I shall not spend more time explaining my shock in reading it, as a woman named Hester Prynne is forced to wear a scarlet letter "A" because she was condemned for committing adultery. I do not comprehend the word scarlet, but I am appalled by what this woman went through while her child's father remained in high standing within his community. I found it an utter relief to learn he finally confessed his adultery before his dying breath. Despite my distaste for its history, this book struck me deeply—and I must confess, in its conclusion, it was one of my favorites to return to when I have a quiet night for such indulgence, but just for the ending alone.

I scavenged through yet another pile as Elior continued his search not more than twenty steps away from me. Four others caught my eye, and I placed them into my pack along with the first three books of documented history. These four appealed to me as they were most likely written as childhood bedtime stories and tended to fetch a higher price.

I have never read anything about magical ruby slippers. I am unsure what rubies are, but the artwork revealed a much brighter royal crimson that shined like Mystic Silver. The flying monkeys gave it away for sure, although I was undoubtedly skeptical from the beginning when the talking scarecrow was introduced. This first bedtime story I found was called *The Wonderful Wizard of Oz* by an author named L. Frank Baum.

The next one I picked up was a book entitled *The Wind in the Willows* by an author named Kenneth Grahame, with one also cited as the character illustrator Ernest H. Shepard. What a peculiar little story of talking animals— one an odd Toad with an unquenchable wild persona, another a Badger, well distinguished, almost to the extent of reminding me of my father in a way. It must mean that I am the Toad, as Badger and his other friends, Ratty and Mole as they are called, constantly tried to curb Toad's unruly behavior. However, I am likely more unruly from within rather than the outward expression displayed by Toad.

I blew a hunk of dust off the next book I raised from the pile to reveal its title, *Charlotte's Web,* by an author named E.B. White. This one had talking animals as well, along with a talking spider. Believe me, if I ever heard a spider talk, I would crush it! The thought of running into a spider in the Unlight still turns my stomach. Once documented, yet again by our famous explorer, Sandulf Collins, is what we know as Mystic Menardis. They are an arachnid breed, described to be just larger than a normal-sized residence door. As authenticated, they are found throughout the Unlight but habitually remain in humid places. They collect dust from Mystic Silver and ingest it. The creature's webbing is highly resilient to tearing or breaking. It is not hard to spot, mostly appearing like giant glowing bulbs in the dark as Mystic Silver makes their abdomen illuminate bright gold and jaffa. The rest of their body is a splatter of royal crimson and dark cocoa. Highly intelligent, the creatures prefer the taste of Gloom Gnawers rather than trying something new like human flesh. It was also documented that the creature can vocalize its thoughts but this became dismissed on pure conjecture.

In selecting my last book from the dusty pile, *Where the Wild Things Are* by an author named Maurice Sendak, I peered toward Elior, staring face-to-face with one of the creepy, eight-legged monstrosities. I felt my blood freeze but stared as Elior stepped bravely forward, and the creature slowly backed into the shadows. Yet its body still shimmered, its eyes peering back from the darkness. The creature's abdomen began to glow brighter gold and jaffa, revealing a transparent heart beating at ease. It was not frightened.

Elior peered back at me with a smile and motioned me to come and stand next to him. I cannot say I did not hesitate, but his grin comforted my racing pulse. After a few moments passed, I joined Elior before the enormous arachnid, serenely staring back. The MKR whispered to me to hold out my hand, palm facing upward. I trusted Elior, yet I did so tremblingly.

My eyes shut tightly, and I could hear Elior softly chuckle. I slowly began to feel a hairy leg caress my hand in a circular motion, its texture springy and coarse. The eight-eyed dome peeked out of the shadows and into the light of my lantern. Dare I say I felt like the spider was smiling back at me through its dripping fangs?

"I am still terrified," I uttered to Elior.

"So is she," he replied. "Do not take your hand away till she pulls away. She is getting to know your taste, which will insult her if you do so."

I watched as the Mystic Menardis slowly pulled its hairy leg back from my hand and nibbled on it.

"She will know you from now on," Elior said. "She knows now that you are trustworthy and likely to share your taste with others like her."

"How does she know that?" I asked.

Elior explained that Mystic Menardis could taste anything—fear, greed, hope, love, gratitude, sadness, joy, evil, and much more. And if it had tasted something awful like evil or greed, it would have killed me.

"I am still terrified," I said again.

"Good," Elior huffed out another chuckle. "It means you respect them. They are private creatures and should not be tampered with. But, should you return to the Unlight, know now that you have an ally in the shadows."

"Likely not going to happen," I conveyed.

Elior just smiled back at me. It was the first time I did not appreciate seeing it. He stared into my eyes and then turned his gaze downward where the spider huddled. I followed his eyes and saw a dusty book lying under the arachnid. I turned my gaze back to Elior. He motioned to me.

"Will you be so kind as to retrieve that book?" he asked.

I felt a lump in my throat too large to swallow. A cold sweat swarmed all over my body. I heard a gasp just behind me. Elior and I turned to see Cenobia, struck just as fearful as me. The MKR put up his hand and ordered her not to scream. I turned back to Elior, who raised an impatient eyebrow as if to say, "I am still waiting."

For whatever reason, I trusted Elior. I slowly approached the shadows and bent on one knee to grasp the book. I felt a gentle tap on my head from the spider, almost the same way you pat the head of an obedient child. I picked up the book and wiped the dust off the stern, leather-bound cover. I am unsure what type of hide it came from, but I stood and glanced at the title.

"What does it say?" Elior asked me.

"The book is by an author named Jules Verne," I replied. "The title is *Robur the Conqueror*. Is this..."

"It is one that belongs to me," Elior interrupted and took hold of the book.

"Begging your pardon Master Keeper," Cenobia politely intruded. "Would you be able to share with us what that is about? What history lies within those pages?"

Elior kept his smile, seeing the two of us were intrigued. "It is historical. They are a couple of the last novels by this writer who wrote its sequel, 'Master of the World,' at the time his health was failing him. He was fearful in his precedence about the rising of tyrants."

The explanation confused Cenobia and me; Elior could see it on our faces. Cenobia seemed disinterested in hearing more and respectfully took her leave. I also believe she was having difficulty being so close to the eight-legged monster. Yet Elior could see my concrete curiosity, and he began to elaborate more, but not about Jules Verne.

"This book is not exactly what it seems," Elior kept his voice low as if the walls had ears. "Look closely."

I looked closer at the cover as the MKR held it up, and then I heard Elior whisper words in a language I had never heard before.

Seoda sa Ceapach i dhúiseacht. Lig dom do rúin a ghlacadh.

Astonishing—is the only word I could use to describe the indescribable phenomenon. The book in Elior's hands began to morph and change into a completely different bound book. The cover changed to show a burned design of tilting trees reaching toward one another. The tangled roots stretched down and around to create a circle of thorns, surrounding what appeared to be six Oculus objects.

"What was that you said?" I inquired.

"Open the cover," Elior replied with a smile, handing the book to me.

I did as he told me, and I saw the exact words he had spoken written just on the inside of the cover as if precisely etched in and illuminated by sunlight.

Seoda sa Ceapach i dhúiseacht. Lig dom do rúin a ghlacadh.

"What does it mean?"

"Gems in the Glade awake. Let your secrets be mine to take," Elior replied, his voice hushed. "Keep these words hidden only with you. There is great evil seeking to find this and unlock its secrets."

I began turning through the book, and Elior could see how puzzled I was that all the pages were blank. I looked back to the MKR as he pointed to the only phrase visible inside the cover.

"Memorize it and its meaning," he explained. "Once you do, in time, the book will reveal more to you. If you are in danger, the book will hide itself as it did before, even from you. So, you must know the words to awaken it again."

"You are giving this to me?" I asked, almost breathless.

"To keep for a time," he replied. "There are many who wish to possess this, and if I walk out of the Unlight with it, it will be known the book was found. I will come for it in time."

"Why do you trust me?" I wanted to know.

Elior did not cease grinning. He grasped the book from my hands and placed it in my pack. Without another word, he slipped away from me. I desperately wanted to scream, frustrated as I had suddenly become, to demand an answer. His warning, the burden he had just placed on me, made me fear for my life. I pulled the book from my pack and opened the cover, ensuring no one was watching. I gazed at the etched shimmering words in front of me. I did my best to remember how Elior pronounced them. I spoke the words softly again to the book, and the words illuminated brighter. I did it again, and the words grew even brighter still.

"Aagneya?" I heard Nirnasha's voice behind me.

I snapped the book shut.

"What have you got there?"

I heard his footsteps moving toward me, and I turned to see his face but kept the book at my side, facing away from him.

"Just a book that appeared interesting to me," I said, noticing my voice was shaky.

I could tell he was reaching for the book, and I almost pulled away, yet he had already grasped it. He held up the cover to the light of his lantern.

"Robur the Conqueror by Jules Verne," Nirnasha said. "Why, Aagneya, you got yourself a rare find indeed. This one does not appear damaged at all!"

"I was hoping no one would take notice," I said. "I know it is a rare find, and I did not want anyone trying to take it from me."

Nirnasha smiled. "No worries. I know what you mean. I, too, found a mint condition book with three titles bound within the cover."

"Really?" I asked, trying to deter his attention from Elior's book. "What are the titles?"

"I could probably retire on it," Nirnasha replied, placing Elior's book in my hand. *The Lord of the Rings* by an author named J.R.R. Tolkien. The three titles within its pages were *Fellowship of the Ring*, *The Two Towers*, and *Return of the King*.

"You might regret selling it," I said, slowly placing Elior's book from my hand back into my pack.

"Regret?" Nirnasha appeared surprised. "I would sell it because that is what being an explorer is all about."

"I am not sure I agree," I explained. "I mean, that…I truly love the feel of books in my hands, and not because they would make me wealthy. I find the reward is knowing the history they entail and the stories they portray."

"You sound more like a professor than an explorer," he chuckled. He then motioned for me to follow him. "Come on professor, rejoin the others. I think we are about ready to depart with our loot."

Both of us ceased in our steps, noticing a noise from the dark. I thought it was the Mystic Menardis moving further upward through the ruins. But it stopped moving, and I felt we were being watched by something more unusual and dangerous.

Our next moments were remaining still with our lanterns. Perhaps one of the other explorers was trying to scare us. Yet the resounding soft echo that tickled my ears again came like a crunching and suckling noise. Nirnasha and I peered upward. A shadow came into view, rapidly falling toward us, and we jumped out of the way of Pramyan's broken body.

Nirnasha shoved his hand over my mouth to keep me from screaming. He swiftly examined the body, shining his lantern over the corpse. The top of Pramyan's skull appeared gruesomely torn, but not from the fall. With a closer look, I saw several bite marks all over his legs and arms, exposing the insides of his muscle tissue. Nirnasha quickly turned his gaze upward, and my eyes followed. Several more shadows suddenly landed in front of us and just behind us. I screamed but yanked my drill gun from its holster, firing and hoping two things would occur. One, hit and kill the thing. Two, alert the others. But of course, I missed it.

When my drill bit ricocheted off the ground, the creature reared back but then began pressing forward like a hound on all fours. The thing appeared humanoid yet lacked the posture to stand upright. Its skin glistened as if covered in a slimy substance but was darker than sable. More appeared above us. All of them screeched ear-piercing echoes, unhinging their jaws to reveal unnatural jagged teeth.

The blade of a machete flashed in the light of my lantern and swung wildly at the creatures in front of us. It appeared to take them off guard, and they swiftly leaped aside. My feet were in a full sprint before I even had another thought. Cenobia, though an older woman, matched my speed with Nirnasha right behind us.

We heard the screeching fiends bearing down on our heels as we turned down the departing corridor, flickering with the lantern lights of the others. A bright beam flashed, and I felt a hot blast race by me. I dared not look back, but another light illuminated me. Again, another beam of heat whizzed by. I looked to see it strike one of the monsters that had just leaped to grab me. I lost my balance and skidded on my back, screaming as another one bared down and pounced. In mid-air with its face about to feast on me, another beam of light cut clean through it. Whatever juices resided in its flesh, dark and sticky, bathed me from head to toe as the two halves split and fell on either side.

Fortuitously, I did not have my mouth open. I felt Cenobia and Nirnasha rip me from the ground and pull me to my feet, and we were off running again. As we reached the others, I heard buzzsaw rifles zinging out several rounds. Elior was among them.

"Pleased to see you are in one piece," he told Cenobia, Nirnasha, and me. "I did not have time to be in two places simultaneously."

"What do you mean?" Cenobia asked.

"We were also attacked," Bartus interjected. "We got Prowlers trying to eat us and..."

"That will be quite enough," Elior concluded by holding up a glowing hand, somewhat reinforcing Bartus' understanding of who was in charge. "I assume Prowlers ambushed you."

"Yes," Cenobia replied.

"If Prowlers are about," Elior stated. "Then the Lurker horde will not be far away."

"Why do I hear more buzzsaw rifles outside?" I asked.

"The captain is ensuring the Prowlers do not block our escape," Elior explained. "His soldiers are in good spirits, and we should join them immed..."

Elior ceased his words, catching sight of Nirnasha standing by the dark pool. The boy had an expression of fascination and wonder, standing on the edge of it. He was slowly leaning forward, appearing hypnotized by something in the water. Elior swiftly but silently moved near the pool but did not reach its edge.

"Nirnasha," Elior whispered firmly. "Nirnasha. Do not reach for it!"

Nirnasha glanced slightly toward the MKR, but did not respond. His eyes returned to whatever was mesmerizing him under the water's surface. He bent a knee to reach down, his hand outstretched, slowly reaching to touch the surface of the black pool.

"Nirnasha," I yelled at him. "Nirnasha. What are you doing? Stop!"

"She is going to make me one of them," he fumbled back a reply.

"No," Elior insisted. "She only wants to eat your heart."

"She loves me," Nirnasha stuttered out. I could see sweat beating down his brow. "I know she does."

"She does not," Elior pressed, his eyes illuminating brightly to their golden hue. I saw his hand behind his back begin to manifest a ball of light. "Nirnasha, if you reach for her below the water's surface, you will endanger us all. She is a Tide Maiden. She is not going to give you what you desire."

Nirnasha's eyes peered upward to meet Elior's again. He was trembling profusely. It did appear he was hearing Elior's words and wanting to follow them, yet he could not do so. The tension held between the two. Suddenly, Elior thrust his hand forward, releasing a beam of light. Before Nirnasha could react, his right arm became severed from his body. The young explorer reared back, blaring in agony, and his arm fell into the water. It sank into the darkness, and two other veteran explorers quickly nabbed him from the water's edge, his missing limb cauterized below his shoulder.

"Sorry," Nirnasha mumbled out of his intense wincing. "I am sorry. I am sorry."

"I believe you," Elior reassured him. He watched the other two explorers help Nirnasha to dress the cauterized area and inject him with a numbing agent. Elior turned to me and spoke firmly. "Stay away from dark pools."

"What would have happened?" I did not realize the question had escaped my lips before I received an answer.

"I would not fill your mind with such nightmares," the MKR replied. "We must leave before the Tide Maiden alerts any others, and they surface to nab more of us. We do not need to deal with more abominations when the horde of Lurkers is likely near."

Bartus led the way with some others to rejoin the soldiers outside the ruins. We all exited through the narrow, winding path leading out into the great open cavern. The captain and his soldiers were still holding their ground. I pitied the motionless ones, cradled by the smooth cavern slate. The captain held their name tags in his hand and ripped another one from the neck of the deceased. Not many soldiers were left—and not as many books would be leaving with us either.

"They were waiting for us," the captain sighed as Elior and the rest of us reached them. "They are still waiting. We thought there were only a few. We were wrong."

"I am sorry, friend," Elior replied.

"I need not your apologies MKR," the captain quickly retorted. "I should not have given the order to charge. We should have driven them back and then waited in the light. We should have…"

"Your wishful thinking will not help us live," Elior placed a firm hand on the captain's shoulder. "We must keep our wits and be clever, much more than we anticipated."

"What do you mean?" The captain asked.

"Hardwin, you know there are worse things in the dark than Lurkers or Tide Maidens," Elior explained. "Wendigo is here. The horde follows him."

"We cannot go back the way we came in," Hardwin replied. "We will have to push through and look for a different passage back to the surface."

"Was this a suicide mission or something?" I belted out, feeling my frustration erupt from my toes and build into my face.

"It was more than that," Hardwin shouted me down. He paused a moment, realizing his voice was echoing throughout the cavern. He returned his tone to normal and then spoke to all of us. "We needed to secure an artifact. Yet we were not able to find it."

"What was this artifact?" Bartus demanded.

"A book," Hardwin replied. "A book filled with secrets of magic."

I saw Elior out of the corner of my eye. He did not even turn his gaze toward me. I knew the book Hardwin was speaking of, yet my heart held my tongue and shut my mouth. I had been entrusted with the task of guarding the *Gems of the Hidden Glade*.

"We need to find our way out of this place," Elior interjected. "We will have greater troubles if Wendigo gets anywhere near us."

Elior began trekking in the opposite direction from whence we had entered the cavern, severing more Lurkers with his beams of light as he went. I quickly followed him, not only because I was frightened, but because I desperately wanted to speak with him about the name or creature he kept mentioning as if everyone was supposed to know it. Elior waved my question off and told me to focus on staying close to him. Cenobia chimed in on my question, whispering to me in hushed-filled tones.

She told me about a slender, upright humanoid abomination with a body of dense bone and cartilage. I did not find it surprising that Elior was the main contributor to the documents Cenobia had read, but I did find it peculiar Elior did not wish to tell me himself. Perhaps it was the same as with the Tide Maidens. Yet even Cenobia only gave me small details from what I believed to be thorough manuscripts of the creature. She delved deeper into its appearance as we followed Elior to a new route out of the cavern.

Wendigo's skull is similar to a human, yet protrudes six prehensile serpent-like tentacles from the sides of its head, three on each side, and have small, snappy heads of their own that bear razor-sharp teeth and the ability to taste the scented air around them. Its face has nothing, no eyes, ears, or mouth. Yet it has eyes on the back of its elongated hands with only two elongated fingers and one opposable thumb. The eyes on its hands glow royal crimson, but Wendigo does not use them for seeing. Instead, they vibrate its unsettling presence.

"Enough," Elior stepped in to cut off Cenobia's words. "We do not need Aagneya more frightened as she is right now."

"What is not clear in the manuscripts about Wendigo is whether the creature is real or is a spirit that embodies a vessel," Bartus chimed in, which only made Elior turn with a glare on his face.

"I said enough!" He reprimanded the both of them. "I shall not have the poor girl frightened more than she is. Keep your tongues from flapping!"

"I am not as frightened as you suppose," I said. One of Elior's eyebrows lifted.

"Tell me, Aagneya," Elior replied as we had now halted our quickened pace in a pitch-sable tunnel. "Do you want to be?"

I could not believe it when I felt my shoulders shrug and saw another grin on Elior's face that was not so peaceful, but slightly terrifying.

"Captain," Elior called him over without taking his eyes off me. "Take the others on ahead. The horde is behind us now. Miss Aagneya and I shall catch up shortly."

I was not too fond of the sound of that. But I did not resist. Hardwin and the others continued onward. Cenobia insisted she remained behind with me as well. Elior's eyebrow raised again but complied with her request. We stood in the gloom, our lanterns dimmed. Elior laid one hand on Cenobia's back and the other on mine, gripping our clothing. His eyes began to glow gold like starlight, and the light from our lanterns brightened, no doubt by his magic, to illuminate the figures lurking toward us.

"Wendigo embodies the spirit of starving lusts," Elior uttered. "When its eyes glow from the top of its hands, they pierce and weaken the spirit, destroying the will of any living thing to give in and believe the taste of flesh is all that matters. I am unsure what will happen when Wendigo draws near, but you will feel the hunger rise. You will want to run, but you will not."

My lips quivered, and my body quaked. I do not know how, but I felt a presence that began stirring something in me. I could sense Cenobia was feeling it as well. The weight of Elior's hand on my back gripped me tighter. Then in the haze of the illuminated tunnel, a slender figure came into focus, standing approximately ninety-six units in height. Its body appeared pale and dullish. Its head indeed protruded six prehensile serpent-like tentacles from the sides. The creature had no eyes, ears, mouth, or face. I peered downward at its hands, showing only three long, boney phalanges. I saw the eyes open on the back of its hands, emitting a glow of royal crimson. Wendigo was surrounded by undead trailing him as if the monster were their champion—they continued to draw near to our lights.

Again, I felt something clawing at me, as if from the inside. I could feel the heads on the tentacles tasting my scent. The air around the creature whispered its name, sharp like a dagger penetrating all my senses, making my eyes swell with tears. I was enveloped in uncontrollable sobbing and an overwhelming sensation to feed on the flesh beside me.

I locked eyes with Cenobia, my mouth drooling and temperament escalating to savagery. Yet I was still terrified by Wendigo, swiftly now, racing toward us. The resounding of its name escalated louder, and feverish drips pulsed down my head. I blinked, and then Wendigo was gone. Cenobia and I fell, gasping for air, almost like something choked us violently. The cravings for flesh remained coursing through my veins. Yet Elior reassured us it would pass as he continued holding us apart.

"We must move quickly to the others," Elior said, helping both Cenobia and me to our feet. "From now on, you shall know when Wendigo is drawing near. You have tasted him and lived. You will know when he is coming whenever you find yourself back here in the dark."

I found breathing difficult, but I began placing one foot in front of the other. My joints were stiff, and my soul shaken into a haze, with a churning sensation in my gut. I heaved out a liquid substance, one not of bile but a sparkling, pale goo mixed with blood. Cenobia did the same. And periodically, we continued vomiting it as we raced to catch up with the others. My mind slowly returned to me, but the cravings for flesh did not fade from my bones maybe within the second hour. The hunger dwindled just as we caught up with the others.

Every explorer drew weary from the weight they bore, but refused to throw their books away, ridding ourselves of our wilderness bedding and other gear. Some even rid themselves of the extra ammo they carried. The veteran explorers had taken up much of the load the soldiers were supposed to carry back to the surface. But the adrenaline rush soon ended for the group, and I could see that we were beginning to decelerate significantly. We were not going to outrun the horde or Wendigo.

Hardwin halted us and motioned to speak with Elior. The MKR approached the gasping captain. This time, I was not close enough to hear the conversation between the two, yet I suspected it had something to do with Elior assisting us in our escape. I saw him nod to Hardwin, and the captain ordered us to continue. We moved slowly, following in the captain's footsteps. But Elior did not move.

He captured the concern in my eyes and smiled to put me at ease. He whispered to me that he would see me again.

"Keep it safe," I heard him say. "Do not let go of it."

I watched Elior pull light from my lantern and form it into a hovering ball in his hand. The light of my lantern did not fade as it appeared Elior reproduced the glow from one power source to create his own.

"What do you call that spell?" I asked before I joined in following the others.

"Not sure," he replied. "I have not thought of a name for this ability yet."

"It would seem to me that you are revealing the replication of light," I said. "Why not call it something like Radiant Reveal?"

"It has a nice ring," he replied.

I turned and hastened my steps. I took only one glimpse back at the MKR, seeing the light source grow brighter and brighter into a ball of great size. It floated high above him, and his arms fell to rest at his side. I would see him again, which is the only reason I can explain what happened as Elior waited.

After about a two-day journey, I felt a soft touch on my shoulder in the middle of my slumber. Cenobia roused me that Elior had returned to us. I popped up and hurried to see him sitting by the bright lamplight. Hardwin was sitting beside the MKR, who appeared wholly weary. His top hat was gone, his hair muddled, his face smudged with muck, and his clothes tattered. He sipped water from a canteen as I sat across from him. He looked up and did not hesitate to tell me not to be concerned with him. And he did not wait for me to ask any questions. Instead, he began from the time I last saw him.

Wendigo came with the horde shortly after Elior ceased hearing our footsteps. The Lurkers did not care for the light source the MKR created and remained hesitant to approach. Wendigo, however, was not affected by the brightness. The eyes on the monster's hands remained shut as the slender creature approached Elior. The MKR began blasting it with beams of light that should have cut and burned through Wendigo's body. Yet the beams only shoved it back, and the penetrations remained shallow like scraping a dagger across a rock.

The abomination kept charging him, doing its best to grab hold of Elior. The MKR kept to his tactics, disappearing and reappearing away from Wendigo's grasp. But the light source Elior created dimmed and shrank each time he used magic. In his last efforts, Elior shot a beam of light into the crowd of Lurkers, cutting down several into an explosion of intense light, setting ablaze the area of Lurkers, sending all screeching in retreat. The bright light and fire stole Wendigo's attention, allowing Elior to slip away.

"How did you not succumb to Wendigo's cravings?" I asked.

"I ignore it," Elior replied, chuckling when he saw my reaction.

The creature, Wendigo, sounded more frightening to me the longer Elior described his encounter. Elior could see my concern, or at least I felt he could. But I desperately wanted to know the MKR's answer to how he could resist the cravings. His response did not provide the comfort I was seeking.

"I know you can still feel the cravings," Elior looked at me. "They are not as strong, but they will burrow into your dreams, even give you nightmares. You shall not be rid of them."

"Is there a way?"

"Not unless Wendigo is killed," he replied. "But there is something I can try to help you ignore the cravings the way I can."

"Do it then," we heard Cenobia firmly state from the shadows. I was startled, and I had completely forgotten she was with us. Her body appeared worse than mine, feverish and teeth grinding. I was worried for her, and I could not believe I did not take notice when she awoke me earlier.

"Her body is dying." Elior's head slowly perked up. "She is giving in to the cravings of Wendigo."

"Why did you show us Wendigo?" I demanded. "If you knew this would be the result, why did you not make us leave?"

Elior ignored my questions and stared intensely at Cenobia, as did I. Her skin was beginning to peel, revealing muscles decaying—her eyes milky like staring at a corpse from the grave.

"We must get her to the surface," Elior said. "It should not be long now. If we can get her into the sunlight, I can heal her."

Hardwin swiftly assembled his remaining soldiers, and they quickly followed not far behind him. Elior held them to a whisper and told them what must be done about Cenobia. We swiftly broke camp, and everyone began to trek upward through the steep tunnel. On my way into the tunnel, I noticed over a dozen gold lights illuminating the shadows, radiant like the same abdomen of the Mystic Menardis I had met earlier in the ruins with Elior. The MKR was not far behind me, with two soldiers carrying Cenobia, who had her bound in case she fully became what I hoped she would not.

"I thought only Mystic Silver turns dead things into Lurkers," I said to Elior as we pressed hard onward and upward.

"For most cases, yes," the MKR agreed. "Yet Wendigo can turn even the living into becoming his own. If one cannot fight or escape the hunger, they succumb to it. Think of it as a sort of ethereal poisoning."

"You mean the existence of the celestial?" Bartus interjected with a scoffing tone. "There is no such thing."

Elior and I moved aside and let the soldiers hasten in front of us. Bartus did the same. We began moving again, and soon I saw a brightness I had not seen in many days. I stepped out, feeling the warmth of a mid-afternoon on my skin. After basking briefly in daylight, I knelt beside Cenobia, lying down, still shivering, losing her color, and being pulled into death's grip. The MKR stooped beside her and brought a ball of light into his hand. He placed his other hand on Cenobia's chest.

"What do you believe in then, Master Explorer Bartus?" Elior asked.

"Are you trying to debate me about the existence of the ethereal?" Bartus scoffed again.

"You see magic with your own eyes, something far beyond your grasp. You do not have faith that there is such a place as the ethereal?" Elior asked. "I do find that odd."

The MKR's retort drew somewhat of a crowd of us, even Hardwin, inching closer to hear Elior's words and see a miraculous sight. Cenobia began to appear less pale, regaining her color. Her shivering began to ease, and her breathing commenced to draw in a peaceful posture. I could scarcely believe her body being magically healed. However, Bartus made it challenging to enjoy the moment. He started babbling again, trying to best Elior in knowledge. But no one shouted him down, not even the captain. I believe we were all enjoying seeing Bartus educated by a Master Keeper.

"Faith?" Bartus spat. "Faith is nothing more than religious rubbish. I believe in what I can see. I can see magic plain as day. Yet it is absolutely foolish to believe in what you cannot."

"At last, we agree on one thing," Elior interjected. "Religion is nonsense.

However, faith is not the same as religion. Am I to assume correctly that you wake up each day and, when you can, gaze into the mirror and not have faith you are breathing? You cannot see the air in and out of your lungs, but you can feel it. Faith is no different—it is what makes the unseen tangible."

Bartus appeared at a loss for words. I could see he was trying desperately to find an argument for his reasoning.

"The cosmos is a vast wealth of knowledge that cannot be attained in one lifetime, nor a thousand lifetimes," Elior continued. "As an educated man, you should understand that even though you may know much, what you do know is very little compared to all of the knowledge in the universe. To believe the ethereal does not exist, you, dear Master Explorer, have faith that it does not. The only reason you do not have faith that the ethereal exists is that you cannot prove that it does not exist. And you will not have enough time in your life to do so.

Faith is much like magic. Magic is what I am, not what I do. Every man, woman, and child holds the power to change the way they think, walk, act, talk, and develop. Faith is given to us so we can be awakened to what is already inside us. Faith rouses us to what is not seen. Yet faith is given to us only by what we cannot see. Thus, to assume such things do not exist without seeking them out first is foolish.

Which of your accomplishments can you take with you to the grave? What colleagues will stand beside you when you no longer have eyes to see? What will define you then? You end up living a life full of accomplishments only to waste away, only to find that after your last breath, the things you did see no longer matter. They cease to exist as you can no longer see them."

"We are all destined for that day," Bartus managed to state.

"Really," Elior grinned, rising to his feet and stepping away from Cenobia. "Then I shall speak plainly. You are indeed blinded by what you see. Unlike you, I have never seen my body whither, my mind fade, or my heart cease beating forever. But I will see yours do so and many more after you are gone and forgotten. So, when I speak of the ethereal, I suggest you gain the knowledge and receive the faith of its existence before you even think about trying to debate about it because at least one of us has been there and remains seen to speak of it."

We heard a hovering sound above us. It shook us all from the shock of Elior's confirmation about the ethereal. We turned our eyes upward to see a Westmain wairship, low and dropping a platform to the ground. I turned to see our captain holding a Magic Bean.

Hardwin sent a distress signal with his SHC when we reached the surface. The wairship was a patrol craft that, thankfully, was already close by and I held a thankful heart to not be walking home. After welcoming us aboard, they assigned us to our quarters, but I remained mainly in the medical ward with Cenobia, scribbling notes of what I had seen and heard. I cannot honestly explain the terror I still feel when in the dark. I often remember being in that place when the sun cradles into the horizon and gives way to dusk. Then I know the land shall rise in shadow, and I may have nightmares of my first journey to the Unlight. And yet my dreams held the image of a superb protector named Elior, who brought peace to my thoughts as I closed my eyes.

SKIES OF WOE

The vigilant nurse tending to Cenobia ensured I also ate dinner that night. The physical trauma to Cenobia's body had not fully healed, as Elior could only bring her back from becoming a Lurker, yet her skin remained covered in open sores. While I ate, I took the opportunity to glimpse around at the soldiers who traveled with us. Not one was unscathed, and only twelve made it back alive.

I witnessed Hardwin speaking with them. I could sense the empathy in his posture. And he did not approach them as captain but as an equal. He laughed with them, communicated informally, and even sneaked in a bottle of Jaffa Blossom Wine. I had never witnessed a high-ranking commander act toward his soldiers in such a manner. In fact, I noticed formalities practically ceased aboard the whole vessel. The nurse was kind enough to explain that formalities aboard this particular wairship are only necessary when tradition is observed. Direct questioning and direct responses were the admiral's leadership style, and informalities were often necessary to maintain loyalty and morale—a shared ideology I witnessed with Hardwin and those under his command.

The nurse then shooed me out of the ward once Cenobia stirred to consciousness. She encouraged me to my quarters under a soldier's escort, insisting I be forced to rest. The nurse commended me for remaining beside my friend, but there was "no need for another patient" for such an easily treated condition as exhaustion. I kissed Cenobia's forehead and leaned on the soldier escorting me back to my quarters. I could scarcely keep my eyes open. We were not to return to Langdon for another week or so. We were fortunate that the wairship remained on patrol longer than its schedule. Its next objective was to assist in transporting military might to reinforce the Westmain city of Starvel in the southern region.

Westmain, much like Nod, had its own civil conflicts. Fortunately, northern Westmain held the military might for a time, controlling the skies and fortifying positions along the southern regions of Triune, Starvel, and Harvenger to prevent a full-scale invasion. Yet Starvel continued to be the target of the rebel's push, as the city would be a foothold into the north. Despite the military advantage of the northern army, its weakness (I believe) is in the government arena. One side held the debate of full-scale invasion in high regard, while the opposing members stood unwavering in diplomacy with the rebels in the south. The arguments remained drawn out so long that the southern forces could build their numbers, acquire upgraded weaponry through criminal market trade to Nod's northern kingdom, and amass a strategy to challenge Westmain's vantage points. Total war broke out, with the rebels taking much of the southern realm, staging from Reave and Folesk to capturing Botel. It took Westmain's forces by surprise, pushing them back to make their stand at Starvel. Without hesitation or consent from the congressional governing members, the northern forces created a strategic blockade preventing the rebels from advancing.

By the time the congressional agreed upon a declaration of war, the northern military was already in action, reinforcing the front lines. New blockades were erected to create a new border that helped quash enemy advancements. Suddenly, the North and South remained locked into a stalemated conflict that lasted several years before I attended Langdon University. It was not difficult to piece together why our expedition was so crucial. While we were to receive compensation for the books we brought back, the North of Westmain devised to sell the books at a higher value to Eastguard or North Nod to pay for the war, perhaps even in exchange for higher quantities of Mystic Silver.

"Have you kept it safe?" A soft voice reached me from the other side of the door to my quarters. I did not go to bed as directed but instead found a burst of energy to stay awake and write down the details of my venture. And no sooner did I shut my eyes after climbing into a warm bed did I realize that I journaled all night. Again, the voice reached me, and I scooched out of bed, fully recognizing the individual. I approached the door after putting on my robe, a borrowed accoutrement from the nursing ward that was kindly left by my soldier escort. Strangely though, I could not see any sunlight underneath the cabin door. I first deemed that maybe I was wrong and the MKR's visit was not during waking hours. However, I opened the door to a gust of strong winds and saw inauspicious clouds beating the wairship with rain. Unsure of how I heard such a soft utterance from Elior kept me perplexed. Yet I glanced over to my left, and there he sat poised on a seat just outside my room. He lifted his head, pulling back the brim of a new dark cocoa top hat, one slightly shorter than the one he lost, revealing his charming and childlike grin.

"Was it you who asked me, 'Have you kept it safe?'" I pulled my robe tighter around my chest. The chilling winds became more brutal as I tried to step outside. Elior slowly rose and stood before my door, keeping the winds from touching me.

"I believe it was," he replied. "I hope you slept well."

"For what trauma befell us," I conveyed, "I slept as good as one could hope."

"Then you are ready to take another look at the book?" Elior asked.

"I did not envision I would be revisiting its pages," I said. "I thought you would reclaim it in time."

"Indeed, I shall," Elior admitted. "For now, I wish you to learn more."

"Why do you wish such a thing?" I found my tone to become somewhat demanding.

"I believe you would do well with the book's secrets," Elior replied. "Shall we waste time here so people start to gossip, or shall you get dressed and follow me?"

His demeanor did not diminish in kindness, but I could feel he was pressing me to make haste. I nodded my compliance and slipped into some thermal tights before wrestling with skinny denim trousers cut just a hair smaller than my size. Undoubtedly, they were new and needed my round south end to stretch them out a bit. As I have said, I do not usually like to discuss my frame, but I have received so many compliments from college bachelors that I have learned to accept it as my lot in life. While my frame might be petite in a way with hardly any voluptuous melons to be pressed up into a corset, I have bruised many handsy gentlemen who were influenced by their biology and intoxicant inner monologue ramblings trying to squeeze my hindquarters. Whatever the reason, I gazed at my figure abnormally in the mirror that day. And with a huff, I dismissed my critical thoughts, throwing my fit and flare frock over me as I swung open the door. My frock had just been thoroughly drying out by the fire after a nice soap soak and scrub to remove the stench of the Unlight. My cozy relief from wearing the thing was short-lived when I stepped out into the bone-chilling air again into the rain, accompanying Elior to one of the three study quarters on the wairship.

I carried my pack with me, containing all the books I recovered from our journey—including the infamous secret book belonging to Elior. I was certainly interested in knowing more of the secrets of the book. But what intrigued me even more—why the MKR wanted me to learn them. I could feel a small smile come to my face, sensing Elior pressing against my lower back as he opened the door, a gentleman's way of being well-mannered to lead a lady into a private conversation. I felt my hastened heart rate diminish when I noticed Nirnasha sitting quietly in the corner of the room.

In the dim light, his sable skin kept him mysteriously in the shadows. He pulled up his right arm, a newly equipped prosthetic molded from folded steel and enchanted with Mystic Silver, making it essentially indestructible and fully functioning as an artificial limb to replace the extremity Elior had taken from him. It shimmered in the lantern light as he gave Elior a slight wave and another grateful thank you before he bid me good morning.

"I do not understand," I whispered to Elior. "Is he supposed to be here?"

"I wish the both of you to have a seat," Elior beckoned us, motioning to the table in the center of the room.

I joined Nirnasha as we moved to sit. Elior waited for both of us to settle in before joining us.

"What I am about to divulge to you can never be uttered from this room," the MKR explained. "Therefore, I will not speak it aloud. But commune it another way. However, you must agree to keep this secret for all time. Otherwise, death shall befall you."

"Why would we die?" Nirnasha asked.

Elior's eyes glowed brightly in their golden hue. His hand came up, and a ball of dim, swirling light began to appear.

"Asking stupid questions can also bring sudden demise," Elior's voice echoed, but not aloud. Nirnasha was just as startled as I was to hear the MKR's voice speaking to us in our thoughts. I could not only hear Elior, but I felt his presence inside my mind somehow. I admit, I almost wet my trousers.

"Do not speak aloud," we heard Elior's echo within us. "If you wish to speak, simply think of what you wish to say."

"I am confused," I thought. I heard my voice echo all around me, and Nirnasha's eyes shot toward me.

"I can also hear you," Nirnasha's echo returned to me. "How is this happening?"

"Quiet your minds." We heard Elior's echo overwhelm our own. "There are secrets that are too precious for spoken words. For even the wind can have ears."

"Please tell us what you wish us to know," I shifted excitedly in my seat. I saw Nirnasha nod from across the table. Elior reached into my pack. He pulled out the book that belonged to him, *Gems of the Hidden Glade*, disguised in magic as another entitled *Robur the Conqueror*.

Seoda sa Ceapach i dhúiseacht. Lig dom do rúin a ghlacadh.
(Gems in the glade awake. Let your secrets be mine to take).

The magic of the stiff leather book awoke, and the MKR opened it. He withdrew a glowing metal, which I knew was Mystic Silver, and reached into the ball of light still pulsing from his other hand.

"The world needs more of us," Elior began. "I have chosen both of you."

"Chosen us for what?" Nirnasha asked.

"Your will is to remain your own," Elior explained with soft and gentle persuasion. "But I desire your assistance. I have need for you both. War is not the only shadow on the horizon for this world."

"Begging your pardon," Nirnasha resounded. "Can you please be more direct?"

"Is it not obvious?" Elior replied. "I am awakening you both to become Master Keepers."

"How is this possible?" I replied, realizing even my audible inner monologue was demanding when sparked by curiosity. "I have already touched Mystic Silver. How can you awaken us?"

"As have I," Nirnasha chimed in agreement. "What if this shall kill us both?"

"Do either of you know how an MKR is created?" Elior grinned. "A Keeper cannot become an MKR because they have already been awakened. To try and take them farther would destroy them. The only way to awaken someone is for Mystic Silver not to affect them at all."

"Are you saying ordinary people can become Master Keepers?" I chuckled to myself. Elior did not appear as amused as I, and Nirnasha did not seem to find it amusing either. I sank back in my chair.

As the moments passed, my thoughts increased in fascination, jumbling my blood with a thrilling sensation at the notion that I could become like Elior. I could see Nirnasha pondering the wonders of living as an MKR. We soon wholeheartedly agreed to Elior's request. We watched him place the piece of Mystic Silver on the table, and suddenly, its radiance faded completely, manifesting a ball of light coming out from its center. The ball of light in Elior's hand glided to merge with it, and when it did, the illuminating essence swirled and sparkled the walls as sunlight through glass.

"Many cannot understand that Mystic Silver does not bring us progress," the MKR explained. "Mystic Silver holds us back from becoming what we could be."

The ball of light in the center of the table violently split in two, one turning toward me, the other toward Nirnasha. Then we heard Elior whisper aloud:

Léiríonn rúin an Ceapach mo chroí. Lig do taisce mo shaol a oscailt óna chéile.

The translation pulsed through me, surging tremors up my spine as the ball of light coming toward me fragmented in two again and leaped forward into my eyes. I was blinded for a moment, all but an intense frenzy glow, and then I could see the words take form before me—"The Glade's secrets mark my heart. Let your treasures open my life apart." I blinked several times as if waking from a deep sleep. When I opened my eyes, I saw nothing more than dim lantern light in the room with Nirnasha and Elior.

"Can we speak?" Nirnasha said aloud.

Elior smiled, bringing forth a light chuckle. "Yes, you can speak."

"Where is it?" I asked. Elior knew I was referring to the book. He told me he had slipped it back into my pack.

"Hang on to it for me a while longer," he said. "Make sure you and Nirnasha study what it says and keep it safe. In time, I shall reveal the final words to unveil its most guarded secret."

"It would appear you and I will have to become friends," Nirnasha teased.

"What did you mean by 'shadow?'" I asked Elior, ignoring Nirnasha's comment.

"Until you both know what power you possess, I cannot say," Elior replied. "Both of you are awakened, but you must discover what that power is and decide what you will do with it."

"What do you mean?" Nirnasha interjected, keeping his voice soft. "Do we not have the power of light you possess?"

"You may, perhaps," Elior explained. "It is more likely that you have an entirely different power. The knowledge of your power can increase by studying the book I have given you and practicing what you discover. Should you decide to assist me, I shall be grateful. That is all I can give you for now—and my gratitude."

"What if we do not wish to assist you?" Nirnasha probed.

"Your decisions are yours to make," Elior continued. "Though, there will come a time when you must choose what you will do with your power and what purpose you will serve. Should you give your service to what lies in the dark—I assure you the ending is not pleasant."

I did not want to seem ungrateful for what Elior gave me. And it seemed both Nirnasha and I decided to reason our way out of assisting him in his endeavors. We respectfully declined to join him, with myself using my parents as my excuse. I explained that I missed them dearly and was sure they felt the same. However, in the back of my mind, I honestly doubted that was their heart toward me. The grin never left Elior's face. He promised he would be back for the book in due time.

Out of the study, Nirnasha bid me good day while Elior slipped away without another word. From there, I went straight to see Cenobia in the medical ward. She appeared considerably in better health, with a lift in her spirits seeing me approach her bedside. I did not dare speak to her about what happened in the study quarters. After learning she would be released in a day or two, I felt her squeeze me more tightly than my mother or father. Her embrace warmed me, and I knew she meant motherly affection. She asked me about the books she and I had gathered. I reassured her they were safe in my quarters, keeping her pack hidden. I also placed the etching of the plaque and banner with her books. I felt she deserved a little more after what she went through.

Cenobia began to doze off about an hour after I came to visit. Though the rain had ceased, I could see the sun still hidden by thick clouds in the distance. Our destination bound us to fly further into them. Cenobia kissed my forehead, and she laid her head down. Then I felt my vision begin to blur. I managed to rise to my feet, surmising fatigue settling in as I had not slept at all the night before. I made haste to the deck outside, grabbing the ship's railings to steady my balance. The feeling grew heavy, and I suddenly saw jaffa and crimson lights darting around me. A sudden touch on my shoulder spun my eyes around to see the face of my sable-skinned fellow explorer, who appeared to be sharing in my discomfort.

"There is no need to be frightened," I felt a voice echo. Despite my mind spinning, I knew it was Elior. "Consider this your first lesson."

"Are you hearing him too?" Nirnasha whispered to me. I nodded.

"Those who are awakened can feel my voice and sense my heartbeat," Elior continued. "They can also use this ability with one another should they desire."

"Why is our vision blurry?" I felt Nirnasha inquire.

"You both are transforming," Elior answered. "Transformation is not always easy, but it is effortless—since the power of light is the one changing you. You may experience discomfort or moments of uncontrollable joy. I can never recall which comes first."

I heard the MKR chuckle, this time just behind me. I turned but saw no one standing there. Nirnasha squealed, and our heads darted to look behind him. Elior appeared with a smile on his face. I looked at Nirnasha, gripping my right arm tightly with his left hand as if some deadly creature had pierced his back.

"I did not mean to frighten you," Elior explained. "I merely tapped your shoulder to get your attention."

"You got it, you dunderhead!" Nirnasha shouted. "What sort of prankster are you? First, you take my arm. Now you are..."

"Making you squeal like a child," I interjected.

"Are you finding this hilarious?" Nirnasha snapped at me.

"Not at all," I replied sharply, keeping my tone within only our ears. "If Elior were something from the darkness, we would be dead already because you were not watching your back."

"A decent observation," Elior admitted. "But Nirnasha is more spot on. You see, I have not had this much fun in many lifetimes. I do not normally get to share this with others. I only had a bit of fun for a laugh."

My jaw dropped.

"Are you a child?" I demanded. My question wiped the smile off Elior's gentle face. His eyes intensified, and I thought he would reach into my chest and rip out my heart.

"You listen to me, children," Elior's face drew in extremely close. "If you cannot overcome the games I play with you, then how will you ever overcome an adversary who truly wishes you harm? You may not wish to assist me, but that does not negate me from the responsibility of being your teacher."

I reached up and took Nirnasha's hand, seeing the MKR's eyes turn to their viridescent hue.

"There are creatures quite fouler than Wendigo," Elior continued, his words slapping us across the face as if we misbehaved. "There is even magic greater than mine, more ancient and sinister than neither of you can begin to imagine."

I shall not forget Elior's words to me and Nirnasha on the deck that day. Both Nirnasha and I blinked, and Elior had vanished. Seeing this and heeding the MKR's warning, I gripped Nirnasha's hand tighter and led him to my room, despite how others might have seen it.

We ran into Bikarma and Garvish, who boorishly cheered Nirnasha's conquest as they saw us holding hands and practically dragging him into my room. But it was undoubtedly for more essential matters. I locked the door behind us, pulled the secret book from my pack, and spoke the revealing words allowed.

"We should not take this lightly," I told Nirnasha. "We have crossed into a different world, something we took upon ourselves that we cannot comprehend in the slightest."

"Agreed," Nirnasha replied. "While we are on this vessel, let us do what we can to learn what we have become—together."

It is not every day a book echoes its thoughts and brings visions to your mind. We were vulnerable yet secure, feeling a new power surge within us. The book held our fascination as if it were a natural person speaking to us from a time long forgotten. The manifestations were so tangible that they touched all our senses. We could feel the fumes of fire, smell the scent of crashing tides, taste the sweet scent of the wind, and see the way our world once was eons ago.

At such a time, they did not possess Mystic Silver or have knowledge of Elior. Yet their culture fascinated me in seeing them imagine what having magic would be like. They created books and moving picture stories around such things. But it was all make-believe. These moving picture stories were called movies. And nothing of the kind exists anymore.

We watched people walking by in unusual attire and driving machines called automobiles as if they were specters in the room. Many of their machines, like the automobile, were powered by a substance known as oil and byproducts from it. I could not imagine another fuel source besides steam or Mystic Silver. But what impressed me the most was the architecture, and the people of the culture created. They built monumental cities that were havens for art, science, rhetoric, fine cuisine, entertainment, and coffee. Everywhere I turned, I could see people delighting in conversation or study, drinking coffee. And if you did not enjoy it, you had several other beverage choices. "Coffee shops" could be found at almost any location in their cities—one such metropolitan referred to New York.

As if peering through the eyes of some distant memory, New York held buildings that reached far into the sky, much like some of the towers of Langdon. Yet the towers of Langdon are watch towers used for spotting incoming airships, not places of business or residency. And as time moved forward in the manifestations, Nirnasha and I witnessed the fate of New York City's beauty.

There was a great rebellion. We did not see how it came to pass. But the banners the rebels carried depicted strange symbols, which appeared abstract, and I squinted to make out the lines of paint moving outward from two oval shapes in the center. The lines squiggled down like dripping water breaking as they went. My attention swiftly shifted from the banners to the many innocents slaughtered by those who fought under the precarious banners. Smoke climbed high above the city's buildings as continued destruction pushed its residents out of their homes, fleeing for their very lives.

We witnessed yet another great city's fate, a place known as San Francisco. Like New York, we witnessed the city before its demise. During a grand celebration, the land erupted in violent shaking. The land collapsed, and San Francisco fell helplessly into the roaring tides. Its once beautiful bridges and places of fantastic art and cultural treasures became swallowed in the deep.

Then another city called Lagos revealed millions of people who perished from an infestation from another land. No one knew where the disease came from, but it reached throughout the world into other great cities known as London, Paris, Berlin, New Delhi, Beijing, and Tokyo. Lagos' once wonderful city of art and business economy decayed from this spreading decay, and war soon followed in many of the world's kingdoms. A furious leader brought forth his army from the north, believing the disease would not reach him or his army. He won many battles and burned the land as he went. However, years into the mighty feud, he perished by contracting the pandemic.

Nirnasha and I suddenly found our minds standing in front of the significant buildings with very familiar columns and archways. Above us, I could see a banner waving in the wind, and I recognized it—the one Cenobia and I found while exploring the Unlight. The library we saw in ruins stood clearly before me, and suddenly I caught a glimpse of the plaque "Library of Congress, Thomas Jefferson Building." To my delight, I did not realize I physically thrust my arms upward and hit Nirnasha across his cheek. After apologizing, we returned to the spectacle of the manifestation.

Pleased to see this place fully intact, I reached for the door, and suddenly darkness loomed over us. The entrance was gone, and we were back in the Unlight. The building was as it was when we discovered it. Yet, we did not sense any danger as we could still see the outer walls of my quarters. A dim light appeared in the room, taking the form of an elder-looking gentleman. He did not move like one, though, walking elegantly in youthful steps, dressed in fine dark cocoa skinny trousers and a gold gentlemen's vest. His fit and flare frock appeared with the shine of freshly pressed Gossypium, and his shoes held a tinted glow of gold, greased to the finest shade of mystic midnight I had ever seen.

"Who are you?" Nirnasha asked.

"I am the one who holds the secrets of the hidden glade for my master," the elder replied.

"Who is your master?" I asked.

"He weaves light like the air he breathes," the elder-looking man answered. "You certainly know him or would not know of my existence."

A simple nod from both of us told the elder that we knew Elior. I motioned to the ruins of the building behind the man, curious to know more about what I was sure caused the catastrophic collapse.

"The Great Collide is what caused all this," he explained. "It was necessary to keep humanity from destroying one another in their madness, lust, fear, and most of all their pride."

"What do you mean it was necessary?" Nirnasha interrupted.

"You would do well to know the darkness that is being reborn," the elderly man expounded. "One, you will know in time. There are three bound to it. They are the doors to find the key to ending its grasp upon the world. So, it would be best if you grew strong. Nourish what others cannot."

"Our magic?" I asked.

"The power awakened in you," the elderly man continued. "If magic is what you wish to call it, then yes. But do not be fooled and deceived by any desire. The power placed in you is yours only because it was given to you. You did not earn such a gift, nor were you born with it—this is the message my master commanded me to pass on."

"If you are reckless with it, then it will consume your essence and chain you in darkness," Elior's voice echoed inside me. I turned to see Nirnasha had heard the same. We both turned to see the MKR standing inside by the locked door, his eyes glowing with gentle gold.

Nirnasha and I were back in my quarters, and the visions had vanished. The book had returned to its hidden form and lay closed on the bed. I peered down to see that Nirnasha and I were still holding hands. Oddly, I did not pull my hand suddenly away from his, but he abruptly jerked it away from mine. I was embarrassed, though I did my best to keep my head turned, not to reveal my face. Elior spoke again, this time aloud to us.

"We are reaching the borders of the southern region," Elior said. "When we reach the fortress city of Starvel, we shall go our separate ways. However, I will come to find you both again. I highly recommend you remain together as you head back to Langdon."

"What about what we saw?" Nirnasha hastily asked, his tone dropping exceedingly. "What about...you...and...the...darkness?"

"The power of life and death are always at odds," Elior answered. "You will either draw your power from one or the other. You cannot draw power from both. Either serve one or serve the other. Meditate on what you have discovered, what you learn, what becomes revealed to you, and what you can selflessly do for others—that is the way of life. The way of death is to serve only yourself, and in the end, your chains shall bind you to an existence of torment and suffering. And you will believe that you are grateful for it."

"I believe I wish to draw my power from life," I quickly stated, standing to my feet. Nirnasha swiftly replied his concurrence, making Elior laugh. His wonderful grin did not leave his face.

"Come," the MKR said. "We are close to our destination."

An unbearable pitch and a sudden thunderous boom thwarted our pleasantries. Elior rushed out of the quarters and to the railing with us in tow. To our dismay, the city of Starvel suddenly ignited into leaping flames. Elior's gaze turned a slight distance out from the city. A wairship had just passed over Starvel, dropping EDOs upon its fortified walls.

"That is an Eastguard wairship," Elior appeared almost stunned.

"Why are they attacking Starvel?" Nirnasha shouted.

"I do not know," the MKR answered. "But it appears our admiral has decided to find out."

Our wairship engaged in battle formation, with soldiers darting to their stations and stabilizing buzzsaw firing guns. The clicks of the guns locked and loaded reverberated throughout the ship. Cannons were swiftly loaded, and the shouts from soldiers covering their positions with buzzsaw rifles were suddenly quiet as we approached the wairship from Eastguard, now heading directly away from us. It was moving into position to turn and make another EDO run. I can only assume it did not spy us in the heavy cloud cover. Before the blasts of the cannons, I heard Elior whisper to Nirnasha and me, "I may not be leaving you after all."

The buzzsaw firing guns followed the cannon fire, spinning projectiles of doom toward our foe. Our wairship had drawn dangerously close to the Eastguard wairship, preparing to pile on another barrage.

"Stay down," Elior echoed to us. "And draw your weapons."

As we ducked behind the fortified railing, we instantly heard buzzsaw fire wisp over our heads. The Eastguard wairship was retaliating. The cries from our soldiers pierced the ears of those around them and then silenced into the arms of breathless slumber. The decks erupted and splattered with the lives of several as they were suddenly drenched in crimson on both wairships, now evenly parallel.

A familiar voice shouted a command just below us to our soldiers to "pour it back into them." Hearing Hardwin's voice bravely rise above all the clatter felt comforting. I spied two familiar characters crawling on their hands and knees toward the three of us—Bikarma and Garvish with drill guns in hand.

"Can you do something?" Bikarma shouted to Elior. "Use your magic or anything?"

"Not to that wairship," Elior replied. "I am waiting for the other one."

"The other one?" Garvish shouted. "What other one?"

A loud humming approached us from above. It began to open fire on our ship, landing cannonballs on our decks. The echoing of screams followed as the circular projectiles shattered into our ranks.

"Get to the bridge!" Elior told me. "Take them with you. Tell the admiral I said to head for the west wall of the city. The Eastguardians will give chase. That is what we want them to do. Tell him to do his best to outrun them."

Elior pointed toward the bridge. We were not far from it. I crept low, and the others followed me. I could see our wairship was turning approximately toward the west wall anyhow, so I figured the admiral would oblige the message from the MKR.

We reached the bridge, and I shouted to the admiral that I had word from Elior. He ceased his panicked commands to his navigators, and I told him what the MKR had told me. At first, he was not inclined, but the other three with me confirmed. He reluctantly followed Elior's command and opened the wairship to full speed. He shouted commands to the engineers to get our damaged propellers working again. Fortuitously, our balloon cage was not punctured.

Nirnasha, Garvish, Bikarma, and I watched the city of Starvel burn from the bridge. The destruction made it unbearable to think of the number of bodies to be pulled from the wreckage, whether burned or broken. As I tried to keep my thoughts from throwing me into a full-blown breakdown of tears, I felt Nirnasha take hold of my shoulders.

"Do you see what I see?" He whispered. I was not convinced he and I were gazing upon the same city set ablaze. Swiftly, I felt my mind shift to visions of Elior as I was about to answer Nirnasha. I could feel my heart thump, and I could feel Nirnasha's do the same. Then I sensed Elior's. In my best possible explanation, I saw more precisely through the MKR's eyes than my hand in front of me. He was aboard the Eastguardian wairship that was just behind us. Breathless, I only heard one phrase from the MKR.

"Finally decided to tune in?" He asked with a playful chuckle.

Elior unleashed his drill guns from their holsters. Abruptly, the MKR became spotted on the Eastguardian bridge, and every soldier pulled their weapon toward Elior to fire. Before any of them could fire a shot, the MKR appeared next to all of them—each in a split moment. I watched through Elior's eyes as he held his drill guns point-blank to each soldier's head and pulled the trigger. Before they even felt the drill bit, Elior stood where he first appeared in the center of the navigation deck, with both his guns lowered. And in another split moment, every soldier and officer plopped lifeless to the deck after a burst of crimson flew from their cranium. I counted the bodies, twenty-four soldiers in all.

"Did he even reload?" I heard Nirnasha gawk. "When did he reload?"

A burst of laughter escaped me, knowing Elior had heard him too. I turned my gaze toward the ship now under Elior's control. It was turning and flying all ahead full toward the other Eastguardian wairship still tailing us.

We had reached the west wall with enough distance that we then watched the wairship controlled by Elior crash into the other Eastguardian warship from above. The explosive impact caused an ear-piercing collision, and the admiral desperately spun our wairship away from the oncoming fireballs now hurling toward us. The two destroyed Eastguardian wairships crashed far enough away, outside Stavel's western wall. After a few moments, a familiar voice startled us on the bridge.

"Well done, admiral," Elior was standing just behind us. "You may have saved Starvel from destruction."

"If you had not assisted us, we all could have been destroyed ourselves," the admiral replied. "My thanks to you, Elior, for your assistance. As always, you are welcome aboard my wairship any time."

Elior gave a slight, respectful bow, removing his top hat. Nirnasha, Garvish, Bikarma, and I followed the MKR down to the main deck, where Hardwin stooped over a bloody mess of lifeless soldiers lined up to be identified. Elior stood beside him, and the four of us remained silent, keeping a slight distance out of respect. Yet, we all could overhear their conversation.

"You have saved us once again, my friend," Hardwin said with a heavy sigh.

"It was my pleasure," Elior replied. "Seeing that Eastguard has broken its treaty with Westmain only makes me believe one thing—the Emperor of Eastguard no longer respects my council."

"Most likely," Hardwin agreed.

"Will you stay awhile in Starvel?" Elior asked.

"I shall remain awhile to make sure the rebels do not gain a foothold here," Hardwin confirmed.

"I shall remain as well," Elior assured. "But the rest of our party will return to Langdon when the wairship is ready."

"I shall do no such thing," I interjected. I was taken aback by Elior's grin at my rude interruption, yet I continued. "I cannot bear to return home without aiding my countrymen, and such unforgivable shame will be on any of us standing here if we do not assist."

"I can speak for myself," Bikarma answered. Garvish followed with his concurrence.

"I am not about to let some uggo speak for me," Garvish harshly jested. I turned swiftly and landed my closed fist on his jaw, sending him soaring onto his back.

I heard Elior disarm my temper with an authoritative, "Aagneya!"

Nirnasha drew Elior's attention to my eyes as Bikarma slowly backed away from us.

"Your eyes are glowing like crimson fire," Nirnasha gasped.

"It is not all that is glowing," Elior pointed out. "Look at your fist Aagneya."

I turned my gaze downward with the hand I had slugged into Garvish's face. It was set ablaze with the fire halfway up my arm without devouring my clothes.

"You are an MKR!" Bikarma squealed. "You are..."

Elior's hand clasped quickly over Bikarma's mouth. "Keep your trap shut."

Elior removed his hand from Bikarma's mouth as I began to calm my nerves. I doubt Garvish would ever speak to me in such a way again. Yet Elior helped the slender explorer back to his feet, holding him steady till he found his footing. Bikarma told him I hit him, which made the boyish brat stand back from me a bit more.

"You two are coming with us," Elior said with a somewhat forceful inflection. "You will help me protect these two and keep their powers a secret."

"What? Is Nirnasha one too?" Garvish asked, popping his jaw back into place.

"Why do MKRs have need for us?" Bikarma asked. "You can destroy wairships by yourself. She can summon fire. And Nirnasha is also..."

"I do not need to explain my reasons," Elior cut in. "I have chosen you both for this task. If you do not wish to fulfill it, I must kill you both before you are tempted to blab."

I had never heard Elior threaten in such a way. I turned to Hardwin, who gave me a wink unseen by the rest.

"Can he do that?" Garvish reached out to Hardwin.

"He is an MKR," Hardwin replied. "He has done many great deeds. Should he kill two misfits off, people shall believe he had good reason to do so. And no one will mind."

I saw Elior almost laugh, which put me more at ease.

"As it stands, then," Bikarma said. "It appears we do not have much of a choice. But like I said, why do MKRs need two 'regulars' like us?"

"You have skills that shall assist us," Elior assured. "Both of you survived the Unlight, where our journey shall certainly retake us. We need good explorers like you."

"You are not going anywhere without me," we heard Cenobia pipe up from the shadows. "You will also bring me along, as I know your secret."

Her smile held great comfort for me. Elior gave out a small laugh and motioned for her to join them away from the underdeck.

"I believe it is improper for a lady to travel alone in such company," Cenobia continued. "If I were along, you would raise less suspicion."

"Agreed," Elior replied.

We landed in Starvel. The panic and fear beaming from its citizens' faces troubled my mind. Among the haste of soldiers running to protect the walls, citizens had begun to loot shops and the dead. Hardwin led many soldiers off the wairship to assist in terminating the looters, who were shot on sight. What a pity that many only think of themselves when death and destruction arise.

We heard rebels pouring into the city from the east wall, almost entirely blown into rubble. Some of the fortress walls still stood. Yet the enormous holes allowed for rebels to pour in and onslaught the wounded or the few numbers of Westmain soldiers trying to regroup. Elior saw the need for his magic to help in the east, while the fortress commander commanded Hardwin to move to the south of the city. The five of us, Nirnasha, Cenobia, Garvish, Bikarma, and

I, followed Elior toward the east wall. Yet following behind us was a dispatch from Westmain's Elite Guard stationed in Starvel, each armored head to toe in copper plating interwoven into full-body dark cocoa uniforms. Azure paint was strewn across their face to display their patriotism and loyalty to Westmain, as is the tradition of Westmain's Elite Guard.

Westmain's Elite Guard troops hone their bodies much further than typical soldiers. For instance, Elite Guards are sharpshooters and highly trained close-quarter combatants. Where typical units in Westmain may have a regiment of sharpshooters, Elite Guardsmen can be removed from their position should they miss their target. They are trained unmercifully, and some do not even survive the trials to become one. They are a hardened brood, trained to lose sight of their fear of death and bring that fear of death to their enemies. Each one must maintain their spectacle of perfection in strength, wit, and tenacity.

An Elite Guard's weapon of choice is, first and foremost, a buzzsaw rifle with a military-grade drill grip attachment. However, the Elite Guard's buzzsaw rifle model holds a much larger clip of blades, which makes the rifle slightly heavier. Secondly, in intense close-quarter hand-to-hand combat, Elite Guards carry slightly curved machetes with saw teeth near the hilt. No one is allowed to carry such designed weaponry unless they have received a permit from the Westmain government. Along with their weaponry, Elite Guards carry a Mystic Silver enchanted armor plate attached to their forearm. This plate of copper can expand upon their command to become a protective shield, varying depending on the size of the soldier.

I watched the Elite Guards hurry to move in front of us as we drew closer to the onslaught. Westmain soldiers were trying to flee toward us. Some tried to carry the wounded to safety, fired on like helpless animals. When the Elite Guard formed their lines, one row dropped to a knee while the other stood. Their commander ordered them to aim and then pointed his finger intensely, screaming for them to fire. I have never witnessed such marksmanship. Westmain soldiers that were fleeing felt whizzing sawblades race past their heads, just a few fingertips away, but sink into the rebels charging from behind them. The rebels began to take cover among the rubble, allowing more of Westmain's wounded to escape. The Elite Guard opened a way for them to pass through their ranks before finally closing the lines.

An eerie silence crept over the streets as we stood where all the east roads in the city diverged into one main street. The only sound was the crackling fires from destroyed buildings, still ignited from the EDO blasts. The east wall had now become an Elite Guard unit of Westmain. The front row expanded their shields and advanced slowly down the sloping street. From our vantage point, I could see several rebels still taking cover. Some carried buzzsaw rifles, citizen single-shot models rather than the rapid-fire of the military grade. Others had nothing more than weapons used for close quarters. I could not believe they were much of a threat. That was until a few moments later.

Out of the night, we heard steam loudly release from the gears of a crawling machine raised high above the ground, with plated steel covering its axles. Smoke emerged from its five exhaust pipes that shot straight into the air. Its two long arms held raised platforms attached with two buzzsaw firing guns each. Rebels controlling the guns locked their weapons into place and aimed at the line of Elite Guards advancing. More rebels were aiming with buzzsaw rifles positioned on the machine. The Elite Guard commander resounded an all-attack command. Each soldier expanded their shields and began running toward the machine that now appeared more like a metal beast in the dim light.

"What is that thing?" Garvish shouted.

"A steam-powered Mech," Elior replied. "They used machines like this before Mystic Silver. They still do in many industries as Mystic Silver is too highly-priced to obtain."

"Where did this one come from?" I asked, feeling panic reach my throat.

"The timber industry, most likely," Elior stated. "You can see the two arms made to raise loggers so they can cut trees high up."

"What do we do?" Nirnasha chimed in. His voice seemed more panicked than mine.

"Let them entertain the beast," Elior said. "We have other matters to attend to." I wanted to argue, but in moments the rebels let loose the firepower of their fabricated weapon upon the front line of Elite Guards. I thought they would be eradicated but discovered how wrong I could be. While a few fell in a frighteningly bloody mess, many more held their ground, protected by their shields. The others moved in with shields covering them, creating a protective shell-like formation as they moved toward the rebels.

"Garvish. Bikarma, Cenobia," Elior grabbed our attention. "Stay here. Wait for us."

Surprisingly, the two blockheads did not argue. Cenobia joked she would make sure they did not wet themselves. Before following, I watched the Elite Guard reach the Mech and disperse beneath the buzzsaw fire, climbing the thing as it moved. Rebels on the lower region of the machine soon met a merciless fate from machetes slicing through them. I chuckled and took one last look at the courage of the Elite Guards, then followed Elior and Nirnasha into the shadows of a blown-out building.

"Why did you not destroy that thing like you did the wairship?" I asked Elior, speeding up to join the two.

"If people become too reliant on magic, then they will not know how to defend or think for themselves without it," Elior pointed out. "Westmain's Elite Guard has fought against worse odds and with fewer soldiers to gain victory."

We climbed up the rubble to reach what endured of the rooftops. Elior continued speaking to us about the dangers of solely relying on magic.

"It is good you have lived without magic for so long," he explained. "Hold onto your wits and strength you have learned without it. Now that magic is what you have become, make it rely on you."

"I have only seen magic," Nirnasha said. "I have yet to do anything like what Aagneya did."

"Now is your chance," Elior replied.

"What do you mean?" Nirnasha asked.

"The gap between these buildings is too far for us to jump," Elior explained. "Do something about it?"

"How could I possibly do that?" Nirnasha was still confused. Elior gave him a grin.

"I know what emanates from you," Elior continued. "I knew what emanated from each of you before I awoke you. You were given the book for a reason, to learn what is possible. Now show us."

"I still do not know what you mean," Nirnasha boyishly complained.

"Begin with why you want to do something," Elior continued. "We need magic in this situation because we cannot move on without you. Let go of how to do it. Think about why you want to do it, then do it."

Nirnasha peered over the edge of the ruins. With a heavy sigh, he said, "It would be easier if the ground came up here so we could walk across."

"If you believe that," Elior said. "Reach out your hand so it can."

Nirnasha stretched out his hand. I felt his mind bring forth the thought of the ground moving to rise to meet it. The soil below began to shake, ascending to his hand. Nirnasha's eyes popped out of his head. I think mine did too.

Elior was the first to plant his footing on top of the pillar of soil. He passed by Nirnasha with an enormous smile as if to say, "Well done." I motioned for Nirnasha to follow us as I walked across after Elior. I called out his name, and he awoke from shock, crossing over to meet us. He continued to move us along with his newly discovered ability, passing us from one gap of rubble to another. We were moving around the rebels in the dark. However, I believe their attention remained locked elsewhere.

The Elite Guards were now swarming the Mech, similar to insects I studied in Langdon. Unlike most specimen studies, we observed these creatures in their natural state and introduced obstacles for the species to overcome. Many of these observations introduced larger insects, predatory in nature, to study how the nest unified and adapted to overcome—ants, I believe they are called. The pragmatic tactics became applied by students planning to join officer military academies or wilderness survival training. At any rate, I could see the Elite Guards had mastered the mindset. The brutality which sealed the rebels' fate was masterfully executed, and the machine suddenly turned against the onslaught of invaders trying to penetrate the city's infrastructure.

We, at last, reached the eastern wall. Elior slid down the rubble as if wings were attached to his feet. I nearly tumbled, but the MKR caught me by the arm just before my face met the ground. Nirnasha created steps for him to travel down. He sent an obnoxious sneer my way, which I returned with a glare.

"I see a light up ahead," Elior said after a few moments of peering toward a large clump of trees just outside the Dwelling Gates.

"Is that from the rebels?" I asked.

"No," Elior swiftly replied. "That would be our other business. Our invitation to talk awaits."

Nirnasha and I shared a bewildered look toward one another, but Elior continued.

"Do not agree to anything," Elior explained. "Do not believe anything you hear."

We followed Elior out into the night, a small distance away from the city of Starvel and into the Deadlands. There was a clearing in the woods where the light of a fire glowed and violently crackled into the sky. On the other side was a familiar sight, to me at least, a tiny man with slithering hair and a frightful face. His eyes were milky white, though I doubted he could not see. His long sharp fingers pointed and welcomed us to draw closer. His skin was lightly brushed with daylight sky, yet he appeared deathly ill. He pushed back the brim of his tattered-looking gent's top hat and revealed his pointy teeth when he greeted us with an enormous, vile smile.

THE FALL OF FOLESK

"You appear a bit low this evening," Elior poked a pun.

The tiny man slowly rose from his seat, still smiling, keeping his composure despite being greeted with a jest about his stature. It was the first time I had a better look at him. I estimated he stood no more than one-and-half arm lengths tall.

I took notice of the thick fog rolling in and the beady eyes glowing from the treetops. I knew they were birds by flapping their wings and low squawking. The forest was dense, and I felt a chill run over the back of my neck. I thought it was Nirnasha breathing behind me, but no, he stood next to me, as did Elior.

"I have seen this one before," I said to Elior. "In the Unlight, when he temptingly contravened me."

"I merely wished to see what sparked Elior's interest," the tiny man's voice rasped. "Surely, you cannot fault my curiosity. You nearly put a bit in my skull, my dear."

"Shall I try again?!" I spat, reaching for my drill bit gun.

"Oh, she is a fiery lass," the tiny man chuckled. "I do believe I am beginning to like her more."

"Enough of the banter," Elior calmly interjected and grabbed ahold of my arm to keep me from pulling my drill bit gun from its holster. The MKR peered upward, drawing a deep breath, making the tiny man snicker again.

"You have not changed," the tiny man teased. "Still seeking all these years, yet still afraid to look in the one place you know you should."

"Where might that be?" I boldly stepped forward. The tiny man's posture turned toward me, and his eyes squinted harshly.

"Why, in the gloom, of course," he replied.

"What did we come here for?" I heard Nirnasha pipe up to Elior.

"Good question," the tiny man perked up. "What did you come here for, my dear Elior? Was it to introduce me to your two new pupils or talk some more about the ones you have lost?"

Elior did not appear to be phased by the questioning at all. He removed his top hat and scratched the back of his head, then proceeded to place his hat back upon his head.

"What is he on about?" Nirnasha asked.

"I told you," Elior replied. "Your life would utterly be in danger if you agreed to become what you now are. You have remained with me, and thus you are following me on my quest."

"Still calling it a quest?" the tiny man teased again. "At this point, I think you would start calling it a sacrifice."

"I will find him," Elior replied.

"The longer you play the game," the tiny man sang. "The stronger he becomes, the more likely he will find you."

The fog rolled in, and the tiny man disappeared, quenching the fire and most of my boldness. He had laughed vilely before taking his leave, and it still echoed, fading as the sound of the wind blew through the trees and took hold of the night. Elior was staring at where the tiny man once stood. His face had never held such concern before as I knew him, and dare I say, a portrayal of fear emanated as his eyes kept their gaze.

"Who was that?" Nirnasha demanded, breaking the eerie silence.

"He is one of the three," Elior replied, not turning to face us. "One of the creatures of nightmares."

The first was Wendigo, as Elior elaborated, and I had already experienced its power. I interjected to describe what I had witnessed to Nirnasha—Wendigo's insatiable influence to torture the spirit to starve, turning hunger into a despicable lust for human flesh. Elior then repossessed the conversation and spoke of Wendigo and his previous encounters with the abomination. In Elior's first encounter, he spoke as if Wendigo had almost killed him, and each time he faced Wendigo alone, he was so exhausted that he had to run.

"So, is that why you need us?" Nirnasha blurted out. "If you, an MKR, cannot kill the creature, what makes you think we can?

"Is that what happened to your other pupils?" I joined in, feeling somewhat anxious. "Did Wendigo kill them?"

"No," Elior replied. He stared at both of us with sorrow in his eyes. "I did."

"You!" Nirnasha shouted. "Why did you...?"

"Because I had to!" Elior's eyes glowed a fiery gold that threw Nirnasha and me back on our heels as he whipped his head to face us. "They betrayed me!"

"How did they betray you?" I boldly stepped forward after seeing Elior's eyes calm.

"I thought I would take a different approach this time," Elior tried to explain but did not reveal details of what he had done. "I brought you out here to meet him, instead of trying to protect you from him. If you met him, I thought it might sway you not to be led astray."

"Then, please clarify," I pressed.

"His name is Rumpelstilzchen," Elior whispered. "Do not speak his name aloud any other time. Else he will hear you and know where you are. He carries magic that can lure and torture the heart. He pries to find what is vulnerable, then exploits it for his gain. It is vicious magic that grants him the ability to persuade and induce. He tempts hearts to move into the dark, thus betraying everything they hold dear, including what they once loved. The winds that bring him are swift, with a chill greater than death. Unlike Wendigo, he does not remain in the Unlight. He goes where he pleases and does what he pleases, only bound to the greater shadow."

"You are describing the Suzerain Efah," Nirnasha gasped.

"What does that mean?" I asked. Nirnasha sent his gaze toward me.

"It means Sovereign in the Gloom," he replied. "This creature is well known in Nod…at least in bedtime stories."

"He is no story," Elior reassured. "He brings an existence of nightmares to those who trust him. He burdens families with a price too high to pay for their desires. And in the end, they are consumed to be his shadowy puppets."

"Is that why you had to kill your pupils?" Nirnasha asked, his eyes almost pushing out tears. "Is that why you warned us that you would kill us if we betrayed you?"

"What choice does Elior have?" I interjected. "If that monster turns hearts against one another, then…"

"Then there is no bringing them back," Nirnasha concluded.

"Twice this has happened," Elior elucidated. "Twice I have gained pupils, and twice they turned. Twice I tried to protect them. Twice I tried to keep them away from him. I needed to do something different this time."

"How did he turn them?" I asked.

Elior could not say. Nirnasha and I drew closer to hear the MKR's voice roll into a hush. "He will tempt you. But take nothing from him. Please do not believe a single word from his mouth. Fighting him takes more than magic. It takes your heart to know the truth."

"And what is the truth?" Nirnasha kept his voice as low as Elior's.

"The truth is your heart can gain nothing from the promises of another," Elior urged. "If you truly desire something, put in the time and effort to attain it. But even if you attain what you desire, it always carries a price."

"So be careful what you wish for," I added with a grin. The MKR smiled back. What I believe was a heartfelt moment was interrupted by rustling. We turned toward the darkness to see the tiny man had appeared again.

"I thought I would give you a moment to explain to these younglings who I am," Rumpelstilzchen teased. "Did you really think I had gone, that I would miss continuing our little game?"

"I knew you were still around," Elior confessed. "I appreciate your generous time to let me introduce you to my pupils privately."

"Private," the tiny man scoffed. "Dear friend, I heard every word. Also, you mentioned that I was only one of three. Were you planning to explain who the third is, or perhaps you hoped they had forgotten?"

The chuckle from the tiny man was eerie. While Nirnasha and I stared at him, who had certainly returned to our presence to entertain his sickened mind; I did my best to study him while Elior took a deep breath to begin telling us more. Yet before he could, the tiny man jumped on his words.

"Or maybe not," Rumpelstilzchen shot out. "Do you think they would believe you? I do not know of anyone who would believe such a thing. Unless, of course..."

"Perhaps you are right," Elior agreed with a grin that confused the tiny man. "Out here in the cold does not seem like the proper place. Maybe we should adjourn indoors to a nice fire and a fresh brew of jaffa tea."

"If you are afraid to tell them, Elior, then maybe I could enlighten them," the tiny man cheekily offered.

"Now, where is the fun in that?" Elior held his grin as if he had gotten the better of the wicked imp. "You would ruin the surprise."

The tiny man scoffed with a loud laugh, and we slowly began walking away from him.

"Oh, you have started the game differently this time," Rumpelstilzchen called to Elior. "I look forward to seeing how this one pans out."

Daylight had come upon the fortified city of Starvel. The sun revealed more destruction than we had anticipated. Walking back into the ruins, we saw Westmain's Elite Guard clearing the bodies of the dead, along with other citizens who offered to help. We had spent the rest of the night in the woods, meeting our enemy, one of which Elior thought was a greater threat than the rebels.

No one asked where we were. No one accused us of running off from the fight. No one looked at us as we made our way to the citadel, the last line of defense that was miraculously intact and untouched. EDOs had destroyed the city square, completely breaking the eastern and southern walls. Westmain soldiers were still dispersing toward both locations to fortify their positions. But the north tower still stood, which was a welcoming sign that the city remained vigilant to attacks.

I shall never forget how Nirnasha looked at his people who were finding themselves pulled back into bloodshed by the rebellion in Westmain. As a first-year student at the university, I remember seeing Nodian refugees seeking asylum in Westmain from the Civil War in Nod. They had journeyed to Langdon, only to find their home in a poverty-stricken district. Our government pushed to relocate and house them in different areas so that disease and crime would not rise in the streets. Starvel was one of them—now a war-stricken place to remind them of home. I pitied them.

There was an inn just before the entrance to the citadel. I admit I felt ashamed that my thoughts moved from poverty-stricken and war-torn refugees to my comforts, a nice cup of tea, and a warm bed. Maybe if anyone else had just faced the dark evils of a tiny and sinister madman, they might throw a little sympathy my way. Perhaps or perhaps not.

Elior's hand reached for a kettle as soon as he entered the inn. He filled it with water and placed it on the rack over the fire. The innkeeper was a soft and pudgy woman with soft lines running through her face and a fancy robe tied around her.

"How may I help you today, sir?" she embellished her kind tone.

"Just the tea and whatever breakfast you have—and your largest and cleanest room," Elior replied politely. "I shall pay double." The woman's eyes widened, and she hurried away upstairs.

"Do you know what this place is?" Nirnasha lowered his voice to both of us. "This is a rumpy-pumpy lodge."

"I know," Elior replied. "But they have the best food and tea in the city with the softest beds."

"Bet no one will disturb us," I added. "At least not you."

"What do you mean by that?" Nirnasha asked.

"They will not want to touch you since you have a face only a mother could love," I teased.

"Very funny," he snapped back. "If your chest were a little bigger, I would encourage you to apply for a position."

"You two can kill each other later," Elior sighed. "Right now, pipe down, eat, drink, and rest up."

When we finished our tea and breakfast—the best jaffa tea I have ever tasted—I opened the door to a room with three beds. I remained hesitant to go in with two other men, even though Elior was one of them. We were in a house with a particular reputation, after all. But the pillows and dark cocoa sheets were so inviting. I practically leaped to find my head had never felt a softer pillow. It was a joy, almost like sleeping on a cloud in the sky. Elior told us he would take the first watch.

"The first watch?" Nirnasha asked.

"The game has begun," the MKR explained. "We are safer here. Yet that does not mean the darkness will not try to reach us."

"Will you tell us about the third creature?" I asked, sprawling out wider on my bed.

"Some other time," Elior bowed as he plopped down in a chair by the window. He pulled a wooden pipe from his inner frock pocket and packed in sweet-scented sage and mugwort. Smoking sage and mugwort is often a relaxing way to pass the time, at least for sophisticated gentlemen, and is usually improper for a lady to take part.

I rolled my head away from looking at Elior. I am unsure how much sleep the MKR expected us to find early that morning. I closed my eyes and still saw the tiny man's wicked smile while recalling my encounter with Wendigo in the Unlight. Something else, however, stirred while I tried to slumber. I felt aloft, but I could not understand what was happening. I had blurry visions of a meadow surrounded by trees and a soothing evening breeze sweeping over me. As I thought I was dreaming, I believe I caught Nirnasha out of the corner of my eye.

Voices in the room finally swayed me to open my eyes. Cenobia had joined us, along with the other two blockheads, Garvish and Bikarma. The room was peaceful, with low mumblings between Nirnasha and Cenobia. I did not see Elior anywhere. Garvish and Bikarma enjoyed a juvenile joke fest, daring one another to sleep with the ugliest wench available.

"That would mean Aagneya," Garvish sneered softly.

"I am going to burn your face off." I sat up with a quick threat.

Garvish and Bikarma froze, grabbing tightly to their chairs. I could feel my eyes blaze with a fiery essence. I glanced down at my hand, seeing a fireball swirl and form within it, and this time much larger than I had manifested before.

"She really should," Cenobia agreed. "You boys are too stupid to take anything seriously. If you are not careful, you shall die worse than the others did in the Unlight."

Elior entered the room, ignoring the squabble, and slowly shut the door behind him. He asked Cenobia for a cup of tea, and we all gathered around the table in the room next to the fireplace. When we all had sat down, Elior voiced his plan.

"We must learn why Eastguard attacked Starvel," he stated.

"We mean to travel there then?" Nirnasha asked.

"Yes," Elior replied. "But not by air. If Eastguard is indeed at war with Westmain now, traveling in the sky is compromised."

"Would you not do the same thing you did to the other two ships that attacked us?" I interjected.

"No." The MKR shook his head. "Crossing their borders now, even in a merchant's ship, will raise suspicion. Best we make it appear as if we are simply peripatetic and have no idea what has happened."

"Many know your face," Cenobia joined in. "I am sure even in Eastguard, they will recognize you. And certainly, they will know us by how we dress."

"No one knows what I did to those two ships," Elior replied. "Even now, a rumor about the admiral's prowess who brought us here is being spread. People shall believe he destroyed the Eastguard ships, not me."

"Then we dress like Eastguardens to keep the cover and the intent of our visit," Bikarma said. I was surprised by his willingness to participate.

"Perhaps," Elior pondered.

"Does not sound too hard," went Garvish's loud mouth, as I expected.

"The only problem is we would need a cargo that would not be expensive," Elior ignored the comment.

"Wait a moment," I said. "What if we were not merchants at all? But instead, we are who we are, explorers who just found books in the Unlight?"

I saw Elior smile wide at me.

"Are you suggesting we travel to Eastguard with the books we picked up from down there?" Bikarma sneered.

"Listen, you stupid Sus." I felt my eyes light up with fire again. "Pay attention if you do not want me to fry your hide. We can sell the books we have anywhere we want. They will go for a high price, and our alibi is true. The merchandise is already in our possession. Let us go to Eastguard with the excuse that we have heard we could get a better deal for our tomes."

"Duh," Garvish mocked at Bikarma.

I almost chuckled, seeing them bicker among each other now. Nirnasha voiced his approval, and Cenobia joined him.

"I believe this is a marvelous idea, Aagneya," Elior said. "But if anyone asks, you are not from Westmain. Let them know you are from Nod instead, from a clan in the North."

I had to ditch my royal crimson garbs. Although I needed to stitch a few hems back together, I could not be seen even traveling with them in my belongings. Most explorers from Nod wear tan hide clothes. I even had to hock my lucky gold and pin-striped ruffle shorts. I traded my clothes to one of the ladies who worked at the inn and thought about what new ruffle shorts I would buy next to make them my lucky ones. I acquired a tan hide clincher ruffle skirt—an ankle-length skirt in the back that only drops to about the upper thigh in the front, revealing a woman's bare thighs and garter. The skirt is worn mainly by young women, strategizing to attract a union bond or perhaps wanting some attention. Commonly, clincher ruffle skirts are fashionably worn with knee-high boots with knee-high socks, which the woman obliged not to allow me to trod off as a fashion nightmare, and threw in a pair of her own.

The skirt was exceptionally darling, with a stone damask design stitched into it. And I can honestly say that it made my thighs appear somewhat thinner, leaving much more room for my posterior than my skinny denim trousers. Elior then assisted in purchasing two more pairs of tan hide skinny denim trousers as I needed them, along with more thermal tights from the lodge's head private collection. Admittedly, I never thought I would enjoy shopping in a rumpy-pumpy closet. When I emerged from the room with Cenobia, I noticed my clincher ruffle skirt caught the eyes of both idiots and Nirnasha. It feels good for a woman to turn some heads.

Our travel plans, Elior believed, needed to go through the south to Folesk, one of the three rebel cities. From there, we would find a boat and move along the southern coast to reach Ye and Poe, two small outpost towns in Eastguard. Then we would catch an Eastguard airship traveling to Havensire, the mega fortress and capital of the kingdom, ruled in part by the Raven Caste Clan and the Pure Bone Clan.

Starvel was not far from Folesk, and we trekked out into the Deadlands under the cover of night. The moon did not shine, and we followed Elior's dim light for miles until we reached a clearing to see the town just after our third sunrise. Gladly, we made it to Folesk without incident. But I never would have imagined the poverty stench filling the air in such a hot, steamy mess. I was sure I would contract an incurable disease, moving through the crowds of people, breathing heavily all over us, and sending solemn gazes our way as we entered. Sewage piled high in the streets as we ventured further in, noticing people vomit on the street corners from the rank, then moved on as if nothing had happened.

"I have never been to Folesk," I told Elior, grabbing his arm to get his attention and then holding my nose with the other hand.

"Folesk has an interesting story," the MKR replied. "People used to be friendly here. Then the rebellion broke out, and the town fell into chaos. All their leaders joined the war, and now there is no one to take care of the town."

"I am not sure I know what the war is about," I admitted. "All I heard is the rebels want a new system of government."

"True," Elior continued. "They believe everyone should profit from one another, under a system of government that prohibits private ownership, where merchants should not benefit from a private profit but instead be taxed heavily to support the people."

"That does not make sense," Nirnasha chimed in next to us. "If a business cannot turn a profit, how does it grow to provide further openings for new employment or generate economic growth from its services?"

"They would grow much slower," I replied. "But it would not help free market trade, which essentially delivers to us the ability to buy and sell at the value of supply and demand. Essentially, we would have to sell our goods from exploration at a set price instead of being able to sell to the highest bidder."

"True, because the government would control the price," Nirnasha agreed.

"Westmain has already implemented systems to help support its people," Elior explained. "But the rebels wish to overthrow the government for more reasons than abolishing the free market. It is a power struggle that the leaders of the rebellion are striving to attain. Once in power, there would be a new type of corruption, and the government would be in full control to not listen to the people's voice."

"Fortunately, not all of us care about such things," we heard a voice behind us.

We had made our way to the docks of Folesk, where a new foul stench had invaded my nostrils. I peered toward seven rowdy-looking individuals standing behind what I considered an ugly child. Instead, it was a short and stout man, with muscles bulging from every orifice of his frame. His long, scraggly beard held bits of food and chew, a sight I had never seen. His top hat had a torn brim, with teeth marks all around it, appearing as if he chewed on his hat. His dark cocoa eyes were bloodshot, and his shirt sleeves ripped off, revealing his biceps, thrice the size of my thighs. His arms were scarred with provocative tattoos, apart from one that was a simple heart that read "mother." The others with him appeared no better as they were all covered in grease and grime and stunk like rotting fish from the sea.

"It has been a long time since I have seen you, Elior," the short man piped up.

He was not as short as Rumpelstilzchen, mind you, but his height was not far above, hunching over as if the muscles on his shoulders and neck were trying to throw his face into the ground.

"How are you, Meik?" Elior asked with a grin.

"How am I?" the short man replied with enough enthusiasm to rouse curious looks from every bystander within five hundred footsteps of us. "I'm Meik Feenk, King of the Sea and the best blazon steamboat captain. Before I could open my eyes, I was the only infant to refuse my mother's milk and trade it for my father's booze. I'm a reg'lar screamer of the open waters, who only loves women, wine, and the waves. I'm half bull and half Ironclad. I can out-talk, out-run, out-jump, out-fight, out-shoot, out-brag, out-drink, and out-maneuver any man who dares challenge me. I'm a no holds barred, rough-and-tumble jack knob, who cooks sea monsters for my breakfast and kaks out sunshine with tremendous thunder. I'm the craziest and meanest explorer you've ever seen, and my snapper can jibber-jabber and bite off a man's head simultaneously!"

"Give me a break," Garvish sneered under his breath. The gaze Meik sent back his way was murderous. He quickly walked up, grabbed Garvish by his privates, and pulled him down to his level, making Garvish give a high-pitched squeal.

"Are you looking for some exercise today, boy?" the steamboat captain gritted his teeth. I could see Garvish's face flushing up as his head had quickly dropped down just to where Meik wanted it to be, in range of his fist. "Cause if you are, by the time I'm done with you, you won't know if you've been brawling or if you were someone's prison bait."

"No need," Elior kept his calm grin. "The boy has a mouth on him, but I believe he has learned his lesson and should apologize before he loses something more than his pride."

Garvish nodded and managed to squeak an apology, which seemed to suffice, and Meik let him go.

"Where you headed?" Elior asked. The crowd began to disperse, seeing that no blood would be spilled. What a pity.

"Getting ready to head out for Ye and Poe," Meik answered. "You know my traveling schedule so well." The short man's mouth opened with a wide smile.

"Can you take on some passengers?" Elior lowered his voice.

"I can," Meik matched the MKR's tone. "But I'm guessing you don't want people to know where you're headed by how your voice is dropped."

"You know me so well," Elior's reply dripped with amusing sarcasm. "How much?"

"Thousand per head," Meik bargained.

"There are six of us," Elior said. "That seems reasonable. There is me and the rest here." Elior motioned toward us. Meik took a big sigh when his eyes landed on me.

"I don't think she can come," he said. "My crew would want to touch her very much."

"I understand that," Elior agreed. "But make them understand that if they do touch her, I will slice off their arms and pluck out their eyeballs."

"Ain't that just the thing." The short man let out a bellowing laugh. "I knew I liked you, Elior. But that'll make the price go higher."

"How high?" Elior asked.

"Ten thousand," Meik made no hesitation. "Take it or leave it."

Elior stared at the short man, who did not budge from smiling. I watched Elior's eyes move from their viridescent meadow fields, sunny day azure skies, and golden starlight, but his face remained deadpan. It brought Meik's smile down to a nervous grin.

"Seven thousand?" The short man finally suggested.

"We have a contract," Elior nodded.

"Finally," Meik replied, regaining his composure. "We set sail tomorrow morning. Now, if you'll excuse me, you're keeping me from glugging."

We were not far behind Meik and his band of misfits. Elior seemed to know the waterfront well enough, so again, we would bed in a place of disease-ridden ladies and cozy beds. We had time to wash and rest just before the banquet hall opened. I sat beside Elior and Nirnasha in the loft seating, observing the commotion below. Meik's crew emerged spotless from the shadows of the ground floor entrance, each basking momentarily in the smells and, no doubt, the brawls that awaited them.

I hardly noticed Meik approaching our table with Cenobia by his side. They both sat at our table, and I could not help but feel something peculiar had transpired between them. Cenobia was beaming, and Meik appeared less on edge than when we first met him. Elior pretended not to notice, but I knew what had occurred. I stared wide-eyed at Cenobia. She caught my gaze and gave me a shrug.

"Don't be so surprised," Meik said. "Cenobia and I have explored together before."

"What is this about?" Nirnasha asked. Of course, he would be oblivious.

"Never you mind," I snapped. "Just keep out of it."

"Sweet girl," Cenobia nabbed my attention with a gruff tone. "Why not mind your own business?"

"Because I am completely lost," I snapped back.

"Remain calm," Elior insisted. I peered down at my hand, beginning to burn red.

"It's quite all right," Meik interjected with a pertinent smirk. "It's obvious what's bothering you, missy. You think you're better than I am."

"Of course I am," I ruthlessly replied. "You are a scoundrel."

"I'm also a father, little turd." Meik leaned forward and fired back.

"Keep it civil," Elior interjected. "We are not going to turn this into a mountain."

"I was a father." Meik eased his shoulders, shifting to a less aggressive posture. "You don't know who I am, and you don't know Cenobia, and you don't even know my crew. Yet you insist that you're better than us. What have you lost in your life? What makes you the judge and jury of how we're supposed to live?"

"He has a point," Nirnasha muffled with a mouth full of food. "You do seem to think you are better than everyone at times, even me."

The room suddenly went pale, and the faces of everyone became faded. Only Elior appeared in clear view, keeping a comforting countenance. His eyes were glowing, and it felt like considerable time passed, but only one thought held in my mind.

"What are they all talking about?" I asked.

"Your anger stems from pride," Elior said plainly. I could not believe my ears. "Even now, in your heart, you feel as if everyone is turning on you, even me."

"You are!" I shouted.

"No," Elior shook his head. "Though he is unkind in his approach, Meik is not wrong. Deep down, you know this—I am not here to condemn you, Aagneya. However, if you do not take correction where you can find it, to search within yourself what wisdom you must learn to become what I know you to be, then you shall continue to doubt and keep others away, even me. You will shut people out and succumb to the darkness."

"I do not wish to feel this way," I admitted. "I do not wish to feel that I am better than everyone. It must be something from my mother."

"You cannot control the power awakened within you without humility, should you desire to use your power for good," Elior explained. "Learn it wherever you can, even if you truly believe you are right. Being right does not matter when it swells up obscurity within your heart."

I blinked, and everything returned to what it was before. I knew Elior had been inside my mind, speaking to me, teaching me, and helping me see what I needed to know.

"I am sorry," I said calmly and clearly. "I did not mean to be so critical."

"That was unexpected," Nirnasha admitted, making me want to shove my fist into his face. But I breathed a heavy sigh, and Cenobia nodded to let me know I was forgiven.

"Sorry," Meik blabbed. "I don't need your half-lipped apology. You can go..."

"Manners, Meik," Elior interceded, his eyes flashing gold. "Let us turn this into a more pleasant evening? Tell us about who we shall be sailing with?"

Meik reluctantly changed the subject by downing a colossal gulp of booze. And I listened to the steamboat captain speak to us about his "shipmates," as he called them.

Foremost, Meik alluded to his first mate aboard the "Seaborne Scoundrel," Darby Krokkett—a tall, slender man with lanky muscles, dark cocoa hair, tanned creme veil skin, and a handsome jawline. He sounded like a quiet and humble man when he greeted us as he passed by, but I could tell he was no stranger to the perils of being an explorer. I had come to know that he held a gentle spirit unless trouble brewed. Elior whispered to my thoughts that Meik was amusing to Darby. He was also a better shot than Meik and much cleverer, but he allowed Meik to be the leader as Darby did not like drawing attention to himself. A slight giggle rang out from me, which halted Meik from speaking.

"Sorry," I said. "Sometimes I just laugh."

"Are you well?" Nirnasha asked. "You are mentally slipping."

"It must be that time of the month, emotional things," I replied. "Please continue, Meik."

Next was Darby's best friend Reggie Gusel, another tanned creme veil with almost sable hair. He was reasonably competent when not drinking—an extremely talented engineer who could fix anything on the Seaborne Scoundrel but had a more challenging time fixing his mouth when he knocked back a few. He stood a step down from Darby's height, but also with a slight stoop in his stance, big, sphere stone shimmering eyes, a scraggly jawline of whiskers to fill in a patchy beard, and a consistent goofy and crooked smile.

The next crew member Meik pointed out was a woman by the name of Kassy Bones—an Eastguardian oval eye, creme veil woman with long, shiny, and straight sable hair tied into a tail on the top of her head as if she was ready to fight. She appeared to be able to outmuscle most fit men. I immediately interrupted Meik to explain why I cost more than the others just because I was a younger woman.

"Did you not say that your crew would try to touch me? Why do they not try to touch her?"

Meik's answer made me feel somewhat fearful but poked a chuckle out of Elior.

"She would not want to touch you like the others," the sea captain said, taking back another gulp. "She would touch you with her fist. She does not like pretty faces other than hers. Drunkards try to take advantage of her, and they regret it the next morning when they wake up with a broken jaw or worse—maybe they do not wake up at all. My crew has learned to respect her."

"Her hand-to-hand combat can rival even Meik on his best day," Elior poked.

A comment that only made the sea captain roll his eyes. But I turned my gaze toward Kassy. A little make-up and styling would have made her more femininely presentable. Her bright, viridescent eyes kept darting around for anyone who gave her the wrong type of glance. In the short time we had spent chatting, I had witnessed her get into four different brawls, ending quickly with her, yes, breaking the jaw of one man, hearing it crack all the way from where I sat. The other three went down completely stiffed out and likely concussed.

Meik introduced another crew member, Wild Willy, as he came up to drink with three different women, scantily clad and drunker than he appeared. His skin held a rich cocoa veil, and his teeth glistened with an unnatural heaven hue. He described Wild Willy as twice the joker, three times the lover, and four times the fighter—a brash mouth but had the skills to back up his claims. He was an ex-soldier from one of the finest sharpshooter divisions of Westmain. He could reload faster, shoot keener, and love a woman faster than it takes to pour him a shot. I watched him for a while, keenly seducing the women to his chambers when he pushed back his long sable hair from his azure-speckled eyes. It turned my stomach.

Meik seemed to lose interest in the conversation when the last two of his crew joined us in the loft seating area. A large, heavy man and a small boy sat in the opposite corner with hot plates of food and two large glass goblets of wine.

"Is that boy drinking?" I asked, feeling my mandible drop.

"Folesk is an outlaw town filled with rebels against Westmain," Nirnasha said. "How does that surprise you?"

Elior did not flinch at my question. He watched Meik grab Cenobia by the hand and lead her around the balcony to a hallway. They disappeared into the dim lighting and likely into a room for what I could only assume was another round of sensualism.

"That is Will Byde," Elior said, redirecting my attention away from the two twitterpated spectacles and toward the large man sitting with the boy. "People call him 'Wide Berth.' He was once a man with a family..."

"Now a presentable drunk," Nirnasha teased.

"Now who thinks they are better than everyone," I replied sarcastically.

Nirnasha rolled his eyes and waited for Elior to continue. I saw that Wide Berth dressed fancy, but his pupils were glazed over from drinking. He seemed quiet, though, peacefully pouring in his intoxication with his shaky sable hands.

"He is a troubled man," Elior explained. "He lost his family to a boating accident many years ago. He and Meik can identify with one another. Watch your words about him around Meik, or the steamboat captain might cut your head off before I can do anything about it."

Wide Berth was indeed very round but built like a boulder. He presented a slicked-back styling of his sable hair, and a clean shave, except for a well-curled mustache. His face appeared to swallow his dark cocoa eyes, and he hardly chewed his food before stuffing his cheeks again.

"Who is the child with him?" I asked.

"That is Dok Ferias," Elior answered. "He avoided me mostly the last time I traveled with them. He is a baby-faced charmer one minute and then picks your pocket the next. His tiny, nimble fingers are impressively terrific at sleight of hand, which I guess makes him a great cheater at cards."

"He looks adorable," I admitted.

The boy's dark cocoa hair drooped over his cocoa veil face and curled up on the ends. Then I watched one of the ladies of the house approach the boy's side of the table. She sat beside him flirtatiously and ran her fingers through the boy's hair. Again, my chin dropped, seeing the boy responded by placing his hand on her thigh. His eyes lit up as she cooed over him.

"I cannot believe this," I said, turning away. "She is trying to woo him."

"Welcome to the unfeigned world." Elior grinned. "You are experiencing the sleaze that ensnares many souls—even the young."

Nirnasha looked down at his plate and slowly pushed it away from him. I did the same and then took an enormous gulp of water. I looked up at Elior, who suddenly appeared to be distracted. I did not know what it was or how he could hear anything with the racket of music and drunken theatrics. Then, I began to feel the floor trembling, ever so slightly at first. A sudden quake knocked me out of my seat, and Nirnasha collapsed with me. He caught my head under his arm to keep it from slamming into the floor. I peered up at Elior, who had not budged but remained perfectly balanced. When the enormous tremor ceased, he slowly peeked over the railing.

"What was that?" Nirnasha stammered out.

"The game is afoot," Elior replied.

Another tremor shook the foundation again, and a large hole collapsed in the main floor next to the bar, with several patrons swallowed by the opening and their screams abruptly silenced. I regained my footing and peered over the railing to see fur-covered creatures. Each stood on their hind legs and snatched helpless folk into the grasp of their claws before clamping down with prominent buck teeth to end the screams of their helpless victims. Metal armor was scattered across their shoulders, thighs, chest, and long snouts. Their eyes beat crimson with a hunger I could only describe as lustful, as when Wendigo began to take over me.

"Gloom Gnawers!" I heard someone shout, only to realize Wide Berth had aimed with his buzzsaw rifle and began firing into the fray.

"Use what you know," Elior told us as he drew his drill guns and began firing. "Nirnasha, see if you can seal up that hole."

Nirnasha began to stretch out his hands when something yanked him to the ground. A Gloom Gnawer had snatched him, and the treacherous vermin bit down on his Mystic Silver prosthetic arm as he lifted it to defend himself. The vermin's teeth shattered, forcing it to rear back in agony before receiving a drill bit through its head from Elior.

"Close it up!" Elior shouted again to Nirnasha. The MKR's eyes suddenly darted toward a doorway where he and I noticed a tiny man grinning with sharp, jagged teeth. A dark bird squawked from its roost atop his torn hat while two others latched onto his arms. I did not wait to mix words. I felt my body ignite, my entire arms lighting up with wilder flames than anything I had ever conjured. Rumpelstilzchen's eyes widened, seeing the display of my power. I hurled a blazing ball of flame in his direction, blasting the wall outward and bringing dwindling sunlight through smoke and fire. Unfortunately, I did not see a scorched tiny body in the haze. Elior touched my shoulder to let me know I did well.

"Regroup!" I heard a familiar steamboat captain's voice shout. Meik fired off a couple of rounds from a buzzsaw rifle into a Gloom Gnawer, blocking the path of Kassy Bones coming up the stairs. She wielded two razor-sharp machetes and did not have too much trouble cutting through the vermin as they came at her. Wild Willy could hardly stand, but his accuracy stayed precise as he stumbled out, seeing what disturbed his night of pleasure. He hit each Gloom Gnawer accurately through the cranium with every drill bit he fired from his elaborately stylish drill bit guns plated copper with Sus hide wrapped handles, even with his pants barely buckled around his waist.

Nirnasha began to try again as I saw Kassy join us, cutting down Gloom Gnawers trying to come up the stairs. They were jumping up to the railing from the first floor, only to be shot off by Meik and his crew.

"I am having a hard time," Nirnasha admitted. "There are too many distractions."

Elior did not answer. He took a deep breath and manifested hundreds of bright orbs that rose from his body. In a single moment, the orbs erupted into beams of light striking through the overwhelming numbers of Gloom Gnawers climbing through the hole. Screeching bounced around the room as the monstrous vermin were sliced into sizzling pieces. And for a moment, all remained still.

"Show off," we heard Dok Ferias break the silence with his unflattering, cracking voice. But another voice unexpectedly came to us, and I felt it. I felt a presence that began stirring something in me. Wendigo was beginning to climb to the surface.

"There are no more distractions," I stammered to Nirnasha. I could feel the voice of hunger intensify. "What are you waiting for?! Close up the hole!"

"Something is not right," Nirnasha replied. "Something is preventing me from touching the earth to collapse it!"

Across the way, Elior's eyes locked with the tiny man, his grin still scoffing at us.

"Everyone to the Scoundrel," Meik shouted. "We're getting out of here!"

"Through there," Wide Berth earnestly pointed to the burnt-out hole in the wall.

Elior waited for all of us to pass by him, feeling the echoing ripple of hunger. I felt, as could Elior, I am sure, Wendigo had ceased climbing. If the creature had pressed onward, all of us would have been touched, never to forget the unbearable possession of hunger it imposed on the spirit.

"Rumpelstilzchen has been trying to get Wendigo to come into the light for some time now," Elior said with a look, his voice echoing in my mind. "But Wendigo is a creature that desires the dark. However, this is the closest I have ever witnessed him finding his way to the surface."

We stood momentarily, allowing the others to jump to the ground first, then Elior and I followed. More sawblade and drill bit fire followed. I grabbed Nirnasha's arm, yanked him to his feet, and noticed him fighting to remain stabilized. Nirnasha admitted to me later that the creature's hunger had indeed reached him.

We treaded swiftly behind the others. Wild Willy was making sure his wenches remained close, although the one, who was nearest Dok, was suddenly nabbed and devoured. Wild Willy blasted every round of his drill bit guns into them, but it was too late. His eyes pulsed with rage as he began to reload.

"Move it!" Meik shouted to him. "She's gone, and you're not staying here."

Wild Willy reluctantly followed Meik and the rest, pushing the other two women onward in front of him. He appeared highly protective of them, shooting any rodent that remotely came within range. Gloom Gnawers were overwhelming the town now, and many more emerged from various holes in the ground. We were not far from Meik's Ironclad and had moved away from the soft soil beneath our feet. The vermin pursued us, even when we reached the dock where the steamboat waited in the harbor.

I heard sawblades whiz over our heads—coming from the Ironclad. Its engines roared to full steam, and I could make out Darby Krokkett's figure on the upper deck, reigning down cover fire for us. Kassy Bones chopped one of the rope ties and swiftly approached the second, waiting for us to get aboard. Wild Willy and his wenches leaped to the deck, along with Wide Berth and Dok. Meik and Cenobia climbed aboard, followed by Nirnasha, Elior, and I. Surprisingly, Garvish and Bikarma were already aboard the ship, following Darby and Reggie aboard earlier that evening. They were bringing up a buzzsaw firing gun from below deck. Nirnasha jumped in to help them carry the boxes of ammo. The two idiots mounted the gun to the side and jammed in the large clip of sawblades. Bikarma began pulling the trigger into the ravenous vermin almost to the boat. Kassy cut the last line and jumped aboard.

Meik was already in the helm house on the top deck and pulled the blow horn—a signal to the engine room that the boat was ready for departure. He grabbed the helm and wheeled it away from the dock, setting the Seaborne Scoundrel into the waters. The steamboat captain started laughing while some other crew members wildly joined him.

"You don't see that every day, lads!" Meik proclaimed with a smile. I found it insensitive that they were laughing, considering everyone else in the town was most likely corpses. But I said nothing. Meik's laughter was short-lived as we watched three other steamboats take off from the dock.

"Those things are sailing the steamboats," Darby called out. There was just enough sunlight to see who was on board. And I did not need spy spectacles to see the ugly, disease-infested crew of the other three ships. The Seaborne Scoundrel held high dependability when facing weather conditions and crashing waves but not so steady when trying to outrun lighter steamboats filled with flesh-eating monsters.

"Looks like we're going to have to dig a few watery graves," Meik enthusiastically bellowed. "Get ready for some fun, lads!"

I watched Kassy emerge below deck with a buzzsaw firing gun herself. Wild Willy followed behind her with two boxes of ammo. They went up to the second deck, and I followed them, cutting the wenches off.

Darby uncovered what appeared to be a cannon or at least the barrel of one, as there was no pipe attachment to the breach. He began packing a black powder into the muzzle and then placed a cannonball in after it. He also took notice of the confusion on my face.

"This here is an antique," he explained with a grin. "But she still works."

He cut a small piece of rope, or so it appeared, and placed it into what he called a touch hole. I thought he was being vulgar, but he reassured me that it was the proper historical name. The cannon sat on a wooden platform with four wooden wheels and tied to a pulley system. Darby tugged on the rope to ease the cannon forward and waited for the vermin-filled steamboats to draw closer to us.

The first boat began coming alongside the Ironclad when Darby lit the rope inside the cannon. He told me to cover my ears, and just in time, I could still clearly hear the thunderclap blast. It shot out the cannonball, which exploded into the hull of a Gloom Gnawers' steamboat. Bits and pieces of wood flew in all directions, even landing back on our deck.

"That is how you drown rats," Wild Willy hollered. There was a roar of cheers from the crew, and Darby began reloading the cannon. With the other two boats not ceasing their pursuit, Kassy and Bikarma began firing sawblades into the other boats. Yet before the sawblades hit their marks, they bounced off what appeared to be thin air. As the boats drew closer, I could see some type of magic was parrying the sawblades.

"Protection spell." Elior broke my gaze from the boats for a moment. "See that dim crimson light where the sawblades are hitting around the ship? It repels metal objects from penetrating through."

"What do we do?" I asked.

"Use magic, of course," Elior replied. "Now is another great time for you and Nirnasha to practice."

"What can I possibly do out here?" Nirnasha startled me. "I control soil and rock, not water."

"True," Elior admitted. "But that does not mean you cannot reach the soft soil beneath us. Reach down and pull it above the waves."

Nirnasha shrugged and said he would try. We each targeted a boat and began conjuring what we could. I concentrated on summoning a ball of fire larger than I had ever done before. I could see Darby's eyes widen as he watched the ball of flame grow bigger than my body, hovering in a mass above my head. I began feeling weary, took aim, and hurled it onto the boat I was targeting. The massive ball of flame landed on the bow and erupted into ashes. The steamboat suddenly swallowed water, and the rest dove violently into the sea. Nirnasha, on the other hand, was having trouble again.

"Something is wrong," Nirnasha said. "I cannot seem to feel any power to do what I want to do."

"Take a breath," I could hear Elior speak into Nirnasha's mind. "Your emotions are clouding you from what is true."

I could see Nirnasha relax. His hand remained outstretched toward the steamboat swiftly approaching our port side. He took several deeper breaths before loudly shouting and shoving his arm upward. Nothing happened. His head sunk low, and stared back at Elior. Nirnasha's disappointment quickly faded when a violent burst of muck and sand flew up from the sea bed, so massive and close that it almost capsized the Ironclad. But it flung the Gloom Gnawers' steamboat into the air and then, as if grasped by a giant hand, yanked it back down below the surface of the sea with an explosive splash, slamming more unforgiving waves against the Ironclad and threw all of us to our backside—apart from one.

"You do much better when you are calm, Nirnasha," Elior said, standing over us. "I can see the power inside you is growing."

"What the bloody balls was that?!" Meik's voice roared as he hopped back to his feet.

"Sorry, Captain Feenk, sir," Nirnasha tried to apologize, getting to his feet. "I did not know it would be like that."

"Never mind that stupid boy," Meik replied. He pushed past Nirnasha to stand before Elior, almost knocking the stupid boy back down. "What are fiends like that doing on the surface, and not to mention sailing steamboats like they know what the bloody balls they're doing?! They belong in the Unlight!"

"Things are not going to remain where they belong," Elior serenely stated. Meik huffed, shook his head, and then walked down to the main deck.

"You did great," I heard Cenobia's voice behind me. I gave her a slight smirk, but she could tell I felt exhausted from the ordeal.

"You appear exhausted. You should lie down." Cenobia reached out for my hand. I let her take it, and we walked down to the ship's cabins.

The Seaborne Scoundrel was more sizeable than I thought when I first saw it briefly from the waterfront—as we were all rushing to get aboard. There were plenty of rooms, but only a tiny space for a bed and the door to slide shut.

"Would you tell me more about you and Meik?" I asked Cenobia as she opened the door to an available cabin. She sighed heavily but then nodded her consent.

"It has been over ten years ago now," Cenobia began. "Meik and I had a child together. Our boy was so beautiful, and I, a joyful bride of the best steamboat captain on the sea. Meik was a bragger back then—a witty merchant who rapidly became wealthy. We both shared a love for adventure, even when our baby came along. We did not want to stop seeing the world together."

"What was your baby's name?" I asked.

"Pelagios," Cenobia replied, her eyes swelling with tears. "One day, a storm swept upon us without warning. I was holding our baby with Meik on the upper deck, sailing back from Crye. Before I could get below, an enormous wave crashed against our boat and ripped my baby from my hands. The sea nabbed him, stole him from us. I vowed I would never set foot on a boat again. But Meik loved the sea. Despite the tragedy, he could not find it in his heart to stop sailing. So, he and I went our separate ways. And now, here I am, back where he is and breaking my vow."

"You just left him?" I asked. "Does that mean you are still married to him?"

"I guess it does," Cenobia admitted. "Meik has his reputation to uphold. He may pinch a wench's rump now and again, but deep down, he held true to me. He confessed that to me earlier this evening and would hate for you to know. Do keep it under your hat."

I smiled and hugged her goodnight. "I will. I promise,"—until I write it down later. It is all for historical purposes, after all.

REALM OF DREAMS

I desired to sleep, yet my eyes were open. I could hear my breath echo, reaching far off into the distance of a dimly illuminated landscape, softer than twilight. The walls of the Ironclad cabin were gone, the steamboat itself nowhere in sight along with the sea. My bed lay in a vaguely familiar misty meadow, once blurry, now fully lucid. Everything by my bedside remained near and appeared to be emitting steam. Even the blooming flowers and grassy knolls appeared hazy with vapor. The trees that encircled the meadow held a solid silhouette, with branches swaying steadily back and forth. However, I felt no wind touch my skin. Then, I could hear it whisper through the canopies as my breath resounded back.

The stillness held a pleasantness at first. But then I felt a rage of sadness sweep over me, followed by heartbreak, fear, and anger. I inhaled and tasted the stench of such things on my tongue, as I can only describe it—such vile sensations choked my throat. I leaped out of my bed, not quite finding my feet. I stumbled, still nauseous and looking to vomit the taste out of my mouth. Yet I could only dry heave when I fell to my knees. In the next few moments, I felt a gentle hand on my head, bringing something sweet to my tongue. The calm swept over me as I breathed in again, and I could taste joy, bliss, and peace—delightful and satisfying. I could feel myself become weightless, and my mind drifted to ease. Elior stood over me, his hand still softly on my head. Nirnasha was with him, holding tightly to his forearm.

"What is this place?" My voice carried far off into the distance.

"Nowhere," Elior replied, his voice resounding the same. "And everywhere."

"I got the same answer," Nirnasha sighed. "Now that we are together, maybe he shall finally tell me more."

Certainly, he did. Elior conveyed we were in the ethereal realm, a place between life and death, a convergence where existence sauntered, yet time became a memory. While in the ethereal, our bodies could rest while our souls could learn more to train and increase our power.

Elior continued speaking with us as we walked down a narrow pathway into the forest that surrounded the meadow. Dreaming for an MKR, as he described it, is a gateway—one in which our souls had finally transitioned and arrived, reaching the state where our bodies had utterly surrendered to the awakened power within us.

The dangers of the ethereal were many, much for an MKR who lost their way or fell in the ethereal. It did not surprise me to hear Elior explain how a spirit dies. The very fabric of their existence is cleaved from ever-knowing consciousness, with only one thing remaining—the continuum of an empty void benumbed never to wake again.

"When did you witness a spirit die?" I asked.

"It was long ago," Elior replied.

"How does one kill a spirit?" I heard Nirnasha interject with a similar curiosity.

"If you have to ask," Elior replied. "Then you are not ready to learn how to kill one."

Refusing to say any more on the matter, Elior stopped at the edge of the tree line. We were gazing out upon land that would have appeared no different than the Deadlands in the physical realm. Elior had created a haven in the ethereal, where Nirnasha and I could come at night and train together. But he warned us not to yet go beyond the forest. Even stepping out from the tree line would expose us to dangers we were unprepared to face.

We turned and made our way back to the center of the meadow. My bed was gone. In its place was a long pedestal with a familiar book, Gems of the Hidden Glade, that Nirnasha and I had explored together, and existed in both the ethereal and the physical.

"What were those things I felt and tasted?" I asked.

"What other spirits feel," Elior answered. "It is normal for this place. Just be careful you do not embrace what they bring to you. For even joy in this place can turn your soul to madness."

Nirnasha and I watched Elior fade from our sight. Again, we spoke the words to reveal the book's spirit. A dim light appeared and took form in the shape of the elder-looking man. He briskly moved toward us in his youthful step, dressed in his fine, dark cocoa skinny trousers and gold gentleman's vest. His fit and flare frock appeared with the shine of freshly pressed Gossypium, and his shoes still held their tinted glow of gold. This time, he met us with a smile.

We remained listening to the book's spirit and practiced the only spells we knew how to cast. We did not stay long, or so it felt. The walls of my cabin in the Ironclad appeared once more. I was disoriented yet rested. All remained weightless, lifeless, and ready to disappear for the next few moments. Then my sensations felt weighted or even heightened like the warmth of my heart beating inside me. I could hear the splashing of the sea colliding with the steamboat. Shivers surged up my spine when my feet touched the icy floor, and I swiftly pulled them back up to the bed. The feeling of cold momentarily alarmed me. Again, the icy sensation burst against my skin once I had slipped into my boots and opened the cabin door, the chilling winds pressing hard against me. It was early morning, with choppy waves slapping violently against the Ironclad. I reached for my frock by the door, wrapping it around me, and stepped into the crisp spritz of the open tide.

Elior met me with a kind candor to follow in his footsteps. My legs were shaky. Yet I steadied my balance and followed the MKR into the lower deck, where dusty lanterns made the dining hall appear abandoned. Meik stood with his arms spread out over a map that lay unraveled on a table. I could scarcely believe my eyes. There were many charted cities, a detailed layout of the three kingdoms, and bodies of water. I was not aware of anyone else holding such a valuable possession.

"Where did you get this?" I gasped.

"I stole it," Meik brutishly replied.

"Do not be like that," Cenobia said. "Tell her the truth, or I shall not fix the Sus strips the way you like."

I saw Meik about to begin a debate like all men do. Which, I did not let him start in about it.

"Tell me, how did you get this?!"

"Why don't you ask your mentor?" Meik spoke plainly and turned his gaze toward Elior. "He is the one who made it for me."

"How is that possible? How did you make this?" I asked. I could not help the words escape my lips. Of course, I should have realized by then that if there were any impossibilities, Elior found a way to do it.

"You are going to have to stop being an unbeliever," Elior replied gently. "How is it you still do not see what you are capable of doing? You are an MKR now. The impossible will happen if you have the eyes to seek it out."

"He used light," we heard Nirnasha interject. "Elior is an MKR who controls light. It is simple. He soaked the paper in a Mystic Silver chemical compound and burned the light into the paper."

"Well spoken," Elior replied. "I assume that you were studying a little longer than Aagneya."

"I did," Nirnasha admitted. "I believe I learned more than I thought I would."

"Aye," Meik spoke up and pointed at Elior. "Be careful where you go at night, especially with this one around. You never know where he might take you."

"What do you mean?" I asked.

"Don't believe for a moment the dead don't dream," Meik continued. "They walk the ethereal just as real as you do. They lust to devour life and make it like them."

I turned my gaze toward Nirnasha, who looked at Elior. When the MKR felt everyone's eyes were upon him, he sighed and asked if we wanted to know the truth.

"I knew one day I would be old enough to hear bedtime stories again," Meik chuckled. "But I believe I've already heard the one you're going to tell." The steamboat captain sent both me and Nirnasha a wink.

"Best get some food then. It will be a long one," Elior motioned to another table where Cenobia was preparing plates of food.

The dining hall grew crowded with the rest of the crew, but they kept their distance from where Elior sat. His words reminded me of stories I had read in old, dusty books, not as ancient as the ones we found in the Unlight, but they indeed held a nostalgic flavor for my senses. Nirnasha and I happened to be the only seemingly interested individuals for the MKR to speak. Still, I caught Cenobia brushing Kassy aside from her view to see what Elior was doing.

"Before the beginning," Elior began, his tea still piping hot next to his pressed hands in front of him. He picked it up and blew steam across the table, illuminating light like stars within the cloud. "There was oneness and togetherness, manifested in three distinct individualities, yet equally one in essence. Face-to-face, out of the void and the gloom of nothing, they remained abiding freely with one another and freely expressed their light into the darkness. From the ever-existing light came all things with breath, all things palpable, all things ethereal, and all things virtuous.

Yet the darkness would not be tamed so easily. It grew jealous of the light. It was bitter and desired to corrupt what the light had made. One creation of the light sought to make it so. It allowed itself to be tainted and engulfed by a lust for power. The light, however, was not fooled. They cast down the servant of the dark and those it had besmirched and gave them an enslaver over them. The slave master was none other than humanity, created in the image of the light and chosen to subdue and rule over the darkness. Humanity was chosen for such an honor and was the only one of its kind. They were forged within spirit, and their ethereal presence became housed in flesh and bone by the very breath of light. Just as the light desired, the spirit of humanity would not only feel the light in their ethereal existence but know what the light had created with the touch of their hands. Humanity could wield the light in the realms and find pleasure in living in its domain.

Yet the dark had other plans. It slithered into the spirit of humans and corrupted their hearts as it had done to those before. Thus, they who became created to rule over the dark betrayed the light just as the first servant of darkness did. The light knew the allure of the shadow and promised it would one day put an end to the deeds the darkness inflicts. This is the story my father told me—and my brother."

"You have a brother?" Nirnasha chimed in before I could. Elior did not respond. He sipped his tea like an old, proper gentleman.

"I was seven years old then," Elior continued. His hand waved, and suddenly the realm of the ethereal became projected in light all around us. The crew startlingly pushed away from the walls and joined our table in the center of the room. Elior began illuminating silhouettes of young boys and their father emerging from the growing steam.

"How are you controlling the steam?" I asked aloud. "I thought you could only control light."

"As I said before, when you are familiar with the ethereal," Elior replied. "You will find what you can control and what you cannot. In your case, how do you know what fire is and what is not while in the ethereal?"

He turned to Nirnasha.

"How do you know what is earth and what is not? Elements in the physical mean nothing in the ethereal."

He had a point. And I believe I was finally beginning to comprehend how magic must be understood. Though what may seem chaotic to some is, in fact, orderly to the one who carries wisdom to learn and recognize its function. In the physical realm, logic and reason can be applied because barriers and boundaries define their limitations. Yet magic is a convergence of both ethereal and physical, each affecting the other. Certain things have an essence in the ethereal such as humanity, consisting of body and spirit. However, only some funnel their energy from one realm to another, and fewer still if something more remarkable has awakened within them. Then, I began wondering what Elior had awakened within me and how he did it.

"I did have a brother," Elior continued as the silhouettes of two young boys pranced at play around us. "Together, we devoted our lives to know the light, the one who brought all things into being. Just as the explorers of today, my brother and I believed we could discover knowledge in the light like seeking treasure."

Elior, the creator he described, was distinct in expression yet completely defined as one harmonious deity that unified as one above all realms and held an ever-existing presence. I could scarcely imagine such a thing, but it elated me to hear the MKR's tone trembling with wonder.

"Sod off," Kassy Bones scoffed from the other side of the cabin. "You expect us to believe this bedwetting bedtime story?"

"Keep your tongue trapped, wench," Meik snapped back. "The next time you speak ill of Elior, I'll feed you to the Tide Maidens!"

"Enough," Elior spoke out calmly. "I do not expect everyone I tell to believe me.

Yet if you wish to know how and why I have walked existence for so long, it may be wise to follow the words of your captain."

"Sod off," Kassy spat. "No great light made me. I owe nothing to no one. I go where I please, say what I please, and do what I please!"

She stomped up the steps, slamming the door behind her. Wide Berth followed her with Dok in tow. Their posture did not show they cared much to hear anymore, either. The others began excusing themselves to return to the upper deck.

I could not understand why no one seemed to believe him. Then I heard Meik say something to Elior as he began making his way out, with Cenobia following behind him.

"It's not your fault, Elior," Meik sympathized. "They don't know you as I do."

Since then, I have learned much about the fragility of the human psyche. What is surrendered to one's imagination of the truth is never accepted as reality. In other words, it never matters how much time is spent speaking what is true, spending time proving something is true, or even showing them a demonstration of the truth's power. It is rejected because it is not what they desire to be real. In many ways, I could see Nirnasha's mind contort to avoid believing what Elior was saying. Soon, even he left the cabin, leaving me and Elior sitting in silence.

"Even an awakened MKR is not always ready to have ears to hear," Elior admitted. Then he turned to me. "Are you not leaving with the others?"

"You have not finished yet," I replied.

The MKR's grin lit up my heart. I confess that a part of me wanted to pull away. But I knew it was because I had never heard anything like it. And somehow, I knew my heart was telling me his story held validity.

"Perhaps another time," Elior said.

I did not argue with him. We returned to the upper deck, where Meik and Darby navigated us to the narrow straits using the map we had first seen that morning. He stepped away from the map and approached me outside the helm house, leaning against the railing and pointed toward the distance. The sea held a cloudy mist before us, but it remained clear enough to see the shore and a large opening in a bulbous rock formation.

"That is where we need to go," Darby said. "I saw what you did with those other boats chasing after us. Could you scale it back and focus more on not bringing down the entire caverns or setting the boat on fire?"

"I could try," I replied.

"Good," he sighed. "I do not mean to frighten you, but we nearly perished the last time we went through the Narrow Straits."

"What happened?" I asked.

"Well, we lost the only two passengers we had due to our fires going out," Darby admitted. "The place is crawling with Tide Maidens. They do not like fire too much but are not above trying to put it out if they are famished. Never been so terrified in all my life."

He motioned toward Elior.

"Tide Maidens do not like light too much either," Darby explained. "But they hate fire. Somehow, they destroyed most of our torches, and we did not have much of anything to fight them with, mostly because we could hardly see. Meik yelled for all of us to get to the helm house, except for Reggie, who was down in the engine room."

"What does he do down there anyway?" I asked. "Mystic Silver powers the only vessels I have been on."

"This one is as well," Darby replied. "But not in the usual way as you might think."

He smiled when I scrunched up my nose in confusion.

"Meik is actually a Keeper," Darby clarified and did not pause hearing my shocking gasp. "The engine and boiler are made from Mystic Silver and Iron. It allows less fuel to be burned and produces higher amounts of steam to power the pistons. Meik enchanted it to keep the boiler from overheating and the engine at a reasonable temperature. Reggie stays down there to ensure all the pistons remain working as Meik messed up the enchantment. Sometimes

Reggie has to beat on them with a wrench."

"Wait a minute," I interjected, seeing Darby amusing himself with the thought of his friend hollering and hammering away. "Are you telling me that we had the ability to outrun those vermin back in Folesk?"

"Meik used only enough speed to stay ahead of them," Darby replied. "Elior requested it."

"Why would Elior do something like that?" I said, thoroughly doubting Darby's words.

"Because you needed an opportunity to test yourself," Elior's voice came from behind us. Darby moved away from the railing. Meik stood beside the MKR, who drew my attention again to the Narrow Straits.

"That is a place it will be tested again," Meik assured me. "No doubt Darby told you it is crawling with Tide Maidens. I also want to make one thing clear. The only reason we're even out here sailing back through is that we have three MKRs with us. We were all planning on an extended stay in Folesk before Elior made me an offer I couldn't refuse."

"I know," I replied. "Your big money contract."

"Blast the money, lass! Don't think you're the only one Elior speaks to up here." Meik boasted, pointing to his skull. "While we be speaking about credits, there was more negotiating going on. Elior knows what I'm seeking and showed me how to get it. We will be needing his help, and probably yours too to get it."

"What did you promise him?" I demanded Elior to answer me.

"Mystic Silver," Elior replied. "Down in the Unlight. Heaps of it."

"He said there was plenty to share." Meik chuckled. "Plenty for my Scoundrel. Plenty for me, my crew, and even some left over for you."

I could not believe it. Elior had promised to find out what Eastguard was up to, and here we were, sailing for what was essentially another treasure hunt. I was beginning to wonder if we were explorers or just pirates.

"Sometimes it feels like both," I heard Elior whisper in my mind.

"Do not invade my private thoughts ever again!" I whispered fiercely under my breath. "Or I will incinerate you from the inside out."

I turned to see Nirnasha had joined us, but I pushed past him. I almost felt Elior's eyes latch onto me as I hurried down the steps. I felt tears streaming down my face, knowing we were journeying back to a place I never wanted to venture to again. I felt my thoughts turn dark toward the MKR I adored so much. Then he was suddenly in front of me.

"Why are you angry?" Elior asked. "Why do you fear so much? I am with you."

"I refuse to be a part of this," I replied. "I shall not go on another treasure hunt in that place."

"You have a power that not only gives you light but can reach out and destroy anything it touches." Elior placed his hands gently on my shoulders and stared into my eyes. "With such power, I know you will journey many times into the darkness. But never believe it will overcome you."

"How can you be sure?" I managed to press out from my sobbing face. I could feel myself trembling just at the thought of returning.

"You are much more stubborn than any other I have awoken," Elior assured. "Cling to what is good and hopeful, and no gloom shall take you."

"I never dreamed I would do this," I admitted. "I do not believe I will ever stop being afraid."

"We never do," Elior admitted. "But fear is not the enemy. It is our comfort that destroys us. So, dare to dream vaster than anything you ever thought was possible. For the only dreams that die are the ones never attempted."

Something unexpectedly impacted the Ironclad, ringing it like a bell. I was put on my back, but Elior swiftly pulled me to my feet. We heard more high-pitched whistling overhead, and several hefty splashes threw water onto the lower deck. I could hear Meik shouting and cursing from above. Elior and I raced back to him.

"How did those ball snatchers get so close to us?" Meik shouted to Darby. "Who's the lookout?!"

"Dok and Wide Berth, I believe," Darby shouted back as more whistling projectiles landed near us.

"They are never where they are supposed to be," Wild Willy appeared on the deck. "I just thumped them for sleeping in the storeroom. Making them bring up the heavy ammo."

There was a cease-fire from the other steamboats that were now no more than approximately one hundred arm lengths away.

"Don't bother," Meik revealed a vile grin to Wild Willy. "I know exactly how to take care of these parasitic lubbers."

Meik called down to Reggie to oil up the pistons. Reggie's voice argued for a moment in the pipe speaker, suddenly overthrown by Meik barking back at him. He spun the helm clear around, facing the other steamboats, and I could feel the Ironclad pick-up speed. Wild Willy caught my arm and told me to hang onto the railing to brace myself. The other steamboats began firing projectiles again, but the Ironclad moved too quickly for the other boats to aim accurately.

"Are those pirates?" I asked Wild Willy.

"Yes," he nodded. "Now, hold onto that railing good and tight."

The Ironclad's momentum elevated the front of the boat out of the water, exposing its jagged bow-like teeth from a monster of the deep, sending Meik into hysterical laughter. I could see most of the pirates frozen in terror as we drew near the first vessel.

"The sea loves me," Meik shouted. "For I am the madness that will feed it your corpses!"

The Ironclad slammed through the steamboat, cutting through it like a spinning bandsaw blade through a Sus' hide. The impact jolted my insides and almost yanked my grip from the railing. Then another hard turn from Meik slammed unforgivably into the next steamboat and splintered it apart. A third hard turn of the helm and Meik found yet another to shatter. This time, he did not go clean through it. The Ironclad had slowed, but the steamboat quickly took on enough water to sink within minutes. I regained my bearings and saw the other steamboats fleeing. Three sunk out of the five. Nirnasha's eyes were wide, but I could see a grin begin to form on his face. I had almost forgotten my fellow

MKR was with us. He turned toward me with a now glowing smile.

"Was that not the most thrilling thing you have ever experienced in your life?!" he exclaimed.

I did not want to, but his dumb look made me burst out a giggle. Wild Willy stepped between us and brought our attention to the remains of the steamboats. He pointed to some of the survivors who managed to live through the carnage of the Ironclad. Nirnasha and I watched from a distance as the survivors, men and women, some young and some older, snatched and dragged beneath the surface. Their screams were unforgettable, and I took note of the crimson that suddenly filled the water. I wanted to help, but every survivor was gone before I finished the thought.

"Tide Maidens are hungry today," Wild Willy teased. Then his tone transformed completely to worry. "That is why I hate the water. Do not even much like taking a bath."

No one said much when we reached the entrance to the Narrow Straits. The gloomy shadow forced my mind back to the Unlight. It did not appear any different. Elior summoned some magic light orbs that floated all around the Ironclad. We stayed away from the edges of the boat so as not to be seized overboard by the crafty maidens. Most of us remained on the top deck and did not bother venturing below.

We were silent as the time came for us to rest. I was having trouble concentrating on going into the ethereal and practice. Whenever I shut my eyes, I thought about a Tide Maiden crawling up the steps to secretly drag me away. I would open my eyes again to the soft drips of water from the cavern ceiling bouncing into the ever-growing still waters. It dripped like my bathroom faucet back home. That should have comforted me, but my home was not a place I remember where I felt secure. Even having Elior with us did not help me sleep soundly.

Each time, Nirnasha tried to lure me away to the ethereal to train. But I could not keep my eyes shut long enough to dream into it. Fear of death held my thoughts captive. Nirnasha admitted he had trouble keeping his eyes shut as well. He hoped that if we did it together, we would be better prepared if anything happened. Together, holding hands, we finally found our way to Elior's meadow, surrounded by trees shifting into the silhouettes of twilight.

We discovered we could imagine particular objects in the ethereal if our minds were calm enough to concentrate and summon them into our presence. We started with small objects like candles. I sought to practice controlling my abilities and summon small flames. Nirnasha summoned small mounds of dirt and tried to mold them into various shapes and sizes. Then he summoned roots from the ground to intertwine and take the form of a tree. Impressed in seeing his progress, I became envious as I had difficulty even summoning the tiniest spark to light one of the candles. When Nirnasha's tree began to glow, I allowed myself to remain distracted.

The tree's fruit held a viridescent shimmer, surrounded by golden threads. Nirnasha saw that I was standing next to him. He grinned and told me he dreamt of such a tree as a child and never forgot it. The tree began breathing, and then it moved. Two openings appeared toward its canopy, burning with the same haze as its body. Its roots pulled together, and it stood upright like a human, spreading out long branches that contorted to reveal arms and hands. I could scarcely believe it when Nirnasha began speaking to it, and the tree spoke back. Their language was foreign to me, but I remained listening intently. The tree turned away from Nirnasha and walked away from us.

"I told him to explore this realm," Nirnasha said. "I know Elior told us not to go beyond the trees surrounding this place yet, but I figured we could send something else to give us word about what is out there before we see for ourselves."

"I believe that is a wonderful idea," I admitted.

"It shall go beyond the tree line and then come back to tell me what it has seen," Nirnasha explained.

"What if you are not here?" I asked.

"Then it will tell the trees surrounding this meadow," Nirnasha smiled. "That way, I shall know it is doing fine."

I smiled back and congratulated him on his clever idea. He began encouraging me and I did my best to learn. While I did not manage to summon something so spectacular as Nirnasha's tree, I remained steadfast to finally summon fire and sense how I could harness the magnitude of the flame by assigning specific colors to certain emotions. For example, I thought of azure, a calming sky, to summon just a spark to ignite the candles. I imagined giving full vent to my anger would summon an immense flame. But my goal was to generate emotions behind my power with a strategic purpose and not to lose control of my wits. Funneling through what I felt turned my mind toward my parents once more.

Both my father and mother believed I was too spirited as a child. Even in my adulthood, they could never see why things touched me so profoundly to the point of crying or becoming hysterical with rage. I would guess that when your parents are hardly present during your childhood or criticize every accomplishment you are able to do—one could ponder why I often feel like a fire waiting to burn out of control. Spending time out of their house when I was going to school somehow soothed me from wanting to rip my hair out each day. I assumed I had enough pent-up aggression toward my parents to fit my need for a huge fire blast should I ever need it. It certainly worked against the Gloom Gnawers. I had no idea Nirnasha could hear my thoughts about my parents until I looked up and saw his sympathetic expression.

"Why are you in my head?" I snapped.

"We are in the ethereal," he replied. "It is kind of hard not to hear one another's thoughts. Remember how I told you about that tree I dreamt of as a child?"

"Wait." My tone stumbled with confusion. "You were not speaking that out loud?"

"No," Nirnasha laughed. "We do not have mouths in this realm. The only way to communicate is with our minds. You did not pick up on that already?"

"Of course I did," I sneered, despite the fact I knew he was right. Judging from the look, he shot me, he knew he was too. But I continued to persist in the falsity. "I probably just forgot."

"Fine," Nirnasha calmly concluded. "Just remember that even those inner thoughts you think you have are not private here."

"Unless you learn to hide them." Elior made both of us jump, me to the point I almost returned to the physical realm.

"Why do you always do that?!" Nirnasha exclaimed.

"How do we hide them?" I asked, pushing past my fellow MKR. "And aren't you supposed to be on watch?"

"Darby and Wild Willy are on the lookout," Elior replied. "I shall make this quick so I can return to them. While you are here, I recommend you learn from one another, especially how to hide your thoughts and secretly share them with one another. Sometimes, the knowledge someone else possesses can inspire us to acquire more about what we are capable of as well. Learn and listen."

"I wonder if we can tie a bell around his neck," Nirnasha wondered after Elior had vanished.

"I know what you mean," I agreed. "But I have noticed that Elior only gets in your face if he knows you are close to discovering something special."

"Then I guess we should share what we have learned with one another," Nirnasha admitted.

I learned that Nirnasha had taken to the ethereal with a much greater adaptation than I did. He was able to feel the solidity of the physical realm, such as rock, soil, and plant life, in the ethereal. The only difference is how those things were interpreted. He was unsure of what to call his ability to feel the physical realm from our dream state. He implemented the descriptors "tone" and "melody" that connected with certain substances in the physical realm. He then followed that melody back to its source in the ethereal to summon what he wanted. I stared blankly at him, believing my mind was about to melt.

"Are you trying to tell me that you hear music?" I asked. The taste of scoff hit my tongue with bitterness and then an unbearable burning that made me reel.

"Does that taste good?" He replied sarcastically. "That is what unbelief tastes like."

When I regained my composure, Nirnasha placed his hands on my shoulders so I would look at him in his eyes.

"I have been in this place much longer than you have," he explained. "Ever since we learned that we could come here, I have taken every opportunity to learn what I can. I started doubting myself, believing you would teach me something because you do not seem to have a problem summoning your powers in the physical realm. But now I see that you need me because you have difficulty recognizing how to summon your power in the ethereal."

"Then I guess we truly do need one another," I replied. "I shall do my best to help you in the physical realm, and you do your best to help me in the ethereal."

Nirnasha smiled and let go of my shoulders.

"Do you remember what fire feels like?" he asked. "Try to remember, and then listen for the melody in the ethereal. Once you hear it, follow it with your mind to touch the physical realm, then try to summon your power here. This way, you will learn how the ethereal interprets fire."

Nirnasha reminded me then of what the power of music has on people. Music transcends what is played in the physical realm, touches people's emotions, and often inspires their essence. It should be no surprise that music is the tether that connects both realms. One can always tune out music if they so choose. But I have realized that all of existence comprises many different songs. They outnumber the stars in the skies. I know how strange this can sound because it would be strange to see how my body began to dance, as it is always odd to those who cannot hear the music. But I did as I remembered the elegance and warmth of fire igniting through me to set my arms ablaze. Nirnasha knew I was hearing it, too, claiming he could feel the vibrations emanating toward me. The manifestation took hold and came to fruition. When I felt the unabridged melody finally engulf my presence, everything about it held a familiarity.

My fellow MKR described the experience of watching me ignite and interchange between royal crimson, then gold, viola, and azure as a "phenomenal spectacle." I have never been called that before. It appeared as if my whole body had become kindled, flickering, and leaping with flames that pirouetted in a rhythm all around me. Even my eyes churned with the presence of the hues I emitted. Seeing Nirnasha's reaction and a tear roll down his cheek flattered me to the point of feeling my own tears stream down my face with my heart overwhelmed by a joy I had never tasted. The palate of it stuck to the roof of my mouth, rolling on my tongue like fresh honey. I peered down at my hands, wondering what I should summon. I looked deep inside my heart as I kept elegantly dancing, searching not for what I wanted but for what I truly believed I needed. I closed my eyes and reached out with my hands, and a vast blaze sprang forth from my chest.

The release of fire swirled and crashed just a ways from the both of us. The inferno took shape and formed into a womanly figure, tall and debonaire, something I was not. Her skin was like molten crust, the color of dark ash but smooth and shimmering. Her hair swayed like flames in a calm breeze. She interchanged the way I did, between the four colors, emitting a transcendent beauty I never fathomed. She appeared perplexed for the moment but soon stood in front of me and held out her hand. I was unaware I had fallen to my knees, and I rapidly sensed my strength had left me.

She reached out again for me, this time with both hands. I felt her warm touch upon me, raising me to my feet. And then her welcoming palms held my face, and she stared deeply into my eyes and whispered a saying much like the secret phrase to unlock Elior's book. Yet the meaning never reached me. Her voice sounded much like Cenobia's but with a far echo coupled with a crackling fire. She pulled me to my feet and embraced me. I began feeling my strength return to me as my heart grew hot, like a soothing steam bath, calming every fiber of my being. At that moment, she spoke her name—Lasair Neamhbhásmhar, meaning immortal flame. She is the protector of the living flame, just one spark of creation that lives in music, hope, inspiration, love, innocence, wisdom, and chaste desires—existing for many eons but never heard the call of one such as me.

"Once there was a king who spoke highly of me," she told me. "I tutored and counseled him. Now, shall it be for you, but in the ways of fire and the heart. The stronger your flame becomes, the more you shall know my power. Call on me when you need aid, and I will open the gates for Dancing Desire to keep you safe."

I awoke, still with the warmth of Lasair's arms around me. Nirnasha held a smirk on his face, just next to me. Elior stood over us, looking down with a much larger smile.

"You are doing much better than I expected," he whispered. "You both have found your snares, it would seem."

THE MAIDENS' CALL

Elior revealed that having an ethereal snare is vital for an MKR to remain protected from perishing. The snare emits life to the body and maintains a MKR's spirit if death is experienced in the physical realm. Specific conditions to the way an MKR dies could prohibit them from returning from the ethereal and be reborn. He warned us that even though he knew what our snares were, to keep them secret from anyone else, as it is possible for another MKR or ethereal being to learn the weakness of the snare and destroy it. It can render the magnitude of an MKR's power and perhaps even kill them off in the physical realm, binding them to wander endlessly lost in the ethereal.

"A snare continues to feed power to an MKR, heightening one's abilities," Elior explained. We would learn as much from the snare as we would learn from the book *Gems of the Hidden Glade*, perhaps even more. While the book would help us unlock secrets of our capabilities as an MKR and assist us in learning about the past, our snare would guide us in using our specific powers, whether in the ethereal or physical realm.

Another night of training in the ethereal passed, and I awoke in the helm house next to Nirnasha. He stood and lent me a hand, pulling me to my feet. For all the hype Darby made about the Narrow Straits, it was sorely becoming a boring boat ride while in the physical realm, at least. All we did was sleep, eat, and stay as quiet as possible. I could not believe I complained that no danger was befalling us. Yet I was eager to use what I had learned, and I thought an opportunity would present itself in the blindness of the rocky tunnel. I could sense my fear of dark spaces waning as my confidence grew.

We walked out on the deck, and I saw Wild Willy leaning against a crate, but I did not see the two women he had brought on board. Bikarma and Garvish were tightly clenching buzzsaw rifles as if they were getting ready to fire them off. I felt Cenobia grab my hand. I turned to her, and she leaned in with a whisper.

"Elior did not want to wake you and Nirnasha," she uttered. "But now that you are up, you might as well know what happened."

I waited for her to take a couple of deep breaths as I could see the news that she wished to give me was difficult. I sensed fear in her trembling tone, but not just for herself.

"Wild Willy went down into the kitchen with Elior not too long ago," she continued. "They were looking for Wide Berth and Dok, who escorted the two women down there to bring back food. Elior and Wild Willy found them in the mess hall. And Wide Berth and Dok were strewn on the tables with the two women devouring them."

Nirnasha had leaned in also to hear. He and I had no words in response.

"They succumbed to the Maiden's Call." She sighed heavily.

There is a well-known children's rhyme in Westmain, perhaps translated differently in parts of Eastguard and Nod, that I learned in school as a young girl. Traveling by sea was known for young girls and older women going missing. I had even heard bizarre tales from Ye and Po about young girls walking off peers or boats in the middle of the night, never to be seen again. No one is clear about who wrote the rhyme, but it always held a disturbing narrative—and I never forgot.

The Maiden's Call can find you near
The Maiden's Call can find you far
You do not need ears to hear
Just the tune of the enticing star
Do not let your heart be wooed
Or the sea shall call you home
While vile things become your brood
Forever beneath the waves, you shall roam

Elior silently cut the women's throats afore Wild Willy could even fire off a shot. They were already manifesting their appetite and transforming with scales appearing all over their bodies.

"How did you not stop this?" I asked Elior, who was now standing just opposite Wild Willy. "I thought you would see them changing or at least hear whatever enticed them to heed the call."

"I cannot hear the Maiden's Call," he answered. "For it is magic meant only for women."

"I warned the girls to keep a song going in their mind, as I do," Cenobia said. "I even tried to teach them one so they would not succumb to it."

"Why have I not heard it yet?" I inquired.

"Could it be because we have spent so much time in the ethereal focused on other things you could not hear?" Nirnasha speculated. "In fact, your snare is a melody that you heard and awoke within you, which would explain why you do not appear to be struggling in maintaining your sanity like Cenobia."

"Your logic seems solid," I admitted. "But what about Kassy?"

"She is curled up in the helm house with her fingers in her ears," Cenobia responded. "I am returning there now to do the same."

"Perhaps we can experiment," Nirnasha almost let his voice rise above a low tone as Cenobia walked off. "Maybe you could listen for the Maiden's Call to learn what it sounds like."

"You could risk it," Elior interjected. "But if you heed the call and begin to transform, I will have no choice but to kill you."

I gazed at Nirnasha in the dim light projected by Elior's orbs scattered across the deck. He appeared regretful even speaking the idea. I closed my eyes and listened to the melody of the ethereal. Dancing Desire soothed my soul, and I could hear Lasair speak comforting words.

"If you become lost, I know where to find you."

I opened my eyes and nodded to Elior. He drew his dagger, which I assumed he had slit the throats of the other two who succumbed to the call. I took a deep breath, closed my eyes again, and tried to sense the melody meant only for women. It did not take very long.

I first felt pulsations in my feet while a rapturous sound vibrated up my spine and latched onto my thoughts. The rhythm swayed like a child's lullaby but dipped ever so slightly into a reverb that intensified to become a sharp sensation up my spine. Suddenly, lyrics from a language unknown to me beckoned my impulses to devour the hearts of men. The lust to rip flesh from bones swelled, much like the hunger when I felt Wendigo nearby. I began seeing the waters below in my mind, feeling the heartbeats of Maidens, gliding through the current. Their tails began to move back and forth, faster and faster. I saw hundreds of them reaching out to grab ahold of the Ironclad.

"They are coming," I said as my eyes flew open.

I glanced down at Elior's dagger dripping with crimson. I shot my gaze upward to his eyes, gasping as he held me, but only for a moment to hear him say, "Find your way back quickly." My vision spun into darkness, and I awoke with Lasair standing over me.

"This your first time?" She giggled.

"My first time?" I said, perplexed. "What do you mean?"

"You are dead," Lasair explained. "You followed the melody of the Maidens."

"I did it because we needed to know about the them," I refuted hostilely. "How am I supposed to help them now?!"

"Return," Lasair continued, "I have kept your essence alive so that you can do just that."

"You mean be reborn?" I pressed. "How long will that take?"

"I am your snare." Lasair laughed. "Do you not know the power you possess? Death in the physical is not the end, especially for one such as you. Find the fire that calls you, and you will return."

"How do I do that?" I asked.

"I shall guide you," Lasair assured. "I know where your body lies. And the one who awakened you has just lit the flame to guide you back."

My snare pointed to the horizon. A bright flame churned from the skies, and I could hear the "Dancing Desire" melody calling to me. Lasair pulled me close and placed me on her back. She sprang high into the air, clear out of the meadow, and landed far beyond it. She continued to do so, getting me closer and closer to the light beaming down from the sky.

No other dangers were presented along the way, my first time outside Elior's glade, but it transcended to be a sight to behold as Lasair sent us repeatedly airborne. From such a height, I surveyed the scape of the ethereal, witnessing marvels that only come alive in dreams. The sun remained held in a state of twilight, forever grasped by the horizon. Lasair's realm came into view, a fortress intertwined with a raging volcanic mountain surrounded by a moat of molten rock. Spreading across the skies above, slithered and swayed an eccentric realm of smoke and vapor. Below, surrounding the fortress and throughout, I could see a land of knolls teeming with high grass, vast forests, swamps, and shadowy mists.

We landed near the swirling fire, right outside the gates of her fortress. It was an enormous pillar where I could hear familiar voices. I could see visions of faces I knew, and somehow felt I had started to forget them. Lasair gently pulled me off her back, telling me I would be stronger once I returned. I did not know what she meant.

"Death for some is different than others like you," she told me. "If it happens again, your soul shall likely know more of what to expect. The first time takes some coaxing to convince the mind it is possible to go back."

"How do I know I want to go back now?" I asked.

"Because the one holding the torch for you is the same one who cut you down," Lasair replied. "I hear his heart hopes for you to return and grow into something greater than you were before."

I guess it is true what they say—the wounds of friends can be trusted. I trusted my teacher and returned to see what I would become. I reached out my hand and jumped into the swirling pillar of flame. My next moment was feeling a deep pain hit my chest and breath rushing into my lungs. Revivification surged my whole body with a prickling agony, and suddenly I sensed my hands grasping tightly to another—Nirnasha, clinging to a torch, and calling me to get up.

The sound of buzzsaw and drill bit fire resounded. I had never seen Tide Maidens before crawling out of the water. They moved swiftly, even on the solid decks of the ship. The Ironclad had several torches lit, and Elior replicated the light from the flame Nirnasha held over me to fill the Narrow Straits. The others were firing and fighting the monsters from all sides of the ship.

"Get up, Aagneya!" Nirnasha shouted. "We need more fire to scare them off!"

I did not feel weak, just dazed as Nirnasha pulled me to my feet. Perhaps the sudden rush of blood to my head made me unbalanced, but Elior reached out and helped steady me.

"Welcome back, MKR," he grinned.

I returned his expression and summoned fire from within me, mounting bigger and brighter around my hands, and sent it in a long wave down the starboard side of the Ironclad. It was just as effective as taking a torch to a hornet's nest. The Tide Maidens climbing up the side were engulfed in flame and fell as sizzling corpses back into the dark waters below. I did the same to the port side, and the Tide Maidens that had climbed aboard from the decks below quickly retreated into the water. All of us could hear several splashes, and then there was silence.

"I think the number of maidens has increased since last time," Meik huffed. "Not sure what sparked them into such a frenzy."

"I listened to their song," I replied, not knowing how I acquired such knowledge. "They felt my power and desperately wanted me to join them."

"So, this is your fault," Garvish sneered.

"Shut it, boy!" Meik spat, sending him a terrible scowl. Then he directed it my way. "So, this is your fault?!"

"Perhaps," I admitted. "But now I know how to listen without falling under the Maidens' call. Now I know exactly where they are and will feel their every move before they do. For example, I know several remain onboard and are hiding in the cabins below, waiting to ambush those who believe it is now safe."

"I already suspected that!" Meik barked. "We always make a sweep after an encounter with their slimy faces."

"But do you know exactly where to look and how many?" I scoffed back, seeing Elior's smirk out of the corner of my eye. "Would you like to come with me, captain, and dispose of them?"

"You bet, missy," Meik gritted his teeth. "And then we'll talk some more."

I learned during this time, though I am still unaware of how—but it came as simple to me as breathing—something new I could summon, a fire that followed the motions of my hands. These hands of fire held firmly to whatever I deemed to be held in mine, and the creatures squirmed and screamed as they melted in the palms of the inferno. The first Tide Maiden to feel this wrath awaited us in the shadows on the second deck, just beneath the stairs, behind water barrels. I flushed her out with a tiny spark that burned her tail. The creature hurried to try and dive back into the water, but my hands of fire clutched and torched her into ash first. We swept through the entire steamboat in no time. All the while, Meik did not say a word—finally.

I could see Elior had stepped aside to allow me to grow into what I had become. Despite the fact he had slain me, I began to understand why it was necessary. It can build confidence once you return from death, knowing that you can take more risks in life than you are used to pursuing. It made me wish I was not so afraid to take risks in the first place. Knowing what I know now, I would have risked so much more if I only had one life to live. I consider it a humbling thing to be able to live over again. For not many do.

Meik sighed when we completed the sweep of the Scoundrel. He admitted he did not know if he could trust me with his secret. Yet he told me the only reason he could trust me now was he knew Elior thoroughly did. He spoke of a treasure in the sky, a floating fortress of some kind, as we returned to his cabin. Meik pulled an ancient book from his locker entitled *Jack and the Beanstalk*, the author's name worn off the cover, and the title page had fallen out. Explorers refer to this as "duration damage." From the bits and pieces I skimmed through, it seemed as if, at one point in time (long ago), a discovery was made of such a fortress in the sky. And it held men on a much larger scale than what is known today, referred to as "giants." Meik then acknowledged his plan for the Ironclad and why he agreed to Elior's proposal. He wanted to turn the Scoundrel into a vessel that could sail the open seas and turn into an airship. However, he relayed the entirety of his plan to me because he desired me to explore with him and his crew one day, believing my fire would be ever helpful in his venture.

"I am sworn to Elior and his task already," I said. "Perhaps, when our quest is completed with him, I am sure I could join you. But I can swear to you, I shall tell no one what you have told me."

"Fair enough, lass," Meik answered. "I would not require you to keep a promise you can't keep. But you'll have plenty of time to think until all this is over. I'm unsure if such a place even exists, but this book allowed me to explore more than what's beneath my feet, though I dearly love the sea."

A light blinded us—not Elior but a welcoming sight for our eyes that spent days in the treacherous night. The sun brought relief to everyone on board the Ironclad. Even Reggie Gusel escaped his post for a much-needed time to bask in the open sea air and the comforting warmth beaming from high above us.

We wrapped the bodies of Wide Berth, Dok, and the two wenches, delivering them to the open sea. Believe me. I do not wish to simply give them a nod. The tragedy of all four deeply cut the crew's morale, especially Wild Willy. While he usually held a bottle of drink in one hand and several girls in the other, he remained sitting still and quiet upon a crate on the upper deck. Nirnasha placed a hand on his shoulder and assured him not to blame himself for what happened.

"Tide Maidens lure men with their eyes and women with their songs," my fellow MKR tried to comfort him. Wild Willy said nothing but did not pull away from Nirnasha's soothing words.

Afterward, we took turns taking baths to wash away the stench of death and burnt flesh and gathered in the dining hall that night, listening to Meik tell us stories about the two lost crewmates. I have never heard of a captain having such thorough knowledge of his crew, but Meik kept the stories coming. I would be remiss if I did not share some to honor their memory. Although I hardly knew them, they were still a part of this larger story.

Dok was a starving street orphan when Meik found him while walking the streets of Resk, a river city in Nod. He was still a little boy, even smaller than we remembered him, his face pressed into the ground by a soldier's boot, about to receive charges of thievery and resistance to arrest. Both could have ended the boy's life, whether he would be judged for execution or die from hunger in the depths of a prison.

Wynster Byde, better known as Wide Berth, was with Meik at the time. Somehow, Wide Berth convinced the soldiers that Dok was his runaway slave. He bribed the soldiers, paid off the merchandise, and slid a plate of potato stew across the table to Dok by the day's end. Meik did not argue Wide Berth's request to bring the lad aboard as part of the crew. And Dok did not leave Wide Berth's side. Even though Wide Berth had to put him in his place occasionally, both proved valuable and formidable as part of Meik's crew. The tragic irony of their demise did not fall on deaf ears.

The two were unrivaled in harpooning Tide Maidens in the open sea. I did not know that Tide Maiden scales were valuable to some merchants, as they use them in makeup and lipstick. I grew repulsed just thinking about all the times I had to use my mother's expensive lipstick when she forced me to attend one of her overly lavish fundraising galas, entertaining all the contemptible upper-class meat sacks in Langdon. My parent's noses were so dark cocoa by the end of the evening I could scarcely recognize them. But Meik enthralled me, and I shall tell at least one story of Dok and Wynster about their obsession to bait and impale a unique Tide Maiden.

They had been raving to the crew about it for months, in the days when Meik saw profit in the industry of Tide Maiden harvesting. Both believed they had seen a golden Tide Maiden, which would have made her a rare catch indeed. Most documented Tide Maidens appeared more of a stone or azure hue. Occasionally, one would catch a rarity of royal crimson running through her hair, perhaps highlighting her scales. All of Meik's crew gave stout approval to hear the story they also experienced. But none more so than Wild Willy, who suddenly entered the dining hall.

"What we need is live bait," Wynster told Dok.

"What about a drifter?" Dok asked. "We could make small slits on his arms, then dangle him over the side of the boat."

"That's awfully maniacal of you," Wynster replied. "Expect a good beating later to remove those thoughts from your head."

"You always say that," Dok taunted. "Never finish what you start."

"All right, smart sack," Wynster said. "Pay attention. We can't use human flesh since we don't have a drifter. But we do have a Sus."

"You're going to kill Oinkers?!" Dok exclaimed.

"Shut your trap and go get 'em!"

Dok reluctantly got the Sus they had picked up in the harbor just days before when Meik and the rest of the crew marinated their organs in cheap ale. The captain commented on the unavoidable necessity to go ashore and then gave a wink to Cenobia, which I can only say made me vomit a little. I dislike it when that short stack makes me picture him naked.

Meik continued his story by saying, "The Sus was then tied up and dangled overboard like a drifter." A week went by without a catch. Yet Dok and Wynster constantly remained vigilant. But the Sus did not even get a nibble. Finally, the two pulled the Sus in for the final time. Oinkers remained unaware of danger but grunted his displeasure at being forced to dangle all day.

"We all grew tired of not catching a thing," Meik explained. "The waters once held so many Tide Maidens. They would practically fly out of the water and plop on the deck of the Ironclad, waiting to be butchered for profit. You could lure them to the surface with anything shiny or dripping animal carcasses. Our decks would be piled with dozens upon dozens. But now, not even live bait was bringing them out. I don't believe Tide Maidens once had a taste for human flesh, but that all changed. I began to believe something else was going on."

Meik spoke of several smaller vessels they encountered while hunting. The crews were utterly gone, almost as if they had abandoned the ship. The wooden planks had deep claw marks and strewn blood all over them, but not a crew member in sight. Then Meik recalled the hazy night when the sea brought in a storm of fog and mist, something of the likes he had never seen. He and his crew lit torches and fiercely kept a lookout.

Dok was the first to draw the crew's attention to the low-clicking noise that escalated shriller. Wynster hurried Dok to the upper deck as he cautiously followed behind him, guarding his backside with a buzzsaw rifle and a harpoon. Meik remembered shouting for everyone to get to the helm house after it reached him too. Reggie Gusel stayed in the engine room like always, keeping the door locked behind him. Darby ignited several more torches on the upper deck, and the rest held firmly to their assigned positions.

Several thumps echoed in the darkness. More grim shrills followed. The flickering torchlight revealed glowing eyes drawing closer, down below the steps. The firelight caught the shadows of creatures, with the upper half of a woman covered in shiny scales and the lower half of a fish covered in the same. Each had four arms with razor-sharp claws, their faces succulent yet held a ferrous intensity like predators about to pounce on their prey. Their jaws dropped to three times a human's average length to reveal their unnaturally sharp teeth.

One creature suddenly scurried up the steps, using its bottom arms like legs and thumping its tail on the steps as it went. Its tail sprang its body upward to reach the top step, only to feel a barrage of sawblades ripping it apart. Wynster ran its head through with a harpoon and kicked it back down. The Maidens all began to scramble, even climbing like spiders up the sides of the boat from the deep.

"You could hear them savagely scream their bloodlust," Meik described the memory. "Not much different than we witnessed. But Dok had climbed up on top of the helm house. I had never seen a kid more accurate with a drill bit gun. Every hit drilled through a Maiden's head, almost like a young version of Wild Willy."

"Do not forget the scary part," Wild Willy interjected, taking a long swig of wine from his mug and cracking a half-cocked grin.

"I'm getting to it!" Meik retorted. "I was just coming to it."

Dok had almost met his end. Behind him grew a tall, lengthy shadow. Wynster saw what was behind him. Reflecting in the firelight, a large Tide Maiden with scales illuminating in a golden hue came down hard-pressed on the Dok's backside, practically crushing him underneath her weight, keeping him there with one arm.

"You could hear the boy's bones cracking," Meik embellished.

A harpoon soared into the Maiden's chest before Meik could turn his weapon and lay down a shot. She screamed as Meik fired into the arm, holding Dok down. His pinpoint accuracy sent several blades, severing the Maiden's arm entirely. Dok, surprisingly, sprang up and away from the creature with one arm limply tucked in close to his chest. Wild Willy leaped to the top of the helm house and fired twelve rounds of drill bits into the Maiden while Meik grabbed another loaded buzzsaw rifle. The monster's cries appeared to stun the rest as they stopped their advance, seeing the giant golden Tide Maiden be shot to pieces before their eyes. Wynster came up the other side and butchered her head off her shoulders with his machete, forcing the rest back into the depths.

"After that day, we all had enough of hunting Tide Maidens. But that gold Maiden's skull is hanging back above the grill," Meik pointed out. "Skinned her scales like all the rest. Got a pretty price for them too. And the only casualties that day was Dok's broken arm with a few cracked ribs, Wild Willy's forearm scar, Darby's broken nose, and my chipped tooth. Good ol' Wynster didn't have a scratch on him."

A NIGHT OUT

The cities of Eastguard, Ye and Poe, finally came into view. Over four months aboard the Seaborne Scoundrel, my legs begged for dry land. I had not heard or seen much of Garvish and Bikarma, as they spent most of their time down in the engine room with Reggie Gusel since the Tide Maidens attacked. The two spoke with Meik just before we docked in Ye, and I overheard them asking the captain if they could join his crew. The captain's response was no surprise. He began shouting orders to them to prepare to go ashore. Garvish and Bikarma were hesitant about what to do precisely, making Meik bark more orders and childish insults.

Wild Willy jumped from the lower deck onto the dock once we were in the port. Kassy joined him shortly after, tying the Ironclad to the dock. I had already gathered my belongings, and Nirnasha followed me off the ship, with Elior, Meik, and Cenobia being the last three to set foot on the dock. Darby and Reggie bid us farewell as they had volunteered to remain behind and guard the boat.

The entrance of Ye's port into the city had two large public elevators. A fortified wall and gate blocked the way as each of us was herded into a line to be documented, giving our name, ethos descriptor, and reason for staying in Ye and Poe. Elior, ever the copious celebrity, was recognized by one of the officers officiating the documentation. The MKR's voucher for all of us made the processing speed up quite dramatically. We were earnestly, yet politely, escorted to a private elevator strictly for high-ranking officials.

"You four should stand back here," Elior motioned to Nirnasha, Garvish, Bikarma, and me. "It is quite breathtaking once we rise above the wall."

He was not wrong. Elevating above the enormous barrier drew our gaze to a different sea of steam and machines bustling loudly along the streets below. Above us, a canopy of catwalks and more elevators connected back and forth to buildings that reached far into the clouds. In the distance, I spotted a massive, polished bridge that spread over the river, joining the cities. On each side were rail tracks with steam engines pulling freight compartments full of passengers and cargo. In the middle were Mechs, walking upright and carrying scrap metal and ore for refining—the ore coming from the vast iron mine in Vlok northwestward.

"Eastguard never rests from refining its infrastructure," Elior elucidated. "The monarchy refuses to be unprepared. That is why every city in its kingdom works tirelessly to build, strengthen, and upgrade at all times."

"I have never seen such a thing," Garvish said, widening his eyes.

I had never seen or heard him be so authentic. Usually, he remained in a state of mockery and sarcasm. Bikarma also followed up with childlike excitement, acting like young boys presented with gifts for no reason other than being born. I felt an unpleasant snark swell up to my tongue, but I bit it before releasing any sound. I believed we all needed to enjoy the moment. So I allowed my mind to become amazed by the numerous catwalks and buildings suddenly lighting up with every coloration imaginable as the sun fell below the mountain peaks in the West.

The elevator doors opened, and we stepped out high above the noise of the streets, with the haste of chilling winds seizing the skin on my face. But I stood too excited to pay any heed to it. Elior led us down a dazzling walkway, where he suggested we find food to our liking. We were to meet at the "Ye Downs Lodging and Hotel," a bright shimmering building dazzled by rich viola lights and five gold waving spotlights.

Eatery vendors were set up in linear shops, built along each side of the catwalks, lighting up their stalls either jaffa, royal crimson or viridescent to portray the type of food they served. Jaffa lights were a soup dish, usually comprising noodles, various meats, and veggies, but more importantly, the combination of herbs and spices for customers to choose to their liking. Royal crimson lights meant a hearty meat dish with minimal veggies, cooked over roaring fires beneath iron gating—each meat variant specially sauced and seasoned by the chef. Viridescent lights presented a hearty veggie dish with minimal to no meat. I would venture it would be for those who are dieting to lose weight as my mother often did. The meat of the royal crimson lights enticed my senses more than any other vendor—animal chucks with glistening crunchy skin and a sizzling melody that tantalized a tune to my tongue.

Nirnasha joined me just before large crowds gathered around us. We sat down on stools and placed our arms on the high countertop. A woman with a friendly smile and a thick Eastguardian accident asked what looked good to us. I wanted to sample all of it. With a slight chuckle, the woman sliced a little bit of everything and placed it aesthetically on a plate. Just before we handed her our credits, a familiar hand reached behind us and delivered our tab. I turned to see Elior with his usual smirk, depicting his uncanny politeness.

"And what would you like, Master Keeper?" The woman asked.

"Your crispy Gallus and smoked Acer sauce," Elior replied. "Also, I think a bottle of Jaffa Blossom Wine would be nice."

"She seems to know you well," I told Elior when the woman stepped away to prepare his order.

"Being well known does have its advantages," Elior admitted. "However, she is herself, a Keeper. Take a look at her power generator."

I looked toward the back corner of the alcove establishment and saw steam rising from a machine dimly glowing azure. It was fueling the flames below the iron gating laid over the top of them.

I remember seeing food cooked in such a way during my travels to Eastguard with my father. As this cooking was completely foreign to Westmain, my father deliberately passed on the opportunity to taste the sensuous eruption of spices and sauces I now indulged in. Elior, never reluctant, shared what was placed before him, a succulent and crunchy Gallus smothered in a divinely gooey sauce.

The delicacy nearly brought tears of joy to my eyes. And it felt like the first time I had genuinely laughed during a meal. We faced so many frightening things together, certain doom for most, if not for being under the guidance of a certain MKR. Despite the large portions we consumed, I felt a burst of energy to explore the city further. Elior urged us to check into our lodgings, where we would meet up with the others. He assured us we would see more sights and sounds later in the evening.

The Ye Downs Lodging and Hotel welcomed us as if we were royalty, with two stewards at the door dressed in gold frocks and respectfully bowed as they opened the way for us. Inside, the chandeliers alone overwhelmed my senses with awe, cut from precious metals and crafted into immaculate works of art. They dangled down like blossoming tree limbs in spring. The carpets were a rich royal crimson hue with golden threads weaving an immaculate PrimaDonna pattern. The walls sparkled in splashed hints of gold, matching the threads beneath my feet as we were each escorted to our rooms with the complimentary hospitality of our host. Once more, Elior's renown proceeded him in Eastguard, though I should not have been surprised. Not even those in Westmain showered a well-known face with such praise. Our host mentioned how Elior had rescued several guests from a raging fire that broke out on the third floor more than twenty years ago. Since then, Elior has been welcome to stay free of charge with any number of guests.

Cenobia, Kassy Bones, and I entered one of the finest master suites, with three large, fluffy beds, fancy lamps, chic furniture, and a fireplace with a tea kettle ready to be boiled. I laid down and sighed deeply to commit the comforts to memory. That moment did not last long as I opened my eyes to Kassy stripping off all her articles of clothing within seconds, even before the master caretaker who escorted us to the room had closed the door. Guests out in the hall gaped and gasped, and she smirked, showing she knew full well the embarrassment she displayed to her own people. I, for one, and Cenobia, for another, were not surprised, and we refused to give her the satisfaction.

I leaped from the bed, apologizing to our host and guests outside the room, swiftly aiding the master caretaker to move his body and bulging peepers out of the room, then shutting the door in his face. I could hear a slight chuckle from Kassy as she made her way to the bathroom. Seconds later, Cenobia and I heard the water running.

"A bit of a savage," I said quietly to Cenobia. She nodded but gave me an expression of sympathy and uttered, "Somehow, she feels empowered to act in such a way."

"Enough of her," I stammered out. "Will you come to explore the city with me once we get cleaned up?"

Cenobia smiled. "Of course, dear. I heard Elior say he wanted to meet us in the lobby when we are all ready."

Our suite had three bathrooms, which allowed me to freshen up in a much more pampered way. The water aboard the Scoundrel was ice cold, brought in from the sea, and held no comparison to the scalding relaxation of my first hot bath in months. The scented soaps lavished my muscles, and my mind drifted away momentarily, and I realized how different I had become. Truly, it was a moment I missed having a 'normal' life—as to what end that means, I am not sure.

And while we bathed, the hotel service washed our attires, along with providing us with fresh new ones for a time at no charge. As Cenobia and I enjoyed posing in different outfits before deciding which one to wear, I felt my curiosity seize the better of me. I hesitated momentarily and asked Cenobia why she had decided to room with us. Her reply was genuine yet somewhat concerning. Since she and Meik had rekindled their affections, she still felt the need not to rush into rekindling their pledge to one another. After all, he did nothing to prevent her from leaving when they lost their child. Then Cenobia mentioned the other reason.

Her concern lay with the unpredictable Kassy, confiding in me that she noticed the young lady became much pricklier on the return to her homeland. She was not sure what Kassy would do, especially when she mentioned she wanted to share a room with me. Knowing the brutish lady had requested such a thing did not sit well with me. Yet Cenobia quickly and adamantly renewed her feigned excitement that the women folk got to share a place in such an outstanding abode. Kassy shrugged at the comment, but Cenobia and I noticed a scowl on her face when she turned to return to the steaming room from where she bathed. We left her for the time as she dawdled to get dressed.

Nirnasha, Garvish, Bikarma, and Wild Willy met us on the way to the lobby. Meik was already with Elior, who welcomed us in newly pressed mystic midnight attire. Each man wore a finely hemmed top hat with pearl buttons and cufflinks with gentleman's formal attire. I had chosen a gold lace bustle dress with ruffled backing and a royal crimson sleeveless top interwoven with a shimmering Leaf Damask pattern that pushed my bosom toward my chin, accentuating but certainly making them appear larger than my actual size.

Before heading out, Elior led us to again meet our generous hotel host in the lounge with four of his other associates, where the women were surprised with the privilege of choosing a jewelry piece that would represent the hotel during our night out. Cenobia wanted something elegant yet simple. I decided completely the opposite. I thought, why not enjoy and embrace such a rare opportunity? The centerpiece of my outfit befitted a proudly adorned heaven gold choker holding a three-unit viola stone. When I re-entered the lobby, I was met by three wide-eyed boys who suddenly ceased their banter. I pretended not to notice Nirnasha, Garivsh, and Bikarma's pupils popping out of their heads. I thought I noticed Wild Willy's creepy gaze falling on me from the corner of the room. However, he was sending his stare past me. I turned to see Kassy Bones practically falling out of a dark cocoa clincher ruffle skirt and adorning a viola diamond choker similar to mine.

"Are we all ready?" Elior asked politely to all of us.

"Some are more ready than others," I muttered in my mind, to which Elior raised an eyebrow, knowing I was referring to the scantily clad trope shaking her goods behind me. Every man's eye in the room appeared glued to her except Elior and one surprisingly young MKR. Nirnasha bid me a gentlemanly compliment, even tipping his hat in the process.

"You have an astounding taste for refinement," he said.

"You say that as if you prefer me this way," I teased, watching embarrassment rush into his face. But I chuckled to ease the moment, and Nirnasha joined me.

We made our way further up the catwalks of Ye into an establishment shaped much like the hotel but frosted with flickering royal crimson lighting, wide-open floors, and glowing paint spattered all over the walls. The ceilings were shoved high above us, with people dancing on every single level, from the ground floor to the fifth. The foreign music captured my interest swiftly, played by the Music Master whose station stood high above and attached to the far wall. I could tell the music was extraordinary, historical from ancient times. Yet despite its catchy rhythm and sound, I found it challenging to comprehend the lyrics. I had no clue what "poker" could be, yet it had something to do with the face of the woman who sang the song. I did my best not to try and start discussing the historical context of the lyrics with Nirnasha and pushed myself just to enjoy the night.

The man who owned the establishment was a collector of rare and ancient music before the Great Collide. Once more, I learned how people catered to Elior as he sold his music findings exclusively to the club's owner. Astonishingly, we were there to meet with him because the owner was an MKR. His name was Easton—no last name or proper introduction. He sat in a glamorous alcove with a fancy table called the Owner's Box at the back of the fifth floor in the prestige section known as the VIP. It held a large circular booth with high-rise walls surrounding it to soften the lively melody and the noise of the dancing crowds. Surprisingly, the table had an open spread of food with women dressed just as classy as me. The dirty stares the women gave to Kassy as we approached made her slow her steps, and I will not lie. I enjoyed the moment, knowing I was appropriately dressed for the culture.

"Elior!" Easton belted out. "I am always so pleased to see you. What can I do for you?"

Easton had a comprehensive, bulky build and slicked-back braids neatly tied into a bun. His skin held a cocoa creme veil leaning toward a sable spectrum, with intricately tattooed arms. I admired one in particular—the artistic head of a Bos Taurus revealed on his bare right arm as he wore a well-designed mystic midnight vest inlaid with gold embroidery over his bare chest, keeping his rippling physique exposed. I am sure his mystic midnight trousers fit neatly around his waist as he stood to welcome us, with a Bos Taurus buckle and belt for show. His smile was almost as welcoming as Elior's, yet he appeared wilder and chaotically mischievous.

He hurried past the women on the left side of the table and placed what appeared like a death grip on Elior's forearm. The two exchanged pleasantries before Easton invited us to his table. I sat down next to Elior with Nirnasha beside me. Cenobia and Meik sat across from us, with Garvish, Bikarma, and Kassy. I had lost sight of Wild Willy until he came trotting toward us with five girls dressed like Kassy.

"Kassy," he blathered. "Come have a drink with us."

"Bet you two would like some fun too, eh," she teased Garvish and Bikarma. "Sit here and listen to business or have fun with us."

Her succulent chuckle piqued the boys who followed the wild party down one flight of stairs. Most of Easton's women had dispersed but were not far from us. The one he referred to as his favorite remained under his arm as he reclined.

"It is always business with you, Elior," Easton teased. "But most of your business I find fun these days as it brings me more musical genres to share with my guests. So, let us hear it."

Elior stared at him momentarily but refused to speak until drinks were served. His convincing remark of us all having a long journey and deserving to enjoy the night a bit before serious affairs were discussed made Easton laugh, yet our host obliged, calling one of his women over to bring back several bottles of Jaffa Blossom Wine and Honey Milk Mead. The latter is one of the finest drinks I have ever tasted. Honey Milk Mead, a mix of honey and spice mead, fermented with smoked suckles and aged inside Acer barrels. As wealthy as my parents were, they never had a bottle of Honey Milk in their cellar. The cost of one bottle priced more than likely the salary of the average individual. However, Easton poured it out like water from the tap.

Now, I admit, I may have over-indulged myself. But I turned to Nirnasha, who was only on his first glass. I could feel my vision blur, yet I could tell something was peculiar about him. His eyes were shut, and he reclined against the wall behind him. I turned to look at Elior and Easton, who were doing the same. Despite my spiraling state of consciousness, I knew what they were doing. I closed my eyes and concentrated, sailing my soul swiftly into the ethereal. Sure enough, the three of them were standing in Elior's meadow, where Nirnasha and I trained in our dreams night after night.

"Rude!" I shouted to the three of them, seemingly just a couple of strides from me. "You did not…me…not…know we were going…here."

I began stumbling toward them, the feeling of my lips numbing—even in my own mind. Easton placed his hand on Nirnasha, who appeared to begin moving toward me. He stepped around him with a massive smile on his face.

"This should be entertaining," Easton said. "I know people are more truthful when they are drunk. I prefer a more direct approach myself."

Elior remained silent.

"I know you, Elior," Easton continued. "You shall keep me in suspense of your reasons why you need so much Mystic Silver. But I am more interested in what we all truly desire."

I finally reached them, barely feeling I could stand.

"Only one of us took the bait," Elior said. "And drugging her will not slow her down."

"You…me…drugged me," I glared at Easton. "Me…you…me…drugged!"

I lit both of my arms up with fire. Easton did not flinch. He sneered and turned toward Elior.

"Her fire magic here cannot hurt me," Easton said. "She would have to find my snare."

"Actually," Nirnasha interjected. "She just has to know what color works on you. That is what she practiced with me."

"What does that mean?" Easton scoffed.

I did not wait for any more words. I displayed what I had learned to Easton—summoning fire in the ethereal to be whatever hue I chose. Each hue had a different effect, allowing me to explore what hurt Nirnasha's mind when we last practiced together. I named my new ability "Bewitching Bonfire." And though I could barely stand, the longer my soul blazed, the clearer it became to Easton I was sobering up.

I began with jaffa, hurling fireballs at Easton. Elior and Nirnasha stepped swiftly away. Easton laughed, but I was not done. I switched to azure, then to viridescent, and finally to viola. Viola sent Easton screaming backward to the ground, almost to the tree line. However, he regained his composure and stood straight up as if nothing had phased him. His eyes appeared crazed and untamed.

"All right, little girl," Easton huffed. "You want to play? We can surely rumble."

Though I could still feel the effects of the drugs, I had a snappy revelation that I had just enraged another MKR, one I knew nothing about. It appeared Elior would not even try to step in this time.

Easton's body turned pure molten copper, like impenetrable armor, and he began to charge toward me. He roared like a madman, and I felt a fear I never felt before. His footsteps pounded as I stood frozen, unable to process what I should do. Suddenly, the soil beneath me elevated and threw me over the reach of Easton as he ran right underneath, crashing through the dirt that had saved me. He slid to a halt and turned back. The Molten MKR remained bewildered as Nirnasha solidified behind him, rising from the earth. Easton barely turned around before Nirnasha brought a giant fist of rock and muck up to meet his chin. The MKR flew over me to the tree line again, where I had sent him before. After landing with an unforgiving thud, he did not as swiftly find his footing again. Nirnasha came and stood next to me, congratulating me on landing on my feet even in my wobbly condition.

"If you want to fight her," Nirnasha said. "You must fight me too."

"You have a couple of good students," Easton told Elior. "But how well do they fight what cannot be seen?"

Easton's body instantly became translucent. We heard a rustling that went into the trees. But afterward, there was nothing but silence.

"I feel him," Nirnasha said. "I feel him moving along the ground. He is making his way around to get near us."

"What do we do?" I asked.

"Throw viola fire where I tell you," he said softly. "But let him get a little closer before we pounce."

I set my arms ablaze in viola, waiting for Nirnasha to direct my fire. I saw a tree root spring up, tripping something, creating a loud thump against the soil.

"There!" Nirnasha exclaimed.

I brought forth the flames with all my strength. Easton screamed again while squirming on his stomach, turning visible again. This time, I did not let up and kept the blaze on him.

"Enough!" Elior's voice resounded as thunder clapped across the skies.

I ceased, but Nirnasha kept the tree root wrapped around Easton's ankles.

"Enough, Nirnasha," Elior insisted. "This is done."

Elior waited for Easton to return to his feet as Nirnasha pulled away the tree root from the battered MKR.

"Are you ready to talk now?" Elior asked Easton. "You witnessed their power. "

"I shall help you get what you need," Easton admitted. "But you should know that I do not desire money. As I said before, let us know what we all desire."

"And what do you desire?" Elior inquired.

"When you have harvested the Mystic Silver and returned to the surface safely," Easton began, still breathing heavily. "You will assist me in building a haven in the Deadlands."

"Why would you want such a thing?" Nirnasha imposed. "It is impossible."

"Implausible," Elior corrected. "Not impossible."

"I felt fear from you when setting you ablaze," I said. "I thought it came from thinking I was going to kill you. But that is not the case, is it?"

"How could you feel my fear?" Easton sneered.

"It happens sometimes," Nirnasha replied. "Call it a side-effect."

Easton stared at the three of us for a long time and then peered into Elior's eyes. He pronounced he needed to get away from the city and far from Eastguard due to what he referred to as a cataclysmic threat.

"A man dressed in heaven," Easton expounded. "He commissioned my factories to manufacture metal for him. He even promised me six deeds to the Raven Caste Estate distilleries for meeting my quotas. I have never had so much wealth. So no, money is not what I seek."

"This man," I inquired. "He is obviously extremely wealthy himself in order to wear a color such as heaven. But what is so 'cataclysmic' about what you are doing for him."

"He is building something," Easton replied. "I know not what. But it is something much bigger than a wairship, yet I know it is going to fly. My factories have made over eight hundred propellers, and each one is about the size of a normal wairship."

"What did this man look like?" Elior introspectively inquired. I could see even Elior felt uneasy in asking the question. Easton kept staring at Elior, seemingly trying to muster up the answer.

"The man looked like you," Easton sighed heavily.

We returned to the physical realm, each sending concerned glances toward one another.

"Follow me," Easton said. "I trust Elior. So, I guess I shall also trust the two of you."

"You four were gone awhile," Meik said. "I wish I could have joined you, but the conversation was much more private than what a regular Keeper gets to hear I suppose."

"Follow me," Easton repeated, getting up from his seat.

"Do I get my ship?" Meik asked.

"You need to find the others and return to the hotel quickly. Make sure you are not followed," Elior did his best to keep the remark respectful. "I shall speak to you later about the ship. I need you to do this for me, old friend."

Meik nodded. And Easton led us up a private staircase to a floor that did not stretch the area of the building, tucked away in a corner of the structure. A large metal door slid open and then shut behind us. We stood in an open room with a desk and fancy chair at the far end. Next to the desk was another seating area with a plush leather couch. Behind the couch stood a large bookcase. Easton went to one of the shelves and reached inside it. We heard a lever activate, and the bookcase moved aside, revealing a secret passage.

"If I leave, it will raise suspicion," Easton said. "The three of you can follow this into the city and head to safety. I shall meet you before sunrise."

"Easton, your light does not have to shut off," Elior replied, confusing me. "Though I know you have no choice right now."

"I shall be there," Easton assured.

The three of us made haste down the corridor, running along the building's pipelines. The enormous pathway would have been pitch dark if Elior and I did not use our power. Not too long, I could feel the air of the exit. But before we went any farther, Elior halted us abruptly. Instinctively, Nirnasha and I remained silent as we could hear Elior's thoughts of concern.

"They are waiting for us," Elior echoed. "They have blocked the way out."

He slowly pulled his drill guns out. Nirnasha and I did the same. I heard Elior tell me to double back.

"If they are here, they will want Easton too. Go back to him. Burn the place down if you must—just be sure he leaves with you."

Though surprised Elior had charged me with this task, I quickly obeyed and returned the way we had come. Elior's mind remained open to me, as did Nirnasha, so I could see through their eyes. Both turned the corner to face two figures waiting for them in the shadows. Two elegant-looking women appeared which the MKR of Light knew very well.

First, Marilla Baostin, an MKR with the power of Water and Flood—her face, veiled in creme, appeared wet as she entered Elior's light. She had shimmering azure covering the lids of her eyes and lips and did not seem much taller than me. Her sable hair was tied tightly into a stylish bun, with two curled bangs hanging slightly down along her temples. Her fit and flare frock held a darker stone than I had ever seen stained before, and she wore the same color ruffle shorts with knee-high dark cocoa boots. She had two drill-bit guns strapped to her hips and two more strapped on either side of her chest.

The second, Amaterasu Nasmire, her flesh a beautiful sable, and envious, slanting oval eyes swirling in a viridescent glimmer, and her long, sable hair hung wildly and wavy. The woman's intimidating scowl did not diminish her impressive facade. I practically grew jealous of how royal crimson appeared on her. She wore a ruffle skirt and a tightly woven mystic midnight long sleeve with royal crimson-dyed leather armor, an unusual and unique attire. Her knee-high royal crimson boots glistened like the goldish body dust she wore.

I hesitated to turn back, but I pressed onward when I saw Nirnasha's mind held steady. I watched through his eyes as he brought his Mystic Silver arm upward, ever so effortlessly, and began pointing it toward the two figures. I shall say I was proud of him. His Mystic Silver prosthetic was challenging to get used to, and I do not believe he had used it much before. Although I could feel the power surge through his mind, Nirnasha waited for Elior to make the first move, as were the other two.

The MKR of Light told Nirnasha and me plainly the two women were once his pupils—the ones he killed. I now understood what he meant. He had not destroyed their snares but had cut them off from his mind, a type of death I believe could not be pleasant. Unable to feel Elior's presence, their minds were expurgated from the calm his light brought, allowing Nirnasha to remain composed against the past pupils.

I hastened my pace to return to Easton's office, but when I reached the secret entrance, the wall with the bookcase was shut. I could hear voices on the other side. The first belonged to Easton, and the other belonged to one who came with a chilling breeze, feeling it seep through the cracks in the wall. I could hear the tiny man speaking to Easton but could not make out his words. I desperately looked for a lever or button to reopen the secret passage. The chatter on the other side grew louder, at least from Easton. I knew he was in trouble.

"I am not your slave," Easton shouted. "Our deal is finished. I gave you what you wanted."

"Not quite," the tiny man then shouted back. "To ensure the game goes my way, your snare is required."

"Deal?" I thought to myself, letting Elior and Nirnasha in on my thoughts. "What deal?"

"I knew Easton would betray us," Elior echoed his reply. "I do not believe he had much of a choice. You must show him there is a way out, that he does not need to be afraid."

Backstabbed or not, my rage pulsed and intensified. Just thinking about Rumpelstilzchen devoured my veins in such unbearable disgust that I could feel my anger focus on the wall as I reached out with my hands. Fire stretched before me, taking the shape of much larger clenched fists than I had ever summoned. I let out a screech and slammed one of the flaming fists into the wall. As it collided, it exploded through the wall, setting ablaze every book on the shelf and erupting every particle of wood.

The blast sent both Easton and Rumpelstilzchen back on their heels. The tiny man turned to see one of my flaming fists catch him. He screeched in agony as I made my fiery paw slam downward, bursting an enormous hole in the metal floor, and wrenched him through every level of the establishment, including the foundation.

For a few moments, I felt drained from manifesting such a significant spell, but I knew I would not feel that way for long. As I stepped into the office from the passageway, I began to sense Lasair swiftly nursing my fatigue, and soon I became wholly composed again. Easton's jaw was agape, staring down the holes I had crashed the tiny man through. He finally brought his face slowly upward, his eyes meeting mine.

"I have never been quick enough to throttle him like that," Easton admitted.

"You probably have never been able to take him by surprise either," I replied.

I promptly told Easton that Elior knew he had no choice but to betray us. He tried to deny it, but I recalled that I overheard what he was shouting to the tiny man. I explained that we needed his help and that if the four of us stuck together as MKRs, no one could stand against us, not even Rumpelstilzchen.

"He is not the one I fear," Easton confessed. "The man dressed in heaven is much more dangerous. I do not believe even Elior can stand against his power."

"Then the four of us should stand together with Elior," I explained. "No evil should be that powerful and be allowed to exist."

A slight grin emerged from Easton, but it quickly vanished, perceiving a sinister figure standing in the doorway. She stepped into the light with a scowl that would have skinned a Sus. Her hair was mangled into a curly, dark mess, and she wore a mystic midnight vest with full-sleeve tattoos running up her entire neck and weaving into her cleavage. Her mystic midnight skinny denim trousers were purposely ripped in both knees and horizontal slits in the thighs all the way up to the pockets. She wore leather mystic midnight gloves and dark-shaded make-up, making her light azure eyes pop like jewels in the sunlight. Barefoot and floating slightly above the floor, I had never seen someone fly without the assistance of an airship.

"Still not fond of boots, eh Amara?" Easton teased.

"Never disliked them," the woman answered. "I just have no use for them."

"Hey, kid," Easton said to me. "Meet Amara Monroe, my former lover."

"You wish," Amara mockingly laughed and slowly floated toward us. "I might have fallen for you once if you were not so boring and pretentious."

"Amara is an MKR," Easton kept talking, backing away and pulling me with him. "She has a way with vapor and smoke. I would not get too close to her. She likes to toxify the air around her body."

"O' do not give away my surprise to a stranger," Amara tantalized. "I was surely looking forward to taking her breath away."

"Do not get near her," I said to Easton. "I believe I can manage that."

I refused to continue the pointless back-and-forth conversation with some hovering fashion nightmare anyway. I turned my flames on and blazed two streams of fire in Amara's direction. Before the fire reached her, she vanished in a puff of smoke and reappeared on the other side of the room with an astonishing smirk.

"Why, Easton, you have finally astounded me. I never would have guessed you would shack up with a fiery crimson head," Amara scoffed. Then she turned to me. "You must be one of Elior's new recruits. We have all been in the rookie seat before. I shall try not to kill you too swiftly."

Easton nabbed my arm and raced us both through the office door and down the steps.

"Better if we get her out in the open!" Easton quickly exclaimed. "It will give us more room to stay away from her."

"Or just make it easier to catch us," I retorted. Easton only shrugged but did not flinch as we waited for Amara to join us on the VIP floor.

The skirmish between Marilla and Amaterasu and Elior and Nirnasha had begun with an exchange of firing drill bits at one another, which had now turned into an all-out battle using magic. I tried not to get distracted by Nirnasha struggling against Marilla manifesting treacherous tides against him. He had ripped concrete from the walls and formed it into shields to cover him from her onslaught of fierce water spells. The shields hovered in front of him in an odd viridescent glow I had only witnessed in the ethereal, convincing me his power had grown since we last trained together.

Amara appeared again in a cloud of smoke, soaring above our heads like a wasp getting ready to strike. She disappeared again, then reappeared to our left and then to our right, mocking us as she went. I became fed up with her stupid sneering laughter, deciding it was time to call upon something I was aching to perform but had yet to manifest.

I immediately heard the melody of Lasair. A gentle pulse surged through my body, rippling out, and then an enormous rush of energy erupted from me. I gasped, and Easton fell to the floor, a flabbergasted look on his face. But I noticed I had also caught Amara's attention. And even I was unprepared to gaze upon the two elegant beings materializing, blackened by fire and yet still set ablaze, from a bright gateway. They pranced gracefully upon their toes, floating just above the ground like Amara. The flames that embodied them expanded brighter, and their eyes glowed like crimson glass held up to the sun, taking on my form and setting their focus upon my enemy.

"Burn her and this place to the ground," I commanded, pointing to Amara. The MKR soaring directly above us, no longer showing off snarky grins or mocking laughter. I hurried Easton to his feet.

"You should be afraid," I told Amara. "You should not have made me angry."

The fire beings began to twirl so beautifully, throwing spheres of flames toward her. Amara quickly dodged away and then reappeared in another place.

"Where did you learn to summon elementals?" Easton asked as we both began to rush out.

"Later!" I exclaimed. "We need to get out of here quickly."

Amara appeared in front of us, but before she could make a move, both elementals cut her off, beginning to spray molten rock toward her. She impressively dodged again but cleared out of the way so we could continue down to the fourth floor. This resumed the entire time we moved to escape. Fire surrounded us as the elementals persisted in trying to catch Amara in their onslaught. She remained considerably faster, but I could see her momentum waning. The citizens had caught on to the danger and swiftly moved toward the doors to the outside, flooding out of the building and screeching as they went.

When we reached the first floor, the building began to collapse. Amara finally reached close to us as we were about to exit the front doors. Yet I had a bit of a surprise for her as I anticipated she would try one last time. The MKR appeared just behind us, and I whipped around, shooting a stream of flames from my hands. Amara flew backward to the floor as the fire elementals descended on her, igniting her flesh in a pirouette of fire. Her screams were excruciatingly high-pitched. And for a moment, I regretted destroying her.

We darted away from the establishment as it collapsed in the inferno tearing it apart. Many onlookers crowded the catwalk, but no eyes followed us as we slipped into the shadows on our way back to the Ye Downs Lodging and Hotel.

We arrived without further incident, but the streets were eerily quiet. Before I could open the entrance, a steward swiftly obliged, and in the lobby waiting for us stood Elior and Nirnasha, who now had a thin laceration across his left eye. It would be a hardly noticeable scar, but a scar nonetheless.

"I see you gained a souvenir," I pestered, though it was not my intention. Nirnasha grinned at me and startled me with a hug. He was drenched.

"You are soaking wet!"

He pulled away and laughed, with Elior joining him. Easton laughed along with them.

"You both have survived your first encounter with those who share the MKR mantle," Elior said, his tone sighing with relief. "You both have grown powerful in your own way and have done more than I could have hoped. Well done."

"You should have seen Aagneya," Easton admirably stated. "She made Amara appear like an amateur."

"I do not doubt it," Elior answered. "But there is only one reason for that. Amara underestimated her. You know she will not make that mistake twice."

"Of course not," I replied with a cocky undertone. "I completely destroyed her body."

Elior's eyes shot over to me with an expression that made it seem like he would slap me. He came close, and I had never felt more intimidated by him.

"You must not make the same mistake," he whispered. "Amara is not entirely gone. Unless you killed her snare, she will never be truly gone."

"As long as her snare remains, her body shall reform and return," Nirnasha stated as he followed me into my room. I was not sure why he followed me. My only assumption was he wanted to talk a bit more, yet I did not refuse to wait to change my clothes. I went behind the changing screen, and Nirnasha politely shut the door behind him.

"We should speak of what we learned," he continued. "And try to figure out what their snares could be. Of course, Elior should know."

"That is right," Easton's voice reached us while opening the door.

"Is this a men's room?!" I exclaimed.

"But I doubt Elior holds a high regard for secrets coming to light in their own time." Easton sighed. "It is just his way."

"That is no surprise," I replied, at last fully dressed in fresh clothes. "The truth that Elior tells often holds a hidden meaning of some kind. I already guessed that Amara is not truly gone as I, too, returned to my body quite swiftly, I might add."

"Then you are aware of who pulls the strings on the others' snares," Easton assumed. Nirnasha and I stared at one another for a moment and concurred it was none other than the Suzerain Efah, known to us as Rumpelstilzchen, though we dared not speak his name. Easton could see we knew the answer and continued.

"Long ago, Elior recruited Amara, Amaterasu, and me to go against the greater threat, the one with whom the tiny man is intertwined. Amara and I dug deep together to learn that the greater threat was none other than an MKR, a master of decay and shadow. Somehow, this MKR found a way to snare his soul to three different things."

"Yes, we have heard this," I concurred. "The tiny man is one of them. Wendigo is another. But…"

"Elior will not tell us who the third is," Nirnasha interjected.

"Yes, but it is much more complicated than that," Easton explained. "Amara is the one who learned the most about that wicked imp. He truly does have a mind of his own and somehow found a way to captivate Amara's snare and the others, thus influencing them to do his bidding."

"So, our next move is to kill their snares?" I asked.

"Not necessarily," Easton continued. "Suzerain Efah might have their snares on a string, influencing them to his desires, but if the strings could be cut, they might be free from him. The imp has a way of influencing snares, including his master's other two."

"You mentioned that Elior recruited Amara, Amaterasu, and you. But what of Marilla?" Nirnasha inquired.

"She is much older," Easton replied. "I am not sure how old, but I believe she was at least one of Elior's first pupils. Yet I am unsure if the imp holds her snare captive. Though it does appear, she is no loyalist to Elior."

"Has Elior made any others besides the four of you?" I asked.

"Not that I know of," Easton admitted.

"What about you?" Nirnasha inquired. "How come your snare is not under his control?"

"Because his snare is the forge in Lasair's fortress," I answered. "Which I guess is why she wants to be so well-defended. The tiny man has not found a way to get to her."

"How do you know what my snare is?" Easton's tone suddenly became demanding.

"But she knew she would be," Elior's voice softly reached us. He had suddenly appeared in the room. "The game, which Suzrain Efah calls it, now has two new players. He knows Aagneya is snared with Lasair, one of the most powerful beings in the ethereal realm. And he knows Nirnasha's power consists of things from the earth. He may try to learn of your snare first before infiltrating Lasair's domain."

"Even if he could do that," Easton replied. "He would not find it so easy to control her."
"No, he would not," Nirnasha replied. "Unless he offered something so tempting, she could not refuse."

"Is it possible any other snares wish to be free from his grasp?" I asked.

Again, Elior drew close to me but stared into my eyes with a sense of compassion, and his tone remained heavy-hearted.

"There are some decisions you can never return from," he replied. "We are not saviors. At times, we do not even know we have chosen evil until it is too late. But I do not see the harm in trying."

I grabbed Elior's hand as he began to turn away. "What is the third snare of the greater threat?"

"You will learn in time," Elior assured me. "Please understand when I say you must learn it for yourselves."

"I understand," I reluctantly sighed. "We should say no more and hurry to stay out in front. We need to go find that Mystic Silver you were talking about."

Elior smiled, and Easton followed him out of the room.

"I guess I better go change then. Unless you want me to get changed here." Nirnasha teased.

"If you take your pants off here, I shall burn it off," I stated sternly but also fought back a snickering grin.

Indeed, such a comment made it dreadfully clear that Nirnasha was budding a fondness for me. We had grown close over our time together, especially in growing our powers in the ethereal. But I do not believe my heart sought romance, though from time to time, I did like his ridiculous innuendos. I think I held a friendship bond with him because he was not dull-witted like Garvish and Bikarma. Still, I could tell he was hoping I would give in one day to his twitterpated remarks—maybe I would fall into his arms, madly in love like some pathetic adolescent girl who knows nothing of the world.

I sat down on my bed as Nirnasha left the room. I peered up with a sudden vision coming into my mind. Elior was broadcasting something to me from his thoughts, telling me to remain where I was no matter what. He articulated for me just to watch and listen. I did.

Elior sat quietly in a chair, sipping tea, making me want to brew some for myself. Then, a familiar shadow came and sat down across from him. The tiny man's eyes glowed, and he smiled vilely like always. I felt Nirnasha's mind suddenly join me in watching and listening.

"I am not here to fight," Rumpelstilzchen assured. "I simply come to congratulate you on your well-earned victory tonight."

"Do not insult me," Elior said. "I know you were testing them."

"True," the tiny man admitted. "But if they did not pass the test, how would you know they are worth all the effort you put into winning the game this time? It would be best if you gave yourself some credit. It is due to you."

"You patronize me," Elior replied. "I loathe it when you are this nice."

"I am a true sportsman. What can I say?" Rumpelstilzchen shrugged.

"But that is not why you are here, is it?" Elior stated. "What do you want?"

"I feel like it would be a shame if something happened to your Ironclad while you are away," the tiny man chuckled. "It is such a fine ship, a fine crew, and it would terribly hurt the bargain you made with the captain, would it not?"

"And what is it you want in return for not allowing something to happen to the Scoundrel?" Elior asked.

"I would love to know what the earth boy has snared up within the ethereal," Rumpelstilzchen suggested.

"I bet you would," Elior laughed. "But that is not an even trade."

"You would be willing to sacrifice the Ironclad and its crew then?" the tiny man asked with a look of surprise.

"I would sacrifice a thousand ships if it meant being rid of you," Elior calmly yet firmly snapped. "No deal."

Rumpelstilzchen began to shift down out of his chair.
"Do not let him leave," I heard Nirnasha's thoughts cry out. "Tell him you shall give him a hint."

"Although," Elior said, grabbing the tiny man's attention again. "I think it would be awful of me to let you leave empty-handed."

Rumpelstilzchen appeared intrigued and sat back down in the chair across from him.

"What are you doing?!" My thoughts reached Nirnasha. He swiftly hushed me and began telling Elior what to say.

"Ask him if he would leave the Ironclad alone for a hint about my snare since he likes games so much. How about a riddle?"

"Since you love games so much," Elior spoke up. "Would you leave the Ironclad alone if I gave you a hint about the boy's snare? How about a riddle?"

Rumpelstilzchen scratched his chin, then scratched his brow. He planted his feet on the floor again and stared at Elior.

"Done," the tiny man agreed with a wide grin. "We can play this game."

Elior began to speak what Nirnasha told him.

"I am alone, yet I have many friends," Elior began.

"One moment," Rumpelstilzchen interjected. "I already know the thing is a tree. So, my hint needs to be more specific."

"I am alone, yet I have many friends," Elior began again, nodding in agreement. "I move where I please, yet remain perfectly still. Light and darkness touch my skin, wet and dry are my kin. To find me, you must know where I begin. For death is but a dream."

Rumpelstilzchen stared at Elior for several moments. I kept hearing Nirnasha's thoughts, silently pleading for the fish to take the bait.

"Interesting," he said. "This will suffice for now."

Elior leaned forward and whispered something to the imp, yet it was cut off from our ears and minds. The tiny man nodded, and the next moment, he crept back into the shadows and disappeared.

"We leave tonight," Elior echoed to both of us. "Tell the others to return with you to the Ironclad. I shall meet you all there shortly. I must see a man about an airship."

THE MAN IN HEAVEN

Among those who remained behind in Ye and Poe were Kassy Bones, Darby Krokkett, and Reggie Gusel to guard the Ironclad. I figured Kassy had no interest in leaving Ye and Poe to see the capital again since I overheard her say to Meik that she had already seen too much of Havenshire. Before dawn, the rest of us slipped aboard an Eastguard merchant airship bound for the capital. Nirnasha came quietly into my room late that night and sat in an armchair by the fireplace with a book in hand. He glanced up at me and grinned.

"If you do not mind, the fireplace in my room does not work, and it is too dark to read," he said.

I chuckled, knowing he was drawing up some excuse to be in my company. I did not mind. I also wished to get through one of the books I brought back from the Unlight—*The Legend of Sleepy Hollow* by an author named Washington Irving. I would have thought the entire thing was unbelievable, that Mr. Irving just made it all up; however, too recently, I have seen stranger things than a headless horseman. The historical documentation still felt foreign to me, one such item, the sort of clothing described in the book, such as a cloak. One could conceal objects within it like the fit and flare frocks of our day, but the artwork revealed it to be much looser along the torso and hips. Another example was I had never seen a specter in the physical realm before, and I could only conclude that, at a point in time, the ethereal had much more influence within the physical realm to create such manifestations.

I spoke with Nirnasha about what I had read, and he seemed to agree that my theory held weighty probabilities. He then began telling me about the book he was reading—*A Christmas Carol* by an author named Charles Dickens—also told of multiple specters visiting a man named Ebenezer Scrooge. Nirnasha could only conclude that Christmas was something celebrated at one point in time, at least one day near the end of a yearly cycle. Our conversation became increasingly fascinating, but we were interrupted by an accustomed voice that came after a knock from the other side of my door. Nirnasha opened it for Elior. I was shocked he did not just appear among us as always. But I decided to leave that mystery alone. The MKR stepped inside and slowly closed the door behind him.

"Finding out why Eastguard wairships attacked Starvel is likely irrelevant now," Elior kept his voice hushed. "I sense our tiny friend has heavily influenced the emperor, and I sense the emperor shall reveal his true intentions in time. For now, we need his blessing to secure passage into the Unlight."

"How do we get his blessing?" Nirnasha asked.

"Promise him more Mystic Silver than we need," Elior replied. "There is an abundance, but getting to it will be extremely dangerous."

"Wendigo?" I assumed.

"Likely," Elior said. "But there are other dangers as well."

Elior's eyes drifted to the books in our hands, and smiled at us.

"Are we doing some late-night reading…together, eh?" he teased, shifting the conversation.

"It is not what you think," I swiftly spoke. "We are discussing the history of the books we found."

Elior sighed, and then we began hearing his voice in our heads. "I know a secret that is so secret I refuse to even speak out loud for fear of anything eavesdropping."

"What is it?" Nirnasha anxiously spouted.

"Those books are only historical in that they were written as fiction long ago," Elior bounced back a reply. "Most of the books you picked up are fiction."

"What is fiction?" I thought.

"It means they were made-up stories." Elior grinned again.

"That makes no sense," I reverberated.

"Why would anyone write down something if it is not true unless it is a bedtime story for children?" Nirnasha quickly concurred.

"Why would any educated adult consume such rubbish?" I asked.

"For entertainment," Elior responded. "Stories are how people passed the time long ago, entertaining one another with fiction. It inspires the imagination."

"It inspires lies," I almost retorted out loud. "These are not historical? They are not worth anything."

"And if you let people know, they certainly will not be," Elior replied, his thoughts calming us. "Ignorance is bliss. But as MKRs, you do not have that luxury. You will need to decipher what is true or not."

"So, all our books are fiction, then?" Nirnasha's thoughts were filled with dire dissatisfaction.

"Not all," Elior reassured. "Remember though, whether fiction or not, whatever the purpose an author writes a story, all stories are written by real people, persons with thoughts, emotions, and breath. All written works are created to be enjoyed and inform readers about the times they were crafted. It is art."

"I still do not understand," I said aloud.

"Not all things can be," Elior replied. "The ones who cannot cope with mystery are doomed to be faithless and hopeless, walking the earth blinded by their own pride..."

"They are the destroyers of the divine, and truly, they bring destruction to all in their wake with a malice they call reason," I interjected. "That is one of my favorite quotes of Darius Hamling."

"Who is Darius Hamling?" Nirnasha asked.

"He was one of the first philosophers of the Secret Arts," I replied. "He is the very reason the Secret Arts are even available to study for non-Keepers!"
"And who do you think gave him the information to do so?" Elior asked, trying to hide his smirk within the shadows.

My mind snapped to the realization after Elior exited that I was under the tutelage of the same MKR who illuminated the philosophical writings of Darius Hamling, one historical figure who had hundreds of documents written about his life due to his wit and philosophical writings.

"Has anyone ever written about you?" I asked Elior, who had joined Nirnasha and me that night in the ethereal.

"No," he replied. "I do not believe anyone ever has, at least not extensively in this present age."

"Then I shall be the first," I answered ecstatically.

Elior did not respond. He gave me another warm smile, but it appeared distant, almost as if he had not heard me. He walked to the edge of the meadow, near the tree line. I followed him, wondering if I had offended him in some way.

"You honor me with your words," he finally said, keeping his back to me. "In all my years, I have never cared for an extensive record. Yet I think now could be the time."

"What about you?" I asked Nirnasha as he joined us. "Would you write about all this and Elior?"

"I am not much of a writer," Nirnasha replied.

"Nor me," I said, trying to encourage him.

Truthfully, I had already begun writing about my travels with Elior in my journal. I just had not thought about organizing what I had written and then publishing it. I have always had a knack for remembering conversations and other important details. It is why I never missed a question on all my exams. At one point, my intellectual memory became challenged by one of my professors, who carried his pride in the difficulty of his lessons, torturing the minds of his pupils striving to receive a passing mark. Yet, in his testing, he became dumbfounded when I could recite his entire lecture script word for word after reading it over once. I made sure the other professors and the Dean were present at the time and took great care in recording my prowess for Langdon's legacy, for I refused to be called a cheater and to be challenged again.

I awoke to a peaceful morning in the sky but witnessed the transformation of the two idiots I knew. Garvish and Bikarma had surprisingly changed into loyal crew members of Meik Feenk—drinking with Wild Willy till they keeled over. The three were passed out on the deck near my door.

Cenobia remained close to Meik for most of the journey, but we found time to enjoy one another's company. I believe she had caught on to Nirnasha's fancy for me. She kept excusing herself each time he found his way to me. Still, I enjoyed Nirnasha's company—he being a wonderful friend and someone I could relate to as a fellow MKR, supporting all my efforts. I did not see much of Easton except when he came up to the dining hall to devour half of what the kitchen staff had prepared. The man's stomach is bottomless.

I was thankful for the days of rest and being able to eat my fill for a change, and I kept swallowing my fear, knowing I would soon return to the Unlight. Yet I did feel more confident in facing its many dangers. A couple of times, Elior dropped in to check on me, once during breakfast on the second day and twice during the late morn of the third and late evening of the fourth. Each time he encouraged me to brush up on Eastguard's etiquette and culture with the books aboard in the airship library. I found some that were most helpful, reminding me how extraordinary Eastguard is and how much I despise some of their customs.

To the people of Eastguard, the Great Collide occurred as a sign from the Divines that the Earth needed to be connected. To this day, the destruction that left billions dead is both mourned and celebrated within the nation as a national holiday, which was set to be three days after our arrival. The holiday, Crimson Regard, upholds Eastguard's most guarded morals—unity and duty, where division and individualism are considered insatiable flaws. Anyone who believes otherwise is strictly matured through the means of enslavement and often remains to ensure they are not a threat to the cultural ideals. The holiday symbolizes the blood lost and spilled to make Eastguard the kingdom it is today—united under the two ruling factions, the Raven Caste Clan and the Pure Bone Clan. None publicly honored unity like these clans, arranging marriages between one another or making blood pacts with one another by slitting their hands and pressing them together to become fused as siblings for life. It is also a time to mourn the sins of their forefathers, reflect on the unity demonstrated within the culture, and celebrate that they remain dutiful people to one cause—forging a nation of one mind.

Above the other two kingdoms, Eastguard truly has no civil war drawn out. The people carry a desire for work and do not cease training and recruiting for their army. Soldiers are recruited and learn how to wield Steam Tech weaponry, drive Steam Tech machines, and fly Steam Tech wairships. They are always on guard, as is their way of life, making sure they are doing their very best to protect the nation's interests, which results in a concrete caste system consisting of the two wealthiest clans I just mentioned and the rest of the kingdom having their proper pecking order between the working class and slaves.

The slave trade is widely recognized as necessary and does not fall into one ethos or biological specification. Essentially, the general rule of the kingdom is what you are born into—there you shall remain. If you are a slave, be proud. For that, it is who you are. The slaves in Eastguard, however, are treated in much higher favor than in Nod. Eastguard views slaves as a priceless commodity. Even the two wealthiest family clans disapprove of the mistreatment of slaves. Abusing slaves can have dire consequences, from losing one's status and becoming a slave or even death—ill use consisting of physical, sensual, or oppressive to one's basic needs.

Yet in the event of slaves rebelling, as Eastguard has experienced only three uprisings, they are swiftly put down with unforgivable force. Those who surrender are blinded and sent to Drac, the Holy City of the Fallen—to be servants of the curators who upkeep the tombs of monarchs, heroes, and soldiers of Eastguard. There, the slaves continue their lot in life, whatever that may be.

Ten years ago, during the third uprising, the Pure Bone and Raven Caste Clans led the way in crushing the rebellion, with Emperor Dejan Pure Bone, his brother Takato Pure Bone, and Bastian Raven Caste (Dejan's brother-in-law) being the star attractions. Eastguard boasts that it gives rise to warriors, yet many do not believe they need warriors if they deem themselves a kingdom of peace. This, of course, was a popular debate theme during my years at Langdon University. Eastguard, however, is not a democracy, nor is it a republic. It is a complete totalitarian monarchy. And they have repeatedly strived to showcase Westmain and Nod that it is the best form of government.

On the final night of our journey, I was in the airship's passenger lounge and noticed Elior leisurely take a seat across from me. This visit was not to encourage me but to inform me.

"Dejan Pure Bone is Emperor of Eastguard," Elior began. "Married to Sabia Raven Caste, he believes in keeping well-groomed, so you must do the same. Otherwise, he may find you insulting. You must address him first before anyone else in the room. No side conversations."

I noticed Elior had neatly trimmed his beard for the occasion.

"He wears an officer uniform of royal crimson, custom made to his liking, bearing the Pure Bone Clan's skull with triple cross-hatch markings on the forehead, signifying purity of the clan. In the common language, the cross-hatches mean 'Bones Never Lie,'" Elior continued. "Do not ask him about the symbol. He will find it insulting."

"Is there anything he will not find insulting?" I asked with a tone riddled with sarcasm.

"Not really," Elior replied, giving no sign of being amused. "Just know that even though he is not a Keeper or MKR, he is a trained warrior in many combat styles and carries the famed gun-blade, something of his own invention. It is not a conventional firearm widely used except by his kin. His gun-blade is virtually indestructible, and it is enchanted with Mystic Silver with the ability to fire nine drill bits before needing to reload."

"Why are you telling me all this?" I interjected, seeing he was holding something back.

"You have to promise not to be angry," Elior sighed. "But you and I shall be the only ones to see the emperor. You will be our bargaining chip to get an audience."

"Wait a minute," I blurted out. "Why me?"

"He likes royal crimson hair," Elior answered. "He also will like it when we tell him you are a virgin."

"What?!" Came my immediate reaction, which I felt had flames beginning to ascend from my fists.

"He will not touch you," Elior reassured. "Calm yourself and hear me out. He needs to believe he will receive you as payment once the expedition is complete, which means he must not know you are an MKR."

I could not believe what I heard. The sum of our plan was to entice and deceive the emperor into thinking he would acquire me as payment to have an audience with him. Once there, we would tell him of our expedition and gain his support to bring back several hundred units of Mystic Silver and, of course, my baby maker.

"This is quite a generous offer," Dejan admitted.

We had indeed gained our audience. He was a slender creme veil, yet well-toned to match his unique soldier-like abilities. The only reason I could tell was from his open silk robe, showing off his bare chest. Thankfully, he wore pants, unlike my father in such cases.

"How much Mystic Silver do you think is down there?" The emperor continued.

"At least three hundred units," Elior quickly estimated.

"You only want 103?" Dejan replied. "And you want to give me the girl?"

"Three nights only," Elior said. "She has a high slave value in Nod as a virgin, but it will diminish much after you have taken the first, second, and third prize. But she only becomes available after our return."

"I see," Dejan smiled. "So, she really is not part of the deal. She was only the enticement for you to gain an audience with me."

"Once again, you have caught me in my scheme," Elior admitted with a slight bow.

"I am not angry, Elior," Dejan chuckled. "Do you know why?" His question was directed at me, but I did not dare open my mouth to speak. I respectfully gave Dejan my attention.

"It is because Elior has never disappointed me," he finally stated. "Everyone has their own schemes and plots, but not once has this one left me without handsomely rewarding me for my assistance. So Elior, scheme away. Just be sure you do not disappoint me."

"You are wise beyond your years," Elior stated sincerely. "I thank you for allowing us to hold a game of wits before our departure. Yet again, you are the victor."

Then something happened that Elior did not expect.

"You have my blessing," Dejan said. "But only if you take a man in my employ with you. I do not expect it will warm you to see him, but he is set to arrive approximately two hours from now, on the east wing platform, gate sixteen."

"Do I know the man?" Elior asked after pausing for a moment.

"Utterly," Dejan replied. "But I have made my will absolutely clear to him as I will make it clear to you. Keep it civil—no violence whatsoever. He has agreed to these terms, and so shall you."

"I do," Elior agreed. "Does this man have a name?"

"I have my own schemes for my amusement," Dejan sneered. "I would not want to ruin the surprise."

Elior recruited Easton and Nirnasha to follow us to the landing platform. He explained to them what the emperor had said, and they, too, made a vow not to be aggressive in any way. I could tell Elior was troubled, almost appearing both livid and jittery.

We passed down several corridors, illuminated by daylight shining through floor-to-ceiling windows, enchanted no less, as to keep out the unforgiving winds and for a more agreeable temperature in the upper domain of Havenshire's mighty fortress. The stronghold stood carved out of an enormous mountain and held all sorts of hidden metals and gems. But alas, no Mystic Silver vein was ever found in its belly or even further beneath. The ancestors who built it took great care in reinforcing the foundations of its structures with iron and dressed them in highlights of copper. I remember coming into the city from the airship and seeing its towering marvels. The palace and upper districts reached much higher into the clouds, creating their hierarchy of significance and divisions among the populace. When the value of Mystic Silver's properties was discovered, the Eastguardians began enchanting essential structural elements to withstand high winds, and bone-chilling temperatures, creating even more elaborate architecture. However, it was not the only impressive feat.

We passed through the old palace, now the slaves' quarters for the emperor and the bearer of Eastguard's royal art gallery and tapestry history, stitched together in an exquisite form much like the structure itself. Each corridor of the old palace glinted in strewn highlights of copper around some portrait or scape depiction.

It is essential, I surmise that each tier of the city held its specific landing platforms—the bottom tier for passengers of low economic status and transporting slaves. The second tier was for merchants and cargo airships.

The third remained for wealthier passengers and Keepers. The last tier could only be used for welcoming guests of the emperor and visits from family members of the two wealthiest factions, who may or may not be welcomed but are allowed to use the platforms, nonetheless. In witnessing Elior's rush, I knew it had to be someone of great import he was eager to see.

We sat near the cargo bay once we reached our destination. The emperor had told us that his guest would arrive in two hours, yet we had rushed to wait on the platform for much of that time. I could not imagine what had Elior in such a frenzy that we could not explore some of the pleasures of the upper district before this guest arrived. He remained seated, not a word, entirely focused on the landing platform.

The three of us, Easton, Nirnasha, and I, passed the time by talking amongst ourselves. Easton kept our tones hushed, but I knew Elior could hear every word if he wished. I did not feel him in my mind, nor did I feel I could approach him.

"I have never seen you like this," I thought.

I saw Elior's face turn toward me ever so slightly, but his eyes did not budge from the platform. I heard him reply.

"There is only one reason the emperor told us to hold our aggression. He has made a pact, one which I have prevented past leaders of kingdoms from making. It will be Dejan's downfall."

"What pact?" I pressed.

"Somehow Dejan was convinced to allow the one we must defeat into his kingdom," Elior responded. This time I could feel Nirnasha's mind hearing the conversation, also joined by a fourth, Easton.

"I know," Easton said aloud.

"So Elior did not cut you off?" I asked.

"Elior remains connected to those he wishes," the Molten MKR nodded. "But it has been long since I visited the glade."

"Are you referring to the ethereal meadow?" Nirnasha asked.

"The place where you are training while you sleep is the glade, representing Elior's mind in the ethereal…yes," Easton replied.

"So, you have seen everything!" I said to Elior. "When were you going to tell us?"

"You are the only ones who know how to find it," Elior explained. "Since I trained my other pupils, I moved it to keep it secret."

"But now you need me back, correct," Easton scoffed.

"I need you because you were the most loyal student I ever had," Elior retorted. "You ran away, and I let you leave. I could not force you to fight then, and I shall not force you now. Yet you should know it is much different today. The game has significantly transformed."

"How? What is different?" Easton asked, now allowing his mind to be heard aloud.

"There are four of us," Elior reassured. "And you know one of them is watched over by Lasair. He is not more powerful than her, and neither am I."

"Who do you mean?" Nirnasha piped up. "Lasair or Aagneya."

"It could be both someday," Elior's eyes grew soft, focusing his gaze on me. "Aagneya could destroy his third snare. If she became powerful enough."

"So, I guess you want me to protect her?" Easton huffed.

"Both of them!" Elior exclaimed. "Help them as I did you. Teach them, and do not let them be pulled into the darkness."

In the distance, I could see an airship approaching the platform. As I watched the craft land, a man appeared, slowly walking down to the landing pad. His hair flowed straight down to his shoulders, darker than sable, practically taking on an azure shimmer, and with a beard styled much like Elior's. But that was not the only feature likened to the MKR of Light. In his approach, I could see the man's face held its mold proportionally and exactly like Elior's, but with shadowy circles surrounding his eyes. His fit and flare frock, trousers, and even his boots were colored heaven, with a gold vest over his elegant, ruffle heaven shirt. If I had never seen Elior before, I would have guessed the man to be an ashen pale face, not the twin of a creme veil.

He was somewhat thinner than Elior, but the broadness of his shoulders revealed he was no weakling. He held a finely decorated walking stick and wore a heaven top hat with a mystic midnight buckle strapped around the brim. His gloves were the same tone as most of his attire but had mystic midnight stitching running through the fingers. His eyes were the most notable distinction, holding a dull, stone hue. And as he drew closer, I could see streams of viola flowing through them like the blood that trickles out from a paper scrape.

He did not smile at us. He did not speak. He tipped his hat, a curious sign of respect but doubtfully sincere. Elior stood between us, and an awkward, unpleasant silence became frightfully unpredictable. The MKR of light maintained an expressionless stare while his brother fussed with his gloves, pulling them up toward his wrists as if biding time. Elior's mouth did not budge.

"I suppose it is customary to introduce oneself at the first meeting," the brother decided to break the silence. "However, from the look on your faces, I can see my brother has already told you much about me. However, I shall remain customary all the same."

He reached up, removed his top hat, and pushed back his long azurish sable hair from his face. He tucked his hat under his arm and then properly introduced himself.

"My name is Kalabhiti Lystander," he said. "But please call me Kalab. Kalabhiti can get the tongue dreadfully tied up."

"The emperor told me you would be coming," Elior said, keeping a very calm demeanor. "I am aware of his wishes."

"As am I," Kalab replied. "I suppose I should be kind enough to explain why exactly he has selected me to accompany you."

"I would," Elior answered. "But it does not interest me how you persuaded him to align himself with you. I have agreed to his request solely on the merit that I need his permission to explore the Unlight."

"You always did know the good hiding spots," Kalab seemed to tease, but I did not find it funny at all.

"Some of us are just blessed," Elior poked back.

"And some of us are just cursed," Kalab sneered.

"Only by choice," Elior quickly collided with Kalab's remark.

"I suppose you are right," Kalab perked up a grin. "For those who are cursed, we need a savior. Therefore, it is not easy for me to say this, but...I need your help."

Elior turned toward us. His brows pressed down into a frown. Easton raised one eyebrow with an expression that spoke volumes of disbelief. Kalab continued, and Elior returned his attention to him.

Kalab confessed to Elior that their past was indeed filled with being at odds with one another. And, astonishingly, he admitted his faults sincerely, claiming he had grown exhausted with the feud between them. For eons, Kalab remained determined in his quest to destroy Elior, incorporating Rumpelstilzchen into his schemes. Kalab said he had conjured the imp to assist in plotting the downfall of Elior and the world. However, in recent years, the tiny man had grown powerfully rebellious and essentially turned away from performing Kalab's wishes. Rumpelstilzchen had even begun having a significant influence on Wendigo.

"I had many years to contemplate my actions," Kalab admitted. "I do not ask for forgiveness or amends. But I do know my mind as of late. I am tired of trying to extinguish you, brother, and I am bored of seeking the world's destruction. Nothing has come of it."

Kalab then explained that he had made a deal with the emperor to help him build Havenshire higher into the clouds with his advanced knowledge of enchanting.

"What is in it for you?" Elior calmly demanded.

"That you would assist me in permanently ridding the world of Suzerain Efah," Kalab replied.

"Liar!" I could not cease from blurting out. I felt as if my feet were suddenly not in my possession, and they rushed me to stand beside Elior. "Why would you want one of your snares dead? It would mean you are closer to your demise, and I doubt you can stomach that!"

"My, my," Kalab responded gracefully. "You have a pupil with a powerful tongue, Elior. I do hope she has the magical prowess to back it up."

"Why not find out?!" I spat.

"Are you crazy?!" Easton and Nirnasha both shouted at me.

Kalab peered at me with what I assumed was a curious fascination. He grinned for a few moments and then turned his gaze to Elior.

"What do you say, brother?" he asked. "Care to watch your pupil spar with your rival?"

"You know the agreement," Elior said to both of us. "No aggression."

"We could call it practice," Kalab replied. "It would give her a chance to test her abilities."

"If I win, you shall help us kill Wendigo also," I added.

Kalab laughed. "I do like your spirit, girl! If I win, then you and Elior agree to help me."

"If you can win!" I exclaimed without hesitation. I then turned my gaze to Elior, who echoed nothing to me.

"You cannot do this," I suddenly heard Nirnasha behind me. "You have no idea..."

"Leave me alone!" I retorted harshly. "I shall put this monster in his place!"

Kalab and I stepped onto the platform with the known rules of no weapons, only magic. We waited a few moments until the airship took flight and was a safe distance away. I noticed the emperor and his brother, Takato Pure Bone, had made their way to Elior. From their discussion, the emperor appeared delighted to watch a sparing display of MKR power. I turned my attention back to Kalab, who had removed his fit and flare frock and rolled his sleeves somewhat up his forearm.

"I leave it to you to announce when the sparring match begins," he motioned. I removed my fit and flare frock, throwing it to the ground.

"We begin...now," I replied, taking one step forward.

I do not remember taking another breath or another step. My body ached all over, and my head throbbed as if clubbed by a hammer. Nirnasha was kneeling over me when I finally opened my eyes. He had what I would call a ridiculous "I told you so" expression on his face. Undoubtedly, I had lost. And I knew I lost much swifter than Nirnasha began describing. He portrayed Kalab's spell as a conjuring of shadow creatures that flew up from the ground and attacked me all at once in the blink of an eye. I never knew what had hit me until it was too late.

"I am sorry I yelled at you, Nirnasha," I said.

He shook his head at me.

"I do not get you, Aagneya," he replied. "I know you are smarter than this—you took on Elior's equal, an MKR of dark power. You could have died."

"You are right," I murmured. "But I know you are smarter too. Do not tell me you learned nothing from what happened."

"Are you insisting that you picked a fight with Kalab just to see what he could do?" Nirnasha asked, surprised.

"That is exactly what she did," we both heard Easton interject. "It is the only reason Elior allowed it."

"Great," Nirnasha admitted, with sarcasm illuminating his tone. "All we have to do now when we fight Kalab is know how to defend ourselves against a thousand shadow creatures."

THE TENEBROUS

We each received a room for the night in the old palace. The guest rooms had a private bathing area, feathered beds, and a balcony overlooking the rest of Havenshire. Among these indulgences, I enjoyed some of the pampering they offered—a massage, manicure, and a steaming hot bath. Afterward, I sat outside, taking in the remarkable view of the city with a steaming cup of Jaffa Blossom Tea.

I stretched my sight out upon the massive city with the setting sun making each tier glisten in highlights of copper as it came to rest upon the rooftops. The lanterns all over the municipality suddenly came to life, spreading throughout the streets and pathways, making the light of the domain so defined that the shadows danced wildly on the outer walls of the fortress, and the mountain appeared to cling effortlessly to the archways and towers of the upper district. The brightness of the municipal competed against the stars in the night sky, and I assumed they disappeared altogether if one stood down at the bottom tier of the stronghold. I could spy plenty of commotion happening below, but from where I sat, the sound ceased to reach me, muffled by the increasing howl of the chilling night breeze. I decided to ignite a small flame along my skin to remain on the balcony, staring at the wondrous speckle before joining Nirnasha in the ethereal.

As I decided to turn in, I heard voices on the balcony above me. I did not recognize them, but I could determine from the hushed tones that it was undoubtedly a secret meeting. Fortunately, my bout with Easton in the ethereal allowed me to learn something more about my abilities. While controlling the hue spectrum of flames, I summon in the ethereal. I learned that if I tune into the melody and cast the spell while in the physical realm, I can reach out to any flame within a reasonable radius to see and hear from it. I am unsure how else to explain it, but I can see the spectrum of flames near me, in my mind, and transition my cerebral state to them. I think of it as a sort of spy network.

Sitting on my bed, I began feeling and seeing the lit lantern in the room above me. My mind transferred to the flame. I recognized the man instantly. He was with the emperor down on the platform during my bout with Kalab, Takato Pure Bone, accompanied by an exquisite but enticingly dressed young woman. Her alluring wiles and long, sable hair tantalized Takato, who played along. He spoke her name, and I nearly gasped. The woman was Sabia Raven Caste—the Majestic One—also known as the wife of Dejan Pure Bone.

I did not wait around to see them shed any clothing. That did not matter, I guess, as I soon heard what sounded like two Suses squealing toward the trough. I desperately did my best to fall asleep without the grotesque image haunting my mind—difficult. Still, when I did, I immediately informed Nirnasha what I had witnessed after I reached the ethereal. He, of course, tried scolding me for intruding into affairs I knew nothing about. However, I reminded him of how valuable such information could be. He rolled his eyes, and then we began our training. Easton soon joined both of us.

We spoke much of how to watch our step around Kalab and by no means allow him to sway our thoughts. Yet it did not take long for my mouth to start jabbering again about what I heard and saw. With an enormous smile, Easton snorted a tiny chuckle and replied, "Duh. What did you expect from royalty?" I expressed my utter unfamiliarity with Eastguard's high-class drama. Easton began to elaborate on what had been known for years among the populace as well as helping me understand more about the two clans.

Dejan Pure Bone, known as the Light Bringer—self-proclaimed, I am sure—resided as Emperor of Eastguard. And during the third uprising, he prided his normalcy, outshining the Keeper abilities of his brother, Takato, and his brother-in-law, Bastian Raven Caste. In Eastguard's culture, Keepers are believed to have heightened reflexes and even superior strength for some. Dejan had remained on par with the slaying of rebels as that of Takato and Bastian. While Takato relinquished the respect Dejan believed he deserved, he stood furiously insulted by Bastian Raven Caste's disingenuous praises.

Then Easton spoke of the famed gun-blade, the ingenuity belonging to Dejan, and the enchanting done by none other than Takato was well known to the people of Eastguard. Dejan did not rely so much on the "gun" portion when slaying the rebels. The blade's edge held the potential to cut through steel with enough effort. Takato held a similar yet smaller gun-blade of his own, rather than the extended blade of Dejan's, who preferred to keep his enemies at a distance.

Takato Pure Bone, known as The Exalted One, is not only Dejan's younger brother but a talented Keeper and Dejan's most trusted advisor. Takato personally enchants weapons and armor for the Pure Bone Clan. While his mind is mainly focused on science and exploration among the stars, Takato is no stranger to the art of combat and wielding military-grade weapons. He is about the same build as Dejan, slender and well-toned, with sable hair cut short and slicked back into a tightly tied tail behind his head. But he is much more known as a strategic risk-taker, unlike Dejan, who is brasher. Besides the gun-blade, Takato always carries three gold-plated drill bit guns on his person—one strapped to his hip and two strapped across his chest. And yes, it is all too apparent he and Dejan's wife often sneak off together.

Easton continued by speaking about Mileedis Pure Bone, known as The Soothsayer. She is the second cousin of Dejan and rumored as the mistress who bears his children, which is the supposed secret tradition of the Pure Bone Clan. Though not a Keeper, Mileedis has an unusual foresight ability and talents in wielding daggers. Essentially, she is a great muse and an assassin in the service of Eastguard's emperor. One would know her just by sight as she has a rare skin deformity where she has a visual mix of both pale and sable ethos coloration from head to toe, heaven hair, and oval, bright azure eyes.

Interestingly, what is widely believed about the reason for her skin abnormality is that she was cursed by a being from the ethereal while in the womb. None of her children carry this oddity, and Easton claimed her children were born under the guise that Takato is their father. Although it is clear Takato has no interest in her.

The last Pure Bone Easton described was Sheni Pure Bone—The Beguiler. Sheni appeared somewhat frail but did not move like an older woman. She modestly adorned her appearance but carried a vile weapon wherever she went—her tongue. As the mother of Dejan and Takato, Sheni is a mischievous and cunning woman who remained in power till her eldest son came of age. She had married the eldest son of the Raven Caste Clan, but in the many years of marriage, as the hearsay goes, she made sure her womb was only impregnated by her cousin's uncle. She then proceeded to systematically deceive and assassinate her husband at the time. It is believed he died of poisoning, yet it was never proven. Sheni continues to assure the rest of the Raven Caste Clan that her two sons are of Raven Caste descent. To keep up appearances, Sheni elected that Dejan would marry one of his so-called cousins, Sabia, thus keeping up appearances of good relations between the two clans.

Easton stated he believed Sabia was chosen because of her naivety and vanity. Sabia Raven Caste, known as the Majestic One, is a beautiful woman who loves luxury and pampering. Though she was picked as Dejan's wife, she is not ignorant of the fact they do not love one another. She is no stranger to the politics of the two clans and has always distanced herself from caring about such things until it hinders her comforts. Dejan sees to it that she is well taken care of and does not get bored. She loves wearing elegant, revealing attire to show off her alluring wiles and letting her long, sable hair flow freely. For charming fun, she often sneaks off with Takato.

"One thing Sheni did not expect in picking Sabia as Dejan's bride is that Sabia is quite curious and snoopy," Easton said.

"Which is most likely why Dejan would employ his brother to keep her attention elsewhere," I replied.

With a nod, Easton took his time to describe the champion of the Raven Caste Clan—Bastian, The Heart Slayer. He is Sabia's brother, with his own rakishly handsome features, spending his entire life studying the art of combat and matured in a more primitive style that relies on power than finesse, the opposite of Dejan and Takato. Bastian is also a Keeper like Takato, but more so a hardened warrior who pushes the limits of his own body and mind. His build is colossal compared to Dejan and Takato combined, and he hardly ever removes his enchanted plated armor, specifically strengthened in vital points of his body to thwart being pierced by projectiles or close-quarter combat weapons. His title as The Heart Slayer came not only from his charm but his fantastic ability to take the hearts of his enemies quickly—and he is the only one who can claim the people bestowed such a label upon him.

I noticed his prowess when we all gathered the next morn. Bastian, The Heart Slayer of Raven Caste, strutted into the palace courtyard with his chin elevated toward the clouds as if there were thousands of people chanting his name. I peered out of the corner of my eye to see Dejan's displeased scowl at how Bastian gamboled his own praise. Then I became wide-eyed seeing the man who followed in behind him, a familiar explorer, Bartus.

I turned my gaze toward Nirnasha, who also held his face poised in bewilderment. However, Bartus did not speak, ensuring he remained respectful in the emperor's court.

"My dear brother-in-law," Dejan's demeanor wholly transformed into his political persona. "How kind of you to come. But as you can see, we are gathered to discuss important matters."

"Such is why I am here," Bastian admitted. "I ran into Elior yesterday, and he asked if I would be interested in a venture. And with your permission, I am looking to assist in these endeavors."

"You would undoubtedly be useful," Dejan appeared surprised and pleased by Bastian's candor. "I shall grant your request. But who is this stranger who follows quietly behind you?"

"This is Bartus of Westmain," Bastian replied. "He is a veteran explorer who also happens to have books from his travels he thought you might be interested in purchasing."

"I shall hold my interest until this business here is concluded," Dejan stated. "I wonder if your guest would like to remain here. Perhaps afterward, we can all take a look at the merchandise."

Bartus, uncharacteristically, humbly bowed his head to show his acceptance of the emperor's invitation. The palace slaves fetched two more chairs for the assembly of our meeting just as Kalab strode in with his head held aloft, much in the way Bastian entered, but with a different mystic midnight walking cane, decorated with a giant glistening heaven pearl for its top. His heaven attire remained a spectacle of perfection, with his beard groomed niftier than I remembered the day before.

"Gents. Ladies," he began so elegantly. "Our gracious and most esteemed host, the Light Bringer and Emperor of Eastguard has honored and blessed us to accept our noble quest with his approval. Therefore, it is our solemn pledge not to fail his behest."

Cenobia and Meik sat just across from me, with Garvish and Bikarma on either side. Nirnasha sat beside me, with Elior on the other side of him, directly to the emperor's left and Takato on the emperor's right. Next to me sat Easton and Wild Willy. Across from them sat Bartus with Bastian.

Kalab paced back and forth behind us but never behind the emperor as he spoke. He finished his flattering introduction to the emperor, which I was unaware is a formal custom in Eastguard—perhaps only when there is a compensating egomaniac on the throne. Dejan clapped for Kalab's theatrics and then turned his eyes upon us, his seat slightly elevated over our own. His words were like droughted soil, boring me, and my mind wandered to Nirnasha's thoughts, where we held a much more entertaining conversation, daring to try and make the other one giggle. I could see I was winning as Nirnasha shifted, curved his lips, and took deep yet silent breaths.

"He is likely still suckling his mother," Nirnasha heard me. "You can tell by how he positions his lips like a bum hole."

Nirnasha almost lost his composure to a burst of laughter. But he ended up politely and quietly clearing his throat, reaching for the goblet of water each of us was so generously provided. However, Dejan's voice paused, and my fellow MKR and I suddenly realized all eyes were staring at us.

"Something the matter?" Dejan's eyes were particularly wide. He indeed appeared insulted.

"No, my emperor," I swiftly responded. "Please forgive me. I do believe I am eager to begin this venture in your name. I have never had the honor of going on a quest for an emperor, and certainly not one of such high prestige as Eastguard."

"Aye, my emperor," Nirnasha agreed after the water went down his gullet. "I am eager too. I feel I might be too eager as I have allowed my mouth to run dry with nerves of anticipation."

I could not believe Nirnasha and I had just turned into politicians. It appeared to work. Dejan eased his shoulders and leaned back in his seat with an astute grin. I peered momentarily at Elior, who gave me an unforeseen wink. I guess one really can play the game when the need arises. Although, I felt my true feelings beneath—how desperately I wanted to burn Dejan's smirk clear off his face.

"I believe our two youthful adventurers are correct," Dejan stated. "I find myself eager as well to get this venture started. Let us state the finality of the agreement, and then we shall be underway. First, Elior, you stated that your harvest needs must be no less than 103 mass units. As emperor, I have agreed to allow you to enter the Unlight in my lands upon the agreed sum that you will match my price of mass units with your required sum, totaling your required harvest to be no less than 206 mass units. You have also agreed that any extra mass units shall go to me. If, in the event, you cannot harvest the required mass unit amount of 206, then all mass units shall be divided into a percentage in my favor, 70/30. Do you and the rest of your enterprise agree to these terms?"

We were all required to raise our hands individually and swear we agreed to the terms. Although, I certainly did not. I had never heard of a harvest of Mystic Silver ever being 206 mass units. How could the rarest of ores ever be in one place?

Once our business concluded, Dejan motioned for Bartus to show him the books in his possession. I was also curious to see what the oaf had found during my first dive into the Unlight. He had only two books. The first was called *To Kill a Mockingbird* by an author named Harper Lee. The second was called *One Flew Over the Cuckoo's Nest* by an author named Ken Kesey.

"I think they will make a good addition to my collection," Dejan said. "What say you to 3,000,000 credits each?"

"Most generous, my Emperor," Bartus replied. "However, I was hoping for a bit more."

"How much?" Dejan's nose began to crinkle up. "I believe 3,000,000 each is ample. But what price is flashing before your eyes?"

"I was hoping to receive 6,000,000 for each," Bartus said.

I had never seen Bartus look so nervous. The man looked like he could barely swallow. Seeing it was magnificent as he had made so many other students, including myself, squirm in our seats. I was hoping the emperor would threaten him in some fashion so I could see his eyes pop out of his head. But no such luck. After several moments of staring down Bartus, Dejan agreed to his price.

"Did you want to sell the books we found?" Nirnasha asked me once we were walking to gather our belongings. "For 6,000,000 credits each—an exemplary compensation."

"You could have spoken up to sell yours," I replied. "Why not?"

"I guess now that I know what they are," Nirnasha sighed. "I feel like they are too valuable to sell. I truly enjoy reading them."

"I feel the same way," I said with a large grin.

We gathered our belongings, including the packs still holding the books we found in the Unlight. Elior's thoughts reached Nirnasha and me as we passed by him to step aboard the Eastguard wairship.

"It is the most dangerous place you can think of—your first venture to the Unlight will feel like you were school children, innocently playing on a playground."

"What of Wendigo?" I thought.

"I suspect Kalab will keep Wendigo from interfering in whatever he is planning," Elior answered. "I see that he desires to have a portion of the harvest for himself. It will force us into a fray with Kalab if Wendigo does appear."

"I do not understand," Nirnasha interjected. "How can Dejan trust Kalab? Does he not fully know who he is?"

"Yes and no," Elior echoed his reply. "But Dejan will do anything as long as it benefits himself."

"I still wish we could learn why Eastguard wairships attacked Starvel," I sighed.

"We may learn soon enough," Elior replied. "Likely, the answer is simpler than what we can theorize. As I said, Dejan will do anything if it benefits himself. He sees the other two kingdoms growing divided and likely desires to see them destroy themselves from within. Starvel may have been nothing more than a weakening of Westmain's legs while he tightens the noose."

Our heading relocated us to Kirshan Outpost, mapped northwest of Havenshire. From there, we would tread a three-day journey out into the Deadlands of Eastguard, traveling a precise twelve o'clock bearing from Kirshan. Yet while aboard the Eastguard wairship, Nirnasha and I spent most of our time together, reading our esteemed books and exchanging a book for the time being. I recommended to him that he read from my collection, *The Wind in the Willows*.

Nirnasha's book he exchanged with me was only a fifty-seven-page book, *The Call of Cthulhu,* by an author named H.P. Lovecraft. I found the form of speech in the tome somewhat tricky to follow. It did not deter me from finding it an exciting thrill. If I still believed it as a historical document like most explorers, I would have found it horrifying, to say the least. I could not honestly identify the creature's appearance described in the text. Although I could understand the term "dragon," I vaguely remember seeing ancient artwork of such beasts. Yet I had no frame of reference to understand the terms "octopus" or "cuttlefish." The creature's appearance in the text became somewhat lost, but I picked up on several descriptions, taking notes as I went. At one point, the creature's size was compared to a mountain.

I found it odd that the monster became released unwittingly by sailors. But what struck me most curious about the creature in question was its ability to regenerate after what I could assume was a sailing vessel of some kind called a "yacht" rammed into its head. At the same time, the book mentioned the creature's name and the cult that followed it—"Cthulhu."

"Do you suppose Cthulhu or its cult was ever real?" I asked Nirnasha as we made our way off the wairship.

"I cannot be positive," Nirnasha replied. "I have thought about it quite a bit myself. But do you suppose it could be just another text of fiction?"

"I would assume so," I agreed. "But something about it does not feel fictional. We have seen the ethereal. I wonder if it was a being from there but somehow got released into the physical realm."

"How could it remain in the physical realm, though?" Nirnasha stated. "Ethereal beings remain in the ethereal because that is where they exist. Physical beings remain in the physical. As MKRs, we are the only beings able to exist in both places simultaneously."

"True," I concurred to the best of my knowledge. "But what if other things can exist in both places at once? What if we are not the only beings able to do so, historically speaking?"

Nirnasha did not have an answer and could only relay a shrug to my line of questioning. I did remain to ponder on the matter. However, we heard the call for our landing.

Kirshan Outpost appeared like a nightmare covered in ice and sleet, piercing my eyes with sunlit reflections and nipping my skin with the winds of Suzerain Efah. Widespread, the iron fortress had several platforms for housing wairships and manufacturing wairship parts. Eastguard soldiers guarded every footstep of the walls overlooking the Deadlands. Its citizen population only consisted of those who worked the manufacturing plants, some laboring for wages and others slaves.

We all wore heavy garments insulated with Ovis Aries fibers. Nirnasha had never experienced snow in his life either. He shivered endlessly while I focused my power to warm the blood in my veins. Nirnasha and I remained silently discussing Cthulhu to keep our thoughts off the chilling winds, which I think he was thankful for as it became a wonderful distraction.

"How did you come by such a book?" I asked my fellow MKR. "What prompted you to pick it from the many you could have chosen?"

"I did not," Nirnasha admitted. "Elior asked me to hold it for him."

We had journeyed for three days, bombarded by cold heaven powder, to find our destination surrounded by a clump of dead trees and the resonance of a violent wind that leaped out from inside the darkness. The Unlight entrance lay indeed where Elior said it would be. And he and Kalab entered first side-by-side. During the entire journey, both remained in stride. I could only imagine Elior bartering with or warning him against double-crossing him. I tried to listen in through Elior's mind, but he had blocked me and Nirnasha out. It all became clear once we had settled into the cave to camp for the night.

"I must inform all of you of what lies ahead," Elior began. "Kalab and I have spoken about it while trekking to this destination. The dangers awaiting us to reach the harvest are nightmares none of you have faced. There are worse things in the depths than Lurkers or Tide Maidens."

"I have made a pact with Elior," Kalab stepped in. "I shall do everything I can to keep dark creatures at bay so we do not waste precious time or energy defending ourselves against them. However, two issues must be addressed. You must not wander off or attack a creature without provocation. In many aspects, I know how to distract Lurkers from wanting to harm us. Second, there is a depth into the Unlight where ancient creatures despise intruders and even see me as one."

"In agreement for assisting us with the Lurkers," Elior said. "I have offered my assistance to Kalab's dilemma. However, it does not involve all of you. But after this is complete, it does involve me, Easton, Aagneya, and Nirnasha."

"So do not turn your back on Kalab for a second," the three of us (Easton, Nirnasha, and myself) heard Elior whisper to our minds. "Do not let him speak with you alone, or you may find yourself lost."

There were thirty-one of us. Kalab stood away in the shadows, but the crackling campfire still lit up his feet while Elior told the rest of us about the creatures we would face in what is known as the Tenebrous, the far depths of the Unlight. Wild Willy, Meik, Cenobia, Garvish, Bikarma, Easton, Nirnasha, and I sat on one side of the fire while Bastian and twenty of Eastguard's elite troops sat on the other. Each elite soldier was armed with a gun-blade, much like the shorter design of Takato's, and a buzzsaw rifle.

The Tenebrous depths harbor two dangerous things that Elior and Kalab knew about. Shangores, meaning "Faceless Ones," I learned that Wendigo was once one, undoubtedly corrupted in becoming Kalab's soul snare. Their appearance is humanoid and slender, walking upright and with hardened, dense bone cartilage inside their body. Their head is like a human, yet protrudes the six prehensile serpent-like tentacles from the sides of their head, three on each side. Like Wendigo, their tentacles have heads that bear razor-sharp teeth, with massive biting force and the ability to taste the air for the presence of dead or living things. The creature's face has no eyes, ears, or mouth. Much of their species remain only wandering the vast caverns of the Tenebrous. What normal Shangores do not possess are the eyes on their hands like Wendigo. As formidable specimens, they attack anything foreign to their domain or anything that is not one of them—such as Harleps.

Harleps means "Lost Species," and they are insect-like creatures. Their torso is humanoid with four arms bearing sharp claws yet six spiny insect legs sprouting from their lower half. Their head holds jagged pincers, much like the head of a Mystic Menardis, yet they, too, have no eyes. They listen with tiny ear holes and sense vibrations with them.

Shangores and Harleps hate one another, and they hate anything else that is not their species. Having to deal with any Lurkers, Gloom Gnawers, or Tide Maidens appeared frightening enough to those of us who did not have magical powers. From how Elior spoke, it seemed as if we were walking into a battleground of elite monsters that would surely overwhelm us.

"Wendigo will come nowhere near us," we all heard Kalab interject and step forward from the shadows. "I shall make sure of that. You have my word."
"We shall see how good your word is, Dark MKR," Bastian bravely replied. "I have seen men turn vile in their lust, leap at the throats of others, unbearably hungry for human flesh..."

"Understandable," Elior stepped in calmly. "I have had my dealings with Wendigo before. If we encounter him, perhaps my brother truly wants a final showdown, which I shall gladly give if needed."

"I understand you do not trust me, brother," Kalab answered with what I would describe as a wicked grin. "I have not given you any reason to trust me. Nevertheless, the Tenebrous awaits, and Mystic Silver cries out to be rescued from its belly."

"Aye," Meik chimed in. "I almost hope that abomination does show. I cooked up a little surprise just in case."

Kalab appeared taken aback by Meik's comment, not showing any signs of concern but intrigued. Easton also sent a glare Kalab's way as he stood up and walked to turn in for the night. Then Kalab returned to the shadows, away from the crackling flames.

"I believe I made a mistake," I projected my thoughts to Elior. The MKR did not turn toward me, knowing eyes were watching him. "I have the book with me."

"Then it is safe," Elior echoed back. "He may suspect it found, but he does not know its disguise. He believes I would not dare trust another with it. Which is why I carry a decoy."

Elior sent one final thought to Easton, Nirnasha, and myself that night. He warned us not to enter the ethereal as Kalab could sense them to take advantage. That is when I realized the time had come to physically manifest everything Nirnasha and I had learned from our training.

My mind raced that night about each enemy I would have to face, including Kalab if need be, when it came to my turn to remain on watch. While I surveyed the others, I tried to concentrate back on when I challenged him, doing my best to see how to slow him down, for I refused to let him beat me again. I pondered for so long that I did not notice the sun's light climbing over the horizon. Yet when its warmth touched me, I stood at the cave entrance, marveling at the beauty that reflected off the fresh powder. Nothing but shadow and rock awaited me. And a long time would pass before seeing the sky again or the shimmering dew. The sight of the morning became so much more beautiful and meaningful the first time I emerged from the Unlight. I believed it would feel the same again, perhaps even more so.

I soaked up the remaining heat from the cindering coals just before we broke camp. I leisurely pulled my gloves over my hands to the soft sounds of footsteps beginning to echo deeper into the cave. Not long after, we strangely reached a spiraling set of stairs that appeared to be carved through long ago. The light from the outside world had vanished when we reached the bottom, and we placed our first magic bean in an old carved-out crevasse in the rock face next to the stairs, signifying our last marker in trekking our way back to the entrance. Everyone waited patiently till their SHCs synced to the Nanomite signal.

This may have been my second trip into the Unlight, but it was my first time using the Steam Tech and extensively relying on it. Before, Elior had known the way. Now it appeared like he was being more cautious than I had ever seen him and somewhat dimmer on his directional heading. I could see Elior acting his best to hide the worry in his demeanor, making me even more watchful of Kalab. I knew I needed to study him. I needed to find a weakness in the Dark MKR.

"This place is always changing," Elior said under his breath. He turned left and continued leading us further downward.

We trekked for several days without incident. Nirnasha, Easton, Meik, Cenobia, Bikarma, Garvish, and I remained as close to one another as possible. We walked only about six strides behind Elior, who remained walking step-for-step with Kalab. Bastian trailed behind us while the soldiers kept pace with their buzzsaw rifles, ready to fire.

"Elior…stop," I heard Nirnasha's thoughts. "I feel vibrations that are not our own."

Elior halted immediately.

"What is it?" Kalab whispered.

"I heard something," Elior replied. He motioned for the soldiers to gather in their battle-ready formation and told the rest of us to get ready.

"They are moving silently, but I can feel them," Nirnasha continued.

I wondered how many there were, but Nirnasha could not say. He knew the footsteps were moving to surround us and likely to strike at any time. Elior waited a few moments and then burst forth orbs of light, fully illuminating the cavern.

Hundreds of Prowlers, slender and glistening with mystic midnight flesh, screeched blood-curdling echoes from their unclasped jaws. It is infrequent to see Prowlers travel together in such great numbers. But this horde covered the entire rock-face all around us. For the moment, they were stunned, which gave the Eastguard soldiers ample opportunity to open fire.

"Ceasefire," Kalab shouted. "Ceasefire!"

"What do you mean?" Elior turned to him. "Did you have something to do with this?"

Elior grew enraged seeing Kalab shrug.

"You best explain why I should not dispose of you," Elior spat, seizing Kalab by his collar.

"First of all," Kalab remained calm. "You made an oath to the emperor. Secondly, it is not my fault. They are drawn to me. I have ordered them to keep their distance and..."

"What?! You mean you control these abominations," Bastian stomped forward and demanded. By now, the buzzsaw rifles had gone silent.

"I would not call them abominations, but yes, I can," Kalab replied. "I was trying not to alarm any of you, but then Elior heard something, and you have seen the rest."

"What are you trying to pull?" I chimed in.

"Ready for round two, I see," Kalab mocked me. He turned to Elior. "Get your hands off of me and calm yourself, brother."

Elior let him go, allowing the Dark MKR to straighten his attire.

"If it is unclear to you, brother, or everyone else, then I shall explain," Kalab pronounced. "I promised I would keep Wendigo far away from us, but that does not mean I would not call for assistance from other allies. Do you not think it best to save our strength for the real fighting when we reach the Tenebrous? This horde could protect us from Gloom Gnawers or other unknown dangers."

"Are you saying you want these things to protect us?" Nirnasha's voice squeaked, but he would never admit that it did.

"They shall," Kalab replied. "At a reasonable distance."

"I do not want them near us at all," Bastian spat.

"Careful, big boy," Kalab's eyes grew wide. "I never promised the emperor a non-aggression pact with you."

"If you want to die here," Bastian bravely stepped forward. "I shall gladly end you and your abominations."

"Enough!" Elior shouted. "I shall speak to my brother alone."

Elior may have stated that, but Easton, Nirnasha, and I heard the conversation after they had stepped off several paces away from us all.

"What are you doing?" Elior demanded.

"I told you before," Kalab answered. "I need your help. I shall do whatever it takes to ensure this venture goes as smoothly as possible. That means if I have to safeguard us until we get to the Tenebrous without needlessly wasting precious time and energy, I shall ensure Lurkers or any other creature in the Unlight leaves us alone."

"Why Prowlers?" Elior asked.

"Prowlers are quiet," Kalab said. "Do you want me to draw in regular Lurkers so we can hear them shuffling around in the dark or Bangores thumping and shouting while the others try to sleep?"

"I doubt anyone will be able to sleep now that they know what surrounds us," Elior replied.

"True," Kalab admitted. "But that is more your fault. You have such great hearing, yet you did not bother to ask me what is out in the dark. Remember, this has been my domain for quite some time."

"I know," Elior sighed. "That is why I do not like it."

"I do have an idea of what we could do, brother," Kalab perked up. "Why not have these Prowlers follow us into the Tenebrous? That way, they could help defend us from any creatures there. You know I cannot control Shangores or Harleps. But having a horde of Prowlers for fodder would help us greatly."

Elior turned toward us. He took two steps in our direction. I could not believe he was considering Kalab's offer, even though I thought it was not a bad idea.

"Think of it," the Dark MKR said. "Think of how easy it would be."

"That is what got you to where you are now," Elior replied, turning back toward his brother. Every light orb in the cavern suddenly shot down in one unison strike, cutting off all the heads of the Prowlers surrounding us. "My answer is no."

One orb of light remained, bright enough for us to see one another. I saw the scowl on Kalab's face and grew fearful the two brothers would burst into an all-out brawl. Of course, I do not think we would have picked Kalab's side.

"You say you need my help," Elior stated. "Yet you do not seem to understand one thing."

"What is that?" Kalab gritted his teeth.

"I shall never trust you," Elior grinned. "This may be your domain, but I am King down here and during this venture. We will end this if you choose to go against my wishes."

I could sense his heart racing. Elior's demeanor did not reveal it, but I could hear the pounding in his mind. I tried sending him a comforting echo to let him know he was not alone standing against his brother. Nirnasha interjected his agreement and reassured Elior he had more allies with him who would rather die than see Kalab be victorious. We both received a slight grin from the MKR, and he turned away, replying to Nirnasha and me.

"Thank you—to you both."

I turned my gaze to see Meik and Wild Willy conversing with Bastian Raven Caste. Too silent to understand their words, yet it could not be anything other than what they planned to do should Kalab bring more Lurkers to us.

We stopped to rest. Whether it was night or day, it did not matter. Everybody looked worn and in need of a fresh dose of shuteye. While we were setting our beds down on the hardened rock, I noticed Garvish and Bikarma began whispering to one another. Bikarma had a worried look on his face. Garvish saw my eyes were on them. He turned his head in every possible direction, hoping no one saw him motion to me and Nirnasha to come over. Soon the rest of our allies were gathered around them. Cenobia, Meik, Wild Willy, Easton, and even Bastian grew curious about the huddled group. Bikarma motioned for all ears to move in close.

"We have a problem," he whispered. "One of the most perilous proportions."

"What's the trouble, boy?" Meik answered.

"I just went to check the signal of the magic bean trail," Bikarma replied, keeping his tone down. "It was getting weaker and weaker. Now, there is nothing."

"Which means only one thing," Garvish added.

"Something has obliterated our beans," Bastian glared.

"Most likely," Meik concurred. "One thing is for sure; they knew where to look."

"The only traitor I smell is Kalab," I said, which drew nods and agreement from everyone.

"We shall set out a perimeter guard of about ten," Bastian said. "That way, the rest of you can sleep. I will lead the first watch."

"And I the second," Meik quickly responded.

I volunteered to be part of the second watch. Nirnasha lay slumbering only a few paces away as part of the first. Seeing him slumber made my mind drift to fantasies of being cozied next to him, which brought me to comprehend that I cared for him much more than a friend. I had grown fond of hearing his voice and missed sharing private conversations in a world we had never dreamt of until Elior came into our lives. That is when the MKR of light came and sat beside me, interrupting my thoughts. His mind reached out to me.

"I hear worry from you," his voice echoed inside me.

"I worry for the world," I reverberated. "I worry that such wicked things shall destroy it. Though I am not quite fond of my parents or perhaps just people in general, I want them to be safe."

Elior silently chuckled at my comment. Then he focused on comforting my own, with a slight grin on his face.

"The fate of the world haunted me for many eons till I met one who came with a power I never thought I would see again," he said. "His hands were as heavy as a thousand sawblades. His words cut like them too, but ever so distinctly, gently, and precisely to free people from their burdens and what worried them. I saw him betrayed and watched him let the darkness take his life. No other manner of man has ever lived since, and no other has so divinely mastered what we all fear. Yet he conquered it, redefining the way it means to be an MKR. He was no longer like any of us, cursed to live in a broken vessel, ever so sorrowfully growing in the knowledge of the ages, less we learn that nothing makes any difference, less his heart remains the hermeneutic for the melody of our existence."

"What does his heart say then?" I asked out loud in a hushed tone.

"Seek the helpless and defend them," Elior replied in a like manner. "Pursue justice, make honest gains, and live peacefully because death is only the beginning."

"You speak as though you knew the man long before," I whispered.

"He is how my brother and I came to be," Elior confessed. "His form the second time was distinct, taking on a shell of flesh and bone. Yet, the first time we met him, his face was brighter than the sun, his eyes blazed like fire, and his hair the brightest shimmering heaven. He wore a robe of untarnished gold, and his voice crashed like tides against the cliffs. He held seven lights in his right hand, and his tongue cut like a double-edged sword, just like when I met him the second time. He was our teacher, master, and the father we never knew."

"What happened when you met him for the first time?" I asked.

"He smiled," Elior replied with a grin of his own. "His presence made my brother, and I lose control of our footing to where we fell to our faces. It was an overwhelming surge of both fear and peace all at once. We were both trembling uncontrollably. But he commanded us not to be afraid. And so, we obeyed."

While I listened to Elior, I could also hear the dark caverns dripping moisture onto the solid rock below like a ticking clock. Then for several moments, it stopped. Elior ceased conversing with me and slowly rose to his feet. I joined him. He manifested light to fill the cavern, and in those moments, we both saw a single faceless terror with its six tentacles protruding from its head, kneeling, and drinking from the small pool. It did not appear to have detected us. I refused to allow it to do so. I broke into a fierce run, my steps waking the rest of our party and drawing the attention of the others watching. As I began to summon fire to incinerate the thing, Kalab grabbed hold of both my wrists. Elior was the first to reach me.

"Calm yourself, brother," Kalab said. "Remain calm, all of you."

I looked at the creature in front of us, still drinking from the pool as if nothing had disturbed it.

"What have you done?" Elior demanded.

"What dark magic is this?" Meik also piped in.

"Because my brother refused to allow me to use creatures to protect us here," Kalab began. "I have found another means of keeping us safe."

"What are you talking about?" Bastian demanded. "What have you done?"

"I have simply cast a barrier around us that eliminates our sound, scent, and vibration to anything outside of it," Kalab explained. "We are like shadows in this place."

"He speaks the truth," Nirnasha relayed to Elior's mind. "The only vibrations I can feel belong to the creature."

"Would you rather the rest of them become alerted to our presence?" Kalab asked, staring intently at all of us. "Or would you rather I maintain this spell long enough so we are not ripped to shreds in our sleep?"

More faceless ones appeared out of the shadows, Shangores, that towered over all of us. They could not see the light Elior had cast, but we could see them pouring in around us. In a matter of minutes, we were surrounded.

"I do not want to waste time fighting," Kalab insisted to Elior. "I am not trying to deceive you when I say I need your help."

"Shielding us is fine," Elior admitted. "As long as you do not bring any abominations to us."

"As I said, I cannot control the Shangores. I have never been able to do so," Kalab replied. "However, he can. And most likely, he has them hunting us."

"You are saying Suzerain Efah controls these things?" Nirnasha stuttered out his question.

"Not just them," Kalab responded. "I am sure he has sent an army of Gloom Gnawers to hunt us as well. Unfortunately, my shield will not stop them from spying us in the dark."

"Gloom Gnawers favor an ambush," Meik said. "Best we have Nirnasha take the lead from now on to see if we can sense what's ahead of us."

I could see Nirnasha trying to muster his courage. I grasped his hand to steady his nerves once we broke camp. My MKR companion pulled me with him as we went. I promised him I would walk with him if he let go of my hand. It was not that I did not want to hold his hand; it was just that I felt uneasy, catching Kalab's eyes sticking to me.

"Do not worry," I whispered to Nirnasha as he let go. "I shall roast us some rat meat before they even reach us."

"I have never told anyone before, Aagneya," he nervously smirked. "I hate rats. And the idea they are waiting to pounce on me is my worst nightmare, even though I know I hold great power against them."

A man I had not spoken to in over a week began walking behind us. Wild Willy snickered a bit when I turned around to see who the cocky footsteps belonged to—he was strutting. Meik had charged him with guarding both of us. Soon, we were joined by Garvish and Bikarma, who amazingly remained silent. For many more days, the five of us led the pack, while Elior remained toward the back with Kalab and Bastian Raven Caste began shadowing our footsteps more closely as the days went on. I had grown fond of Bastian, to be honest. I found he held endearing protective qualities and remained fearless in his demeanor. Easton moved about with Cenobia, Meik, and the twenty Eastguard soldiers spread throughout our line, but none moved to be in the front with us.

Day nine, or so I had to assume, we came to a vast cavern with ancient-looking columns, still holding the structural integrity of an ancient civilization. There were no ruins of buildings about to say it was part of the Great Collide, so I could only theorize that once a race of beings lived deep in the earth and had the minds for sculpting underground cities.

"Harleps once thrived in this place," Elior spoke to my mind. How he always knew my inquisitiveness had perked did not bother me, especially when so many questions were racing through my mind. "They are shy like Mystic Menardis and often allied with them. Yet Shangores have viciously decreased their numbers over the centuries. Since you have a bond with one of their allies, Harleps will know your scent as friend."

Nirnasha suddenly paused as we approached a large opening at the other end that would take us into another vast cavern. A strange glow up ahead brought heat that warmed my soul. The others felt it; I knew it could be only one thing. I tried to step forward, but Nirnasha's arm swung before me. The rest of our party gathered behind us, where we all silently relayed that Nirnasha could feel the vibrations of furry-clawed creatures ahead, hidden in the rocks above the entrance.

"Are they moving toward us?" Elior asked.

"No," Nirnasha whispered. "They are digging in, softly scratching, perhaps in anticipation."

"Well, they are in our way," Elior replied. "If we engage the Gloom Gnawers, most likely, the vibrations shall attract more unwanted guests."

"I would not be able to keep us hidden should that happen," Kalab said. "Not from the rodents nor anything else."

"It would seem we have a wall at our back to protect us," Cenobia interjected. "I think rousing other unwanted guests could work to our advantage. Gloom Gnawers are no allies of any creature down here."

I was surprised at Cenobia's response. However, I knew she was right. So did Elior. As Kalab was not controlling any of the atrocities, Cenobia's idea sparked a plan in Elior.

"We should set up a defensive position near that column," Elior said, pointing to one near the large opening with the glowing heat. "We shall be able to fire on the Gloom Gnawers from there and have a greater chance of defending ourselves from things charging us."

Once we were in position, I manifested several fireballs to light upon the rocks overlooking the entrance to our destination. Every Eastguard soldier took careful aim, and as the fire landed on the rocks, we all could see the gnawing faces of enormous rodents standing on their hind legs. They screeched as my fire clutched to their fur and set it ablaze, giving the Eastguard soldiers torches to see their targets. Elior lit up the entire cavern for us once our surprise had hit our enemy.

I am unsure if I felt it before anyone else, but I know many others were familiar with the chilling breeze that pokes at the back of your neck when a confident tiny man has drawn near. I turned to see Rumpelstilzchen standing at the passageway where we had just come.

Into the light stepped faceless creatures, one in particular, a much larger Shangore champion that glistened, covered in Mystic Silver dust. Then coming out of the glowing heat entrance marched hundreds of Gloom Gnawers, blocking the other way. The Eastguard soldiers had all but ceased firing, and so had I. The cavern lay silent, with every creature standing perfectly still. We could only hear the cackling laughter of the tiny man taunting us. I heard Elior's thoughts grow increasingly perplexed that Rumpelstilzchen had united the creatures against us.

In the next instant, Elior's voice connected with Nirnasha and Easton. He told Nirnasha to collapse the way we came while Easton and I cleared a path through the rodents so the others could get through. The tiny man shouted to kill us all, and every monster began charging us all at once. Nirnasha quickly reacted, breaking boulders into the passageway with ease. However, several Shangores had made it through, including the Shangore champion.

Easton had already begun his onslaught in what I came to call his "Impenetrable Incarnation," creating his skin to become metallically indestructible and his strength heightened to unknown properties. I hesitated to join him somehow, seeing the Shangore champion bearing down on my fellow MKR.

"Look out, Nirnasha!" I screamed.

The Shangore champion unleashed a vicious strike on him, sending Nirnasha flying and hitting the cavern wall further behind us. He gasped and coughed, trying to draw breath into his lungs. I knew I went against Elior's instructions, but I could not let Nirnasha go unassisted. I rushed toward him, hearing Bastian and the other Eastguard soldiers charge into the fray with Easton. Wild Willy let up on his shots as I passed by him. Cenobia, Meik, Garvish, and Bikarma did the same, following behind Bastian. I did not see Kalab or Elior anywhere near our position.

I reached the Shangore champion before he could get anywhere near Nirnasha again. I laid a bursting, continuous flame on the monster, making its six tentacle heads screech in agony. I could see the others had also reached me, so I widened the flame to fillet the flesh off their hides. Each one collapsed into a crispy corpse pile of bone and charred flesh remains, except for the Shangore champion. It was still writhing, but its skin would not melt off its frame. My strength began to fade in trying to keep up such a powerful manifestation.

Finally, I fell to my knees, exhausted but saw the Shangore's skin healing swiftly from my attempt to melt it. For a moment, I became terrified, seeing it rise as if nothing had happened. In an instant, rocks cracked open and encased all around it. The Shangore violently hit the formation, but it was no use.

"If you will not burn," I heard Nirnasha cry out behind me. "Then let us just squeeze you dry."

The encasing of rocks slowly began caving as if a hand tightening its grip. I turned to see Nirnasha propped up against the wall, still on the ground. I turned back toward the creature, now writhing in pain again as it was slowly crushed and its bones snapped. Its head, the only visible part in the rock mound, oozed out a dark azurish gel before I turned away, feeling ill to my stomach but more concerned to attend to my friend.

I crawled to him and placed my hands gently on his face. He felt colder than usual, and crimson dripped from the corners of his mouth as his breathing began to wheeze.

"This shall be my first time, I guess," he said. "What was it like for you?"

"Strange," I replied. "Almost like being born. But when you come back, whatever caused your death is repaired."

"Will you wait with me until I return?" Nirnasha asked. "Even though I know I shall, I am still scared to face it."

"I know what you mean," I answered, a tear escaping to run down my cheek. "Yes, I shall wait for you."

TWINS OF FORESIGHT

I watched Nirnasha's eyes roll back in his head as his breathing shortened, and he gasped his last from his crushed rib cage that likely pierced his lungs. And despite knowing he would return soon, my heart mourned his passing, pushing tears out of my eyes. For in Nirnasha's death, I felt sorrow for all those who faced their end someday.

Elior and Kalab were suddenly standing next to me. Rumpelstilzchen had escaped into an upper tunnel passageway, and Elior insisted we move quickly.

"I am not leaving him," I said to Elior. "I promised him I would wait."

"I shall stay with her," I heard Wild Willy volunteer from behind Elior.

Elior nodded.

"I am sorry I did not follow what you directed," I spoke up once Elior began walking away to join the others, knowing my actions aptly brought six Eastguardian soldiers to meet their end.

"You followed your heart," I heard his thoughts reply. "I shall not fault you for laying down your life to save a friend, even if it is another MKR. It is one of the few things that keep us connected to our humanity."

It took longer than expected, yet life returned to Nirnasha's body. Perhaps an hour had passed before I heard his ribs pop back into place, air shoot back into his lungs, and his senses return to him. I knew the feeling of regaining physical consciousness, as the nerves in your body fire off all at once, and your mind tries to comprehend where you were is unbearable. And in another moment, your muscles ache as they reset to find their strength to stand again. Watching it happen from the other side held a particular fascination, but nothing I would want to spend years of my life studying. I also remember not fearing death as much in my return, knowing it would be a feeling I could share now with Nirnasha.

Wild Willy helped him stand. Knowing the others were about an hour ahead of us, we did not waste time in catching up. Nirnasha looked like death had done him some good, as I had not seen him exert the stamina he presented as we found our stride. He kept pace in front of us, slowing only to sense the vibrations of our party. Nirnasha had become a finer tracker, and the vibrations through rock and soil heightened after his demise.

I had experienced death beforehand, yet I did not recall feeling any stronger when I awoke. However, it became the first time my endurance was tested in this fashion, and I realized I kept pace with Nirnasha without gasping for breath—peculiarly, neither did Wild Willy. I do not know if Nirnasha took notice, but I suspect that the man known as Wild Willy is not all he seems to be.

When we finally caught up with the rest, we traveled deeper and closer to the hot glowing mass. A spire of tunnels twisted us downward to at last reach a large opening with a wide bridge and superbly crafted archways of rock and metal, drawing our vision to the other side. There, a large iron door glowed with the glistening of Mystic Silver.

"Is that what I think it is?" Bastian asked.

"It certainly is," Meik spoke up. "I recognize a vault door when I see one."

"I thought we would be mining," Bastian interjected. "Looks like we will not have to work hard after all."

"Do not be so sure," Nirnasha said. "That door is most certainly enchanted. And it will not budge so easily."

"It will," Elior grinned. "Now that you are here."

I could see everyone appeared puzzled, and so did Nirnasha.

"I know everything about that door," Elior said. "I was the one who enchanted it long ago. There is no key or lock, password, or phrase to have it yield what it guards except for MKRs who can move it without opening it."

"I know no such spell," Easton said.

"The key is not just one spell," Elior explained, turning his gaze toward Nirnasha and me. "It must be two working together as one."

I peered down the long plummet from the bridge into molten earth and flame. I drew Nirnasha's attention to it. He heard my thoughts, but I sensed it would still be difficult. The two of us would have to work together, one harnessing the earth of molten rock and the other the fire it sparked. Nirnasha reached out and grasped my hand. I could feel the power of his magic surging through his thoughts and flesh. I knew he felt the same surge from me as we both began to try and lift the molten rock to us.

A pillar slowly churned upward, and the intensity of our combined power began to writhe our muscles and bones. I almost collapsed, but Nirnasha held tightly to me, keeping me upright. I felt faint, my vision blurring when the pillar of fire and earth drew close to the door. One more push of strength, and we would be able to hurl the liquid mass onto it. I remember screaming, feeling as if my insides were about to burst. Nirnasha still did not let me fall. The pillar splashed on the door, melting it swiftly along with part of the surrounding rocks.

I fell backward. Yet Nirnasha still held me up. I caught my reflection in his eyes, strangely glowing in a viridescent hue before all went dark. When I awoke, I was surrounded by bars and coins of gold. There were gems I had never seen, ancient weapons and armor piled high in every direction. A gentle hand came across my forehead with a dry cloth. Cenobia was caressing off the cold sweat. Nirnasha knelt on the other side of me, still holding my hand.

"You waited for me to wake, so I believe it is polite to do likewise," he said.

"How is it you did not pass out as I did?" I muttered.

"I am not sure. But I have a suspicion this has something to do with it," Nirnasha replied, holding up his Mystic Silver enchanted prosthetic. "I saw my arm begin to glow while I could feel your strength waning, yet mine did not. I was… growing stronger."

"We need to rejoin the others," Cenobia interjected. "They are waiting for us."

Both helped me sluggishly find my footing. I remember my bones feeling brittle for the first couple of steps, as if every fiber of my being had been drained of strength. Every nerve in my body began firing through my flesh like needles, almost like I had died, yet I had not seen the ethereal.

I did not fall behind the others as we made our way down even further, spiraling toward a darker abyss, barely catching the light of the molten flow beneath.

Deeper still, until the molten light was no more, but only the flicker of Cenobia's lantern, giving us enough vision to see the ever-whirling steps coming up to meet our feet.

We touched an unvarying rock surface, with a large tunnel opening leading into more flickering torchlights. I could see several stacked piles of glowing ore of Mystic Silver being loaded into soldiers' satchels. With fourteen soldiers and each one able to carry at least 20 mass units, we would have more than enough to meet our demand. Even Bastian shoved nearly double the ore chunks into his back satchel. Wild Willy, Meik, Cenobia, Nirnasha, Garvish, Bikarma, Easton, and I filled our satchels with what we could carry. To our estimation, our party had the ability to carry out over 312 mass units. That would leave 103 mass units for our purposes and over 209 mass units for the emperor.

I noticed Elior standing in the middle of the vault room, lit up the shadows with tiny orbs of light, and staring suspiciously at Kalab, who also began drawing my qualms. The Dark MKR appeared to be searching the piles of jewels and chests for something. I drew near Elior, who turned to me. I could hear his thoughts that we needed to begin moving the Mystic Silver ore out of the vault. Yet before I could pass the word along, I turned to see a tiny man blocking our escape. I found it frightening that I had not felt the chill of his presence, but there he stood. Everyone gathered around Elior, Easton, and Bastian, carefully watching Rumpelstilzchen. Kalab had finally played his hand.

"Where is it, brother?!" He spat. "Do you think you can hide it from me?"

"The answer to that must have a bargain attached," Elior replied. "I knew all along we never stopped playing."

The vault echoed with a low cackling of the tiny man. Kalab expressed his amusement with a slight grin and began playing along.

"Very well," Kalab said. "It is rare for you to catch me at a disadvantage. Yet I suppose I can deduce what you desire."

Elior motioned for him to proceed with his deductions.

"I could destroy each one of you," Kalab boasted. "But then I would not find out what I wish to know. However, I know you want all the Mystic Silver carried back to the emperor to fulfill your contracted obligations. I cannot allow that.

If you wish to bargain with me, you must also choose to betray the emperor."

"I thought as much," Elior did not hesitate to reply. "I was prepared for such a deed long before I entered the darkness."

"After all these years." Kalab scoffed. "You still remain a delightful opponent. I tell you what—in the efforts of good sportsmanship, I shall allow you to choose nine thralls who shall walk out of this room."

I did not understand the Dark MKR's frame of reference. Though, it did not appear to phase Elior. The MKR of Light went first and pointed to Easton. Then he followed on to Wild Willy, Meik, Cenobia, Garvish, Bikarma, Bastian, Nirnasha, and finally, he pointed to me. With his glance, I could hear Elior whisper to my mind. It was a plea to retreat to the surface swiftly. I also saw his eyes turn to Nirnasha with a thought, but I could not hear it over my chest thumping.

In an instant, shadow creatures popped up from the dark floor and stood behind each Eastguard soldier. With one swift motion, they fell all fourteen.

"The rest of you may go now." Kalab sighed. "Go on. Your meaningless existence awaits you above."

Each one of us slowly passed by the tiny man, who gave each of us a snarky grin, trying to intimidate us, yet oddly winked at me.

"You may proceed with telling me what I want to know," I could hear Kalab say to Elior as we exited the room. I remained connected to Elior's eyes to see the outcome.

"Not until every one of them reaches the top of the stairs and safely crosses the bridge," Elior replied. "I know there is an ambush waiting. Just make sure the 'thralls' have a decent head start before you begin hunting them."

Kalab laughed. "You, brother. So clever."

"We are not getting any older," Elior said, making me feel like he was stalling. "I would not mind hearing a bit about what you have been up to since I last saw you."

"Always the same," Kalab replied with a conniving scowl.

I began telling everyone to pick up the pace. A third presence stepped out of the shadows with Kalab and Rumpelstilzchen. I could feel Wendigo's spell of hunger began to reach for me. Then I could see him appear through Elior's eyes.

"Hurry!" Nirnasha shouted. I knew he felt the anxious pull of Wendigo's hunger as well.

At last, the darkness of the spiral stairway became penetrated by the light of the molten earth and fire. Our next steps swiftly carried us across the bridge, where everyone coughed to catch their breath except for the three remaining MKRs and Wild Willy. Nirnasha stepped forward, bringing his arms high above his shoulders. The ground began to quake, and I watched the bridge crumble.

"Stop!" I screamed. "What are you doing?!"

"Elior does not want us followed," was all I could hear over the roar of splitting rock.

I searched my mind again for Elior's sight. Easton and Nirnasha both grabbed hold of me. But I could still see the MKR of Light staring down all three as the dust from the collapsing stairway tumbled down to seal off the only means of escape.

"What is this?" Kalab sneered.

"Your treasure left with one of them," Elior grinned.

"Of course, it did," Kalab scoffed. "I knew one of your pupils had to be holding your little book. Yet I find it is much more fun this way. You think trapping yourself as the martyr while the rest of your thralls all perish before they even know what hits them—a tasteful end, I think. My brother, this vault is the perfect place to keep your body trapped forever in darkness."

"You have indeed been having trouble with one of your snares," Elior interjected. "Rumpelstilzchen has divulged much. So much, in fact, that he has named his price. And I have delivered."

Kalab's face slipped into a frown with deep lines of confusion as Rumpelstilzchen stepped forward, standing next to Elior. The MKR of Light pulled out a glowing crimson oculus, radiating immense power. He handed it to the tiny man who cackled vilely, feeling mighty sneaky in his betrayal.

"Traitor!" Kalab spat.

"Not traitor," Rumpelstilzchen impertinently replied. "Trader. I shall be free from you and become my own. No more listening to you whimper about your brother and your plans. With this, I control the very hearts of man while your power diminishes. Right now, you can feel your power on me weaken, not just because of my will, but because I hold the Oculus Stone of Teallach Tine—the Hearth Fire of the realms!"

"You know not how to wield it!" Kalab screamed as if the stone was causing agony within his veins.

"I shall learn," the tiny man roared back. "But even now, with the power it gives me just by being in my possession, I am rid of you!"

The tiny man disappeared, fading into the dark until he completely vanished. I recalled our last night in the Ye Downs Hotel, where I remembered seeing Elior whispering to the imp, something I had been cut off from. Yet now, I knew the MKR had struck a bargain with him, making us believe Nirnasha's riddle about his snare had sufficed to keep the Ironclad safe. The bargain had concluded, leaving Kalab dropping to one knee as if something had suddenly been ripped from his soul.

"I have one more surprise for you, brother," Elior announced, pulling his drill bit guns from their holsters. "The bits I need were already forged before we came."

"You wanted to be trapped here!" Kalab gasped. "You tricked me."

"No, brother," Elior replied. "I bested you."

"Kill him," Kalab shouted to Wendigo, who suddenly emerged. Kalab hurried back into the shadows while Elior pulled back the hammers of his drill bit guns, his fingers slowly beginning to squeeze the triggers.

Undoubtedly I was elated by how Elior had played everything out; however, I pitied the MKR of Light, having pursued his obsession to the point of trapping himself down in the dark with the abomination and his brother. I had to believe there was more to Elior's plan than being a sacrifice. Yet perhaps he did not do such a thing out of fixation alone. Maybe the words he spoke to me before about laying down your life for a friend held a far greater meaning than I can fathom. Somehow, Elior believed in us, knowing the bounty of Mystic Silver would serve a greater purpose than him becoming lost in the dark. And somehow, he believed he would find his way back out.

He stood still with only twelve shots as Wendigo charged him and then unleashed the drill bits from his gun—none missed. The bits ripped clean through Wendigo's armored skin, sending the monster to fall flat on its back. Elior's final two shots were at point-blank range, standing with a smirk over the abomination's corpse and sending the last two bits straight through its head.

I could see the light of Elior's orbs fade in the gloom. Soon, the only light remaining became the glow of the Mystic Silver drill bits that had ricocheted off the walls after sailing through Wendigo's body and the rest of the ore we left behind. I could hear Elior's footsteps moving toward each drill bit, picking them up and loading them back into his guns. I could only hear his breathing as he held the last one in his hand, standing and waiting in the depths of the Unlight.

A sudden surge of fear, foreign in every way, snapped into Elior's mind. I could feel it, and it ripped me away from connecting to his eyes. Just before, a vision of a shadowy creature took his sight away from mine. Its eyes were mystic midnight yet glowed with a hue of crimson, a large abomination that held an enigmatic familiarity.

"We have to go back," I suddenly halted. Easton and Nirnasha were somewhat astounded by my sudden burst of strength. Yet I repeated myself. "We have to go back!"

"Elior told me we cannot," Easton said. "He told me no matter what, we need to return to the surface."

"He told me the same," Nirnasha reasoned.

"We cannot," I tried to explain. "Something ripped me from his mind, something with immense power."

"Elior knows what he's doing," Meik tried to reassure me with a whisper. "He told me where to meet with him again."

"He will not come," I tried to explain. "I am not sure what has happened, but something has taken him. We have to go back."

"Lass!" Meik shouted and then brought his volume back to a whisper. "Listen to me. We cannot even get to him. It will take months to try and find another route to find him. Elior has survived longer than this in the wilds of the Unlight. He has given us specific instructions."

"I cannot let him stay down here alone!"

"Aagneya, we are about to be ambushed," Nirnasha pointed out. "We will see him again on the surface."

I glared at Nirnasha but knew he was right. There was an ambush waiting for us. Admittedly, I foolishly sprinted ahead into the next cavern, where I could see Gloom Gnawers waiting in thick masses, suddenly charging me. When the others had finally caught up to me, I already burned holes through their lines. Just beyond the Rattus were Shangores that had broken through the cave-in that Nirnasha had performed just before he experienced death for the first time.

Easton took no time dawning his impenetrable incarnation armor and barreled through the rest of the cave-in, which I foresaw in the first place. What I did not foresee awaited us on the other side—an entire army of Shangores, shoulder-to-shoulder, blocking our path in the cavern halls that led back to the surface.

I wasted no time, continuing to burn my way out, pulsating in an enraged exhilaration, racing through my blood, pumping magic into my core. Indisputably, it was my fury and the Mystic Silver I carried with me. Now I understood why Elior sought to get us our own.

Nirnasha's power flowed with the same ease. He pulled rocks from the cavern walls like paper and rolled them through heaping masses of Shangores. He even put up an eddying shield of stones around himself. The straggling Shangores that escaped the massive boulders hurled at them were greeted with blunt force from one of the rocks in his shield, knocking them to the ground and crushing them beneath. The rest of our band then took it upon themselves to finish off any wounded Gloom Gnawers or Shangores that lay helpless. I caught a glimpse of all who appeared to be enjoying the ease of staying in the rear, effortlessly killing our foes. Bastian and Meik laughed together as if they had been drinking, which I believe is worth notation. Because weirdly enough, we were all having fun. The fear of the Unlight had faded from my mind, and in that time, we became inebriated in the shedding of monster blood.

Easton, too, showed no signs of stopping as an indestructible force. I doubt any Shangore head was left uncrushed who faced him. But while my fellow MKRs used brute force to open our way, I decided to switch gears and take a different approach. I summoned the spirits of fire through Dancing Desire, wholly astonished to see how many came alive in my summons this time. It is strange to see even one depiction of myself in a fiery essence, let alone twenty. The battle dance elegantly shifted back and forth from cutting monsters in half with lines of fire to heaping flames upon them until they melted into cinders. With each one's demise, I could feel a tremendous increase in magical power within me, suddenly setting my entire frame ablaze and drawing Nirnasha's attention toward me.

"Show off," he teased.

We fought through the halls of the Unlight. The dramatic shift in the numbers of the Shangores and Gloom Gnawers began significantly thinning. Many were running from us until none were in sight. We could have continued to trek onward, but it was not possible with the others. Even Wild Willy showed signs of fatigue. The other reason we could not continue was that we did not know which direction to head.

Nirnasha covered our entire party with a dome of rocks formed to blend in with the rest of the cavern walls. He and I sat beside one another, with Easton just across from us while the others slept. Nirnasha was putting the finishing touches on the dome, minor cracks ventilating the air in and out. I kept my eyes on him, and he caught my gaze.

"Show off," I teased.

He smiled at me. I could hear his thoughts laughing along with my own. My mind quickly turned from laughter to a sigh, worrying about Elior. I felt Nirnasha gently grasp my hand, beckoning me to tell him again about my vision. The shadow creature I saw filled my mind, and I watched Nirnasha's eyes expand, trying to piece together what I saw. We invited Easton to join our private conversation, where he could see my vision. Easton's immediate response surmised that it had to be a creature of the ethereal, just by its appearance. We did not doubt his theory.

Nirnasha swiftly switched the conversation in our minds and alerted us to the footsteps he felt. They were familiar to him and known to be villainous.

"Kalab is here. He is stopped—he is staring directly at us."

Easton and I did not move. We could not hear any slight shuffling of feet shifting along the cavern floor, but Nirnasha swore he felt him. He informed us of Kalab's movements, describing them as if he were searching for something. Perhaps it was our whereabouts. The Dark MKR may have turned toward us, but he soon picked up the pace, traveling farther away. I thought it might be a trick, but Nirnasha reassured me that Kalab's steps were fading.

"I can sense where he stepped," Nirnasha's thoughts began getting excited. "We could follow him to reach the surface."

"I fear that is where he is heading," Easton replied. "And Elior is not there to challenge him."

When the time came for the others to wake, we set out cautiously. Gradually, we picked up the pace, reaching some familiar tunnels. Although, everything can start looking the same when you have spent much time in the Unlight. Our supplies were beginning to run low, which did not affect the MKRs. However, with the weight of the Mystic Silver on the backs of our other comrades, we began resting more often. All we could hope for was to return without facing more casualties.

At last, sunlight pierced our vision, and we returned to the bitter frost winds of the Deadlands, getting ready for another three days journey on foot back to Kirshan Outpost. Yet we were met by blurry shadows blocking the sun as soon as we exited. Elite soldiers of Eastguard's army stood at the ready, surrounding us and aiming more than six rows deep aiming buzzsaw rifles. Neither of us wanted to admit it, but we knew betrayal had greeted us on our return.

Takato Pure Bone stepped forward as bravely as he could. He hid it well, but I could see he was fearful. He demanded that we hand over the Mystic Silver we had recovered.

"What of our contract?" I shouted. "We have retrieved enough for our share and plenty more for you."

"Due to the higher interests of the Eastguard Empire, it is null and void," he shouted arrogantly. "Either relinquish what is rightfully the emperors, or you shall perish where none will mourn you.”

We were all surprised to hear a drill bit gun go off. Wild Willy stood with one of his pointing straight out, smoking from one single shot. Every soldier's eyes followed down their lines to just one soldier suddenly falling to his knees. I saw Wild Willy give a taunting smooch and a wink, making me nervously laugh. Somehow, the shock lasted a few moments longer before Takato shouted a curse for defying him. Nirnasha took that moment to yank boulders swiftly from the ground to surround us with cover before Takato finally gave the order to fire.

Sawblades ricocheted off the rocks as we kept low, unholstering our drill bit guns to return fire. I sent a wave of thoughts to Nirnasha to see if he could raise more rocks from the ground to make our coverage higher than the Eastguardians. The ground began shifting beneath our feet, and we were suddenly on higher ground than Takato's forces.

“By this betrayal, the Pure Bones have declared war on the Raven Caste Clan!” Bastian shouted.

“Then I assume we have an ally in Eastguard,” I replied. He nodded.

Wild Willy timed another window to get in another shot. Another soldier went down from his pinpoint accuracy. Garvish and Bikarma joined Meik, firing out from our left flank, while Bastian, Wild Willy, and Cenobia guarded our right. Easton had resorted to using his firearm as well.

“You know, eventually, we will have to use magic to end this,” I told Meik.

“True,” he replied. “But there's no harm in having a bit of a rest and some fun first. Let's show Dejan and Takato they picked the wrong day to be the hole of an arse.”

I was not surprised by his answer. Being in a firefight stood as a sign to Meik and his crew that they were embracing life.

“I shall second that,” Bastian exclaimed. “No prisoners!”

Nirnasha did not appear to be in a playful mood. I could hear his thoughts were tired of the pompous actions of Eastguard. Giant roots began to reach from the ground like enormous tentacles, slithering as silent serpents and working their way to deathly grip soldiers. The terror on their faces still haunts me. The roots wrapped around many, squeezing them so tightly that their screams went muffled within a blink, leaving only the sounds of their throats being crushed. Other roots held their captives fast, while another slithered into their mouth, eradicating their victim's gasps for air in a more painful demise.

I turned to see Nirnasha's eyes swirling fiercely in glowing viridescent hues. He looked at me, and he could sense I was truly petrified. His intense stare calmed, and the roots eased their advance as every soldier broke into a full retreat despite Takato's threats to kill them all for their cowardice—he, himself, outrunning most of them.

Nirnasha sat back, and I could hear his thoughts were full of rage, oddly more toward himself.

"I should have gone back with you," Nirnasha echoed, his heart pulsing with sorrow and guilt. "We should not have left Elior behind. I am sorry, Aagneya."

"I do not blame you," I replied.

"I am scared," he admitted. "Kalab terrifies me."

"Me too," I admitted aloud.

"I do not want to be scared anymore," Nirnasha relayed, keeping his words still silent.

I can understand why Nirnasha held such ire. Despite the might of our powers combined, we knew we were not strong enough to face Kalab together. Easton had listened to our echoes back and forth. He agreed even the three of us could not defeat Kalab with our current strength. We could surmise by the tone of his inner monologue he was just as fearful as we were.

I could sense killing monsters felt much different to Nirnasha than slaying humans. I find it unusual that the monsters we face are often ones that appear more like us than the abominations found in the Unlight. I became more fearful of what Nirnasha would become because of this—I remember hugging him to try and steady his nerves. Hearing his heart beating transmitted the rhythm of his spirit's melody, one I had not heard before but unforgettable—a crescendo like the roar of machines plowing earth at the beginning of a new dawn, shrouded in an unknown chaos that reached for me. For some reason, it was beautiful. And I suddenly realized I held love within myself, escalating for him. He was not tuned to my thoughts, but I hoped he felt the same.

"Best we start moving," Meik spoke up. "I'm not sure how we will get our supplies and return to Ye and Poe or even how we will be able to carry the Mystic Silver without drawing attention to ourselves."

"I have a way," Nirnasha sighed. He moved away from my grasp but caught my hand to turn me to follow him. "Head for those trees over there."

"You mean the forest off on the horizon?" Garvish inquired sarcastically, showing the old Garvish I remember.

"Follow him," Meik shoved him onward.

We were in the Deadlands, along the border of Eastguard, moving even further out of its territory. The landscape could transform at any moment, or something stranger could happen. The latter met us. We could see they were moving as we drew closer to the trees. Nirnasha heard my cautionary emotions rushing through my mind but spoke aloud to reassure everyone that everything would be fine.

Routinely, Dendros' behavior is to migrate constantly. So, they can be found in various locations within the Deadlands. Their species are not usually passive, as they always feel threatened. They can be any type of tree, typically remaining in the migration family with their kind. It is almost impossible to tell a Dendro apart from a regular tree until it begins to move. Until now, we had only viewed them from a distance when we first began. Now, they were like living creatures with souls of their own and did not appear like abominations at all. Nirnasha dropped my hand and told us to remain where we were, nonchalantly approaching the creatures. They had beautiful, blooming foliage, and I spied fresh fruit from their branches, which somehow turned on my hunger.

"How goes it?" I echoed to Nirnahsa.

"They are wondering how a human can speak to them," he replied aloud for us all to hear. "I told them I am a Master Keeper, which they are aware of what that is, and I mentioned we know Elior. They seemed pleased to know that for some reason."

"What else?" I asked, seeing one Dendro had stepped forward and appeared to communicate with Nirnasha through a series of rustling and handlike gestures.

"They want to know what kind of MKR I am," he replied. "I told them my power has much to do with the ground and timber, which is probably why I know how to communicate well with them. They seem not to like that as much."

"How do they know Elior?" Meik interjected.

"They know him because he has migrated with them many times," Nirnasha answered. "When they need water, he helped them dig for it."

"Could he have not just used his magic?" Bikarma questioned.

"Perhaps," Nirnasha replied. "Except they do not care much for magic."

Nirnasha further clarified our need to return Ye and Poe far to the south. In his bargaining, he asked them to escort us, feed us, and even carry us and our Mystic Silver. In exchange, we would find and do all the digging for water that they needed. Reluctantly, they agreed.

Every bite of fruit I plucked from their canopy held a succulent flavor, sweet and thirst-quenching, yet not sticky, entirely unlike anything I have ever eaten. Cenobia joined me immediately as we settled in the high branches of the Dendro that carried us. Meik and Nirnasha sat below us, leaning against the larger branches. Its bark felt smooth but held a firmness like armor. Its long strides kept a level pace like a cozy rocking chair, moving back and forth. Then, I sensed a heaviness pulling my eyelids down and leaning my head back.

I awoke to see Nirnasha sitting on a low branch and a large pool of muddy water beneath him. It stretched out in a wide diameter where every Dendro stood with their roots digging deep into the soil. I made my way down the branches, doing my best not to wake Cenobia or Meik. They were in a profound sleep, seemingly spellbinding. Nirnasha, though, heard me coming.

A soft, warm breeze touched my face as I sat beside him, and I saw the wind frolic across the tall grass under a moonlit sky. The stars felt closer and brighter like blazing lanterns, spectators overlooking a majestic show of nocturnal splendor. I turned my head toward Nirnasha, who locked his eyes on the sight before us.

"It is good to be out of the dark," he uttered. "I want to always remember this night should I be tempted to fall away from the light."

"You are not evil," I assured him. "You may enjoy feeling powerful, but your heart longs to be at peace."

"How do you know my heart?" He asked.

"I felt it," I replied. "I have heard its melody."

"Then, you would know I long for another thing as well," Nirnasha said, turning his gaze into mine. His hand slowly reached out and caressed the back of my neck, and then he began to draw me closer. I could feel his lips press against mine before they were even there. My heart soared, sensing his blood rush as we kissed passionately without holding back. We became so that we forgot we were sitting in a tree. And suddenly, we both slipped off the branch, splashing into the muddy water below.

I awoke with a groggy yawn and sat up as if waking from being knocked unconscious. I looked downward, seeing Nirnasha sitting on the low branch beneath the large pool of muddy water. All was as it was when I held visions of Nirnasha and me. However, when I sat down on the branch next to him, the words from my vision were not the first he spoke.

"I think the Dendros are beginning to like my magic," he said with a large grin. "I can feel the water in the ground. I direct them to stand in a spot, then gently open the earth to let the water rise to meet their roots."

"Why does it look like everyone has a spell cast on them?" I asked. "I can feel the magic radiating from them that keeps them dead asleep."

"I believe that would be the Dendros," Nirnasha replied, continuing to explain what he had learned about them, at least this family of Dendros. "The magic particles they emit are also found in their fruit, which has a high concentration of sleep toxin. It will not kill anything, but you may not wake up for a long while."

"How is it you are not asleep?" I asked. "I watched you eat more fruit than me." "They asked me the same thing," he answered, holding back the giddiness in his tone. "I do not feel its effects. I guess it has something to do with my power."

"Most likely," I concurred. "I would like to save some fruit to study its effects further."

"Already on top of it." Nirnasha grinned.

We sat for a while, staring at the night sky. I hid away my thoughts about my hallucination dreams from the fruit, but I could not hide the desire I felt.

"It is good to be out of the dark," I uttered. "I want to always remember this night should I be tempted to fall away from the light."

Nirnasha met my gaze. I thought he would begin to reach out for me, to pull me in and meet the embrace of a passion-filled kiss. His lips began to quiver, but instead, laughter roared out from his mouth.

"That toxin must be messing with your head pretty bad, Aagneya," he laughed.

So, I shoved him off the branch. He plunged into the muddy water below but quickly found his footing.

"What did you do that for?" He scowled, raking mud from his face.

"Sorry," I replied, meeting him with a scowl of my own. "The toxins must be messing with my head."

ESOTERIC ENLIGHTENMENT

Lasair soon reverberated a melody within me, manifesting a spell to burn away the Dendro's sleep toxin before I fell under its influence. Not only did the fruit contain it, but the creatures housed the toxin in the budding flowers upon their limbs, shaking free pollen for us to inhale with each step they took. Her spell strengthened quickly, and I could hear Lasair's melody sing even from Easton's soul, which soon made us both immune.

Nirnasha continued to examine the fruit of the Dendros, discovering while it may be toxic, their fruit held extensive bio-mystical properties that generated a slowing of the digestive process—meaning the fruit would continue to feed and hydrate over a period of approximately five to six months, should one remain under the toxin's influence—the very reason why the others remained in slumber, and were in no danger of starvation or dehydration.

In the days that followed, I began spending more of my time higher up in our Dendros' canopy, surveying the Deadlands that seemed so easily navigated by the creatures. In some instances, the landscape would shift, becoming a barren waste, and then it would become a lush grassland cluttered with forestation. The more I surveyed the Deadlands, the more I could not help but feel something was amiss. Much of the terrain transformed every few hours, but not with what I would describe as a few hiccups. Strangely, I closed one eye by chance, and a vast forest appeared before my vision. I opened my other eye, and the forest disappeared.

I turned my gaze upward, not fully staring into the sun, but sensed an aura of intense power emanating from its light. Could it be? Knowing Elior, I do not understand why I doubted it for a moment. The MKR of Light had most certainly cast a spell on the sun or at least on the light springing from it. My revelation reached the thoughts of my MKR companions, who turned their attention upon me.

"You jest?" Nirnasha's tone held more awe than disbelief.

"That would explain how Elior navigated the Deadlands so effortlessly," I replied aloud. "The illusion he created does not affect him."

"But how does that help us?" Easton asked. "How can we navigate it without Elior?"

"Try closing one eye." I grinned.

The other two gasped when the forest suddenly appeared on the horizon. Promptly, the Dendros turned toward it. When we reached the edge to enter it, we could see everything with both eyes, as if the vast trees suddenly sprouted before us.

"The spell uses depth perception and changes the refractions of the sun's light. I am sure that is how it works!" I exclaimed.

I shuddered at the thought should any kingdom learn of this secret. Of course, how often does one close one eye? Even should one do so, it is most likely one would believe the Deadlands were playing tricks on their sight. I could not help feeling that Elior had planned this, and even still, I felt as if he wanted us to seek something out within his illusion. Knowing this secret, we could explore the unknown depths that separated the three kingdoms. I could not fathom the possibilities of what we could find. A gurgling howl broke my deliberations. The attention of the Dendros and the other MKRs were drawn to it as well, which began to turn louder and soon hailed an entire horde of growls.

We first distinguished their eyes and only swift glimpses of their dullish stone fur. Our encounter with Reverie Hounds on our first journey was brief yet frightening. The musculature of those that now followed us appeared much more massive than the ones before, and their exposed spines were considerably hardened, breaking outward to armor their legs. Their eyes peered from the forest's shadows in a crimson hue as they darted in and out of sight.

The Dendros huddled close, with the larger ones shaping the outer rim as we marched on. I could smell the rain before it began falling from the forest's canopy, with honey-like stickiness, and the scent drove the hounds into a frenzy. Suddenly, several lurched out from the dark and snatched a large Dendro by, what I assume would be its ankles, brought it to the ground, and tore it to pieces. The screams of a dying Dendro are nothing I would wish anyone to hear, nor do I desire to describe. Its limbs were ripped from its trunk, a light crimson solution gushing forth from its body, and swiftly consumed by the ravaging hounds.

"They say it is like this every time they march," Nirnasha spoke. "One gives up their life for the rest. The old protect the young. It keeps the hounds from pursuing them for a while in case not all hounds get their fill."

"What is that liquid coming out of it?" I asked.

"They call it life," Nirnasha replied. "But if it is sustenance for those beasts, then my guess would be it is more like blood."

"Is there something we can do to help them?" I sounded more desperate than I anticipated.

"Maybe another day," Easton stated. "We need to keep moving."

The Dendros never broke stride, moving through the darkness of the forest. After a time, we reached a clearing, and I saw bright fires of industry with steam and smoke rising. We were near the fortified city of Ugnis Ro of Eastguard. I could see its famous glistening towers, coated in the enchantments of Mystic Silver, believed to be indestructible, proving the city tremendously vigilant of the land and skies along the kingdom's border. The towers climbed ever so distant into the skies, yet I ducked into the canopy of the Dendro, keeping only part of my head and eyes fixed on them. Whatever enchantments they generated, I somehow sensed their vision reached further than I perceived. The city's light still peeked through, as if reaching out for us, as we trekked into the covering of trees again and then dissipated from the sight of the towers.

We moved out into a clearing several days later. In the distance, I saw what I believed could only be Vlok, the mines of Eastguard. Prisoners of Eastguard were sent there to work until their sentence was complete. The mines were surrounded by high, wooden spiked barricades, long razor-edged wire, and anything else to prevent people from escaping. Wairships were landing to empty their cargo, whether supplies or prisoners, I could not tell which. Again, we heard howling. I raced down the Dendro. The herd of walking flora had ceased, waiting for another to be taken.

"This will not happen again," I spat, igniting a flame in my hand.

"Put it out!" Nirnasha urged. "We cannot risk giving away our position. I have a better way."

I knew Nirnasha was right. Though I hesitated and huffed my frustration, I went to stand behind him. He stepped out and away from the herd of Dendro as the Reverie Hounds appeared. This time, the sticky rain fell upon us all like a mist.

The hounds appeared confused by such a tiny morsel standing out and alone from the rest. Yet they did not leap at Nirnasha. They only peered him up and down until one, much larger than the rest, came forth, placing my wits in shock to hear it speak.

"You are either stupid or powerful," the hound's voice held a malevolent snarl. "Which is it, I wonder?"

Roots sprang upward and captured several hounds, entrapping and yanking them to the ground. The hound pack leader turned its head to and fro to see what had befallen its followers.

"I can kill you all easy enough," Nirnasha replied.

Without hesitation, the hound leader leaped at Nirnasha, only to fall flat on its belly, as roots had stealthily snatched its hind legs. Before it could move, more roots sprang up and held it tightly to the soil, allowing Nirnasha to approach its snarling, muzzled snout.

"You will find another food source, or I shall call them over to stomp you into the ground."

"Do so then," the hound managed to muffle out. "You have sentenced us to starve."

"What do you mean?" Nirnasha demanded.

"What food does the land provide except these? We are constantly at war with other packs, guarding what preciously sustains us. But we cannot hunt anything else. For nothing else satisfies our hunger."

"We should be rid of these filthy hounds," I interjected. "Let us slay all of them!"

"That is not wise," Nirnasha replied. "I hear this from the Dendro's melody." He turned to face the pack of living trees, looking on as if grief-stricken.

"What else do they say?" I asked.

"I am told the hounds are essential. They bring fear to those who would carry ruin to the Deadlands. If the hounds were gone, they believe our kind would war and destroy the land as we did long ago."

Another great, old Dendro stepped out from the herd and moved past the hounds. Nirnasha stepped back into my reach. With great dismay, he released the hounds. Off into the distance went snarls and howls to chase down the willing Dendro that gave up its life.

"I cannot deny the logic," Nirnasha said. "Without fear of monsters, our kind would war to gain control of the land."

"Sometimes the only solution is not pretty," Easton said. "Our kind often wars no matter what."

Wild Willy, Meik, Cenobia, Garvish, Bikarma, and Bastian Raven Caste all awoke two days after the Dendros had left us near the Eastguard border. It would take us about a week or so to walk into Ye's harbor. I directed any questions they had to Easton or Nirnasha as I enjoyed watching them try and explain the last few months of our journey. Meik appeared the least amused that he remained knocked out for so long by a sleep toxin. Still, I teased him that at least it was quiet.

Darby Krokkett and Reggie Gusel were still aboard the Ironclad, but we soon learned Kassy Bones had not returned to the boat for over a month. Meik refused to leave her behind. And we spent another week searching Ye and Poe—time I believe we did not have. However, knowing her appetites better than anyone, Cenobia finally located her in a red-light district in Poe, just beneath the catwalks of what is known as the Glamour Heights. Kassy was weak and covered in filth I can only describe as potent excrement. Her fix streamed through her blood like venom, and a fever held tightly to her skin. She had no clothes to cover her, completely stripped and left to perish. Doubtfully, she was robbed sober. Cenobia had found Kassy like this once before, practically on the brink of death due to self-destruction.

That was the first time I had ever seen Meik shed tears. It felt as if he had just found his daughter in the gutter. He scooped her up in his arms while Cenobia found a vendor to purchase a blanket to wrap around her. Kassy held despair in her soul. I could sense it immensely—an abused orphan, a childhood filled with provocative trauma. Time and again, Meik and Cenobia had brought her back from the brink of her calamities, hoping she would get better. But she remained the rebel, angry at the world, which turned inward many times to herself. Her despair now placed us in a dangerous position as our trek back to the Ironclad would not be easy.

Eastguard soldiers arrived, patrolling the streets, almost abruptly climbing out of the shadows and undoubtedly hunting us. Taking several back alleys and doing our best to stay hidden in the crowds, we finally reached the edge of the docks only to find the Ironclad and its crew in a standoff against a large force of Eastguardian troops further down the pier. I could have cast fire upon them all, but I would have put civilians at risk if the entire wooden dock became engulfed. I reached out to the minds of Nirnasha and Easton, letting them know our location. Moments later, the Ironclad steamed up and began to move out into the waters.

To my dismay, I recognized Marilla Baostin, the MKR of Water, after seeing her once through Elior's eyes. She confidently strolled in on our flank. Liquid began spurting up from underneath the docks, ripping the boards and foundation to pieces. We were blocked from moving at all. I did not hold back my instincts, conjured a fireball the size of my chest, and hurled it toward her. Water swiftly sprang up in front of her and drowned the fireball into steam.

By now, the Eastguard soldiers knew our location and were firing at us, and the Ironclad that moved toward our position kept a covering fire for us, sending a few soldiers to their demise. Meik and Cenobia stayed low with Kassy, with the only cover for us being a couple of wine barrels, while I did my best to delay Marilla's approach. Yet my every attempt could not get through her reflexes as she doused my flames. Then I felt the earth tremble and rift. The ground beneath the dock waters ripped open, and Eastguard soldiers began falling into the cracks. The ground sprang up and slammed into Marilla like a landslide, sweeping her away in a river of mud and sand, coming to a sudden halt at the base of Ye's dock wall near the public elevators.

I turned toward the Ironclad, seeing Nirnasha standing on the upper deck, his eyes still glowing a viridescent hue. However, my smile faded as I peered down at Meik holding Cenobia in his arms. Kassy was still unconscious, but Cenobia had expired in the fray. I had not noticed. My eyes realized her demise much sooner than my mind as tears poured down my face, but my thoughts could not believe she was taken from us. Two sawblades had pierced her face, one in her cheek and the other directly above her left eye. Meik also had sawblades stuck in him, one in his left shoulder and another in his right. That is when I realized the agony in my side came from sawblades that had shot through the barrels we hid behind.

Staring down, I noticed a sawblade had pierced my left ribs, undoubtedly slashing through a couple. Two more had sailed into my thigh on the same side. One more had plummeted deep into my chest. My breathing quickly shortened, and my vision grew increasingly dim. I fell back and only remembered sable arms catching me before I awoke in the ethereal knowing death had reached me a second time. Lasair was there to greet me.

"They have lit a candle for you," she said. "I can hear its melody. But it is quite the risk to reach it."

She brought me to the shore's edge, the waters filled with distant echoes and impenetrable shadows.

"Do not follow the echoes," she explained. "Do not look down. Your feet can walk upon the waves as if solid ground, but should you fall under their spell, you will be lost forever."

"What are they?" I pressed for more of an answer.

"They are 'The Forgotten,' much like mortal souls once," she elaborated. "Yet they no longer resemble what they once were. They have become like wild things—untamed, imprisoned, drowning in their despair forever."

"This place feels empty to me," I said. "I feel as though you purposely brought me here."

"I did," Lasair replied. "If you are to be snared with me, your mind must grow stronger and your heart greatly steadfast."

"Are you afraid I shall follow Suzerain Efah one day?" I asked.

"He is formidable," Lasair admitted. "Yet he is not the prodigious reason. Go now. Pass my trial, and gain wisdom from it. The longer you remain, the more likely you shall become lost."

The melody of the flame moved farther from me. Lasair rushed me out to meet the waves, where I leaped over the rolling tide. My feet planted as she said they would. I could sense screeching beneath the waves to get my attention, but I kept my sight on the horizon, focused on the melody. Yet it grew softer and softer. Soon, I could not locate the direction from which it came.

A strong gust came upon me and shoved me to my backside. I did not turn over to push myself to my feet. Instead, I closed my eyes and sat up, quickly placing my feet under me. When I opened my eyes, I recognized Amaterasu Nasmire, the one I refer to as the MKR of Air and Skies. Her sable skin glistened like starlight, and her hair blew wildly behind her brow. She held out her hands as she slowly descended to stare into my eyes. Though I had already ignited my arms for battle, it appeared she did not want one with me.

"I must be brief," she explained. "Suzerain Efah does not know I am here."

"What do you want?" I retorted, refusing to drop my guard.

"We are enslaved to him, Aagneya. The tiny man holds us captive," Amaterasu reasoned. "Your snare has allowed me to be here to speak with you."

"Why should I trust anything you say? You and the others you speak, have you all not betrayed Elior?" I scowled.

"Not by choice," Amaterasu reassured. "Even if it was a choice at the time, our betrayal was not of our doing. None of us wish to remain in this cycle. If you were to free us, we would aid your cause."

"You betrayed Elior," I spat. "If I find your snares, I shall destroy them and be rid of all of you."

My response sent Amaterasu to pull back. She hesitated to speak further but continued to reason with me.

"Should that be your decision, then you would be freeing us. Immortality is not glamorous, as you will soon discover. But if you are not careful with your heart, the tiny man will find the root of your desire, exploit it, and enslave you like the rest of us. It is why Easton disappeared, so as not to be found by his charms."

"Easton spoke of you," I said.

"Yes, we were all friends once—Amara, Easton, and myself. Amara was like a sister to me. Easton and I had the same mother. But nothing prepared us for the life we would have when Elior awoke us."

"What of Marilla?" I interjected.

"She is much older than us," Amaterasu replied. "But I cannot speak of her now. If you wish to set us free, you may do as you wish—kill us or not—he will continue to use our power against you."

"How do I proceed?"

"Ask Easton about Gurēsusutā," she answered. "He knows the name. Easton is the only one who knows how to reach her, other than Elior and the tiny man."

Amaterasu's form blew away like chaff in the wind. I focused on the name while trying to listen for the melody of the flame once more. I closed my eyes and heard an echo stand out from the rest. It was Nirnasha speaking to me. I could hear him calling me back from the ethereal. As I followed his voice, my ears soon heard the melody of the flame intensify.

The Ironclad in the ethereal appeared in front of me, far out to sea. The melody led into my room aboard the vessel. As I stood over my body and heard Nirnasha call for me to wake, I noticed the sawblades removed from my flesh and placed in a metal bin beside the bed. When I saw what had slain me, I could sense wrestling in my mind about returning to my physical form, fully healed from being pierced. I realized an MKR's death always poses a ruthless challenge to their soul—resurrection is not only a matter of one's will but a powerful choice between either love or hate, for both carry enticing melodies. Choosing the reason for to return, I believe, steamrolls the path for the type of MKR one becomes. Should it be a choice of vengeance, a lust for power, greed, or any other form of hatred, the manifestation would set my destiny in motion as the clock is wound and ticks forward to the inevitable.

When I watched Nirnasha calling to me, I wondered why anyone would want to return for anything except love. Apart from my body, I sensed its overwhelming taste and all-pervading desire to be physically present. I reached out to my physical form, and my nerves fired throughout my body, feeling my heart pump blood into my veins again. I sobbed violently when I awoke, as I could feel my grief for Cenobia still pouring out as if I had forgotten her in death, yet my flesh retained the memory. The rush of rage and sadness became so overwhelming that Nirnasha almost could not calm me. Easton was with him and held down my legs as fire ignited up and down my body. Nirnasha pulled away, conjuring stone over his skin, and held my arms firmly down. I heard his voice calling to me as I slowly regained my composure.

"I do believe something else has awoken in you," he said.

"We will find out soon enough," Easton added.

"Gurēsusutā," came the first word out of my mouth. Easton did not catch it at first, but I kept repeating it.

"Where did you hear that?" He asked with wide eyes and trembling lips.

I spoke to him about meeting Amaterasu in the ethereal and told him what she said. He did not answer but seemed lost in thought.

"She cannot be trusted," he finally said. "Forget what you heard."

I pressed him, swiftly standing to my feet and getting between him and the door.

"She said you knew how to reach Gurēsusutā!"

"What is Gurēsusutā?" Nirnasha chimed in.

Easton sighed heavily, seeing he would not escape the room without an explanation.

"Gurēsusutā means 'Grace Star.' She is Amaterasu's snare," he explained. "Gurēsusutā is a ghost of space, and she dwells where nothing else does—on an ethereal asteroid orbiting the earth."

"On a what?" I asked. "And what does 'orbits' mean?"

"You both really are newbies," Easton sighed, seeing the blank stares from Nirnasha and myself. "An asteroid is a massive rock that orbits—meaning that it goes around."

Again, Easton saw our blank stares but, this time, grew frustrated.

"Are you serious?" He belted out. "The two of you are becoming increasingly powerful MKRs, yet you know nothing about space?"

"Well, I feel we are fairly new," Nirnasha tried to reason, leading to Easton to roll his eyes.

We both sat listening to Easton explain that there were other worlds besides ours. The earth, surprisingly, is not the center of existence as we were taught throughout our education. Instead, it is known as a planet that goes around the sun. It is a common belief among the world that gravity only exists within the realm present to us. However, Easton revealed that gravity exists outside into greater space, what he referred to as the Galactic Void, a place beyond our concept of the physical realm. It is the place where stars dwell, and massive rocks "orbit" in the gravitational pull of other objects, such as what Easton referred to as planets.

Much like the ethereal realm, other places of space carry other formulas of existence in the Galactic Void, having no oxygen for lungs to breathe. Easton referenced his childhood, long before becoming an MKR, and the Great Collide—an era he called the '90s. In his childhood, they were educated about the Galactic Void or how it was referred to in those days as Outer Space. Contrary to present popularly accepted beliefs, the earth is not a flat surface, nor is it the center of existence, but instead revolves around the sun—a massive star that brings power to sustain life in the physical realm on earth.

"Did you learn about Gurēsusutā back then?" I asked.

"Of course not," Easton replied. "No one but Elior knew about hidden knowledge like that. A snare was nothing more than a concept from someone's imagination."

"When did you meet Elior?" Nirnasha asked with curiosity dripping in his tone.

"It is hard to remember," Easton admitted. "I do not remember the exact time, but I recall being famous and rich. However, the currency that made up my wealth died out long ago. And the height of my fame dwindled as I desired a more private life after becoming an MKR. I also recollect being in love with Amara. Amaterasu went by the name Jackie at the time. She changed it at some point because she liked the name Amaterasu better."

"We are straying off the path," I said. "How do we reach Gurēsusutā?"

"I know Amaterasu betrayed Elior," Easton stared into my eyes and Nirnasha's. "But she is still my little sister. And if she is serious about helping us, she may be one of the very few to aid in freeing Amara as well. You are right that I know how to reach my sister's snare. But in order to do that, I first have a promise to keep with Meik."

RISE OF
THE GULLYWHUMPER

When I reached the top deck, Garvish and Bikarma were nestled against the helm house. The brisk ocean breeze felt comforting as I sat across them against two wooden crates holding ammo for the two buzzsaw firing guns mounted to the platform. The two had not said much to me for the time we were in the Unlight, and neither one said anything to me once they awoke from the Dendro toxin. Yet, I could sense they were just as disheartened as I was to see Cenobia lost to us.

We all gathered and sent her body to rest in the watery depths no more than three days after our departure. Meik sobbed his way through, bidding her farewell, which allowed me to finally see the true man he hid beneath his bulky frame, courageous and still clinging to love. His words drew tears to my eyes, knowing how dearly I would miss her, the warmth of her friendship, and the motherly qualities I found endearing. Each member of Meik's crew placed a respectful hand on him as Cenobia's wrapped body dropped into the water. Admittedly, I had no more tears to cry by that time.

Whether by reminiscing about Cenobia's demise or some other means, my parents came to mind. I had not thought of my mother or father in quite a while. Despite their flaws, I believed they deserved to know their daughter was all right. Our destination sailed us for Crye, in the Kingdom of Nod. Once I reached Crye, I decided to write to both if I could. For now, the Seaborne Scoundrel stayed close to the mainland, each of us taking turns to keep an eye out for Tide Maidens.

"What is it like being an MKR?" Garvish sincerely inquired as he peered at me from across the deck after the ceremony concluded and most everyone had dispersed.

I had not fully comprehended the question to answer before Bikarma laid on another one.

"Do you need anything?"

I shook my head, still pondering Garvish's question.

"Burdensome," I replied to Garvish. "Restless…"

"But purposeful," Nirnasha interjected, sending a grin in my direction as he joined us.

"Do you suppose you could make me into one?" Garvish pressed.

I could not believe my ears. Whatever humility I thought he learned, he again sounded like the old arse face I first met before we journeyed into the Unlight. Neither one of us answered him. Nirnasha leaned back next to me on the railing. He appeared to be considering the foolish request. But of course, we could not, or at least; I did not think we could.

"If one of us tried to make you one," Nirnasha replied. "The chances of you dying are great."

"I am willing to take that chance," Garvish stood to his feet. Bikarma agreed with him, prompting us that he was willing as well.

We suddenly heard Meik cursing from within the helm house as he had overheard us. He thundered out after he swung the door open, with Easton following behind him.

"Listen to me now, you fecal fart fools!" Meik shouted. "None of you have any idea what you're talking about!"

"What he said," Easton chimed in, pointing to Meik, momentarily pausing the short man's embellished fury, but his glare soon slammed back upon the four of us.

"Elior is the only one who ever awakened that power within someone," Meik continued, approaching Nirnasha and me with a softer tone but with the same intensity. "And you two. Who are you? Do you think cause you've learned some strong magic, you somehow know what Elior knows? Huh? Elior has had eons to explore and practice the hidden knowledge he shared with you. Do you think you've mastered it to the point where you can't kill someone who asks to become like you?"

Nirnasha was not taking the passive-aggressive tongue-lashing very well, mainly because he knew it was more directed at him than me, as he entertained the idea of making Garvish and Bikarma into MKRs.

"What's even more stupid and disturbing," Meik pressed, moving closer to Nirnasha's face. "Is to give someone this power who asks for it. I touched Mystic Silver as a child and received, with no logical reason, the ability to enchant. And I can barely contain the madness of my aspirations."

"Then why do you want to enchant the Ironclad to be able to fly like a wairship?" I challenged Meik, especially in coming to my fellow MKR's defense.

"Because long ago, Elior put the idea in my head," he answered with a cocky sway of his head. "He gave me inspiration for what to do with it. But at the time, he knew I wasn't ready. I was a wild man til one day, Elior introduced me to Cenobia! And it didn't take long for me to settle down a bit after we wed. After we lost our child, I blamed her. Then she left me as I would not leave my first love—the sea. When my heart desired to see her again, there Elior stood, telling me that I would soon see her again."

"Wait. That whole encounter with you and Elior was just an act when we first met you?" I asked.

"To keep up appearances, yes," Meik admitted, his eyes pushing tears down his cheeks again. "Elior had found me long before. When I finally saw her walking with him along the docks, I knew I needed her to stay."

He turned around to face Garvish and Bikarma.

"You don't want this power," Meik said. "Every MKR that Elior awoke ends up losing something they're unwilling to lose."

"Mortality," Easton chimed in. "No one should witness the amount of death I have. Sooner or later, you find yourself alone."

"Maybe we should change that," I replied. "I have never felt closer to anyone, including my parents. Some of us have fought for one another in the Unlight more than once. If that is not family, I do not know what is."

"Meik is right," Garvish said surprisingly. "I had no right to ask you. I have never been in this position before. I have seen what happened to Cenobia...not just her...but all the ones who have been slain with us, and I must confess it is the first time I have felt truly afraid."

"I as well," Bikarma admitted.

"Power does not make fear go away," Easton empathized. "It often increases it."

By this time, the rest of the crew had joined us back on the deck—Wild Willy, Darby, Reggie, and even Kassy Bones, who likely heard Meik's voice before, rising over the roar of the sea.

"I have noticed the only time I feel like I have the strength to face my fears is when I believe I shall see the ones I care about again," I confessed. "Truly, that is all of you."

"Then maybe we should make a pact," Meik piped up. "Even if we're separated, we all vow to do our best to find one another again."

"I like that," Nirnasha nodded. As did everyone else except Kassy Bones, who assumed she was too proud to admit she needed us. My anger climbed into my throat, still blaming her for abandoning the Ironclad to seek out her disparaging appetites. We would have left a week sooner, and Cenobia would still be with us. I could not forgive her for that. But that did not stop me from including her in what I said. I felt like Meik would keep a closer eye on her from now on.

Later, I led Nirnasha into my room. I needed him to know my concerns about him considering awakening someone to become an MKR. In our extensive conversation, he confessed that he felt guilty about not searching more for Elior in the Unlight, which led him to feel fearful of losing his way and becoming like the other MKRs, as Elior was not around to keep him focused on the right path.

"We are going to pick up the search again," I reassured him. "Do not despair. We need to learn the right place to begin finding answers."

We agreed Elior was still alive but had nothing to assist us in locating him. But as we pondered and were vexed to remember if we missed a clue, we both decided to continue Meik's mission, enchanting the Ironclad for air travel before revisiting the matter.

In the evening's dinner discussion, Easton claimed he knew of a dockmaster who would lease out an enchanter's wharf in Crye, the best dockmaster who would not ask questions about leasing out an enclosed space. Most illegal sea and air vessels were built and sold on the black market, veiled by Crye's massive legitimate merchant trade. But nothing so spectacular as what we had planned to attempt. We could smelt the Mystic Silver we needed there, with a forge Easton knew could withstand the sweltering temperatures. And although I did not fully explain who or what Gurēsusutā was during my conversing with everyone, I did emphasize the importance of finding the "Grace Star," alluding to the fact that it might give us a clue to Elior's whereabouts. None of the others fully understood. Yet I believe they trusted my words until I felt a dagger held against my throat the next morning, clinched there by Kassy Bones.

Her viridescent eyes stared into mine with a cold, thirstily gaze—an unsettling intoxication. She began mumbling about how all blame for Cenobia's death stuck with me and that we should have left her behind in the gutter where we found her. Though I pitied Kassy, it did not deter me from being offended that she pressed a blade against my jugular with untruthful culpability. Instinctively, as is the best I can describe it, I knew my strength outmatched hers. I swiftly grabbed hold of her wrists, pushing her body upward. She slammed into the cabin ceiling and came crashing down at my bedside, where I had already jumped.

Stunned and staggering, Kassy managed to lunge at me in a fit of rage again with her blade. She missed, plunging and thumping face first on the other side of the bed and into the wall. Her nose poured out streams of crimson as she placed one knee under her to stand. Before she could, I gave her a swift fist that sent her back to the floor. The blow released the dagger from her grip and out of her reach. I pressed my foot down on her throat, not looking to harm her but letting her know that her strength remained useless in struggling against me.

"Cease this at once!" I exclaimed. "You cannot throw the responsibility upon me for Cenobia's death. Do you think she would have left you? You are accountable for her demise! No one else!"

I may have sobered her up with the blow I gave her. Her eyes were vast now as she screamed and cursed me. I pressed more on her throat, and she gagged, ceasing her threats.

"You have been nothing but a worm since we began," I said harshly. "Your behavior is that of a small child, and your actions that of a whore! I would end you if I did not pity you and no one else cared for you."

"If you let me go," Kassy managed to gasp out. "I shall cut your throat and burn your body. To be rid of your kind would be a favor to us all."

My cabin door flew open. Meik stood in the doorway. Without saying a word, he nodded at me as if to say he knew what had occurred.

"Say nothin'," he uttered. "She's mad with drink. Not even I could console her. Knew she would lash out, but I didn't expect it would go so far."

"She was holding a dagger to my throat!" I replied angrily.

"Aye," Meik replied. "She threatened me with it early this morning as well. Best tie her down till she sobers up."

"How could you not see she was a risk?" I demanded.

Meik ashamedly stared at me as Kassy passed out under my foot. He pushed past me, picked her up from the floor, and swung her over his shoulder.

"The only other time I've seen her this bad was when her dear, sweet man drowned. She has never forgotten the pain. You already heard Cenobia speak of her upbringing. She lives in all of it constantly. Cenobia was always the one who brought her back. I believe Kassy is afraid of falling deeper into despair, knowing that her destructive conduct will consume her. Truthfully, she fears death more than you realize."

"Her lover drowned?" I inquired.

"In saving her from the sea, yes," Meik said. "They were both Keepers and merchants once. She fell overboard, and he dove in after her. He got her back to the vessel but swept away in the storm before he could climb aboard."

I followed Meik onto the deck. A warm tear trickled down my cheek as the morning sea breeze danced along to meet us. I learned at that moment, watching Meik walk away with Kassy, I would become familiar with the suffering of others so much more than in a single lifetime. I could hear Lasair singing the melody of both their hearts, tunes of grief speaking of helplessness buried within a forlorn rhythm. Then I realized something more than just greater strength awakened in me. I could hear hearts beating even more so than before like a signal broadcasted directly from the ethereal to my soul's hidden places. And if I reached out, I could determine Nirnasha's location and everyone else on board. With such an awakening, I wondered if I could locate Elior—if only I could locate the melody of his heart.

"Something has roused in you," I heard Easton's voice catch me off-guard.

"How do you know?" I asked.

"My snare is awake when Lasair is using it," he replied. "She is forging to open her knowledge to you, and it would seem, forging a power within you that I have never witnessed."

"What do you mean?"

"I have never felt Lasair forge with such intensity. I am not quite sure what it means. But I do know she is unleashing a monumental power within you."

I could hear the melody of Easton's heart. It sang of a troubled mind. Yet that did not disturb me as much as when I found Nirnasha sitting outside the dining hall, staring at the misty horizon. The overcasting clouds and every pressing threat of a storm loomed around us—perfectly describing the melody that beat within him. The fear that flowed through his tune pushed me to taste gloom, but I would not let it take me. I quickly stepped to him and grasped ahold of his face. He tried to speak, but I embraced him with a kiss that I refused to let up till the song of his heart changed. I could feel his fear surge through my lips, subsiding when his arms slid upward and pulled my body down to him.

"Do not despair," I whispered to him.

That wonderful moment of being held by Nirnasha and embracing him was shattered by cannon fire blasting into the water around the Ironclad. Darby became the first to call out the wairships above us. They were not full-sized but scout ships, closing in on our position. Garvish and Bikarma jumped on the two buzzsaw firing guns and began returning fire as the wairships drew closer in range.

While Meik maneuvered the Ironclad to avoid the warship's cannon fire, Nirnasha assisted Darby with setting up our only cannon, an ancient weapon with an unknown capability of holding it together. I figured hurling fire in the Eastguardian's direction would keep them from getting too close. I summoned two large orbs of inferno, shocked by my newfound strength, and threw them to reach the hulls of the attacking vessels.

One wairship broke off from the rest and drew close to the water near our stern, approaching our port side. Bikarma and Garvish continued their assault against the other two while I followed the third wairship, upkeeping a barrage of fire into it. I could see it had a shimmering gloss of fireproof coating all over its balloon. The only way to pierce it was with a forceful impact, something my fire would be unable to accomplish as it dissipated like water splashing against rocks. I began aiming for the soldiers with buzzsaw firing guns, igniting them into screaming corpses.

Nirnasha heard my thoughts to aim the cannon at the balloon to pierce it. Before he could, they fired their cannons against the Ironclad's heavy armor. Several cannonballs shattered on impact, and others bounced off, all causing a deafening clanging throughout the ship. I had to duck and cover my ears for a moment but quickly found my footing to sail more flames across the waters and into the wairship's crew.

A small explosion came after one fireball hit the hull, most likely striking a cannon's pipe or pressure valve. Scrap metal and several soldiers were lifelessly tossed into the sea, and the wairship struggled to regain altitude. Its hull began skimming deeper along the water's surface when Darby set off the cannon into its balloon. The impact pierced a small hole in its undercarriage, and the ship slammed into the waves.

The other two wairships moved away from our stern, approaching our port and starboard, hovering just above the waters. Meik could not maneuver out of their sights, nor could we outrun them. The Eastguard ships shot a massive crossfire, slamming into our hull and bringing the Scoundrel dead in the water. The wairships flew onward but turned about, heading back for another crossfire barrage that would surely finish us off. Our buzzsaw firing guns were out of ammo, and we knew the cannon could not be loaded in time. I drew another breath to summon more fire, trying to prevent them from sinking us. But something strange happened. Easton grabbed my wrists, and I would have wrestled free if I had not been surprised the wairships hovered close to us and did not fire. Soon, they passed on.

None of us made a noise as the wairships turned around to make another pass. I noticed Easton casting a melody of magic that Nirnasha and I had seen once before in the ethereal—Mirror Mirage, which reflects the environment to create the illusion of invisibility. Easton had cast it around the Ironclad. The wairships passed us again but hovered briefly before flying off into the distance.

We were stranded, but no casualties. Reggie stumbled out of the engine bay, his ears bleeding undoubtedly from the loud clanging of cannon fire against the hull. My ears were also ringing, but the sound of the waves soon returned to me. The rest of the crew made their way to us, flopping down on the upper deck. Wild Willy followed behind Kassy Bones, who was now wide awake. Meik stepped out from the helm house and let loose a heavy sigh.

"I forgot how helpful it is having Easton around," Meik confessed. "Smuggling was much easier."

"You smuggled with Meik?" I asked.

"Just a couple of times til I had the credits I needed to make my own way," Easton replied.

I did not bother to inquire more about the reference. I assumed Easton had known Meik longer than anticipated, much like Elior. My only other inquiry toward Easton held my attention on why it took him so long to cast the spell. He explained casting the spell over other objects held a higher deal of difficulty for him than just casting it on himself.

"You should practice more," I said, slightly joking. Easton only gave me a nod and a grin.

Our only choice to fix the Ironclad was to dig into our ample supply of Mystic Silver, which Kassy did most of the patchwork while Meik inspected any other signs of significant damage. Mainly, the engines were wrecked, and Meik spent most of his time down in the engine bay with Reggie and Darby while Bikarma and Garvish brought up multiple buckets of water to dump back into the sea.

"Another hit, and we'd be sea bait," Meik huffed, returning to the upper deck several hours later.

"We may still get our chance," Darby poked, receiving a pulsing vein glare from the captain.

The sun began to fade below the horizon, and Meik's repairs with the Mystic Silver had not entirely taken effect for the engines to work at full capacity. The current had taken us farther out from the shoreline, but we had not lost sight of our navigation. While not ideal, the Ironclad sputtered and crawled across the tides. We all remained alert as the waters grew dark, and a small storm caught up to us, and so did a familiar melody. Kassy had already plugged her ears with Gossypium and hummed softly. I recognized the lullaby from my caregiver, who often sang me to sleep with it as a child. It was the first time I had heard its lyrics from another's lips.

O' sweet baby, divine
Sweet dreams come to rise
When you shut your eyes
O' sweet baby of mine

O' lovely child, divine
Lovely is the night
When your visions take flight
O' lovely child of mine

O' peaceful girl, divine
Peaceful is your bed
When down, lay your head
O' peaceful girl of mine

All of us were gathered on the upper deck, waiting for the sound of the maidens to begin crawling out of the depths. I could hear the melody of their call grow ever more evident. Though it had no effect on me, I still hummed the lullaby coming from Kassy's lips as it assisted in keeping her at ease.

We remained vigilant all night as the rain drenched us in a downpour and blanketed our vision. I dared to look into the waters and see their glowing golden eyes. Still, we saw none peek their heads out from beneath the waves to approach the Ironclad. Meik took another crack at the engines and cursed until they were fully repaired, enabling the Ironclad to speed up. And I watched the golden hue fade from beneath the waves along with their song.

Unexpectedly, we continued onward without incident and reached Crye within three months after we departed from Ye and Poe. The guards did not willingly welcome our vessel, pointing out their suspicions of the Ironclad's heavily dented cannon damage. However, Meik persuaded them to allow us to dock by offering them a unique small token of fungi that would later augment their mental state when they were off duty.

Getting into the city presented even more of a dilemma, as the docks in Crye were so crowded with merchants and goods that it took all morning to weave through them. Nirnasha, Meik, Kassy Bones, Bikarma, Garvish, Darby, and Reggie remained with the Ironclad while Easton led me and Wild Willy, who insisted on coming to the city gates.

The Crye docks, if you can imagine, stretch out more than four thousand footsteps in each direction along the shoreline. It is the most profitable port among the three kingdoms, taxing all goods that come through. Hundreds of docking platforms for airships are located in the shallows, with catwalks leading back to the mainland, while more docking locations for sea vessels are harbored below. I would imagine that from a view from high above, the Crye docks appeared much like an arachnid web.

I have spoken about the Kingdom of Nod being separated by northern and southern territories. What has been an ongoing conflict between the two regions is separated by an immense chasm flooded with stagnant waters. Just next to the chasm is the city of Deadlakes, which is surrounded by several small bodies of murky waters, marshes, and rocky hills—it is odd as these are unchanging, unlike the rest of the landscape. The engineering of several tall lookout towers is formidable to any aerial assault. Deadlakes is heavily fortified and well-armed, amassing over five hundred buzzsaw firing guns within its city walls and scattering more throughout the fortified rock formations just outside the city. Just to the south, another unchanging small river flows from the mountainside, roaming down to the settlement of Quodon, named after a famous Nodian explorer.

Quodon was once an outpost for explorers looking to stage their expeditions before trekking further into the Deadlands. In recent years, the city has maintained a steady population but has become more of a storage facility for weapons, ammunition, and other supplies. It is well fortified, with the city itself carved into a mountainside and its populace becoming miners of sorts, digging tunnels to store goods and house their populace. Their goods are transported upriver from Nodtides to move on and supply Deadlakes.

Nodtides is the furthest southern settlement in Nod, located almost directly south of Crye. Nodtides is one of the greatest suppliers of iron and copper, rivaling Resk in the north. It is a region of chilling winds but ingenious engineering, without enchantments from Mystic Silver—the engines for refining ore run by utilizing the ocean tides. Hundreds of flume gates remain open, allowing water to rush in to constantly fall over enormous gears and other mechanisms to spin and power the furnaces for operations.

Only one of us knew so much about the southern settlements. That was Wild Willy, who spent some time being a transporter of goods from Nodtides through to Deadlakes. I took the liberty to jot down these notes as we went through a briny and bustling chockablock to Crye's gates. I had never heard Wild Willy chatter so much about his life. It could have been he was reminiscing. Or perhaps it was one of the rare occasions of being sober. While walking next to me, he did not have his usual scent of sage and mugwort or pumca. No matter. Easton ignored the stories, likely focusing on finding the forge station to lease a specific docking house. The forge station came into view just beyond the gates, in a wooden enclosed structure with only a hanging wooden sign depicting it from the rest.

Now, I must say something about forge docking houses. No one cleans up after themselves. After Easton bartered a small portion of our Mystic Silver as payment, we returned to the Ironclad and sailed north along the coastline. On reaching our destination, our forge docking house, number 223, was enough to fit the Ironclad and have room to spare for the planned alterations. Connected to the docking house stood a large forge engineered and enchanted to sustain the highest temperatures of any other in the three kingdoms, at least to Easton's knowledge. He explained the enchantments alone cost more than all our weight combined and took over twenty years to perfect. Since then, Nod has not seen such dedication to Keeper's craftsmanship.

"Who oversaw the engineering of the forges?" I asked.

"Well, if it was not me, who do you think?" Easton scoffed at my question.

"I have not been an MKR for long," Nirnasha interjected. "I see Meik is a Keeper and is Kassy also. They both can enchant, yet I have not learned, nor has Aagneya."

"Well, I do," Easton replied. "Elior is the one who taught me. MKRs can do much greater enchantments than regular Keepers. Our dear captain and our friend cannot accomplish what we are about the forge."

"So that is why Meik needed Elior to transform the Ironclad," Nirnasha realized. "But why did Elior not teach us something so simple as enchanting?"

A large hand found the back of Nirnasha's head. He turned around and saw

Meik glaring into his eyes.

"You continue to show me just how witless you are," he said. "Enchanting for a Keeper takes years of practice. The results can be disastrous if we try to go too big before giving ourselves the proper training."

"For an MKR," Easton interceded. "If you do not have the strength and control of your power, the enchantment will not work. Keepers rely on using Mystic Silver as their source of magic to enchant, whereas MKRs must rely on the power we possess to enchant Mystic Silver and bend it to our will. We are not just enchanting an object, but transforming Mystic Silver to become part of something else and continue radiating its magical properties to perform what we desire."

"So, it is a different kind of enchanting," I smugly grinned near Nirnasha's face. He playfully placed his hand over my head and shoved me away.

"All right," Meik stepped in between the twitterpated exchanges. "Before we can do anything, an awful mess must be cleaned out of the dock house."

Though the progress of cleaning proved to be a egregious task for us all, we kept our spirits high. Even Kassy Bones appeared amused by the camaraderie and banter as we cleansed the dock house and the forge of rust and scrap. It took no more than a week, and soon the Ironclad became shut away inside the dock house like a swaddled babe, concealing our secretive scheme from the world.

We fired up the forge, using a combination of paraffin oil and my magic for fuel. Easton melted down scraps he would purify and mold into pieces for the Ironclad's transformation. The ship itself had to be stripped of all its outer shell, leaving nothing but the initial bones to be built upon. Meik did not say a word or ask questions about how the Seaborne Scoundrel would appear after completion. He only communicated a few requirements he would need in the design.

I saw the blueprint formed in Easton's mind before he created each piece and molded it magically from molten scrap in front of me. Though I never doubted that Easton knew how to use his power to mold metal, I did not know he could picture an airship so perfectly and craft each piece so quickly. First, he devised a way to armor the undercarriage for the balloon so it could not be pierced by cannon fire so easily. For most airships, the undercarriage needed to be open for heat to escape and not combust the apparatus. However, Easton devised an intricate valve system to release heat so that it could be better protected.

Then the helm house became a superior captain's navigation deck, with three steering devices, one to control the Scoundrel in flight and another during ocean travel. It would be Easton's surprise to Meik that the Ironclad could also roam by land. The helms were labeled and connected to a spinning platform facing the navigation view when set to its particular mode of travel. Uncommonly, to the left of the helms held the navigation pane to partition the SHCs. Most airship navigation decks have the SHCs behind them, with a navigator communicating to the captain their position. I believe the design intrigued me and also annexed an exorbitant expanse of common sense.

Next, to the right of the helms, an elaborate communication system led down to the engine room, where a vast network of steam valves and pistons worked collectively to provide power to the rest of the ship. I felt my excitement spike in seeing this part of the design unfold. Four engines were put in place with the requirement that all four be made solely from Mystic Silver. The engines were no bigger than 20 units long and stretched approximately 16 units wide, an astonishingly intricate design and compacted, allowing more space in the engine room to accommodate a contraption I had never seen before.

While I am unfamiliar with the terminology as I am no engineer or ingenious designer like Easton, it had an "on" and "off" switch that could be controlled directly from the helm house. It, too, he molded solely of Mystic Silver. The contraption had an orbiting module of mechanisms that rapidly spun around when it turned on—also clasping and utilizing Mystic Silver as its fuel in the center. My glimpse into Easton's mind continued to amaze me as the machine's function revealed the enablement of the ship to mimic one of Easton's spells— Mirror Mirage—allowing the ship to become invisible.

I noticed Easton had refined the iron scraps and the salvage from the body of the Scoundrel, transforming the entire figure of the ship into enchanted steel, exceedingly dense and completely rust-resistant. There were now six decks, one being the lower deck containing the engines and cargo space. From there, an intricate system of cannon pipes emerged, intertwining and traveling up to all the other levels above. Each one connected to an elite wairship type of cannon, as I would describe it, for there was no cannon of the kind I had ever seen before. A control panel on the navigation deck, located to the right of the helms, initiated the barrels of the cannons to extend or collapse, hiding them behind a shuttered window made of broad, pure steel. Nirnasha remained stunned by Easton's blueprints just as much as me. And nothing prepared our minds for what the fifth deck housed.

Just above the engines and cargo, a sleek steel and copper device formed a cannonball loader that equally fed ammunition up through the pipes and into each cannon on the ship. Again, the controls to open the valves to fire the cannons were located on the navigation deck. But the convenience of restocking the loader was so simple that one person could complete the task of what I would call "nests" holding cannon balls until they were ready to drop down onto a conveyor belt. One conveyor belt fed port side cannons, the other starboard. According to the design capabilities, the cannon balls would take significantly less time to reload than a wairship crew loading them manually.

Living quarters and the dining hall were on the fourth and third deck, along with several spaces for weapon cages to hold buzzsaw rifles and ammo. The only alteration on the third deck became a passenger lounge. And every living quarter held its own waste facility, which made me ecstatic not to have to share with anyone else—some people do not make it a priority to flush. The plumbing for the waste management flowed into large tanks onboard, becoming part of the fuel for the ship's igniter cannons designed to spray out massive flames. Two were located directly on the bow and two directly on the stern, capable of swiveling to cover a half-turn radius.

Buzzsaw firing gun stations were strategically mounted along the second and navigation deck. Each station had a steel shield casing to protect the gunner, unlike any other wairship. The second deck also housed the captain's quarters and the medical facility.

I must admit, I did not catch all the spectacular wonders of Easton's design specs when I first saw them. As the ship began to finish manifesting before us, I noticed another mode of ocean travel I had overlooked. Easton had designed the Scoundrel with the ability to close airtight and dive beneath the waves as an Aquatic Depth Machine (ADM).

Despite Easton's swift molding capabilities, the process of getting to the finished design was no easy task. Melting down most of our supply of Mystic Silver took weeks, as I was the only one capable of performing the exhausting task. Other misfortunes arose as the forge we thought would withstand the high heat cracked. Nirnasha used his power to reinforce it by compacting soil all around it. Temperatures began getting so intense that the others had to wait outside while Easton and I continued to fire and mold the metal while

Nirnasha's support sustained the forge's heat. Meik and the others were charged with finding and bringing more scrap metal to the dock house as the Scoundrel continued to need more materials to be completed.

After several months of grueling work and fortunately not drawing the attention of unwanted eyes, the Scoundrel became unveiled to the sunlight. Meik shouted so exuberantly that I am sure all Eastguard heard him as the propellers sputtered and whirled to life. The balloon inflated once we could steer it out of the dock house. And I swear Meik had tears in his eyes, though he will never admit it.

"What are you going to call it?" I asked him. "Stands to reason it is no longer the Seaborne Scoundrel."

"The Gullywhumper!" Meik replied enthusiastically, his chest raised high in front of him.

To this day, I have no idea what Gullywhumper means. Meik does have a way of making up words and placing meaning to them. Then if he is asked about the connotation, he plays it out like the person is incompetent. So, I did not bother to find out. Here he was, the previous captain of the Seaborne Scoundrel—now the captain of the Gullywhumper—the most intricately designed and progressive vessel ever manufactured.

"All we have left to do is one more enchantment," Easton said. "Aagneya and Nirnasha, meet me on the navigation deck."

We stood close together, staring at one of the last pieces of Mystic Silver in Easton's hand.

"I have placed so much of my power into enchanting each of the Mystic Silver mechanisms on this ship already," Easton explained. "But I do not have the power alone to do what needs to be done and complete what this ship should be."

"What do you mean?" Nirnasha asked.

"The true magic of this ship will be the navigator," Easton continued. "The ship needs a captain to follow. It also needs a voice to communicate with the captain's orders. What it needs is a mind of its own."

"That is insane," I replied. "Why would we want to do that?"

"I know how it sounds," Easton reassured. "But you must believe me that if this ship does not have a mind of its own and falls into the wrong hands, the world will pay dearly. It needs a navigator to sail it, even if all onboard should perish."

"What kind of mind are we supposed to give it?" Nirnasha inquired. Easton held his gaze at both of us, keeping silent for the thought to sink in before he gave us the answer we knew was coming.

"Me," Easton sighed.

I stared, stunned, at Nirnasha, who returned my regard. We both turned our heads back to Easton, ready to argue, but he raised a stiff and swift hand.

"If you want to reach Gurēsusutā," he pressed. "Then you will do this."

We had never enchanted before. But Easton directed us on how to complete the task. He took on his molten metal form and allowed me to, excruciatingly, I might add, melt him down in stifled grits and groans. Nirnasha then touched the Mystic Silver to the puddle of metal Easton had become. It seeped up and around the Mystic Silver as if it were still alive. I placed it into the small opening on the navigation deck where Easton had instructed, which soon shut tight and surged lights to illuminate throughout the ship.

"The machine is alive," we heard Easton's voice echo from the Gullywhumper's frame. "All aboard, and all systems are now activated."

When the rest of the crew joined us aboard, Meik could not believe what we did. Easton's voice echoed throughout the navigation deck and reassured him the right thing had been done. Being reassured made Meik suddenly sparked out of his concern for Easton and shouted for the Gullywhumper to shove off!

"Call the ship what you want," Easton's voice came to him. "Yet as Navigator, you will address me as Easton...Captain Meik Feenk."

THE GRACE STAR &
THE SERPENT

The Gullywhumper effortlessly took flight. The dynamic design of the airship allowed for less turbulence, making it seem as if we were standing still, despite the actual velocity we were traveling. Easton gauged that we were flying faster than any Eastguard wairship he knew of and would likely be built.

I witnessed more of Easton's mind at work, as I assuredly did not understand all the components of the craftsmanship he engineered. Yet now able to observe his creation in motion, I noticed several furnaces were embedded throughout the ship, transferring heat through vents, including the dining hall and all the living quarters. In reaching a higher altitude than any airship could travel, these vents also pushed in oxygen while the rest of the ship shut airtight. I imagine the ship in such a state would appear like a shelled crustacean strapped to a balloon.

Higher, we ascended, and we all explored aspects of the ship that caught our eye. Afterward, I stood on the navigation deck to watch the skies transform from their azure hue to mystic midnight—something I never knew. A far-off, bright, and glowing orb came into view, which Easton relayed as the sun. I never dreamed I would leave the world to see it in its entirety. The earth showed a magnificent azure oculus with a huge landmass in the center. I took notice of a large isle located southeast of the Kingdom of Eastguard, sketching out its shape in my notebook as I did the rest of the land mass.

"Easton, would you know what that isle is below Eastguard?" I asked.

"I do not," Easton's voice complied. "Though I am sure Elior would certainly know."

Even though I focused my attention elsewhere, as I became more curious about the Galactic Void, I kept my thoughts of the isle spinning in the hidden parts of my mind.

The ship's balloon had deflated and harbored safely inside the vessel. The propellers had all but ceased swirling, but somehow, we were still in motion.

"How are we still aloft or moving without the balloon or propellers," I asked.

"Girl, you ask too many questions," Meik piped up. "Why question if it's working?"

"Probably because I am a girl," I replied impertinently. "And girls like to think, unlike their counterparts."

"It is a different kind of sky out here," I heard Easton's voice laugh. "Elior told me that we would just need to release steam. It would continue to thrust us onward. The ship is generating heat from the engines traveling through the vents, many of which travel to the back of the ship and release."

"But I'm still steering the ship," Meik winked.

"Not exactly," Easton replied, widening Meik's eyes. "Since you are not aware of how to navigate our way to Gurēsusutā, I have taken the liberty to place our destination on auto-pilot."

"You scummy little Gnawer," Meik cursed. "You've slithered my captain's command right out from under me!"

"Calm yourself," Easton reassured. "I shall return full control of the helm once we return to our world. Until you understand how to fly in the Galactic Void, I shall assist in navigation and maneuvering."

"Have you been in the Galactic Void before?" I wondered aloud.

"Elior and I created a ship long ago to reach Gurēsusutā," Easton admitted. "Not as elaborate as this one, but this is not the first attempt to reach her."

"What went wrong the last time?" I pressed.

"The ship could not take the pressure," Easton replied. "Elior and I escaped as he brought us back to earth before it all came apart."

Elior had placed the ship's design in Easton's mind. The entire blueprint felt like a traumatic memory of sorts when Easton began conjuring it. The details of the blueprint felt envisioned for more than two lifetimes. It reassured me that Easton was not the enlightened genius I momentarily believed. Although I remained impressed, he had the capabilities to create it, which is likely why Elior chose to keep the plans hidden in his mind.

"When we first set out," I admit sometimes I cannot keep my mouth shut, but I had questions racing through my mind. "Did you not say you wanted to make a haven in the Deadlands? How…?"

"I still do," Easton interjected. "And this ship shall assist in that endeavor…"

"We can speak of this later," Nirnasha sabotaged my line of questioning, likely wanting to know what to expect from a treacherous snare. "How do you know how to get to the Grace Star?"

"I still hold a connection to my sister's heart," Easton explained. "She is not aware, but I gave her a heart valve when we were kids. And she was too young to remember. But when I became an MKR, I felt a deeper connection with her, especially when she learned of her snare. I have known Gurēsusutā has been here for quite some time. Although, she is not always this close to earth."

"Your sister did not feel a deeper connection with you when she became an MKR?" I asked.

"Not that I am aware," Easton recalled.

"What if your valve affected her heart to not be completely taken by Suzerain Efah?" I theorized. "That could explain why she reached out to me for help. It seems more like a characteristic of who you are than her."

"One can assume," Easton chuckled.

We had arrived. Easton did not allow us to ask any more questions but instead swiftly explained that he sensed Gurēsusutā nearby. Nirnasha and I found a place to lounge and then let our minds drift into the ethereal, which held an entirely dissimilar atmosphere while in the Galactic Void.

The Gullywhumper appeared ghostly, shimmering like a translucent mechanical animation with a starry host twinkling upon a dark canvas. An enormous crag was slightly far from us, highlighted by sparkling precious stones and metals. Nirnasha and I were weightless and drifting upward, floating from the Gullywhumper onto the rockface where a somber apparition manifested in front of us, clothed in glistening heaven and skin just as pale. The appearance of decay dominated her lips while her gossamer locks swayed as if blown by a gentle gale. Her hands and feet were bare, yet bound in what appeared to be chains of ice. Vicious hooks lined her back, keeping her face trapped in agony. Dark spheres surrounded her eyes but were lit up with the splendor of a golden tinge. She went to speak as she opened her jaws ever wider—her tongue pierced against the roof of her mouth. How one could be so cruel to surmise such bondage—and yet, I am not surprised by Rumpelstilzchen's cruelty.

Her echo reached out to Nirnasha and me, astoundingly hiding her despair and anguish. Instead, we received a melodious song that politely introduced herself. In her gentle demeanor, she managed to slide up her lips to smile slightly.

"We have come to help you," Nirnasha stated aloud. "I believe you are the snare of Amaterasu."

"O' you know my sweet Amaterasu," Gurēsusutā replied, sounding like a tenderly concerned mother. "You two must be Aagneya and Nirnasha. Amaterasu has told me about you."

By now, I sensed Gurēsusutā's voice hid a threatening undertone. She began hovering ever closer to us, lugging the clinking chains that appeared to give her a longer leash, and I grasped Nirnasha's hand. He sensed my hesitation and concurred with my discernment in squeezing back.

"How can we free you?" Nirnasha asked. "Amaterasu has bid we come to do so."

"Free me?" Gurēsusutā's melody turned minor and eerie. "I am already free. It is you who are imprisoned. But feed me, and I shall wake you."

The Grace Star was not referring to joining us in the ship's dining hall. I conjured Bewitching Bonfire, swirling bright royal crimson flames into my hands. I could feel my eyes intensely teem with a mighty rage, while Nirnasha's entire frame radiated a viridescent hue.

Gurēsusutā remained unphased by the display of our power, making her cravings even more eager to devour us. I threw both flames at her before I soared away from her reach—flattered she sought me out first. Nirnasha ripped a boulder size rock from the crag, forming it into a large, floating hand,

and slammed it into Gurēsusutā, sending the apparition clear across the asteroid. Seeing her swatted like a fly and then sail mercilessly into cliffs on the other side forced a loud snicker from my gut. Unfortunately, her disposition did not shift, and she levitated back up with the same zeal as before.

The flames I hit her with held no effect. I switched my hues to viridescent, viola, azure, jaffa, and gold—sending barrage after barrage of fireballs into her with no promising results. Nirnasha kept her at bay with various spells to manipulate rocks to be thrown against her, sending the specter back into the cliffs. I could see my fellow MKR beginning to wane, and I could not compose another color in my mind. However, we heard cannon fire from the Gullywhumper, taking us both by surprise. Easton had become one with the ship. His consciousness could still move from the physical realm to the ethereal, taking the form of the Gullywhumper.

"My apologies," I heard Easton's voice resound. "I believe I am still getting used to this new vessel's functions."

"How can we kill her?" I urgently pressed.

"That is not your concern," Easton echoed. "You have distracted her so I can get into position."

I had no idea what he implied until the ship's cannons fired again, this time sailing stretched-out nets that seemed like glowing spiderwebs down upon the apparition. The nets entangled Gurēsusutā, and she became enraged, desperately trying to break free. The Gullywhumper maneuvered overhead and opened a hatch bay, dropping an open cage.

"Nirnasha!" Easton's voice reached him earnestly. "Shove her into the cage." Nirnasha, in one last effort, sent a rock-solid fist into Gurēsusutā and slammed her into the enclosure that shut swiftly behind her.

"Did we just capture a ghost?" I asked.

Nirnasha smirked and concurred. "I believe so."

Gurēsusutā was hoisted up into the hatch while Nirnasha and I floated back on board, returning our minds to our bodies. Despite feeling fatigued, I blurted out my astonishment to Easton.

"What did we just do?" Sounding a little more demanding than I wished. "Why did we capture her and not destroy her?"

"She is a Leviathan," Easton replied. "You cannot kill her unless you find out what can destroy her. And it certainly is not any power any of you possess. This creature is far beyond time itself, and she is snared with someone we need as an ally."

"I get it," Nirnasha said. "Now that we have control of Amaterasu's snare, we can control her now."

"Something like that," Easton concurred. "Amaterasu set this up as a trap, but it could not have gone any better if I had planned it myself."

"What do you mean?" I asked, beating Nirnasha to the question.

"The two of you have much to learn," Easton explained. "There is much you are not aware of, yet I will tell you now as we have followed Elior's plan to this point. It was always his aim to regain the lost MKRs. In order to do so, their snares would have to be captured and imprisoned somehow."

"How does one imprison a Leviathan?" I felt like Easton was not explaining fast enough.

"I can hear your heightened explorer curiosity about this equation," Easton laughed. "It only took several eras to plan and build, but your snare, Aagneya, helped Elior and I forge a prison for Leviathans to set them free from Suzerain Efah's grasp."

Returning from the ethereal in the Galactic Void left me more drained than usual. After I awoke, we were already back in the earth's azure skies, and I went to find the Gems of the Hidden Glade, but the book was nowhere in my living quarters where I had left it.

"Is this what you are looking for?" Nirnasha asked me as I clearly leaped into a mode of panic when I had not found the book in my pack. "You should not leave it unguarded."

I slowly reached for the book, and he playfully pulled it away.

"I did not leave it unguarded," I replied, bellowing my frustration and swiftly grasping his wrist to remove it from his hand. "Just tell me next time when you read it."

"I feel like I have almost finished it," Nirnasha grinned. "I think you should take some time to catch up."

"Gladly," I sneered. "That way, I can…"

He stopped my words with a soft kiss, taking me off guard but leaving me with a smile.

"We can talk later," he said, taking his leave.

Concentrating became my first task, as I found it challenging to do so after wanting to be kissed more by him. So, I am not sure how long I sat listening to the book's spirit before I sensed being watched somewhere from the shadows. When the tiny man appeared in the visions given to me by the book, I almost lit my cabin ablaze, but I regained my composure and doused my flames. He acted much like the deceiving imp, but only a projected vision of my mind. Somehow, the book knew I desired to study the Suzerain Efah. And through my perceptions, bit by bit, the book revealed knowledge of the tiny man to me, written into the pages by Elior long ago.

Marilla came to me through my following vision, the MKR, who holds the power of Water and Flood. I had not met her personally, a tiny bout before I died my second time, yet Nirnasha had placed a note beside her name within the

My first MKR battle, Ye & Poe, (signed) Nirnasha Pericles.

It drew my attention to the desire to find out more about her. I am still not sure why Nirnasha did not tell me about her before. Perhaps he wanted me to read it and see the vision for myself. However, when I read Elior's story of Marilla's snare, I scarcely believed such a thing existed despite all I had already witnessed.

In the visions, Elior's travels took him far away, setting foot on sands and marshes, overlooking a vast body of thundering tides. He had caught the soft tune of a heart that grew and felt like it awaited him in the ocean's depths— several nights passed. He sat upon the sands listening to the culminating sounds of birds, waves, and winds. The melody continued to reach above the waves like a radiant song, bidding him to remain and listen.

What appeared out of the waters, more than seven nights after, slithered up an enormous serpent from the sea, covered in glistening azure scales. Its head reached far into the clouds before bowing low to spy Elior with its beady eyes, bound in a heavenly glow. The serpent appeared large enough to rip the entire land into the tides, but it remained moving ever stealthy to coil part of its massive body into the shallows. More noticeably, the serpent's grip on its tail latched tightly within the side of its mouth. Elior had retreated beyond the beach, Bright Bending his frame instantly from the sands to the highest peak overlooking the creature.

I replayed Elior's Bright Bend spell in my mind for a time, seeing if I could learn something about how he could cast it so fluidly. I had watched it happen during our travels together, but it felt like the first time I heard it more thoroughly. His ability to project his frame in one place and then move to another in less than the blink of an eye kept me stunned. So, I did not blink several times while gazing at the vision. I noticed how his eyes flashed a golden hue first, and his frame became consumed in a swift illumination of light, too immediate it would seem to others. Yet I could hear a soft melody remain momentarily from the flash. I wondered if I could perhaps use the melody to find him. I believe it was the clue Nirnasha had discovered and desired to share with me.

"You hold hearts familiar to me, small one," the serpent resounded its hiss, coming to Elior's ears like a distortion of the howling winds. "Should I devour you? The power of such hearts would be lost to the world forever."

"Is that the melody you have been playing?" Elior asked. "Is it a song of your intentions? I welcome you to try."

The serpent's head cocked slightly and then struck faster than anticipated. But Elior had already disappeared and reappeared away from the serpent's strike.

"Why do you hold your tail in your mouth?" Elior scoffed.

"That I may not lose myself," the serpent hissed a distasteful reply. "If not, I would not know where I began or recall where I end."

Again, it struck where Elior once stood, collapsing an entire cliffside. Yet Elior remained well enough away.

"Did you lure me here with the intention to take what was rightly given to me?"

"You are a light-bringer," the serpent held back the third strike. "The sound of your voice makes me believe you are either flying or standing directly upon my snout."

"Flying would be an adventure," Elior teased.

"You are an enigma I have never encountered." The serpent began to slither back out into the ocean. "You have my ear for now, but only till the waves sink back from the land."

"I serve the behest of my Master and Keeper," Elior stated.

"I am aware," the serpent stated, unimpressed. "I have listened to his voice before the corruption befell us all."

"A greater corruption comes even still," Elior continued.

The serpent hissed deeply at the back of its throat and tipped its head in a gesture that made Elior believe it to be snickering.

"There is no greater corruption," the serpent hissed. "That which men have allowed to reign. Indeed, it has swallowed them without pity."

"Has the light not been revealed to you, then?" Elior asked.

"I know the magic that wove together all things," the serpent boasted. "I had felt the rising of the conqueror I knew before the light was ever breathed into the realm. I was one of the first. And I shall be one of the last. You seek to teach me things that you do not fully comprehend. So, make your request known."

"My apologies," Elior responded quickly, feeling he had insulted the serpent. "You are wise beyond what I can truly fathom. I seek to do what my Master and Keeper have commanded me to do. I am to make more of who are snared with the hearts of Leviathans."

The serpent ceased swimming and lowered its head. It had made its way further into what was known at the time as the Balearic Sea and placed Elior down upon a large, inhabited island under the cover of night.

"Heavy is the burden laid upon you," the serpent hissed. "If I should help you, I have a task for you, light-bringer. There is a young girl not more than two-thousand paces up the road. Her name is Mariana. Fetch her, and bring her to me."

"How shall I get her to follow? Who shall I say calls her?"

"Tell her, Chu'mana calls to her," the serpent replied. "Call her by the name I have given her, Marilla."

"Are you to stay here?" Elior asked. "How will you not be seen?"

"I reveal myself to whom I please and hide away from eyes I detest," the serpent assured.

Elior did as instructed, hurrying to find the location of the girl. When he came to a small village, he realized he had no idea what the young girl looked like. He waited for daybreak and began asking for Mariana, cautiously concealing himself as a blind man, placing a cowl over his eyes.

"There are several here by that name," the people replied. "Which one do you seek? Do you know her face?"

"You would ask a blind man if I have seen her face?" Elior infectiously began to chuckle. Many who had crowded to meet the stranger began to laugh as well. But all ceased when he asked his next question. "Is there one who claims she has seen a giant serpent in the sea?"

"You asked for the cursed one?" A bold soul spoke up. "Who is she to you?"

"I believe we are kin in a way," Elior replied. "What use have you of her?"

"She fetches water mostly. Comes and goes as she pleases. But do not touch her, less you want her curse as well," another said.

"How do you know she is cursed?" Elior inquired.

"We see it in her eyes," several replied.

"Well, I cannot see her eyes," Elior continued to chuckle, knowing full well many had the same reaction to the interchanging of hues from his own. "I only wish to speak with her."

Some villagers volunteered to take Elior to the girl. He bid them farewell, and when he felt they had gone, he removed the cowl from his eyes. The young girl held an appearance of youth ready to be wed, with long sable hair and shining azure oval eyes. He spoke the serpent's name to her. Her face lit up, though she did not speak. Willingly and secretly, he led her back to the coast, where the serpent awaited them.

"She does not talk much," Elior stated.

"She does not talk at all," the serpent replied. "This one lost her voice somewhere within me."

"Did you try to eat her?" Elior gasped.

"I succeeded," the serpent hissed with a chuckle. "I swallowed her—her and every bit of the ship she was on. Somehow, she crawled out of me, made me gag when she reached the top of my throat, and so I heaved, almost losing grip of my tail. I had never seen such will from a daughter of men. That was over one hundred years ago."

"Then she is like me," Elior assumed.

"In a way," the serpent replied. "Assuredly, she touched my heart. When she did, she gained its favor. Though she cannot truly possess my power, as I am snared to another."

"Do you wish to be snared with her, then?" Elior asked.

"I do not wish to be shared with anyone," the serpent hissed. "Though, being bound with her heart would be better than the one I am currently tethered. He does not often make me lose control, but I commit evil when he overcomes me."

"Where is this one you are snared to? I shall destroy him." Elior promised.

"He dwells within me," the serpent's hisses resounded shamefully. "He is crafty—a trickster and a plague, born of unknown and dark magic."

"Within you?" Elior could not hold back his astonishment. "You wish I go within you to rid you of this fiend?"

"Time is not your friend," the serpent's eyes began to glaze over. "He knows you are here. He feels you. He is waiting for you."

The serpent opened its mouth, and Elior courageously stepped into the slimy darkness. The foul stench intensified as its jaws closed behind him. To the dismay of the MKR, as the back of the throat warped into several incisions, like thin cracks stretching through glass before shattering. As he touched it, he felt his body fall while his consciousness remained upright. It was the first time he stepped into the ethereal, leaving behind his physical presence, through the gateway to another inconceivable place, and traveling further onward inside the Leviathan.

Hung by chains and ropes were shriveled bodies, dangly in treetops as he went. Crimson liquid soaked him to his knees, sloshing thickly against his movement. Manifesting light orbs around him to cut through the gloom, Elior continued hunting for the snarer through the desolation that appalled him. A small-statured man sitting upon a throne of bones and weapons came into his view, emitting the type of frosty wind Elior would soon become familiar with.

"You are the one who holds the Leviathan captive?" Elior asked.

"What gave it away?" The tiny man cackled.

"The serpent said you were waiting for me. Why?" Elior demanded.

"So many questions with no introductions," the tiny man huffed. "I know you, Elior, but you do not know me."

"Then tell me your name so our introductions may be complete," the MKR insisted.

"Not yet," the tiny man rubbed his hands together. "My name holds a price."

"Your name is bound to the serpent," Elior grinned.

"Clever, boy," the tiny man scoffed. "You have been around a while to catch a thing or two. But can you tell me this, how will you release the serpent from my name?"

"You are an imp of riddles," Elior inferred. "I would do more than guess your name to release the serpent, that is for sure. I shall know your name, its origin, and the power it possesses."

"Seems like you got everything well in hand, hero," the tiny man continued to sneer.

"The aurora of your power is familiar, perhaps manifested, yet not created," Elior continued to deduce. "Your place of choosing to meet me is in the heart of a Leviathan, a place where one's voice dwells, and so does the power of desire. I can successfully presume you are stuck in this place because you lack the knowledge of how to wield the Leviathan's heart."

"Your intellect is astounding," the tiny man clapped. "You certainly know how to play a good game."

"Kalabhiti can only manifest you, but he cannot free you from this place," Elior said after a long silence.

"Kalabhiti?" The tiny man pretended disinterested.

"Kalab is my brother," Elior explained.

The imp's eyes widened. "He is your brother? Are you always spilling secrets like the outpouring of a flooded river?"

"Perhaps," Elior said playfully. "Or perhaps it is part of the game."

It was not intended, but it came to pass that Elior revealed a great magic, a reality beyond the reach of men, even immortals. He did it simply by imitation, remembering when light shines in the darkness, the gloom cannot perceive it, nor can darkness overcome it. By the will of what is and what will be, light has nothing in common with the dark. Thus, it reveals what it wishes to know.

In a burst that erupted into a blinding whirlwind of radiance, Elior's power revealed a whispering melody that did its best to remain hidden in the veil of shadow—melancholy, as if possessed by the very fabric of the despair it portrayed. He had no reference to describe it, nor did he know how to unravel it completely. But he began singing his own song, one of love and repose, to clutch the attention of the whispering captive voices who sang along with the haunting tune in the belly of the Leviathan. He felt one come to him and began singing along with him—the vibrancy of the young girl he sought to snare with Chu'mana.

Taistealaíonn m'anam riamh go dtí d'aghaidh
My soul ever wanders to your face

Tá tú inmholta agus milis
You are admirable and sweet

Imíonn deora ó do shúile fís liom
Tears from your eyes elate a vision in me

Cuirfidh do áilleacht an ghrian go deo
Your beauty forever will outlast the sun

De réir do gháire, tá mé gan déanamh
By your laughter, I am undone

Tú, mo amhrán radanta
You, my radiant song

Fís de gach rud go hálainn
A vision of all things lovely

Ór mo chuid smaointe
The treasure of my thoughts

An lá ar fad a thochailtíonn m'anam
All day, my soul digs on to find

Cén chaoi a mbeidh do chroí i gcónaí i mo chroí
How weaved your heart will always be to mine

The gladness of Elior's heart sang out, reminiscing of love he knew eons past. Her form appeared in his mind and projected elegantly in the light that illuminated the dark. More voices joined in his song, turning away from the tiny man's hold on them. Soon, the imp had no more voices to sing his melancholy tune, and the power of his gloom could not hold the serpent's heart. A glowing azure oculus arose, ridding itself of the crimson sludge and decay, floating like a cloud above the seashore. Elior reached out and grasped it in his hand. He brought it forth to show the tiny man who trembled feebly from the light.

"I know who you are," Elior exclaimed, his eyes turning the same azure brightness as the stone. "The heart speaks to me your name. You are

Rumpelstilzchen—Suzerain Efah."

"I did not know you were so powerful," Rumpelstizchen shuddered. "I shall go. But we will meet again." He looked directly into Elior's eyes. "For I do enjoy a good game."

In a mysterious and chilling wind, the tiny man disappeared.

"You were wrong," Elior said to the serpent once he had returned to the sunlight. "Your heart was caged, not ensnared. The tiny imp is already bound to another."

"You have my gratitude, light-bringer," the serpent replied. "I shall keep my promise to you."

"Your eyes," Elior heard a young girl's voice. "They are ever-changing, more so than before, and I see they shine like mine for a moment."

"Elior has touched Leviathans' hearts and used their power. Thus, it is forever part of us," the serpent hissed. "As are you forever part of me, little one."

"That is a lovely thought," the MKR of light admitted. "But you must snare your heart with her."

"It is done then," the serpent hissed with a sigh. "She shall come to know the power of Water and Flood."

Nirnasha found me pondering the visions as we met in the dining hall that evening. We began conversing about our next move when a sharp pain latched onto my spine. Lasair, distressed and tormented, ripped my attention wholly away from discerning anything else and wrenched my soul into the ethereal.

THE CURSED GATEWAY

I arrived in the ethereal, a daze crawling over me. When my eyes took hold of their focus, the barrier of trees, once a tiny haven for us to train as MKRs, lay torn to the ground, the veil of what felt like a child's secret hiding place, open and bare with each root prostrate and withered. Nirnasha appeared beside me, and for a moment, I could sense his heart tremble like a frightened little boy, lost and abandoned. I grabbed ahold of his hand as swiftly as I could to try and break him of that trepidation, but I could hear his thoughts. If the trees of the ethereal were being devastated, how long would it be before his snare became discovered?

Determined to reach Lasair with all possible haste, I began to run toward the horizon, but I could not get Nirnasha to follow me. He told me he had to find a place for his snare to hide. I could not stop him as he bolted off in the other direction. I knew I could not follow and continued running toward Lasair's melody, still sharp and crying in agony.

When I finally reached the top of the knoll overlooking the ethereal plain to her fortress, I spied creatures spread across the sward like grains of sand upon the seashore, with the fortress of fire not far from them. Appearing pale, sickly thin, and humanoid—the creatures had protrusive jaws and snouts harnessing razor-sharp teeth and claws stretching out from their fingers that were as gruesomely vicious as the jagged spikes along their backbone. Their wings extended out from their vertebrae like gnarly tree branches primarily found in bogs, displaying transparent sable canvases as they stretched further outward. And their eyes were caved inward to their bald skull, with nothing more than glistening heaven pupils.

Lasair's fortress appeared like a mountain of mystic midnight rock, veined with molten magma running through it just as I had seen before. I stared intently to see the one entrance through the abominations obstructing it—a massive, sizzling metal door. Suddenly, the fortress's towers that reached clear into the skies of the ethereal were just as molten as the foundation spewed smoke far into the atmosphere like storm clouds gathering thunder and releasing a chaotic downpour.

Slowly, I made my frame smaller to avoid attracting attention, ducking into the long grass and making my way to the bottom of the hill. I could hear Lasair's melody calling out to me. Her anguish resounded louder in my mind as I drew close. I could feel it beating through my veins. I had only leaped through a flame from the ethereal to the physical realm. I had not learned the melody to allow me to leap from one ethereal flame to another. But as I listened to Lasair, I realized she was trying to teach it to me, and in heightened desperation. I closed my eyes, seeing through her eyes, and located a crackling flame in her throne room. I reach out for it, humming along with her mind deep within myself. When I opened my eyes, her throne stood right next to me.

A loud cry from Lasair reached me, this time outside myself. I looked up and saw her bound, hanging upside down, and slowly being cut with a ghostly blade that appeared to be glowing with the color of frost, held by none other than the tiny man I so desperately wanted to destroy.

"Rumpelstilzchen!" I screamed.

The tiny man turned, looking somewhat staggered. My intuition sensed the hue of azure, and before he could move, I let loose a massive swirling cylinder of fire in his direction. The cylinder nearly slammed into him as he ducked out of the way. The tail of it whipped back and forth like a fin as it glided on by and sliced through Lasair's chains, freeing her to drop to the floor.

I took swift notice of the glowing crimson object the tiny man held in his hand, a glowing crimson—the Oculus of Teallach Tine. Elior had given it to him as the rest of us escaped the Tenebrous. Somehow, the imp had entered Lasair's fortress using the Hearth Fire of the realms. I conjured whips of pure blaze to drop from my hands and lunged them forward at the tiny man's hands. Both whips wrapped tightly around his wrists and yanked him forward to break his pointy nose upon the stone surface beneath our feet.

Even in her weakened state, Lasair reached out and nabbed the oculus. When she did, she burned more brightly than I had ever witnessed. Holding the oculus tightly to her torso, it sank through her outer frame and into her chest.

"The heart of a Leviathan," I gasped. "That is your heart!"

Spirits of fire rose from the floor, transforming into my likeness, and charged the imp. Their blazing arms pinned him down, sending him writhing and squirming like a helpless animal being prepared for slaughter.

"Rip him apart!" I spat.

"No!" Lasair's voice resounded. "Imprison him."

The spirits of fire followed Lasair's command, not mine.

"He knows how to reach Elior," Lasair explained as she turned toward me. "He will not escape my chains."

"How did he enter your fortress?!" I exclaimed.

"My heart is the only key," she answered. "But it is useless if one does not know its true power."

"How did Elior come to possess your heart?" I continued to pry. I could perceive she knew my eyes had seen where the tiny man acquired it.

"I entrusted it to him long ago," she replied. "Yet more pressing matters await us outside this fortress."

She called them "Strigoi"—tortured souls, twisted and vengeful—ethereal creatures that carry the power to desolate, making the plain a habitation for emerging nightmares and coercion to people's minds in the physical realm. They madly searched to feed, their eyes turning bright crimson as they drained the lifeforce of any being in the ethereal. Strigoi are one of the greatest dangers to an MKR while exploring the celestial world. By losing one's life force, a MKR who is also connected to the physical realm can permanently lose their mind—eternal death, and the MKR becomes just like them in spirit. Lasair briefly spoke of how she and Elior banished the creatures to the "Desolate Vales" once, a deep and dark void of the ethereal realm, where the most vilely dangerous creatures of the realm were locked away.

The Strigoi took flight like a great horde of insects invading the skies as the gates of her fortress opened and a bridge extended to the other side of the flowing magma moat. Lasair and I stood upon the steps as they began to encircle us. The Leviathan erupted a massive force of flames into the cloud of creatures, ceasing their onslaught, many of which turned to ash before raining to the ground or landing in the liquid fire below. There were still thousands of them swarming in a frenzy. I conjured Dancing Desire, a hundred or more figures now, taking on my form, and set ablaze with a conjured strength I had not yet summoned before. I felt Lasair's heart thump violently within my chest, and I could feel it surge new strength into me. I began conjuring more figures, each one summoning its own flames to take on the massive airborne army. Lasair conjured a fire shield around us, bringing a brutal end to any Strigoi who flew into it.

We were able to keep up our defense for a time, slaying hundreds of the dark creatures as we slowly made our way across the bridge. But I could sense even Lasair's strength began to wane, and it seemed there was no end to the Strigoi falling upon us. Many of my figures were laid open, their empty shells broken into an ashy heap, the fire from their eyes smoldering out like coals grown cold.

The next moment, a familiar soul reached my own, and I soon heard his thoughts. The ground shook violently, and I could hear Nirnasha laughing as ethereal Dendro charged toward Lasair's fortress. The flapping throng from the sky and terrain-pounding flora multitude unforgivingly slammed into one another, where the Strigoi, though swifter than the Dendro, were outmatched in strength. The tree creatures held their own, springing up vines and branches to snatch the Strigoi out of the air as they flew.

"He's learned a melody to awaken trees," I told Lasair, watching the Strigoi lose interest in us. "Do you suppose he could do the same in the physical realm?"

"Nirnasha's power has grown immensely," she admitted, seeming somewhat astonished. "Only one could teach him that melody and that Leviathan was lost. Yet could it be?"

"What do you mean?"

"Uklallood, the Dusk Wood," Lasair answered as she led me away from the fortress and the battle. "He was known as the Dream Tree, responsible for giving life to trees and bringing about the Dendro into the realm of mortals. Not many things surprise me. Yet the ethereal sometimes manifests a mind of its own—perhaps Uklallood was never truly gone."

We had briskly made our way around to the back of the fortress, where Lasair pointed out an opening to a dark cave.

"The Cursed Gateway lies above us," she explained, turning my attention to something I could sense held greater import. "There is a portal hidden within. It leads into the realm of Enenra."

"Who is that?" I asked.

Lasair pointed to the smoke and vapor rising from her fortress, where the skies formed clouds that stretched out further than I could see.

"Enenra is snared with another you have met before," she explained. "Amara Monroe—she will most likely be waiting for you."

"Am I going alone?" Admittedly, I stuttered a bit.

"The pact between Enenra and I prevents her from setting foot in my domain as it prevents me from setting foot in hers," Lasair continued. "Elior believed the gates to the Vales would be safest where no one would think to look. It also created a permanent bond between my sister and me. The only way for her to come down is to be invited by one bound to me."

"You have a sister?"

"I have two," Lasair replied. "One, you have already rescued, Gurēsusutā. The other is Enenra. The three of us were once protectors of the realms, unbound by the physical plain and untethered from the ethereal. You wished to know how Elior came to hold my heart. Then you should know all began in our creation, as the three of us were given a task—subdue the reaches of the Desolate Vales to the physical realm. Yet the Leviathan, who was imprisoned there, grew powerful in its rest. It emerged here, and we fought it—the Leviathans, our summoned creations, and Elior fought with us. Together, with vast losses that included Uklallood, we fought to push back the Leviathan and its snarer. You know him as Kalabati Lystander."

Kalab and Elior had once fought on the ethereal realm long before the Great Collide and likely much further back in time than I could fathom. Lasair continued her story, speaking of another cave Elior had sealed long ago that was a portal to the Evergloom, the darkest region of the Desolate Vales. It was a place of no light and unexplored even to the ancient ones of the ethereal. Somehow, Elior and Lasair had once followed Kalab and his first snare into the Desolate Vales, returning to seal the gateway behind them successfully.

Eras passed, and the evil lurked in the shadows, pouncing when least expected. Kalab resurrected into the ethereal. Somehow, a gateway to the Desolate Vales opened, and a sea of monstrous creatures came pouring out—the Strigoi. Lasair again summoned Elior to aid her and her sisters, but it would not be a flawless victory. Gurēsusutā was severely injured, almost losing her heart. She abandoned her sisters to return to the stars—refusing to contact them but remaining loyal to Elior's melody, for he had saved her from destruction. How or when she befell Rumpelstilzchen's influence and entrapment, Lasair could not be sure. Yet the damage to Gurēsusutā's soul weighed heavily upon her.

"Tell Enenra I have brought Gurēsusutā back to my fortress," Lasair said. "And I also have the imp imprisoned now. She would enjoy seeing him bound."

"If Enenra hates the tiny man so much, then why allow Amara to be controlled by his bidding?" I asked.

"It is more complicated than that," Lasair replied. "She is embittered, especially toward Elior."

"Why?"

"Because he bound her to guard the gateway to the Desolate Vales," Lasair explained. "Gurēsusutā was not the only one to flee for her life. It was Enenra who abandoned her in the first place. She also fled in the face of the nightmare creature."

So that was it. Elior had cursed Enenra to be the guardian of the gateway for her cowardice. Most likely, Elior forced his hand on Enenra to become snared with Amara. It would not take much to push an embittered heart over the edge, to mar and corrupt the connection in one's favor.

"Go now," Lasair uttered urgently. "I shall see to it that Nirnasha is unharmed."

"I do not believe he will need help," I grinned. "But I appreciate the sentiment that you care deeply for the ones I, too, cherish."

I stepped into the cave, igniting flames in my hands to light the way. I could hear a strange melody guiding me down a chasm of stairways and tunnels. Precious stones started to come into view and soon shimmered all around me, my fire reflecting their azure and viola hue. They appeared like ice and began to dwindle into vapor as I intensified the flames extending from my hands to my forearms. The path grew darker, and I sensed the melody ahead as untrustworthy and then heard a heart quietly kick into an adrenaline rush.

Amara suddenly stepped into the light of my flames, a blank stare covering her face. I could discern she felt threatened by my presence. I had destroyed her the last time, and from how her fists clenched, I believe she remembered our last encounter quite well.

"Enenra wishes to speak with you," she said. "It is the only reason I do not..."

"Burn to a crisp again?" I interjected. "You are trapped in an enclosed tunnel with me, the one whose flames cannot scorch. So, either lead the way to Enenra's lair, or we can dance all over again."

"I do this as a respect for my source of magic and life," Amara replied, keeping her deadpan gaze. "You know just how much the pneuma affects tangible bones and the very breath of the flesh. You believe me to be nothing more than an embittered soul, and such is my only manifestation. But what you do not know is I am not hardened in bitterness. It is a fireproof apathy—and you cannot desolate it, not with all your rage. I simply wait for another day when you will again burn me to ash so I may rise again till I figure out how to permanently cage you like an animal, tortured and helpless, without end."

Amara, let me pass. I did my best to show no expression and kept my heart at a steady pace, knowing that if it began to race, she would have known her words pierced my thoughts. She knew how to cut, that is sure. I had never liked the idea of being trapped in any cage. At that moment, I realized Amara was caged. Her words gave it away. She ached to be free.

"You loved once," I said, keeping my back turned. "I have seen his thoughts. He still cares for you deeply."

"Keep moving, worm," Amara spat. I had struck back at her heart now.

I made my way down another corridor of turns and steps, reaching a small room with a rippling wall in front of me. I could vaguely spot the transparency of the rock as the light of my fire caused it to reflect. I stepped through as if a reflection in the water and into dim light piercing the veil of swirling smoke—a bit unnerving for my mind as I placed one foot in front of the other. Indeed, the spectacle held to a notion of something out of a dream, where walking on smoke clouds is feasible, and the sun burns red through the vapor. The view of the ethereal skyline reminded me of a distant place, my bedroom window as a child, where I once stood to gaze upon the city of Langdon, seeing the light rise above the buildings for a new dawn.

"Beautiful, is it not?"

The voice sounded much like Lasair, a mother's calming tone. I turned to see a face cascading in a young woman's beauty, with shimmering stone eyes and smooth sable skin. Her hair appeared like ash and ascended like ether from a steam engine. Her clothing draped around her as if wrapped in ribbon and dipped in shadow. The sun that pierced through the veil of smoke touched the silky cloth, making it appear like tiny embers sparking to life and then fading away.

"You are Enenra?" I asked.

"I am," the woman replied. "You are Aagneya. Lasair has spoken to you about me?"

"Some, not all," I said as Amara appeared behind her. "I was told you were expecting me. What do you wish to discuss?"

Enenra held her answer. I felt as if she were studying my demeanor and trying to decide how best to proceed. She then confessed that she desired to know why Lasair bound herself to me.

"Lasair never cared to be snared with an ever-living mortal," Enenra said. "I find it suspicious."

"I came to hear what you have to say, but I will not hear complaints about Lasair's decision to be bound to me, less it is of great import," I calmly stated.

"Fair enough," Enenra huffed. "Despite my disbelief of Lasair's true intentions, I admit she has chosen well."

"Flatter me if you wish," I replied. "But I can see you are stalling."

"I am simply thinking things through," Enenra scolded me. "Should I resist you or not? I am calculating the odds."

"We have brought Gurēsusutā back to Lasair's fortress," I imparted Lasair's message, seeing that Enenra was continuously weighing her options. "We also have the imp imprisoned now. Lasair told me that you would enjoy seeing him squirm."

Enenra's face lit up.

"So, it is bribery? You would also lure me away from my realm and imprison me."

"That is not the intention," I urged.

"Then why come find me if not to lure me into a trap?" Enrena demanded. "Lasair seeks to gain the power of our hearts, not free us from our dark coils."

"How do you know this?" I shot back.

"Did she not tell you why I ran and why Gurēsusutā was left behind?" Enenra's tone began to unravel into a malicious bite. "She and Elior have long sought to bring about our end, but we have remained. Despite Elior's curse upon me, I have figured out how to open the Desolate Vales and deliver to my sister what she deserves."

"She mentioned Elior cursed you to be the guardian."

"A continuous burden piercing my existence with torturous intent," Enenra spat. "To where I have allowed another to lessen my pain in exchange for passage through the gateway."

"The snare of Kalab?" I asked.

Her gaze into my eyes revealed her betrayal, but I did not make a move. I wanted to strike down Amara, and battle the Leviathan, to take her heart as she was undeserving of its power. Yet I ceased the thought, remembering just how easy it is to succumb to a power that has convinced the mind of its necessity. Unnerving, Enenra spoke as if her heart belonged to the vile brother of Elior.

"Why allow Strigoi through then? Did he ask you to do that?" I continued to question.

"Yes. And allowing more through the gate relieves the burden," Enenra gritted her teeth. "You shall see more nightmares if this curse upon me is not lifted."

"How do I lift the curse?" I inquired.

"It must be asked for," was her answer.

"I shall desire you to give me the burden on one condition," I said after several moments had passed in silence. Both Enenra and Amara appeared surprised by my words. "I shall ask the curse from you, but you must go to Lasair and peacefully remain with her. Should you leave the fortress, the curse returns to you, and so does your heart belong to me."

"I am to be a prisoner for all time?!"

"Not for all time," I exclaimed. "Only until Kalab is dealt with. I believe we may have a chance, but we must first free all the other MKRs from the imp's hold. If you ally yourself with us, you will return here sooner."

Enenra exposed her disbelief with a heavy sigh. But the more she churned my words over, her face began to soften.

"The only thing that changes in people is perspective," Enenra said. "When their perspective changes so do their thoughts and actions. And should perspective change, so do one's desires."

"Has your perspective changed then?" I asked. "How can I be certain that it has?"

"I would rather be free of this curse and watch the imp rot in the cells of Lasair's oblivion," she replied. "The sooner we are free from Kalab, the better. I accept your offer."

Once we entered Lasair's fortress, I awoke in the physical plain with an agonizing prickling running up and down my spine. My soul felt weighted as if my heart would sink into my intestines, and a feverish chill swept over my brow. The curse once belonging to Enenra now dwelt in me.

The door to my room gently opened. Nirnasha walked toward me, softly grasped my shoulders, and ran his fingers through my hair. I was not aware I had been unconscious for several days.

"We need to talk," he said. Behind him, stepping through the doorway, were Amaterasu Nasmire and Amara Monroe.

I met the three in the passenger's lounge after getting dressed and taking in some, what I believe, much-needed ordinary pleasures. The waft from the pungent aroma of my tea laid my head back with a soothing sigh into a cushy lounge chair, my bare feet near a crackling potbelly stove. I could feel my muscles begin to ease with my favorite delectable jaffa blossom beverage with honey milk stirred into my cup. I could not care less that the other two in our company were previously trying to kill us and perhaps were still plotting against us. I craved to enjoy the moment. Amara did not take her eyes off me as the four of us remained in awkward silence, sipping away and nibbling on dried Sus dipped in a finely spiced Rubus sauce.

It would suddenly come to my attention after this uneasy encounter that the Gullywhumper had gone on a bit of a test run of sorts while Nirnasha and I were battling Strigoi in the ethereal, sacking a merchant airship bound for Nod from Westmain. More unbelievable, Meik and the rest of our crew were able to do so without being seen. Wild Willy, Darby, Garvish, and Bikarma, volunteered to sneak aboard the airship. At the same time, the Gullywhumper flew alongside under cover of night and cloaked with Easton's Mirror Mirage ability. Over the course of an hour or two, they managed to relinquish much of the merchant's precious cargo stealthily. I did not complain, but it did take me some time to shut my jaw from the shock. As I was enjoying the pleasures of what the lounge now had to offer with the others, it did not cross my mind at the time to question whether I was delving into stolen goods and participating in piracy. Finally, Amaterasu ventured the first words.

"I cannot believe my brother could merge his soul with this ship."

"You mean because of how he goofed off before," Amara interjected. "I must agree with you then. How a fool like Easton…"

"Still bitter, I see," we heard Easton's voice taunt Amara over the ship's Nanomite Communicator.

"Enough!" I blurted out. I turned my eyes to Amaterasu and spoke to her in a much calmer tone. "Thank you for breaking the silence with small talk. But I do not believe we have time for that. We have a problem, one that must be resolved swiftly."

"Which is?" Amaterasu asked.

"The distrust in this room could be cut with a knife," I replied. "Nirnasha and I have no reason to trust either of you. And there is no reason either of you should trust us."

"Agreed," both women said.

Nirnasha remained silent. I could hear his thoughts, encouraging me to lead the conversation. He was much more interested in focusing on the two's mannerisms to catch any signs of treachery.

"So, my question to both of you is this," I continued. "Now that your snares are not under threat, and the threat is also imprisoned in Lasair's fortress, what are your plans?"

"I told you I would be your ally," Amaterasu responded quickly. "The power of the imp cannot reach Gurēsusutā so long as Lasair's power remains intact."

"Her power shall not waver," I assured, knowing Lasair had retrieved her heart from the tiny man. Yet I did not divulge that information. "You wish to ally yourself with us, but we cannot trust you. I can feel even Easton is cautious. However, I can promise that should there be any signs of betrayal, Lasair will let the imp go, and the Suzerain Efah shall enslave you again."

"That is not something I desire," Amaterasu sighed, her tone resounding with sincerity. "But do not think for a moment the Suzerain Efah will be unable to tempt either of you. He finds a way into the heart, to see what dark desires lay dormant, and then exploits them."

"How do you mean?" Nirnasha finally spoke.

Amaterasu wasted no time in spilling the burdened story she carried. Orphaned long ago yet remained close with Easton. She adored him, and loved that Elior chose her to awaken as an MKR with him. When Amara, her best friend, became the third recruit to be awakened, she became overjoyed. Together, the four of them felt like family, even when Easton and Amara became lovers. Amaterasu soon after began seeing Elior romantically. Yet when she told him of her intentions, he did not reciprocate. Young and naive, Amaterasu did not take the rejection as peacefully as Elior believed. The one who lay in wait emerged when Amaterasu found herself alone one night.

Like a cunning merchant, Rumpelstilzchen swayed her thoughts to believe that Elior's heart could be hers. The words themselves were like magic, weaving a spell that captivated her into performing a task for him. She held the power to move like the wind, and Rumpelstilzchen desired to do the same. Her task—teach him the melody for this ability, which explained his swiftness. Thus, for Elior's heart, Amaterasu taught the tiny man the melody, which almost cost Elior dearly.

In the following days, Rumpelstilzchen engaged Elior several times, doing his best to trap him. However, Elior remained one step ahead, declaring that Rumpelstilzchen came with a familiar chill, much swifter than the wind. It was then Elior suspected Amaterasu of betrayal. She confessed, but also, in the same breath, again, confessed her undying love.

"Love is not treacherous," Elior told her.

Elior sent her away, cut off from his mind. From then, in the dark, Rumpelstilzchen wooed her to do more of his bidding by teaching her his own melodies. Amaterasu learned how not to breathe, taking on death as life, allowing her to move into the depths of the sea and into the Galactic Void. He also taught her a melody to protect her skin from ice so she would never feel the sting of frost again. The downside, unbeknownst to her, was the more often she used the melodies, the deeper indebted she became to the imp. She found the will of her soul dwindling as his hold on her grew. Till one fateful night, the imp came to her bedside and committed foul deeds to her flesh. She could not even find the strength to scream. During that time, she not only gave up her body to Rumpelstilzchen but gave up the location of the Grace Star. By the imp's words, he swore to destroy Gurēsusutā if she did not continue to do his bidding—and he swore he could.

"That is when she met me in secret," Amara interceded. "That is when I knew Elior was to blame, as it was Elior who banished her away from us."

"Did you tell Easton about this?" I asked.

"I did," Amara gritted her teeth. "And he sided with Elior, against my friend, against his own sister."

"I did not side with Elior," Easton's voice rang out. "I spoke with him about what had happened. He and I even tried to get Gurēsusutā to bring her back to Lasair. But before we could even try, you were gone! You abandoned us!"

"I did not abandon you!" Amara spat. "I was trying to save my friend—to keep that monster away from her!"

"She would have been safe," Easton replied.

"Did you succeed?!" Amara continued shouting. "No. You did not! Your sister was still lost. And you did nothing!"

"Kalab resurrected," Amaterasu interjected, which halted all shouting. "That is what terrified us all."

His appearance sent a shockwave through the physical realm as his form became fully restored—in what Amaterasu referred to as the year 1989, in a place called The Forest of Nisene Marks, located in the province known as California, an era far in the past. The cataclysmic event remained notable in the historical records from that time. Just in his reappearance, Kalab took the lives of more than fifty people.

"Elior said he was preparing us for the day of Kalab's return," Amara continued. "However, Amaterasu and I quickly fell to the might of his power. Elior convinced Easton to run, even while I was still alive. Kalab focused on torturing me, though I know not why, in the forest for hours with no one to hear me scream. We were abandoned."

"You engaged Kalab without us!" Easton's voice boomed throughout the room. "We were supposed to face him together, and you dragged Amaterasu into the fight because she was with you and trying to save you. Do not place blame where it does not belong!"

Amara and Easton began bickering with one another again. Most strangely, it held amusement to see Amara quarreling with a ship, but I needed to reign in the ex-lovers.

"Enough!" I shouted. "I do not care what has transpired. We are here now and do not have time to bicker amongst ourselves."

"We are approaching Harvenger," I heard Meik's voice interpose. "Everyone should come see this."

We all stepped out onto the deck, overlooking the vast fortified city of Harvenger in Westmain, and there, coming down from the clouds—an ill omen. Once, I believed the greatest evil resided in the Unlight, a place of shadows and fears of the unseen. I had witnessed Wendigo first-hand and other atrocities that lie in wait below. But watching, undoubtedly, a vast sky fortress floating among the clouds proved me wrong—the greatest of calamities come from the sky.

The enormous propeller engines made it hover above the earth, with the ever-presence of smoke and steam swirling around it as if harnessed by some orbiting whirlwind. Meik steered us closer to the fortress, where a frightful sound overwhelmed the humming of the propellers. We gazed upon a horde of Lurkers of all kinds, roaring to be let wildly loose on Harvenger below.

"If the city falls, Westmain will be crippled," I told the others.

"Harvenger's wairships are rising to meet it," Amara pointed out. "We need all the firepower we can get."

"Eastguard wairships are coming in behind the floating fortress," Meik shot our gaze toward the horizon. "Westmain wairships have their hands full."

"Then we must take the fortress on ourselves," I said. "We shall begin by bombarding the flying monstrosity with cannon fire. Aim for the propellers. We will need to take it out before it is directly over the city."

"Battle stations then!" Meik exclaimed with excitement that I had grown accustomed to seeing him portray. The itch to take the Gullywhumper into a fight pressed on his mind since it became airborne.

Each of us found a cannon to aim while Meik operated the helm. As I took my station at the cannon, I realized I had never fired one before. Nirnasha, who jumped into position at the next station to my left, heard my thoughts. His burst of laughter resounded as we began our first pass.

"Get ready!" Easton's voice echoed throughout the ship while Meik suddenly pushed the engines to their maximum output. The Gullywhumper sped up and cut through the clouds, coming dangerously close to the flying fortress, which now had guns pointed toward us. Eastguard soldiers lined the walls loading their cannons. But we fired first. The starboard side blasted while the cannons we controlled explicitly aimed for one of the propellers. The armor was so thick that our cannons barely scratched it. We spun around to make another pass to fire from the port side. I took careful aim, trying to locate any weak spot in the structure of the propeller. Again, we barely made any impact. I completely missed it as I discovered I am not a good shot with a cannon aboard an airship moving at maximum velocity. The cannons from the flying fortress fired upon us but flew short of reaching us as we had already moved out of their range.

"Something is familiar about this fortress," I heard Nirnasha's thoughts. "Have we seen this palace before?"

Indeed, we had. It was the palace of Dejan Pure Bone, the very same as Havensire—somehow detached from its foundations to be forced into flight. I ran to the navigation deck, knowing we only had one way to take it down. Meik appeared alarmed when I told him we would have to destroy the fortress from the inside, as our cannons did not dent the propellers.

"Lurkers are on that thing along with Eastguard soldiers," he said. "I afeared to think of what else may be waiting."

"Much like delving into the Unlight," I reasoned. "There is no other choice."

"Let's try to clear some of them off the walls," Meik replied. "It should get you clearance to go aboard."

"Agreed!"

After one more pass, the Gullywhumper fired its cannons in a barrage that sent Eastguard soldiers flying in all directions. As we ascended alongside the cleared wall, more soldiers began moving toward us. Wild Willy and Kassy Bones operated a buzzsaw firing gun each, giving those of us boarding cover fire.

The screams of soldiers being cut to pieces by sawblades pierced my ears as we descended to the wall. The first ones off were Amara and Amaterasu, resorting to using drill guns as a defense. Nirnasha had suggested we conserve energy for any unpleasant surprises we may find inside that would require more powerful means to rout them. Next were the two idiots, Garvish and Bikarma, who would not take no for an answer. Darby and Reggie began sniping Eastguardian soldiers as Nirnasha, and I descended behind them, and they surprisingly followed us.

"What are you doing?!" I shouted to Darby and Reggie.

"Not going to sit this one out," Darby exclaimed. "Reggie and I are both from Prag, and we joined the academy at Harvenger long ago. We are not about to let those soldiers down."

"Westmain would never forgive us if we turned cowards," Reggie added, the first time I had heard Darby or Reggie talk about their past. I truly hoped it would not be the last.

Soldiers fled from the wall, retreating further into the fortress, leaving behind their wounded and many others spread out in a crimson slaughter. As we began to make our way off the wall, what I can only describe as a flash across my sight and a surge of anguish pulsed through my veins. I peered down, thinking some projectile hit me. Yet no sawblade had. Nirnasha took notice of my left wrist, now intensifying with darkened and sickly-looking veins—something spreading, gnashing, and climbing up my arm. I locked eyes with Nirnasha, and he heard my thoughts as I winced.

"The curse of the gateway is starting to ravage me."

CASTLE IN THE CLOUDS

The agony of something sluggishly clawing up my arm made my hand grow numb—the gateway curse began devouring me. I needed to act fast and focus my power to burn intensely inside my left arm. The sickly veins twitched violently, allowing me to see the curse itself as somehow living, perhaps a monster. And like any monster, I knew I would enjoy learning how to kill it.

"If it becomes too much," Nirnasha thought. "Maybe I can help drain some of the pain."

"What do you mean?" I echoed back to him.

"Do you remember when I drained your power to melt the vault door while we were in the Tenebrous?"

"Yes. Where you almost killed me?" I glared at him.

"I think it is not limited to draining power," he responded without waiting for me to finish. "Please, I think I can help if you need me."

I placed my arms around him. Noticeably, the others appeared to think we were taking in a romantic moment, but I did not care. I grabbed Nirnasha's hand, and he heard my thoughts thanking him as I slipped a royal crimson leather glove over my left hand to hide my wrist. The curse remained where it was for now, and my hand regained its sensitivity. We began descending the wall's rubble toward what I assumed were shadows hiding blood-thirsty Lurkers.

"By the way," Nirnasha's thoughts came quietly to my own. "I thought of a name for that draining spell. I call it my Terrestrial Trough."

"Trough," I echoed back. "Is that what you think I was?!"

"I had not thought of that," Nirnasha teased.

He caught the brunt of my glare, which made him quickly change the subject.

"This place reminds me of something I read in one of the books I found," Nirnasha spoke softly. "This boy climbed up an enormous vine called a beanstalk that went up to the sky. When he reached the top, there was a castle with a giant and his wife living there. They had all kinds of gold and magical treasures."

"You and Meik should get together and talk," I replied with the same quiet tone. "You really think we will run into giants here?"

The others turned back to the both of us, wondering what we were so silently conversing about. None of that mattered. Royal crimson eyes illuminated the shadows a moment later, followed by other bright lights. Steam immersed from the sprockets and gears rising upward—admittedly like the giants Nirnasha had described. Yet these were made of steel and copper. More stood up behind it, each upright with two buzzsaw firing guns attached to each of their arms. Mechs, as I had not seen another in operation up close since Starvel, were enchanted with Mystic Silver and did not clunkily maneuver like regular steam types. Each Mech encased a pilot wearing elite dark cocoa uniforms, narrow protector spectacles that glowed gold, and remained tucked away in the machines safely behind projectile-proof glass.

The guns from the Mechs began to rev up, and I must have forgotten that I needed to move. But Darby, Reggie, Garvish, Bikarma, and Nirnasha had already darted for cover while Amara flew into the air to distract them.

I followed Amaterasu in the opposite direction to find cover. Amara easily dodged Mech's sawblades by disappearing and leaving a puff of smoke behind. When she disappeared into the cover of the shadows, the Mechs began searching for us, frantically shining their lights around. We could remain hidden among the cargo of what appeared to be a flight deck. But the only way passed the Mechs was an exposed one hundred and twenty footsteps to a wide-open stairway. We would be easy targets. Even as I tried to think of a plan, one of the Mechs exited the flight deck, guarding the way upward to move deeper into the fortress.

Amara appeared next to me, clenching her ribs. One sawblade had not missed. She gritted her teeth as she pulled it from her body, not making a sound. While an endless flow of blood trickled out of the wound, she assured me it would heal quickly. I watched, astonished the hole shut in a few moments without a mark to be found, just a tear in her clothing where the blade had pierced through.

"I cannot see a way around them," Amaterasu whispered.

An enormous roar echoed from the distant darkness where we had entered. We could dimly see the horde of Lurkers making their way toward us, with more than a dozen Bangores leading the charge—my first time witnessing Bangores directly. The abominations were the strongest of the Lurkers, massively sized with bulked-out muscles, evident brute strength, and surprisingly agile maneuverability.

"I believe that will not matter shortly," I replied, drawing her attention to what noisily charged our way.

Amara swooped out from behind the covering and charged one of the Mechs. I followed behind her. Amaterasu split in the opposite direction toward another, weaving in and out among the cargo. It must have stirred our other comrades from hiding as Nirnasha sprang into action behind the Mech near the stairs. He sprouted enormous roots from his backside that swiftly nabbed the ankles of the Mech when he ran behind it. The roots tensed, and the Mech's legs were yanked out from where it stood, cracking the projectile-proof shield as it crashed face-down.

Amara took to the air, distracting the Mech before us, and shouted for me to send flames toward the pilot's face. I summoned roaring shoots of fire that hit their mark, but with no natural effect until Amara did the unthinkable. The air around her grew toxic and intensified into a flammable explosion that sent me flying backward. I felt my body land harshly against the ground and tumble several times. I knew I could not miss a beat as I rolled into the approaching the Lurker horde. Somehow, I kept flames firing out from my hands to fend off the ones closest to me.

The blast from the explosion distracted the Mech Amaterasu was charging, giving her an opening to strike. I could feel the air become different, and the streaming fire from my hands began to move in waves. A moment of absolute silence came, followed by an incredible shockwave that boomed a tremendous force of energy into the Mech. The machine flew backward from the massive blast, and the shockwave rippled back and outward, slapping against my hands and blowing out my fire. A Bangore came near, about to pounce on me, when a more concentrated shockwave sent it flying backward. I peered to see

Amaterasu somehow right next to me. She sent another shockwave into the oncoming horde, which gave her enough time to pull me to my feet.

Sawblades raced over our heads, hitting the Lurkers on our heels, covering fire from our comrades, Darby, Reggie, Garvish, and Bikarma, as they ran along the flight deck. Nirnasha called out for us to hurry. I tried looking for Amara as we went but could find no trace of her.

"It will take some time for her to regenerate," Amaterasu shouted, seeing my lag to search for Amara. "Until then, we are down a MKR."

The Mech that Amara had taken down lay a shambled, fiery junk heap, and the one Amaterasu destroyed sprawled in complete dismemberment, including the pilot. As we reached the stairs, I witnessed Nirnasha elicit more roots from his back that wrapped around the Mech's arms he had brought down. Lifting it into the air, and seeing the pilot's neck broken, he tensed the roots until the machine yanked apart. The body of the Mech fell and rolled toward the horde of Lurkers, followed by Nirnasha hurling the Mech's limbs in their direction as well.

"Up the stairs," I heard Darby say as we finally reached their position.

More Bangores were swiftly approaching us, but Nirnasha's roots were snapping like whips, with one wrapping so tightly around a Bangore's neck that it popped its head clean off.

"I shall hold them here!" Nirnasha exclaimed.

I hurled a few good fireballs into the horde of Lurkers before I joined the others entering the palace. In reaching the threshold, we were immediately greeted with sawblade fire. Eastguardian elites lined the halls with buzzsaw rifles and wore steel armored military garbs.

"Aim for their neck!" Darby shouted.

We let the boys saw-fight for a bit while Amaterasu and I pulled drill guns to take a shot or two to wait for our next move. A couple of rounds found their mark, which I relished in knowing all my practice with the drill gun was not in vain—as I could not seem to aim a cannon properly.

The Eastguard soldiers began retreating further into the palace after several shots back-and-forth. Reggie hit his marks almost as well as Darby, but Darby never missed—one shot, one kill. I told Amaterasu that it looked like we would not need to clear the hall after all until another Mech, like the ones just moments before, burst through the doorway at the far end.

"I shall knock it down. You melt its face," Amaterasu smiled.

She surged an enormous shockwave down the hall that blew out the floor-to-ceiling windows, tore through the line of soldiers, and slammed into the projectile-proof glass of the Mech, only creating small cracks. The Mech, however, flew onto its back, and I ran the length of the hallway, hearing the footsteps of my comrades behind me. I leaped into the air and landed on the Mech, staring the pilot in her face. Then, I forcibly pushed fire through the glass cracks and roasted her alive.

"Keep going," I heard Nirnasha shout from the threshold where we had just been, the horde of Lurkers closely behind him. They spilled into the hallway like a swarming wave seeking to devour anything within reach, closing in on Nirnasha's heels.

Amaterasu summoned another shockwave down the hall, but not before she shouted for Nirnasha to dive to the floor. He slid to his stomach as the shockwave soared over him. He did not take time to see the devastation it brought to the onslaught of Lurkers and continued making his way toward us. We turned and ran into the next corridor. Upon entering, Garvish was ambushed from above by another familiar Lurker, a Prowler that almost sank its teeth into his neck. However, Darby had already aimed and shot a sawblade clear through its head.

We heard more freakish growling and noticed more creeping up into the windows as Bikarma pulled Garvish to his feet. I brought forth my summoning for Dancing Desire, but strangely, the melody I heard within me awoke something new. An agonizing surge shot out of my chest with enormous flames that became a large, winged beast. It appeared like a reptile, with razor teeth and claws illuminated in bright, jaffa fire. I felt Nirnasha take hold of me, feeling my vision fade and my breath shorten until I awoke in the ethereal, upon Lasair's highest fortress tower. She stood over me with a smile.

"You are ready to know the truest power of my heart," she said. "No one can summon this unless they are bound to me. You are the only one I have ever shared this melody with. Not even Elior knows its tune."

"It killed me!" I shot back. "Quite horrifically! I have never known such anguish."

"The fire of love cannot die, Aagneya, even when it explodes from the heart," she continued, bringing me to my feet. "Out of desolation, love shall thrive—turning ashes to beauty, anguish to joy, and ruins to everlasting cities of light."

"Does the melody have a name?" I asked.

"Azrael, the Destroyer of Men," Lasair answered. "I forged her from the sorrows of my heart and the blessing of the one who made me. In eras past, she has taken on many forms, but her purest is fire."

Lasair pointed toward the skies. Azrael, a melody simultaneously existing in the ethereal and the physical realm, flew toward us, coming to bring me back. As the beast reached down and plucked me from Lasair's tower, I felt a peace, much like when Elior smiled at me the first time. Questions of what Lasair had spoken of raced through my imagination as Azrael soared back to my body in the physical realm. I saw Nirnasha holding me close, with the others ducked beneath the mighty creature's breast. No Lurker remained in sight, and the walls of the hall and corridors were devastated, with nothing more than a walkway leading up another stairway.

Nirnasha continued to embrace me as breath returned to my lungs, and he plucked me from the floor. Still weak from the return, he carried me to the stairway, where I felt the strength to stand again. All of us held nothing more than a couple of bruises and lacerations, but each one had a grin that elated our confidence to believe the flying fortress would surely fall.

"Can you cover us from above?" I asked Azrael. "Make sure reinforcements do not surprise us?"

Azrael took to the air as we began climbing further into the palace. Darby and Reggie were each instinctively convinced the helm for the flying fortress was in the throne room. Undoubtedly, we would find Dejan Pure Bone and perhaps his brother, Takato, there. What we did not expect along the way reached our view in the next corridor after climbing the stairs—another familiar face.

Gravely battered, Bastian Raven Caste leaned against the wall, clinging to a buzzsaw rifle and a slightly curved blade that appeared much like an officer's weapon yet modified to his particular style of brutish combat—the hilt, a formed raven head, with the beak, sharpened like the end of a spear. The blade's guard had a circular pair of wings curled around the blade, which rose upward to approximately more than twice an arm's length. It held a magical glow of azure, which could only come from a specific metal.

I could not determine if he was glad to see us or disappointed. He did not mistake us for enemies, but he certainly did not make any indication he wanted us there, either.

"The Raven Caste clan is gone," Bastian sighed after remaining still and silent for quite some time. "Our estate is decimated. My whole family is now gone. If she has not been killed off, no one is left other than perhaps Sabia."

"What happened?" I bravely asked as my inquiry received a gaze meant to kill.

"We were betrayed...by Bartus," Bastian gritted his teeth. "I managed to survive, and I hunted him back to Havensire. When I reached the city, chaos already ensued—people being taken by Gloom Gnawers, others put into cages, tortured, killed, then raised to become Lurkers."

"Creating more Lurkers?" Nirnasha asked. "How?"

"There is a kind of Lurker that can do such things," Bastian replied. "I have never seen the type with my own eyes, but I watched, remaining hidden—they hold the power to choose the type of Lurker created."

"That would explain the ones we ran into were so many," Darby said. "I have never seen so many Bangores all at once."

"Nor Prowlers," Reggie added.

"I cut through quite a few of them to even get here," Bastian admitted. "I shall cut anything down if I can get to Bartus. Dejan and Takato will be next."

"You have a much better chance of making sure they are dead if you fight with us," I reasoned.

"Perhaps," Bastian answered, trying not to show how he truly needed us. "But no matter what, Bartus is mine."

"I am sure none of us have a problem with that," Darby nodded. "Need to find them first."

Bastian nodded and joined our ranks.

Heading further upward into the palace came with more heavy resistance. However, Azrael efficiently guarded our flanks, cutting off any reinforcements for the Eastguard soldiers standing between us and the throne room. Bastian wasted no time helping us dwindle the soldier's numbers as well. Despite his injuries, his enchanted armor appeared intact as projectiles bounced off. Then his pace became even slower, and he stumbled to his knees, exhausted.

"You still need to catch your breath," I urged, stepping in front of him to hurl a fireball toward the Eastguard soldiers as they retreated into the next corridor.

"I shall rest when Bartus, Dejan, and Takato are dead," he replied, trying to stand again and sweating profusely.

"Let me help," Amaterasu said. To his surprise, she grabbed Bastian's face and pulled his lips and tall frame upward to meet her mouth for several moments, also perplexing the rest of us.

"That should do it," she stated, with no hint of expression, nor did she appear phased by all our flabbergasted stares.

"I am feeling pretty exhausted, too," Garvish spoke up.

Amaterasu shrugged.

"I can only use the spell on one person at a time," she replied.

"How do you feel?" Nirnasha asked Bastian.

"I feel renewed and refreshed," Bastian responded, a grin sprouting from his chops, and effortlessly put his feet beneath him.

"I would, too," Garvish muttered.

"The fatigue in my muscles is gone," Bastian continued, expressing his amazement. "I feel as if I have not been fighting this whole time."

Though impressed with Amaterasu's spell to revitalize Bastian, as I could tell she had more of an effect on him than just relieving his muscle fatigue—I wanted to ensure the spell's effects.

"What did you do to him?" I pulled her aside.

"It is something I do not normally do," she admitted. "But he is a Keeper, so the spell's effects are more heightened."

"What are the specifics of the spell? Does it wear off?"

"In time, it does. As long as he exerts himself, he will use the power of the spell in his lungs, dwindling his vitality while borrowing what is given to him. Thus, I also have the power to cease the spell should I choose."

"You mean you can kill him?" I uttered with contempt.

"Please be calm, Aagneya," Amaterasu reassured. "I shall not take it from him, should he not also betray us. I am a cautious person at heart, and I do not fully trust him."

"I am more worried about you betraying us," I said. "I have fought with Bastian. He has no love for Kalab."

"I promise I shall not betray you," Amaterasu placed her hands gently on my shoulders. "You freed me from a prison I have been in for more years than I can remember."

"What of Amara?" I asked.

"Her mind is still broken. So, I am not entirely sure. I have kept a close eye on her. What Kalab did to her is likely far worse than what the imp did to me. Just because she regenerates does not mean the agony of what befell her goes away. Even in resurrecting, I know her pain is far greater than what I have witnessed of any MKR. In doing so, she relives every moment of her memories instantly."

"So, she feels all the pain she's ever felt each time when she returns?" I said, seeking to understand Amaterasu's words clearly.

"Correct," she confirmed. "The madness that lays dormant within her—what she holds back is unfathomable. At any moment, I surmise she could lose herself."

I remained skeptical of Amaterasu's intentions, and her words about Amara troubled me, but I could not help feeling amused in watching Bastian remain enamored with her.

Love wafted thickly in the air for the boys as Nirnasha pulled me aside before we entered the next corridor, waiting for the others to pass us. As the sawblades began to resound, he pulled me close and passionately brought his mouth to mine.

"I needed a recharge, too," he smiled.

I do not think Nirnasha shall ever know how much vitality his kiss brought to my heart. Lasair was right when she told me that love has great power. We held each other's hand as we darted into the next corridor, my other hand summoning many sawblade-sized fireballs and sending them sailing toward the soldiers. The flames burned through most of the Eastguard soldiers' armor, at least the ones who were not swift enough to duck behind cover. It gave us all the chance to rush them. Nirnasha dropped my hand, and his human arm became like tree roots, rapidly approaching the soldier's position, and began whipping them out from their cover. Once exposed, Amaterasu sent a shockwave toward them. All the while, our other comrades kept firing. The final resistance of Eastguard's elite defense lay strewn around the remains of the hallway, with the entry to the throne room finally in front of us. But even Bastian gave pause once he reached the entryway, surveying the possibility of an ambush. The access to the throne room only had one way in and out to our knowledge, a narrow corridor that elevated into steps toward the end, making it impossible to see anything inside the room from our position. Darby and Reggie leaned against the wall on either side of the threshold and peered down the narrow strip.

"What do you think, Reggie?" Darby asked.

"Too quiet," Reggie replied.

"I have been in the room before," Bastian whispered. "The stairs lead up to a platform. However, a large seating area curves around the platform facing it. It is likely that is where soldiers would surround us the moment we emerge."

I had also been in the throne room months ago with Elior. I stepped forward into the corridor and motioned for the others to follow.

"I can send them on their heels before they take a shot," I said, summoning two flames, one in each hand. "Nirnasha, Amaterasu, and I shall clear the seating areas should any soldiers be there. Bastian will lead the others forward. Find cover as quickly as you can."

My strategy held some risk, but I believed it necessary. When I emerged from the corridor and began climbing the steps to the platform, the seating area held no threats. The only three in the room I recognized were Bartus—the Betrayer, Dejan, and Takato Pure Bone. The three were peering out a large window behind the throne platform, with Takato holding the helm. Dejan turned toward me, displaying a smug and vile grin.

"I see you put my Mystic Silver to good use," he remarked sneeringly and continued to step in my direction.

Those who had followed behind me began to spread out, with Darby and Reggie staying near our backside. Garvish and Bikarma climbed into the seating areas for a better position while Bastian lined up with me. Bartus and Takato joined Dejan, with Bartus standing directly in front of Bastian. The two held their gaze as Dejan continued to speak.

"No matter. I have put all my Mystic Silver to better use."

"Why do you do this?" I bluntly asked. "Trade between the kingdoms has never been more profitable. You are the Emperor of Eastguard and a great warrior. Why do this? Why wage war?"

"I see the mind of greater intellect is lost on you," he replied. "This is not about money or luxury or even infrastructure. It is about order. Eastguard has continued to rebel against my rule, despite my generosity and bringing them good fortune. I noticed the whole world is in the same chaos."

"Do you truly believe people are lesser than you because you are emperor?" I asked. "Is this how the Emperor of Eastguard defends his people, by waging war against the other kingdoms? By allying yourself with darkness and creating monsters of your own people?"

"Defend?" Dejan laughed back at me, his tone becoming more distinguished and prouder. "This was part of the bargain. The people of Eastguard and all the other kingdoms shall become Lurkers making them easier to govern. They shall be obedient in not thinking for themselves. In this way, order shall be restored across the entire world. There will be no more uprisings and only one kingdom!"

"You are the abomination!" Nirnasha interjected. "You did this to your own people? And now to Westmain?!"

"Not if we kill you now!" I spat.

"True," Dejan admitted. "You could kill me in the end. But the fight would take the precious time you do not have to warn the rest of Westmain. Not that it matters."

His smirk remained vile, with Takato now standing ready to fight for his brother and Bartus staring solely at Bastian. I suddenly felt Nirnasha's hand grasp hold of mine. I turned my eyes toward him, and I could hear his thoughts. Could an army be approaching Westmain's capital city that very minute in what could be another aerial fortress, or worse, Skyhaven—the Savior of Eastguard?

"We shall tackle one maniac at a time," Darby said. "We are already fighting for Westmain by making it this far. Let us dispose of these villains, crash this thing, and be on our way."

"Spoken like a true dutiful soldier," Dejan teased. "Except there is one minor detail you left out. You are not going anywhere."

Commotion resounded behind us in the corridor. Eastguard soldiers were beginning to make their way toward us swiftly. Another door opened on the left side of the large navigation window, and more soldiers poured into the room. I wasted no more words, sending fire into the soldiers that had just come through the door. Amaterasu followed the flames with a shockwave that blasted the door and the frame clear through to the other side.

Bastian engaged Bartus, clashing blades like no one else was around. Even Takato had to dodge some of the wild parries. Once he did, he moved toward Reggie, yet noticed two buzzsaw rifles aiming straight at him. He ducked into cover as Garvish and Bikarma began reigning blades down on him from the seating area. Darby called for Reggie to help him cover the corridor we had entered, preventing soldiers from charging up the stairs and into the throne room.

Dejan unsheathed his gun-blade from his scabbard and fired a drill bit directly toward Amaterasu. She moved away before it reached her. Afore he could fire another, I sent a ball of flame in his direction, which he sliced through, veering it to move around him and dissipate without impact. Amaterasu followed up with a shockwave. Yet again, Dejan made a quick slice with his blade to dissipate the impact. Nirnasha tried his luck and sent forth several roots from his body as whips. This sent Dejan back on his heels, but he quickly parried and cut through the roots trying to get at him.

His sword likely held some enchantment to block and disband magic thrown his way, leading me to pull my drill bit gun from its holster and begin to fire. Just as the last root of Nirnasha's was cut down, my drill bits pummeled Dejan's armor but could not penetrate.

"My turn," Dejan smirked. "Takato!"

Takato emerged from his cover and ran behind Dejan as they charged us—his movement, expeditious that I barely had time to step out of the reach of his blade. Takato remained hidden behind his brother. I did not see him suddenly leap out with two golden drill bit guns in his hands, both barrels aiming straight at me. At that moment, something happened where I felt the movement of everything slow, and I could sense Dejan's blade coming again for me. I purposely fell backward to avoid Takato's drill bits and streamed flames upward, making Dejan hesitate in his attack. I rolled backward to reach my feet once more, continuing the stream of my flames, which landed in Takato's face. I suddenly felt the soaring air of a shockwave fly by. Yet again, Dejan cut through it.

"You shall have to do better than that," Dejan taunted.

Takato shook the flames free from his armor and reached up to feel the slightly charred regions of his face. He pulled an armored mask from his belt and slid it over his face. The mask held the appearance of their clan, depicting a skull with a devious smile and three hash marks along the forehead. And Dejan did the same.
"You have made my brother angry," Dejan mocked, pulling his mask over his face. "I wish you luck in living another minute."

"I shall just have to turn up the heat," I replied, with some mockery of my own.

An anguished scream resounded that drew all our attention to Bastian and Bartus, with Bartus kneeling in a bloodied mess, his hands cut clean off. Before he could beg for his life, Bastian ended it. He leisurely walked away from Bartus' body, his sword slung over his shoulder, and the head of the explorer rolling in the other direction.

"Now that that is done," Bastian sighed. "Perhaps you gents would be interested in a real fight?"

Dejan stepped back slightly while Takato drew his gun-blade. We were about to engage the two brothers again when we heard a voice cry out.

"Enough!" Shouted an old woman dressed in fine clothing from across the room. "Hold your fire."

Sheni Pure Bone, the mother of Dejan and Takato, introduced herself, pleading we listen to her words.

"I know of the ill gains and tremendous damage my sons have caused," she began.

"Do you defy me, Mother?" Dejan screamed.

"This is not defiance, my son," Sheni answered sternly. "You are defeated, and I am saving your life. I raised a fool if you truly believe you can defeat three MKRs and Bastian Raven Caste. Should you desire your life to cease and your Eastguard royal line to end here, take a grip of your sword and continue to fight. Let your mother watch you be cut down like a Sus fighting the butcher."

"Your sons deserve to die," I said. "Dejan has declared war on Westmain with his actions. He has slaughtered his own people—turning them into Lurkers is a fate worse than death. I know you do not wish to see your sons perish, but there is no other way."

"There is always another way," Sheni replied. "What is it you seek, and we shall parley?"

"This atrocity must be destroyed," I said. "The lives of the people of Eastguard must not be threatened with this doom."

"This is the palace of Eastguard. It holds generations of memories and the history of the royal family. That cannot be done. Yet, it could be flown back to Eastguard and put back where it belongs, dismantling its enchantments for flight."

"We do not have time for that," Nirnasha spoke up. "Your son, Dejan, claimed that Westmain was in peril, saying that this is not the only flying fortress."

"My son does well with placing thoughts in the heads of others," Sheni answered. "This is the first of its kind, I assure you. Though you may not believe me, I am too old to care for dishonesty. I cannot bear the weight of lies any further. My greatest desire has been to see my son continue ruling Eastguard, but that, I fear, is not in the bargain."

"Surely, it is not," I said. "Should we return this place to its original foundations, then what? What of your sons?"

"Dejan shall turn Eastguard's reign over to Bastian—the Heart Slayer. Then you will banish Dejan and Takato to the wilds of the Deadlands. At least they will have a better chance of survival than fighting all of you."

"I would rather die before allowing these two to run free, even in the Deadlands," Bastian stated. "The price of my clan is much higher than the throne of Eastguard."

"Your sister, Sabia, still lives," Sheni reassured. "She is safe in Eastguard. Assume the throne, and she will help you rule. Take up a wife. Rebuild the clan that you have lost. I ask that you give me a place in the palace to rest my bones till I pass on. I shall neither dine with you nor step foot in your court. I wish to leave this world knowing that my sons still live. It is my greatest wish. In that, I am willing to give up everything. If you wish, take the Pure Bone estate, or burn it to the ground. But you know me, Bastian Raven Caste. You know I do my best to keep the peace, and had I known my son's madness, I would have found a way to reach you before such calamity came to your clan and Eastguard."

Bastian stared at Sheni Pure Bone, seemingly seeking any trickery from the older woman as I continued to do. Yet her words held sincerity, and her beckoning countenance struck the Heart Slayer's mercy with heavy conviction. Her relationship with Bastian was apparent, and they shared a bond of trust over the years, and at this time, he decided to maintain the tie.

"I shall agree to this offer should the Pure Bone clan leave Eastguard," Bastian declared. "But Dejan and Takato must leave all their enchanted armor behind. Dejan must also cut off his right hand and surrender it to me. Takato must do the same. Then I shall allow them to be banished to the Deadlands."

"My throne is not yours to give, Mother," Dejan spat. "Today, we will die like men."

"You will die like Suses," Bastian roared.

"I shall take your bargain!" Takato quickly spoke, which appeared to take his brother by surprise. His eyes turned toward Dejan. "This is foolish! Fight if you wish, brother, but we cannot win this."

Dejan sighed heavily but then charged Bastian, clashing swords with him. Nirnasha pounced with roots that stretched out and wrapped around Dejan's wrists and ankles. Before Dejan could react, Bastian sent a well-placed kick into his chest, soaring him onto his back, which allowed Nirnasha to wrap the roots more tightly around the emperor.

Takato dropped his weapons and stepped back with his hands raised in surrender. Amaterasu leaped into the air while Dejan struggled to get free. Her fist landed on his chest, surging a shockwave onto the enchanted armor. The power of the direct impact created a crack in it and quickly ceased Dejan's efforts to break free. He gasped for breath as Amaterasu swiped his mask from his face. It took several minutes for him to regain his composure. When he did, he stared at flames near his face. He cringed, trying to pull his head away from the heat of my hand.

"Traitors!" Dejan cried.

"I am through with your madness, brother," Takato huffed. "We had everything we could want, but you could not live with that. You needed to take more of what you did not control!"

Takato threw himself at Bastian's feet.

"My Emperor," he implored. "The pain that has been caused to you is great. Should you wish for both of my hands, please take them. But I beseech you, do not banish me with my brother. Please allow me to take my clan out of Eastguard and into Nod, where we will establish a business of trade. For as long as the clan remains, we will pay a tribute of our goods to you and give anyone favorable prices should you command us."

"Give me your right hand," Bastian replied. "But I shall also brand 'coward' on your forehead so that your clan knows what kind of man leads them. Then you may lead your clan out of Eastguard to wherever you see fit to set up trade and pay tribute to me. Yet before this occurs, cut off your brother's right hand now."

Takato slowly moved toward his brother and removed the armor from his right hand, exposing the flesh. He pulled a saw-toothed dagger from his belt and sawed-off his brother's right hand at the wrist while kneeling on Dejan's arm. Dejan barely made a sound. Takato remained kneeling as he lifted his brother's hand to Bastian.

"Good," Bastian said. "Now, take your own."

Takato placed his right hand on the ground. He, too, barely made a sound as he sawed away at his wrist. He then proceeded to lift it to Bastian, who took it and dropped it to the ground next to Dejan's severed hand. He grabbed Takato's neck and pulled a dagger from his belt, carving a symbol for "coward" in the ancient Eastguard tongue upon his forehead. Takato let out a slight wincing noise, but no more. When Bastian finished, he threw Takato back to the floor.

"Now remove your armor," he told Takato. "Stand by your mother in your shame!"

It took Takato some time to remove his armor with one hand, but soon he stood next to his mother in his nakedness. She threw a cloth around him, which Bastian allowed. His focus turned on Dejan.

Nirnasha loosened the grip of his roots, and Dejan slowly moved his left hand to push himself to stand, his sword nowhere near him, and still, the prideful one refused to remove his armor. Enraged by his continued defiance, Bastian bloodied Dejan's face, calculating the placement of his fists to break the emperor's nose, cracked his jaw, and then stripped him of his armor. Dejan lay nude before us, yet Bastian's fury persisted, grasping the sheath of Dejan's sword and beating him with it until the emperor's body was bruised. It continued until Bastian went and picked up Dejan's sword and then brutishly kicked the emperor onto his backside. I turned away, seeing Bastian take hold of Dejan's privates. This made the emperor beg for mercy and confess surrender.

"I swear fealty to you as emperor!" Dejan cried. "I swear my surrender to you the throne of Eastguard!"

"Yes, you do," Bastian gritted his teeth. And though my eyes were turned, I could hear Sheni beg for Bastian to cease, and Dejan also pleaded until his words turned to shrieks of agony.

Nirnasha bound Dejan in tangled roots once more, carrying him toward his mother in his bloodied and battered starkness as if tethered in chains.

While we filed out to the flight deck through the side door to the left of the large glass, Eastguard soldiers filed into the throne room with arms raised, showing they had surrendered and sitting down under the guard of Garvish and Bikarma.

"What did I miss?" I heard Amara's voice reach my ears.

"Everything," came Garvish's cheeky reply from across the room.

"Take Amara with you," Amaterasu said. "I shall help the others stay alert here."

I nodded and followed the others out to the flight deck. Sheni led the way with Takato at her side. Following behind were Bastian and Nirnasha carrying Dejan, and behind them were Amara and me.

"I already ordered the Eastguard wairships to retreat," Sheni said. "No doubt the wairships of Westmain will want to board. Let them know what has transpired and where they can land."

A Nanomite Communicator was located near us just as we walked out. I generated a signal to the Westmain wairships, and after a few moments, I heard audio play through. I explained who I was and that we had captured the sky fortress. I became exhilarated when the voice on the other end recognized me as I did him. Hardwin, now promoted to Major, overseer of Harvenger's defense, replied with a cheerful salutation.

"While I shall say it is good to see you again," Hardwin told Nirnasha and me once he stepped onto the flight deck. "I must say I would rather see you again over tea."

"Likewise," I replied.

Hardwin seemed pleased to hear that we had overthrown Dejan and helped keep the city of Harvenger safe. Yet he pressed the issue on Dejan's banishment, stating that Dejan had committed crimes against Westmain in his attempts to conquer. Good Westmain soldiers had perished in the battle, and Hardwin continued to press that Dejan should stand trial in Langdon.

"These were the terms of his surrender," Bastian stepped in. "I assure you that Eastguard will pay tribute to the families of the soldiers you lost and a stipend to pay for the damages to your ships. I do not ask you to overlook the offense, but I ask that you allow Eastguard to punish Dejan as he first betrayed his own."

Hardwin cringed when he saw Dejan's body, as Nirnasha had set him down. Still bound but exposed, the Major looked over the carnage Bastian had caused to the former emperor.

"This is reasonable," Hardwin finally agreed with a heavy sigh. "I shall write a report to my superiors and give them full details of what has transpired. They and I are not unaware of the uprisings in Eastguard against Dejan. So, I am sure they will trust my judgment in agreeing to your terms and proposal. We do not wish for war with Eastguard."

Meik had never flown a palace before, but he seemed to manage just fine once Hardwin was satisfied and left soon after. It did not long take for the palace of Eastguard to return to its place in Havensire, where much of the great city lay in shambles. The population of the city was nowhere bustling in the streets. And Bastian did not let Dejan leave his sight. The ex-emperor, now in proper chains and recovering from his wounds, slowly treaded in front of us as Bastian paraded him through the streets. The emperor asked people to come out and meet their new protector, but we spotted no movement along the main street.

We reached the marketplace, finding more bodies scattered. The further into the commons ventured, the more bodies we found. I began to believe the entire populace to be massacred until we spied some little ones climbing out from a small shed tucked away in the shadows of a narrow alley—a young toddler held by his older sister, blooming into her adolescence. Soon after, we saw a handful of adults come into view, men, and women, with claws and bite marks on their flesh. I quickly noticed the marks could be nothing but from the Rattus humanoid creatures—Gloom Gnawers. We found where they tunneled up from the Unlight and pounced on the defenseless city. The adolescent girl bravely told us what occurred even though I had not asked her to do so.

"They appeared out of nowhere, giant rat creatures," she said. "Many are dead, but many more were taken alive."

I slowly placed my hand on her shoulder, seeing tears streaming down her face.

"My mother and father, they were taken," she sobbed.

"Why would they take people alive?" Nirnasha asked me.

"I am not sure," a woman interjected. "But I also saw a man dressed in heaven who walked among them, surveying as if he in command of them."

There it was—Kalab had personally taken part in routing Eastguard's capital city with Gloom Gnawers and made it possible to create Dejan's Lurker army. I deduced it to be likely Kalab could now fully influence Gloom Gnawers to do his bidding as the tiny man remained locked away. And peering at the damage his monsters did to the city, I knew, as did Bastian, it would take months to rebuild Havensire's defenses again. Bastian would also have to draw troops from somewhere else in the kingdom, which made me suspicious of Kalab's tactics. He had ransacked Havensire, but the goal was not complete destruction. The more I dwelled on it, the more I realized the most logical solution to defend the capital was to draw troops from somewhere else. Bastian thought the same thing. I believed that wherever Bastian decided to take troops from could be the very place Kalab would strike Eastguard next. Yet something else came to mind as I thought about what had befallen Havensire. I went to Dejan as Bastian stood next to him.

"Where is Skyhaven?" I asked. "Where is the Savior of Eastguard?"

Dejan did nothing but smile with his severely swollen mandible. His smugness soon turned to another mouth full of blood from one of Bastian's fists. Yet what else could Bastian do to him besides end his suffering? His manhood had been sliced from his body, and Dejan spat out the crimson that filled his mouth with a vile grin.

"I believe she asked you a question," Bastian glared. "I suggest you answer it unless I go back on my word to spare you. Your banishment has not taken place, and it is taking real restraint not to run my sword through you. Answer her!"

"He gave me a sky fortress," Dejan answered, sounding pleased to relay his misdeed, and spat more crimson from his mouth. "I gave him a wairship."

In the hands of Kalab, Skyhaven held the capability to cause endless destruction as the largest and most advanced wairship known in all three kingdoms. I became unsure then of Kalab's strategy, as he did not need to attack Eastguard. He could surprise and cripple any city in the world should he choose.

"He does not think logically," I heard Nirnasha's echo reach me. "Kalab is deviously whimsical in the way he thinks, knowing what a logical mind is drawn into."

"To plan for him, we must know what he wants," I replied.

"Not entirely difficult," Nirnasha came back. "Every action he has taken has been a step to be the only one in complete authority. For him to accomplish that, he needs to take drastic measures to seize control of the world with no limits to his supremacy in any sphere of public or private life. He will extend his grip to whatever length feasible without regard to decency. He removed Elior, coerced Dejan, and…"

"Now he is testing the limits of his reach," I said aloud. "He is testing the greatness of his rising power."

"To conquer everything," Nirnasha agreed.

Takato left Eastguard with the Pure Bone Clan, taking his wife and second cousin, Mileedis Pure Bone, and his children with him. They were given an unarmed merchant airship, and we watched them fly off into the horizon. The following day Havensire's Dwelling Gates were open, with Bastian taking the honors of shoving Dejan out into the Deadlands. Bastian proceeded to send messengers to each of the cities of Eastguard with documents explaining his rightful rule and Dejan's treachery and a command to give no quarter to Dejan, even placing a hefty bounty on him should he enter through any of Eastguard's Dwelling Gates.

We spent about three months in Havensire, assisting Bastian in organizing the remaining populace into working and helping rebuild. Bastian decided to pull troops from multiple locations not to weaken the defenses of just one city. Kirshan Outpost sent primarily newly drafted soldiers, while Ugnis Ro gave a few hundred elite snipers and infantry. Ye and Poe delivered cannon engineers and defense experts to tackle the issue of being sieged from beneath. Vlok sent slave workers that Bastian specifically requested would gain their freedom should they work hard to help restore Havensire. After several thousand agreed to the terms, the prison mining camp of Vlok almost reduced to half its incarcerated population. I learned many who knew of the Raven Caste Clan held them in high esteem and were eager to assist Havensire at their new emperor's behest. No word reached us of Westmain being attacked again, and at the end of a long three months, I yearned to return to Langdon to see my home again.

The months we had helped Bastian were somewhat uneventful. I preferred it that way. The constant battles and doing our best to beat back our enemies seemed ongoing for too long. My journey became approximately twenty-four months and twenty-two days since I had set out from Langdon. I thought I would have returned home much sooner. And I finally decided I would sell at least some of my books to buy much-needed pampering and new clothes when I returned.

Amaterasu told us she wished to remain in Havensire to help them. Eastguard was her home, after all, and she swore an oath to us that she would assist in any way she could should we call on her. Amara swore the same and remained on the Gullywhumper while I returned to Langdon with Nirnasha. We bid our comrades farewell, knowing we would call upon Meik and the others again.

I did my best to keep my mind busy, at least organizing my writings as we flew by airship back to Langdon. There were still several unknown factors, including the whereabouts of Marilla Baostin, the MKR of Water and Flood. But I believed she would come out of hiding in time.

I took my books to a bid shop, receiving more than 120 million credits for the only two books I could bring myself to sell—*Moby Dick* by Herman Melville and *The Scarlet Letter* by Nathaniel Hawthorne. I had read them several times and felt I could part with them. But I kept the rest. Nirnasha did not sell any of the books he found, as he told me he still felt they held more value in his possession than as some chauvinist bureaucrat's decor.

What came next was seeing my parents again. Yet I had reservations about Nirnasha meeting them, as they can be a trifle bit intrusive with guests, or should I say just my romantic interests, not that I had many. I deeply cared for Nirnasha, though, and he did not mind once my mother began sputtering out the embarrassment, asking questions like, "Have you seen one another naked yet?" or, "Were you aware that Aagneya snores?"

My father kept unusually silent. I could not tell if he remained deep in thought, but he stared at me with a slight grin. Perhaps it was his way of letting me know he was proud of me. I began to feel relieved to be back in the residence where I grew up while my mother jabbered on. I did not know it would be so comforting, even with the quirks of my parents. Nirnasha could hear my thoughts and reassured me he found them amusing.

We both decided we would not try to explain what we both had become. However, my parents sat with their jaws agape as Nirnasha supported my telling of how we overthrew Eastguard's previous emperor's plot.

"Have you become a soldier as well?" My father asked. "Your aim must have significantly improved."

That last part is his humor, and I decided to record these precious moments with my parents as I desire to remember them. The world is ever increasingly threatened by an MKR we had no way of knowing how to defeat, and my memories of Langdon should be solidified in simplicity should anything befall the beautiful capital of Westmain.

Nirnasha did not share a room with me that night. Jests aside, my mother found it quite improper for a man and woman to sleep in the same room, let alone the same bed, before being properly wed. Thus, Nirnasha's head lay on a pillow in a guest bedroom, the one furthest away from my own. In drifting off to sleep, I heard his thoughts ask me if I wanted to meet in the ethereal to lock lips for a time. I smiled, knowing my parents would never know.

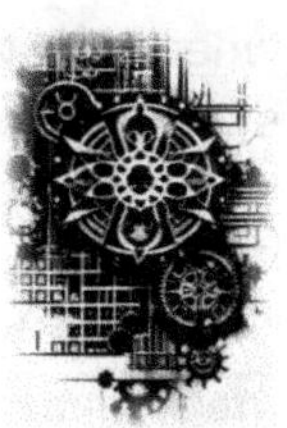

AN ANCIENT SHADOW
IN SHIFTING TIMES

All paths were concealed, entrapping the sight of my soul in a terribly lonely existence, one I could only begin to describe as greatly distressful and cumbersome—no light, no sound, no escape. I could sense agony, but the suffering came as a melody of hush. An overwhelming fear abruptly gripped me, tearing at my mind, and drew me to the shadowy chilling mists now slithering beneath my bare feet. I began to believe I was forgotten, that no one would remember me. No one would say my name again. I felt a multitude of spectral faces stare at me from above and around me, each sitting behind the other like in a courtroom and lifting their proclamations. To no avail, and it drew me deeper into despair and obscurity.

I wanted to journey to the ethereal and meet Nirnasha as always, but I could not. Instead, I stumbled through the pitch dark that held my vision captive. I could not even feel nor hear Nirnasha's thoughts. My mind returned to the day Elior was taken from us and the brief flash of a nightmarish creature.

"Brave light."

I heard a deep whisper surrounding me, even what seemed to be within me. I did all I could to hear the melody of my Dancing Desire. Though faint, I could not conjure my protectors. A barrier of an unknown power—its face flashed before me, its eyes holding the shimmer of mystic midnight, touched with a hue of radiant crimson. This time I saw enormous wings, many tentacles drooping from its face, and large webbed feet and hands brandishing razor-sharp claws. Its form flashed again, monstrous as if it would quickly devour me should it wish.

"Who are you?" I cried out, feeling a madness loom and swell within my veins.

"Names matter not."

The whisper became more resonant, disembodied, gravelly aged, and muffled. The very sound compelled me to shiver violently. I dared to stare upward to where the whisper seemed most profound. When I did, I could see its form somehow, but without light reaching my eyes. I demanded an answer, and the tentacles around its mouth began to move again.

"This one has many names that crack the plains of space and time. Of the many, this one is aptly known as Cin Cxothr'thol—Cthulhu in the young tongue."

"What is it you want? I managed to stammer out.

"This one is curious."

"What about?"

"This one is never fooled, nor does this one care to fool. What is hidden is hidden, and what is revealed is revealed. This one knows more than the lifetimes of a thousand ages and more than what was known before all life began."

"I get it. You are old," I managed to muster some bravery, which lowered my shivering. I wondered if I would fight the thing, despite being completely lost on how I would do so.

"Old holds a meaning of time," the nightmarish creature continued. "Time holds no relevance for this one. This one is not threatened, as this one sees all minds in all times. Yet it remains tethered to the mind of this one because the brave light this one now addresses remains tethered to the mind of another brave light—a brave light that fulfilled its promise to this one."

"Do you speak of Elior?!"

"This one cares not for the brave light's name, nor does this one desire to know the name of the brave light this one now addresses."

"My name is Aagneya," I spat, suddenly finding the strength to plant my feet beneath me. "You should do well to remember it, should you not release Elior."

"This one will remember, though it matters not. It will release its tether from the mind of the brave light so the brave light's promise may become fully satisfied to this one."

"What promise?" I kept my fervor, feeling my fists begin to clinch. I began to feel the fiery heat of my power pulse through my veins, and the melody of Dancing Desire started to come alive within me.

"This one helped the brave light to kill its enemy, the one this brave light addresses as Wendigo."

The creature did not seem to care that I kept asking questions. I kept digging for information to see if Elior was still alive somehow. After some time, Cthulhu stated that my questioning only delayed the inevitable. But I did learn of Elior's promise to the creature—helping Elior kill Wendigo, and in return, Elior would surrender himself to the gloom of the creature, suffering what Cthulhu referred to as the 'Forever Nightmare.'

"You cannot have him," I cried out. "I shall find him and take him from you."

"This one has broken all brave lights. The one this one addresses will be no different."

Its reply enraged me, and my flames ignited all over my body. I could hear a pause in the melody bringing despair to me, and I took the opportunity to listen and summon hundreds of my Dancing Desires to stand around me inflamed. My fire lit up the realm, and Cthulhu became fully visible. The shadows appeared to burn away, and I could see a familiar ethereal realm.

"Such as it is," the creature began to back away and fade into a gloomy mist. "The brave light holds the light of this one's kin, and so it too shall pass away in shadow."

The forms from my Dancing Desire soon dissipated as well. I turned to see myself surrounded by marsh terrain with bare trees, slight fog, and muck-filled pools. Through the fog, I could see Lasair's fortress from afar. With each step, I struggled not to sink into the marsh. I would have just awoken to escape the place, but something held me there. I kept calling out to Nirnasha, hoping he would hear my thoughts. Everything still felt empty. I peered up to keep my eyes on Lasair's fortress. With each step toward it, I felt I moved farther away.

Passingly, I grew accustomed to knowing the feeling of Cthulhu's presence, much like the chilling winds one feels when Rumpelstilzchen is close—and much like Wendigo surging an unbearable hunger through me—Cthulhu brought about a type of hopeless emptiness to break and downcast.

"This is how you are going to break me?" I taunted aloud. "With illusions? Are you not supposed to be a great Leviathan or something? This is how you are going to break Lasair's fire?"

Again, the endless shadows swooped back upon me. Cthulhu brought forth his horrifying image once more. However, something happened I do not believe the creature expected. I began to laugh. Soon, it became an overwhelming joy that I am sure would have appeared like insanity to anyone else. The fire within me manifested in every coloration I could think of, a glorious spectrum of illumination. The shadows again retreated along with Cthulhu's image. This time, I kept the flames ablaze.

"Something tells me you do not like the light," I exclaimed. "Pretty big weakness for one who claims to be so powerful."

"All are brave before this one devours them," came the creature's reply. "The seeds are planted. This one is patient to watch and wait for as long as it takes. Rest well, brave light. This one is always there when eyes are shut."

I awoke from the ethereal but felt as if something sinister pinned me down to my bed, and I fought to break free, sweat dripping from every part of my body. Nirnasha gripped tightly to me, pulling me toward his chest. I could not hear his words for a few long moments. The muffled sound finally attuned, and I responded, "Yes, I'm fine."

"Are you sure? You do not look like it," Nirnasha pointed out.

I did not waste any more time. I threw my hand over his mouth and told him I had much to tell him. While I may have fought to find my bearings, I continued to recall what had befallen me in the ethereal.

"I suppose this Cthulhu and that thing have nothing to do with one another?" Nirnasha asked, pointing at my left wrist, which the sickly-looking veins had climbed slightly up my forearm. "What happens when that reaches your heart?"

"They are connected. They must be," I concluded as something suddenly sparked my deduction, but I ignored Nirnasha's second question. "I think my tether to Elior's mind has grown stronger since I took on the curse."

I did not close my eyes to enter the ethereal for the next few days. Positively, my heart held elation that Elior might be returned to us. I guess hope does not need to rest. Fearfully though, I wrestled with thoughts of facing the shadow Leviathan again. I studied Nirnasha's thoughts as he returned to the ethereal each night to flourish and perfect his skills, which made me conclude that I was the only one connected to the nightmare creature.

I spent much time asking questions of Elior's book, yet it could not tell me much as I did not know Elior's last hidden phrase, which would lead us to its second volume. The book revealed familiarity with Cthulhu, which also bore the title "Estrauth deb Esue" translated as "Torturer of the Soul." I did not doubt it, and it confirmed my thoughts of Cthulhu's nature—a creature that desired the destruction of all light. But for what purpose and to what end, I knew not.

We left my parents' home approximately two weeks after arriving at their doorstep. While they continued to show signs of hospitality, I could sense it strictly for Nirnasha's sake. For years since I left to study at Langdon University, they had a taste of being empty nesters, and I doubt they wanted to keep up appearances for much longer. They tried to appeal to us to stay as we stepped out the door. But I kissed them both and answered that I was now a grown young lady looking to live my life. I thanked them for letting us stay and then departed, moving more to the outskirts of Langdon's foremost residential districts. I had learned of a private residence for sale, tucked away in the city's southwest corner. Nirnasha held no interest in buying it, but I dropped the credits for the owner's asking price—a narrow two-story structure, arched to a slightly steep pitch, and copper paint coating the entire exterior, with dark wood-stained trim around the windows and doors. Unusual architecture in comparison with the surrounding homes, or any other I had seen. I would come to learn the blueprint as the recent works of an upcoming prestigious designer seeking to break free from the norm, and I appreciated it all the more.

The balcony and porch wrapped around the home with elegantly designed iron railings brushed to a stone finish. The interior held a fireplace in the living quarters, three-bed chambers, stained wood floors, and pleasantly crafted caged light fixtures. The kitchen had a full panel sliding door that led into a side yard with a coiled tree doing its best to reach for the clouds. What used to be a personal garden lay in shambles, but I believed Nirnasha would have no problem restoring it to its full glory. The two bathing rooms had long, narrow copper tubs, one of which I put to good use immediately, running the hot water till it ran out. After soaking for quite some time, Nirnasha went with me to purchase furniture and decor for the residence that same day.

It is worth mentioning that Westmain began going through quite a few changes during our undertakings in the Unlight and Eastguard. News of Westmain's civil war had reached Langdon that the rebellion in the south was being beaten back, with its leaders either being killed or surrendering. But another revolution took place, one that had never been seen before. Tailors in Westmain had banded together, placing all their manufacturings on hold and demanding the government allow them to make more colorful clothing styles, including using azure, jaffa, viridescent, and viola for typical styles available to the public. I only learned of the Tailors' success when I happened to step into the market stores on the first day of a newly launched product line. Furniture stores had also followed suit, making more colorful tapestries, drapes, and carpets. One furniture store worker told me a bit of conspiracy that the government agreed only to receive a grander portion of the profits, needing money to pay for the expenses of the war.

I did not pay much heed to him, as I felt every bit of the pride and joy in owning a home with the funds to fill it. I spent the next several days shopping in the crowded marketplaces of middle to upper-class citizens, purchasing furniture for my residence more accustomed to my newly acquired taste in decor—long azure tapestry drapes, woven fireplace carpets composed of azure threads with a dash of gold, and soft azure PrimaDonna Gossypium table cloths. I also sought new fashion for my clothing in a more upscale Tailor shop, high above the marketplace.

The High Nest, as it is called, is not browsed by the majority of Westmain's citizens. Most shops are highly prestigious, with a heaven garment in the front window. They, too, were turning with the times, placing in the new colors to draw more of a crowd of wealthy eyes. The long strip that held the High Nest boutiques had one place of entry—an iron gate well-guarded by private armored security. Eligibility to enter remains merely subjective to the lead guard and focuses on dwindling the line of curious aristocrats. The guardsmen snickered at my approach until I pulled a book I had brought from my satchel—*Charlotte's Web* by E.B. White.

"I suppose I can receive quite a bit of new clothing for this," I stated. "I am an explorer, after all."

The guard motioned to his comrade to open the gate. He even ordered another guard to escort me to whatever shop tickled my fancy.

"See to it, no one hassles her," he ordered to the other guardsmen. "Surely one of our shop owners would love to have her business."

One particular establishment caught my eye; it did not have a heaven garment in its window. I decided to start there, seeing as I became curious about why it did not. The gentleman of the shop seemed a decently mannered man, holding a humble demeanor—unlike most Tailors I had met over the years. Once I showed him my method of payment, he immediately ceased the other two clerks from their tasks to bring them over.

"I would like some custom fittings," I said. "Perhaps you could make something for me?"

"Anything you would like," the Tailor replied.

"I have grown very fond of azure," saying this knowing I held a thrill of imagining my royal crimson clothes burning in a fire. "Yet I would like it paired with mystic midnight."

"Begging your pardon, Miss," the Tailor kept his pleasantness. "Mystic midnight is traditionally reserved for Master Keepers. I carry some material, but I am a man of tradition."

"Glad to hear it," I replied, slowly raising my hand and summoning a small fireball. "For that is exactly what I am."

The Tailor and the clerks watched with tremendous astonishment as I ignited my entire arms with flames, yet it held no effect on my flesh or clothing.

"I have never met another MKR before," the Tailor remained gawking. "I am yours to create whatever garments you desire!"

The Tailor and I spoke for some time about the designs for my new clincher ruffle skirt accompanied with stockings, ruffle shorts, a double order of skinny denim trousers, a bustle skirt, four collar lotuses, two pairs of boots, a custom fit & flare frock, and a woman's top hat—all of which would be created using mystic midnight and azure materials. Upon finishing our discussion and taking my measurements, Nirnasha entered the shop. I could see his thoughts, which surprised me when he desired to barter for new clothes in exchange for one of his books, *Grimm's Complete Fairy Tales,* by authors Jakob and Wilhelm Grimm. I would have teased him about following my lead, but I could also ascertain something troubled him.

"I have found something extraordinary," Nirnasha echoed his thoughts to me.

"I did not realize its importance until I rummaged through my books again."

"Tell me what it is?" I pressed.

"I shall," Nirnasha said aloud with a smirk. "For now, let me enjoy some of the fruits of my labor."

"What would you like?" The Tailor politely interjected.

Nirnasha went through the process as I had done, much more direct, though. He first turned his arm into a long line of roots, which made one of the clerks faint. Undoubtedly, she was the Tailor's wife, and he rushed to her side dramatically, trying to assist her.

"How is it that two MKRs have come to be in my shop?!" the Tailor exclaimed.

"We are sprouting up more than ever now," Nirnasha jested. "Can you customize me something in mystic midnight coupled with one of the new colors? Viridescent is quite dashing, I think. Though, perhaps dye it just a shade darker?"

We made a humble Tailor quite wealthy that day, handing over a book each to pay for our custom garments. In a month or so, I knew I would be wearing the latest style and braving not to hide who I was—an MKR. Before we departed, I asked the Tailor why he did not have a heaven suit in the front of his shop like the rest. His reply brought a chill to me.

"A gentleman came here not too many months ago and bought it off me," he replied. "I had to modify the fit, but he paid upfront."

"What did he look like?" Nirnasha asked.

"Slender, sable hair, distinguished eyes with dark circles, and…"

"Looked a lot like Elior?" I pressed.

"Perhaps," answered the Tailor. "But he did not look well, almost as if he had not seen sunlight in several years' time."

Later as we arrived back at my residence, Nirnasha led me to his book collection. He pulled one from his pile, hidden beneath his mattress. We had read through it before; *Tales of Horror* by an author named H.P. Lovecraft.

Its contents, beginning on page forty-seven, displayed a story from the author called *The Call of Cthulhu*. Nirnasha re-read the story aloud as we both continued to concentrate more this time. In the text, a man named Henry Anthony Wilcox dreamt of the creature's image and woke to sculpt it in clay. I stopped Nirnasha from reading further, as I wanted to know if Elior's book knew anything about the author.

The spirit of the book revealed that Elior infiltrated H.P. Lovecraft's mind during the night while he slept, sharing with him the vision of the creature's image during a time known as the year 1919. While Lovecraft received his inspiration from other sources, it inhabited Elior's intent to release people's minds from the creature's grasp that desperately anticipated returning to the physical realm from the Evergloom.

By placing Cthulhu's image into the tales of the storyteller, the fascination with Cthulhu's image escalated in people's imagination, not their literal consciousness. It only allowed Cthulhu's reach to remain manifested in a cult that existed long before the author received the vision from Elior.

At that time, the cult became part of a series of events leading up to sending the nations of the earth into a second world war in 1939. The atrocities of such an uprising were only a fraction of what could have been.

Elior assisted in thwarting the cult's victory and continued successfully, unnoticed by the soldiers who fought against the cult and its allies. Elior constantly interfered with their plans over the eons, as the book's spirit mentioned, but did not delve into any more details than that. For we did not have the knowledge to ask, nor was it permitted to do so, as the stories of the history of the cult were held in its second volume.

We spent many days studying what the book's spirit taught us and gathered what we could from H.P. Lovecraft's writings. We scarcely left the residence even after our new clothes arrived on our doorstep. Although, I did ceremonially burn my old clothes, giving me a pleasurable moment of satisfaction that I would no longer have a closet full of garments I could not stand. I felt I had become my own person. Nirnasha felt much the same. Dare I say he appeared quite dashing in his new apparel.

After a few months of studying the creature and the texts of H.P. Lovecraft,

Nirnasha turned to me with almost gaping eyes.

"We need to get out," he said decisively.

I smiled and grabbed his hand. "Where should we go?"

I had never felt the irritability and listlessness of being indoors while studying for days, even months. I thoroughly enjoyed each moment of learning and rehashing ideas I already thought through. I witnessed many of my classmates at Langdon lose their minds during the final week of exams, as many spent so much time studying that they became practically insane. Nirnasha certainly seemed to be drifting in the same direction.

We left the residence and discussed our destination along the way while people stopped to gawk, fully surprised that two MKRs were residing in Langdon—a splendid feeling at first, having all eyes notice us. Yet as we stepped into a flavorful and newly established eatery to dine for the evening, some of the eyes upon us were unnerving. My thoughts reached Nirnasha about a group staring at us from the far corner of the room, near the bar, after we were seated. They had followed us into the establishment and were now doing poorly in concealing their gaze toward us, at least from me.

When I first began training as an MKR, Elior taught me that should I ever decide to dress the part, there would be those dumb enough to test their luck. MKRs and Keepers become a target for scoundrels seeking their fortune as they more than likely carry Mystic Silver and carry high-priced valuables.

"Do you suppose…?" I uttered.

"Most certainly, I do," Nirnasha interjected through his thoughts. "I know a place to lead them. But only after we dine. I am starving."

We had little difficulty creating the charade where we were blissfully unaware of the deviants watching us. We forgot they existed for a time as we delved into the exquisite cuisine our waiter had placed upon our table—smoked Sus ribs seasoned to perfection, Agaricus Bisporus, and Brassica Oleracea smothered in a sweetened butter sauce. Finally, Solanum Tuberosum, soaked in oil, cut open, and heavily mixed with butter, a mix of seasonings, and chopped scallions. The Sus rib meat peeled effortlessly off the bone and served with a spiced Rubus dip. Then for dessert—fried Banku, a ball of dough that is usually filled with something tasty. In this case, the delicacy held mashed

Malus Pumila and fried in the juice of the Malus Pumila and butter.

"Let us walk a bit before we go to the place you know," I echoed to Nirnasha.

"Agreed," he replied with a slight nod and an inward belch.

The streets were still crowded as I held Nirnasha's arm, wondering if we could share in the night-air romance before dealing with the scum trailing behind us. My MKR companion and I picked up the pace, making the footsteps following us hasten. We led them to an enclosed alley with a high enclosure toward the end. When we reached the wall, Nirnasha pulled me closer still and brought me in for our lips to meet. I could feel his heart race, and I knew he missed our adventures, many of which ended in a perilous entanglement.

Not long after our romantic moment, our pursuers encroached, and Nirnasha turned his face toward them. He suddenly held out his enchanted hand, the metallic material, and Mystic Silver reflecting in the moonlight. The entire party of ruffians ceased in their tracks. The ground shook, and a wall of earth raised behind them, sealing them in with no hope of retreating.

"Did you think you had trapped us?" Nirnasha glared. "You are all mistaken. It is you who are now trapped here with us."

"We do not give quarter to those who would do us harm," I stated firmly, igniting my arms with blazing fireballs hovering in each palm.

"My lord and my lady," one of the men held out his hands. "You misunderstand our intentions. We are not here to harm you."

"Liar!" Nirnasha spat.

"No, please," the man fell to his knees. "We are not seeking you harm. We did not mean to alarm you but sought you out."

"You follow us in secret," I replied. "Yet you claim you mean us no harm. Whatever for then do you…?"

I thought we were putting up an excellent scare tactic until one of the other men reached into his pocket, and Nirnasha shot up a root from the ground and snapped his neck. He summoned a robust hand made from soil and rock, holding fast the man who had spoken to us, just tight enough not to crush him, while summoning another to block the drill bits fired at us from the others. More roots sprang out from Nirnasha's left arm and whipped the drill guns from their hands, followed by the roots wrapping tightly around their necks, snapping them as well. The only one left was the man who spoke to us, still held tightly in Nirnasha's grip.

"What are you doing?" I belted out to Nirnasha. "There was no need for violence. We had them terrified already."

"Tell me why you followed us!" Nirnasha gritted his teeth, ignoring my query, and stepped toward the man without glancing my way. "Tell us the truth this time."

"The whispers have scattered all over the city about you two," the man grimaced, feeling the solid hand squeeze ever so slightly. "Eyes are always watching the High Nest. We were sent to investigate."

"You are from the government? You are lying?" Nirnasha spat.

"I carry a badge of office," the man quickly replied. "If you can reach my left inner pocket to my fit and flare frock, that is where you will find it."

Nirnasha created a small opening in the hand to reach into the gentleman's pocket. I gasped when I saw his hand pull out the badge and open it. The badge was connected to a leather pouch that held the man's identification papers signifying he told us the truth.

"Why did your man start to draw on us?" Nirnasha demanded.

"I know not what you mean," the man answered. "We do not have many dealings with MKRs."

"I think you are lying to us again," Nirnasha replied. "That badge is a fraud, and you were looking for trouble. Well, you found it."

"Wait!" I cried to Nirnasha, seeing his hand flinch. The man was crushed in an instant. "What have you done?!"

"What needed to be done."

"What?!" I remarked, befuddled. "If it was a misunderstanding, he could have cleared it up."

"No agent of the government conducts proper, friendly business in the dead of night," Nirnasha stated calmly but kept an undertone of surging rage. "He was a fraud. And more will come for us. The next time, we should be prepared to find the head and cut it off."

I found Nirnasha's coldness intolerable. His demeanor shifted so drastically from kindness and empathy to being detached from compassion that I could scarcely recognize each side as the same person.

"Why are you at war?" I finally asked him as we reached my residence, after an arduous walk home, and listening to the melody of his heartbeat waging a feud within as if what made him warmly humane had begun to fade away.

"We are," he replied. "As long as Kalab, Cthulhu, and any other evil are out there, we shall always be at war. I now understand the burden Elior carried, constantly dwelling on doing all he could to keep evil from invading and destroying our world."

"His thoughts were so much more than that. He cared deeply for both of us and to see us thrive," I reasoned.

"He cared only for allies," Nirnasha's voice sank into a harsher tenor. "Which is why I think Cthulhu contacting you is a trick, to get you focused on Elior, who is lost, instead of finding Kalab to send him back into the gloom."

"Do not speak to me of who is lost," I sparked up. "You are the one who is changing for the ill. You were once a man who held high principles and showed mercy. Now, you are addicted to the thrill of slaying your enemies."

"What of you?" Nirnasha stomped his feet. "Do not pretend you do not still feel something for Elior while I am left waiting to have all your heart."

"Is that what this is? Jealousy? How long has this been brooding?" I pressed.

"Call it what you will," Nirnasha answered. "You are holding fast to a fantasy. Elior sacrificed himself so we could live and fight in his stead because he could no longer continue."

"You are most assuredly not speaking of the Elior I knew!" I insisted. "He was clever, and we now have the clues to find and free him."

"You know very little of the creature holding him and the power it possesses," Nirnasha turned away.

"I believe I know where Elior is," I finally confessed. "He is held in the Evergloom."

"You wish to travel there?" Nirnasha's eyes were trembling. "We do not have the power to take on that realm."

"I am the gatekeeper," I replied. "The gate will not shut behind us. We could go in and destroy everything that comes against…"

"Listen to yourself!" Nirnasha interjected. "Did you not see Kalab's capabilities? We barely escaped him. Not only that, but he slaughtered Havensire. We must remain here, in this realm, to prepare for the inevitable of Kalab seeking to destroy the world."

"Then I suppose I shall have to go myself," I retorted. "You do what you must, Nirnasha. But I know we cannot do this without Elior."

He stormed out the front door without another word. I waited for him for several days, but he did not return. Soon a week had gone by. Then, another week passed—still no sign of Nirnasha. I continued to study for more answers, and the confidence in my instinct that Elior was being held in the Evergloom rooted ever further toward complete assurance. I dared to venture into the ethereal, appearing in Lasair's fortress when I kept my thoughts on her and nothing else as I drifted off. Taking control of my thoughts, I believe, became wise training for the battle I desired to take on against a Leviathan who twists them into despair.

Lasair spoke to me of Cthulhu, the once majestic Leviathan. The creature fell away from its created purpose, to bring about dreams to humanity and flourish them in knowledge. But knowledge became a hoarded treasure it refused to share less something was given to it in recompense, darkening its existence to desire all light be consumed in shadow. Kalab, having the same desire, gave the creature something of value in order to be its snare, assuredly, the light of his soul.

I spoke of venturing to the Evergloom to find Elior. Lasair did not like the idea of me going alone. And Nirnasha's disappearance angered her, but she voiced nothing more of the matter. I spent many more days wondering where Nirnasha had gone, but the door never opened to reveal his frame.

In about another week or so, there came a knock, and I opened my door to see two familiar faces. Amara and Amaterasu explained Lasair bid them come to find me, and Amara greeted me, revealing to be much more lighthearted than I had experienced the last time I saw her.

"I am not sure what is in store for us in the Evergloom," I admitted. "I do know that if we go, there is a chance we will become entrapped with Elior."

It did not appear to phase either of them. The three of us sat for several more days, enjoying my residence, sipping tea, and catching up on all that had happened over the many months. Amara had found peace with Easton, not entirely forgiving Elior, but she had accepted a heartfelt apology from Easton. She also remained grateful that her snare no longer carried Elior's curse, and she even admitted I was brave for taking it on.

Amaterasu held word that she and Bastian were now married. The news would have been more shocking had I not remembered how he drooled over her after she healed him during our time in stopping Dejan's plans. She had come to make good on her promise and swore to me that if we came back, I already had an invitation to the celebration, which they had prearranged after rebuilding the city.

I found comfort in their glad tidings. From that moment, I felt a sudden relief in the arm that held the curse. I peered down to see the sickly veins had retreated again to my wrist. I stared, confused, but only for a moment. It could not be that simple, could it? But yes, it was most assuredly—the curse connected to the gateway of the Evergloom, a place of hopelessness that transpired into fear, madness, and despair. I felt it when Cthulhu had me for a time, but I fought against it with hope, a resistance I had no idea held such powerful magic.

"You are looking fancy," Amara howled at me. "Look at those new garments. You are going to let me borrow something, right?"

This was the first thing Amara said to me when I opened the door to them. Amaterasu giggled along, showing her excitement. The three of us were now preparing to board the Gullywhumper, all dressed in custom-made midnight skinny denim trousers with azure inlays, matching mystic midnight fit, and flare frocks with uniquely designed collar lotuses.

About a week or so before, we made our way back to the High Nest, where again I called upon the services of the same Tailor. He told me he received twice as much as he anticipated for both the books Nirnasha and I gave him. Thus, he delighted in rushing an order for more garments of my same design.

After we received our new clothes, we took time to catch up and enjoy some other sights the city offered. Nirnasha may have been right about the government agents being frauds, as I did not receive any looming eyes except those impressed by our prestige. Yet he still never showed. I even had a mother approach me with her daughter, who shyly asked me for my autograph just before we boarded the Gullywhumper. Easton's voice touched my ears first to welcome us aboard, then Meik's, followed by Darby, Reggie, Garvish, Bikarma, Wild Willy, and even Kassy Bones. But one I did not expect reached me as the others hurried ahead.

"I know you must hate me," Nirnasha said. "But I cannot let you go without saying goodbye. You deserve to know I still care about you. Yet I cannot follow you where you are going."

"You are no coward, Nirnasha," I replied. "You must also know that my heart does not belong to Elior. It was yours whether you followed me or not."

"Was?"

"Yes," I began to cry. "You abandoned me. You left without even a word or when you would return. I wanted you to know I desperately wanted you to have my heart. But you stormed out like a child, leaving me behind."

"I am sorry," he replied. "I was wrong. I beg you, reconsider your words. Please do not leave me the way I left you. For I know you deserve better than that. Let me make it up to you."

"What could I possibly want from a man who is so foolish to throw away everything we have been through because of jealousy?" I asked. "You have grown so cold since we fought together for one another in the flying fortress. You killed men without mercy, without even thinking twice."

"They were from the government," Nirnasha blurted out. "They were not frauds. That is where I have been all this time, clearing up this mess, making sure nothing came back on you."

"What?"

"I am not going with you, Aagneya. I owe a debt to the city of Langdon, to the Kingdom of Westmain. I am in their service til the lives of those men are paid in full. They would not take anything for trade except my allegiance and my services."

"So, you are truly not here to go with us," I gasped.

"No," he said. "I am not. I only desire to wish you well and tell you I am sorry. I am sorry for having such a cold heart. But I do know the only thing that warms it is knowing you are safe and that you know I shall always love you."

I fervently pressed my lips to his—"I shall love you always, Nirnasha." He embraced me tightly. I can still recall it. "Fulfill your debt, stay out of trouble, and do not let my house burn down."

"Shall I stay there while you are away?" He asked, seeing my demeanor become more jestive.

"You had better," I uttered, drawing out our kisses as long as we could.

The setting sun began sliding below the horizon when the Gullywhumper took flight, and I saw my love staring up at me til he faded from view. My heart remained heavy, and I sobbed bitterly, knowing it was our first time apart since our first expedition. The feeling was unnerving like a piece of my memory being torn away when no one is ready to say goodbye. I could still feel the warmth of his arms wrapped around me—the taste of his lips lingering until the winds of the skies blew them dry. I watched Langdon become a distant speck, clinging to Nirnasha's mind until the connection became too far away, making me cry more. Amaterasu put her arms around me.

When I composed myself, Amaterasu told me she needed to return to Eastguard to relay the news to Bastian. But she made it clear that before we could venture to the Evergloom, a sizable dilemma needed my help, as well as Amara's.

Bastian held no favor of hearing the news, even threatening to cut Amara and me down to keep his wife from going to find Elior. An empty threat, of course, and she calmed him down with a memorable night, I am sure. As morning illuminated the palace, so did Bastian's demeanor.

"Did you truly have us fly across the world for you to do that with your husband?" Amara asked.

"A good wife knows the needs of her man," Amaterasu replied with little expression. "She also knows her needs, even when they are greater."

The disgusted look on Amara's face made me burst out with laughter.

"I guess you are satisfied, now?" Amara continued, keeping her face scrunched.

"I am satisfied," Amaterasu replied, still with little expression.

"Preparations are complete," we heard Meik's voice reach us, who horribly pretended he had not overheard our conversation by trying to conceal a snicker beneath his smirk.

Over the several months we had not seen one another, Meik had turned the Gullywhumper into a temporary cargo ship, trading goods in Westmain to Havensire for it to rebuild. For our venture to the Evergloom, during such time, Meik believed it best to become a munitions runner for Havensire, transporting manufactured military equipment and ammo from Ye & Poe back to the city and taking a different route each time. The three of us thought it a good plan. Our physical forms would remain safe on board, as I was sure Cthulhu knew we were coming. However, as she stated, there was more to our journey back to Havensire than Amaterasu seeking one last night of romance.

She needed Amara and me for an investigation, in which she unraveled her concerns as Bastian entered the room. Far south of Havensire and east of Ye & Poe lay the city of Drac, also known as the "Holy City of the Fallen." I believe I jotted a few thoughts of it some time ago—the city where fallen soldiers of Eastguard were laid to rest. Amaterasu's attempts to contact the monks, the caretakers of the city, were unsuccessful as of late. Communication with them did not respond to the transport of the last of Eastguard's soldiers who had perished in the Gloom Gnawer's onslaught of Havensire.

Drac rested on a natural formation of catacombs, many of which were sealed off to stop anyone from entering beneath. It did not stop Gloom Gnawers from entering Havensire, as we witnessed. Still, Drac's crust was solidified in iron and other metals, unlike the granite of Havensire, most likely making an attack on Drac's underbelly a cost not worth undertaking. The logical assumption to believe the city had already been overrun did not seem farfetched. The other fortified cities to the west, Kirshan Outpost, Ugnis Ro, Vlok, Ye & Poe, were already on high alert, buffing up their defenses. Drac; however, had no military in the city. And Bastian could not spare troops to go with us.

In the city's center stood the spired monastery that touched high into the clouds. Made from a rock formation, it appeared smooth, eerie, and ancient. Dead trees clung to its surface and appeared more like marbled sculptures than lifeless flora. From its base were high walls of a labyrinth that stretched out for more than three-thousand arm lengths, approximately to a total of ninety thousand units in each direction. The ivy vines were thick along many parts of the labyrinth walls, but the rest remained bare. On our approach, we saw the small landing pad Bastian had mentioned, stretched out from the eastern side of the spire.

It would have been no surprise that Bastian would be the first to step out on the landing platform. Yet somehow, Amaterasu convinced him to remain behind in Havensire just in case this was a diversion. Meik had also ordered some of his crew to remain behind, but they were not Bikarma, Garvish, Wild Willy, and Kassy Bones. Wild Willy remained on board with Meik, who told us he would await us.

Just before we landed, I noticed Bikarma had been busy since I last saw him. No doubt he put his Weaponry Engineering education to good use. With Meik's or Kassy's enchanting assistance, he had created several buzzsaw rifles unlike any other without the proper permits and taxation. I doubt Meik or any of the Gullywhumper crew cared much about government mandates, making the ship their own private kingdom. Bikarma's designed buzzsaw rifles were intricately engineered with sight scopes, auto, and semi-auto triggering systems, a two-clip loading capacity from beneath allowing for eighty blades to be loaded at once, a hand grip toward the front for better stability while firing, and uses the enchantment from Mystic Silver to propel the sawblades out the barrel instead of pressurized air. In this instance, the user of these buzzsaw rifles would not have a limited capacity to fire using an air cartridge.

"Would you ladies like to try it out?" Bikarma asked smugly. I admit I was proud of him.

Neither of us ladies said no, but held out our hands as Bikarma opened a large chest he had pulled up from the cargo bay. It held a new buzzsaw rifle for everyone.

"We have already fired them," Garvish pointed out with a smile of his own. "But not at any monsters. Sorry to say that I hope we run into trouble."

"What is that on your shoulder?" I asked him.

"This?" Garvish swung the rifle around. "This is a sniper version of Bikarma's buzzsaw rifle. However, instead of firing sawblades, it fires drill bits. We calculated that drill bits go farther with the same propulsion due to their shape and size. It is much more accurate but does not hold the same firing capacity."

"A drill gun sniper rifle?!" I did not care if I sounded impressed.

"DGSR!" Bikarma exclaimed.

"Patent it!" Garvish laughed.

The two boys kept their gloating to a dull roar but soon quieted down once we stepped out onto the landing platform, greeted by a stillness I knew all too well—the calm before an ambush. Yet a monk received us at the door to the spire, welcoming us to Drac—unlike the last time Amaterasu quietly pointed out. He was clothed in a royal crimson robe threaded with gold Damask embroidery, his head covered by the hood of his robe, noticing the sun did not touch his face much. His salutation came with a respectful bow, bending at the waist, and then opened the doors even wider.

Amaterasu took the lead in questioning the monk as we followed him inside. He spoke about their communications malfunctioning for the past couple of months, but he kept optimistic that the monks in charge of their tech would fix the issue. He also apologized for not greeting her during her previous visit but assured her that everything remained in order as the monks had seen the bodies drop from the transport. Then he continued to prattle on about the tech.

"The city is well due for an upgrade in Steam Tech," the monk conveyed. "Under the rule of Dejan, he did not see fit to grant our request. We have endured to make do with what we have. Perhaps you may tell our new emperor of our troubles to keep things like this from occurring in the future."

"I assure you Emperor Bastian will take your request to heart," Amaterasu replied. "Rebuilding Eastguard from Dejan's foolishness and greed will take time, but it is being done. Drac is Eastguard's most honored city."

The monk acknowledged Amaterasu's remarks with a slight bow of his head. He led us into an open corridor and a large hall with one stairway spiraling upward and downward. We were now inside the spire, lit up by oil lamps of all things, giving the atmosphere an eldritch yet quiet disposition. Upon the walls were royal crimson tapestries embroidered with strange lines and symbols I believe I had seen before, and I scoured my mind as to where. The spire held no windows or any other openings except for the way we came. Peering upward led only into shadow, slightly lit up by more oil lamps following the stairway of the spire to the top as did the direction downward.

There were three long tables parallel to one another with what appeared to be a kitchen off-center from the farthest wall. A savoring scent or perhaps a stew-like dish emitted its aroma from there and caressed my senses. The tables were already set, and we began seeing other monks wandering into the hall, paying us no mind but found a seat and sat in silence. All of them were dressed in royal crimson robes like the monk who greeted us, except for one. A tall monk wearing a gold robe embroidered in royal crimson Slavyanski design entered the room and approached us.

"We do not get many visitors," his voice slurred into a raspy and deep pitch. "Welcome to Drac. I am the headmaster of this coven, devoted to caring for Eastguard's honored departed."

"There are not many of you," I said. "Do you still have prisoners who help care for this place?"

"We do," the headmaster replied. "Tragically, they are blinded and muted before they arrive here. That has been the punishment for such prisoners who turn to insurrection. Should they survive, they are reproved and come here for the rest of their days. We do our best to see that they are looked after."

"Where are the prisoners now?" I asked.

"As you said, there are not many of us. Some of the seated here were once prisoners, now accustomed to knowing the layout of the Drac spire. It took many years for them to learn how to live without sight or speech. But they can hear every word spoken to them. So, we do our best to teach them the ways of the coven."

"What are the ways of the coven?"

"I am pleased you have such ravenous curiosity," the headmaster grinned. "I do not get to do much idle chatter these days."

He pointed to the tapestries hanging from the walls.

"Each one of these carries meaning," he explained. "There are six 'keys,' as we call them, one embroidered on each of them. These keys you may think of as entities that hold divine insight. They do not speak like you or me, but they hold a certain power of the mind, giving those devoted to prayer and understanding countless purpose in their work here."

The first tapestry embroidered with golden thread held the name Stusra which to me, depicted the flow of waves in the seas but with a vertical pattern. Next came Olui, with lines appearing to me like birds in flight. Thirdly, Pihojm, with broken spheres vertically tapering down the fabric. Fourth, Eotaur wove a more intricate pattern, beginning at the center and spiraling outward. The outward spiral became six different lines, each spiraling outward into twelve of their own. Fifth, Brutaur depicted what looked like another labyrinth. Unlike Drac's labyrinth, it flowed rectangularly rather than spherically—and sixth, Kelisk, which appeared like hundreds of fangs illuminated along one continuous thread.

"What of that one?" I pointed to the seventh tapestry on the wall behind what I would describe as a humble altar. The seventh royal crimson tapestry had gold lines that moved outward from two oval shapes in the center and then squiggled down like dripping water, breaking as they went.

"That is the focus of the coven," the headmaster replied. "No one has learned the knowledge of that entity. It remains clouded and does not reveal itself."

"Looks wicked to me," Amara stated, unafraid of offending our host. He was not but instead remained transparent in admitting that it did have a peculiar presence from the others.

The headmaster invited us to sit at his table as his guests. Typically, tradition dictated the headmaster be seated alone as a sign of respect. But he had no qualms about breaking tradition to honor us. Our idle chatter remained soft as if raising our tone would insult the ears of the others. It did not keep me from prying about the entities the headmaster had spoken about. I especially kept my focus on the one above the altar.

Garvish interrupted and ventured a question in his curiosity about the devotion of the coven and how they chose which one to pray to and about what. In his response, the headmaster revealed that each member chose one of the six to devote themselves to in prayer. They spent years praying to just one of the six, devoting much of their time to meditating and scribing their revelations. The task did not delve so much into asking for knowledge as it did simply receiving it as one purely devoted, a concept that made my mind drift a bit.

"Even the prisoners who came here scribe their revelations," the headmaster explained. "We scribe for them while teaching them how to do it in their condition. Once they have mastered that, their worth of self becomes much grander, and they are more inclined to join in with the coven."

"What of the prisoners who still refuse to be part of the coven?" Bikarma piped up. "And what does the purpose of these beliefs have to do with caring for Eastguard's honored dead."

"There have not been many prisoners to my knowledge who have refused," the headmaster replied. "And to address the purpose of beliefs, most of the revelations we receive deter our very beings from being curators of this place and those who are honored with it."

"How long have you been with the coven?" I asked.

"Practically my whole life. I came here as a boy—the payment for my mother's debt. I took solace in coming here, never seeing her again, which meant not seeing her intoxicated and narcotized. She was unpleasant as I recall."

Dinner came during our conversation, indeed a type of stew. It had a delicious aroma, and I tasted a succulent ingredient I did not recognize. I could feel my muscles relax with each bite as our conversation soon became nothing more than silent slurping noises, shifting creaks of old wooden chairs, and soft breathing echoing throughout the hall. I turned my gaze toward Kassy Bones, who appeared unstable. I then realized that my vision was blurring.

"What is this?!" I shouted at the headmaster, jumping up from my seat. "What are you doing to us?!"

"Do not fight it," the headmaster beckoned. "You are here for a reason. No one comes into the spire without one. And that reason is always to join us."

"We are not here to join the coven," Amaterasu followed my lead. "We are here to investigate why your communications went offline and why no one greeted us the last time we were here."

"All who enter the spire join the coven," the headmaster restated, ignoring Amaterasu's remarks. "We are celebrating your entry. We…"

A loud snap resounded from a drill gun, echoing throughout the hall. Amara, who sat directly across from the headmaster, had just put a drill bit through his head.

"Poisons, narcotics, or any other hallucinogens do not phase me," she spat, getting to her feet. "We are going to get answers, and we are going to get them now!"

Amara's brash action to kill the headmaster did not intimidate as we hoped. The entire hall of the coven slowly stood up and began walking down the stairway until they all left our sight, including the one who had greeted us at the door.

"I do not think I have ever been this high," Garvish nervously giggled. "Not sure I like it. I cannot feel my fingertips."

"Amaterasu and Aagneya should follow me," Amara said. "The effects should wear off soon. But the rest of you should return to the ship. You will likely pass out in the next few minutes."

Bikarma had barely touched his stew, admitting he did not have a good feeling about the headmaster from the beginning. The effects were minimal on him, while Garvish and Kassy Bones could hardly stand.

"I shall see to it that we get back to the ship," Bikarma said. "Take our extra ammo, and we will tell Meik what has happened."

My vision began returning to me as the three pushed back through the landing platform doorway. I turned, staring at the seventh tapestry, and just before my vision returned to normal, the image blurred together where I saw Cthulhu's face.

"The headmaster said they write down their revelations from their prayers," I said. "That means they must have a library somewhere. They worship Cthulhu, and I want to know what they have learned."

"How do you know they are worshiping Cthulhu?" Amaterasu asked.

"That seventh tapestry above the altar—I can faintly hear its melody," I replied. "At first, I could not place the image, but in my blurred vision, I see the monster's face there in the tapestry."

Amara wanted to split up, but Amaterasu and I ruled against it. We allowed ample time for Kassy Bones, Garvish, and Bikarma to make it safely back to the ship. Then, I urged the three of us to go in the opposite direction of the coven. Up the stairway we went, climbing the tall spire. After ascending ten floors, the eleventh had a unique entryway leading into a room shimmering with a strange azure hue. Beneath dusty cloth tarps were mounds of Mystic Silver, which I estimated to be more than 600 (mu). Next to the piles were packs, which gave me an excellent idea.

"We may not have found the library," I said. "But we could fill these packs and take them back to the Gullywhumper, then return to go after the coven. If we need to retreat, we will not leave empty-handed."

"I am beginning to like you a lot more." Amara smiled. "But we should hurry."

"I have a better idea," Amaterasu pushed past us. She made her way to the far end of the room and opened a large window, which let in a blinding light from the sun. "We should signal the Gullywhumper to fly up and hover just here. Then we can load all of it onto the ship."

It did not take long for the Gullywhumper to hover next to the window, with Wild Willy prepped to take the precious cargo aboard. Once we began loading, I wondered what they were doing with the Mystic Silver and how they attained so much. With one last load to go, I saw a strange figure in the doorway, the headmaster, his head still drilled through and dried with blood splattered across his forehead.

"Busy I see," his voice resounded differently than before. "We welcome you into our coven, and you would steal from us? This is unforgivable."

His jaw unhinged and drooped like a familiar creature we all knew too well.

"Lurker!" Amara shouted.

"Since when do Lurkers speak?" I asked.

"Consider me special then," the headmaster drooled.

We had finally met a Necromean, an enchanted Lurker who can create other Lurkers. I soon found out their other powers include blocking magic as I tried to fry him. It revealed yet another ability, morphing its bone structure into an enormous, clawed beast before our eyes. Its face grew into a snout filled with gnashing teeth, and claws almost reaching its thighs. Its robes ripped off like paper as its spine spurted out of its skin.

The three of us leaped out the window onto the Gullywhumper, quickly followed by the abomination. Meik pulled the ship away and raced toward the skies as Amara, Amaterasu, and I began to open fire on the Necromean using our new buzzsaw rifles. The sawblades stuck deep into its flesh but did not seem to faze it for long. We continued to dodge its swipes and bites, doing our best to contain it to the main deck.

"Its body is warded," Amara shouted to me. "It is impervious to most magic. I have only seen magic kill a Necromean when Elior used one of his abilities, cutting it to pieces."

"Then that is what we must do," I shouted back. "But with sawblades."

The new buzzsaw rifles were surprisingly easy to use, and the scope helped tremendously improve my accuracy. I focused my shots on the abomination's knees and other joints, making the creature slow for a time. We needed a better strategy, but it did not take long before one presented itself. A drill bit flew into the back of the Necromean's head and out the other side. The momentum of the drill bit knocked the abomination from its feet, and I turned to see Garvish, still looking squeamish but holding his aim on the Necromean from the navigation deck. Bikarma and Kassy were next to him, now pulling the triggers of their buzzsaw rifles in auto mode.

"Shoot it over the side," Wild Willy shouted. "We are high enough."

We all aimed and continued firing sawblades into the creature to keep it in place while Garvish aimed and fired another shot through its head. The Necromean flew backward against the railing, screaming and trying to withstand the sawblade assault.

"So long, you ugly…" I could barely hear Garvish say before his DGSR echoed a final shot that sailed so accurately that it hit the Necromean directly between its eyes, sending it over the railing and quickly plummeting toward the labyrinth below.

"Meik!" I shouted. "We need to go back."

"I'm right here," Meik appeared behind me. "No need to shout. Tell me why we need to go back?"

"We need to find out what is happening in Drac," Amaterasu said. "The coven is hiding something."

"They have been worshiping Cthulhu," I explained. "We do not know how long they have been worshiping the creature. But a religious cult left unchecked for hundreds of years does not surprise me. We need all the information we can, and they most likely have a library full of what they know about it. We are going back now!"

Meik walked away, murmuring about endless darkness and how we would pull him into it. Yet I knew we were doing the right thing. Anything to help us understand Cthulhu before entering the Evergloom would give us an advantage.

"Are we ready for another go?" Amaterasu asked the others. Garvish and Bikarma replied enthusiastically, but Kassy Bones did not answer as swiftly as they did.

"I am not going," she said. "My head is not right."

"Looks like you will be down one," Wild Willy interjected. "I could use a hand packing away the loot we just acquired. I shall see to it we are ready when you all return."

We packed more ammo and stepped off the ship to the landing platform again. Meik took the Gullywhumper away from us this time, but not out of view of the spire. He ran the ship silently and used Easton to make it invisible. We agreed that our escape would remain hidden if something else went wrong.

The sun began fading from the horizon when we entered the spire again and into the dimly lit dining hall. This time, I took an empty pack to take whatever writings I deemed fit to keep. With no sign of the coven, we slowly descended the stairway, following the dim torches downward. Soon, a large slate floor encased with books and scrolls packed against the walls appeared, and dusty tables and chairs were set in the middle. The coven remained seated at the tables, each quietly reading a scroll in front of them.

"Do not disturb them," I told Amara. "Let us surround them before we start asking questions."

All of us stealthily took up positions surrounding the tables. I boldly stepped out with Amara just across from me. Both of us held our buzzsaw rifles aimed and ready to fire. One of the coven members turned his head from what he was doing but did not seem to heed our approach. I pressed the barrel of my rifle against his head and firmly commanded him to stand. He continued scanning the scroll in front of him. I repeated my command. Yet he continued doing what he was doing. None of the others appeared to mind either that they were under threat.

"What do we do?" I asked Amara.

She firmly grasped the back of another's robe and yanked him out of his seat. The commotion made the rest of the coven look up from their scrolls for a moment but they continued scanning. The coven member Amara had nabbed did not move. He did not raise his arms to signal his surrender, nor did he appear frightened to have Amara's drill bit gun pointed at his head. She released her grasp on him, expressing her confusion to me. The coven member slowly sat back down and began scanning his scroll.

"They will not comply," a voice came from the shadows. Into the dim light stepped a man dressed in heaven—the same, yes, the very same—Kalab.

Amaterasu emerged from her hiding place, covering Kalab's right flank while Amara unshouldered her buzzsaw rifle and pointed at him. I remained holding my position but also pointed my rifle toward Kalab, working my way around to the left of the table.

"This is not necessary, I assure you," he said. "I am merely a shadow emissary, overseeing the will of the one you know. He is not surprised you are here. He knows you are here. He does not care."

"What are they doing?" I demanded. "Why are they scanning through scrolls?"

"Searching for something, I suppose," the emissary's tone dripped with sarcasm. "But you have gotten your answers here. Now, you should be off, should you not? You may tell your emperor he may keep his kingdom how he sees fit. We continue to honor the fallen soldiers of Eastguard, giving them a proper place in the catacombs. But Drac itself belongs to my lord."

"Your coven worships Cthulhu," I spat. "I shall burn this place to the ground before I allow Kalab to take ownership of it."

"Ah, Aagneya. My lord is fond of your 'fiery' passion," the emissary stepped forward to stand before the tables with scrolls strewn all over. "Let us make a bargain then? Since you have learned of the 'revelations' of Cthulhu, I can safely say you are searching for something to help you. You are looking to enter the Evergloom, are you not? I know of the information you seek and can give it to you. However, you must do something for me in return."

"What?"

The coven remained seeking an artifact. The emissary did not explain what it was, but he gave us the tomb's name where the artifact would be found. Find the tomb and retrieve the artifact for the information we needed on Cthulhu.

"The information you need is perhaps in this library," he said. "I shall give it to you, but you must retrieve and place the artifact in my hands. It is best to take this offer as the coven shall find it eventually."

The room suddenly resounded with buzzsaw fire. Each of the coven members remained seated but was thoroughly bladed. In a few moments, the entire coven were strewn motionless; their blood spattered over the scrolls and the floor. The emissary's eyes widened and peered up as Bikarma and Garvish treaded out from the shadows.

"Now they cannot," Garvish grinned. "Now, we are your only hope."

"Nothing good comes from the dark," Bikarma said. "Every member of your coven was Lurkers, which is why they did not react when their life was threatened."

"You brash little insects," the emissary scowled, but soon his face brought forth a grin. "Mortals are truly curious. But you have performed well to even the odds. I give you that."

"Whether you have something waiting for us or not, it better not show itself," Garvish added. "This will be an unhindered treasure hunt."

The emissary's smile grew.

"I see you have thought well ahead to cover your backsides," he chuckled. "I assure you that you will not be disturbed in the least if you hold true to our bargain."

"How can I be sure the information you provide me is what I am after?" I asked.

"The one who hid it, is the one you seek," the emissary brought a cold stare toward my eyes.

REVELATIONS FROM THE GRAVE

I proudly congratulated Garvish and Bikarma for their deductive reasoning. While searching for answers, I did not take the time to realize the coven were mindless, obedient Lurkers under the control of our enemy. While not like other Lurkers we faced, they were still soulless before sawblades pierced their hides. And we left them there as the emissary led the way.

The spire's steps led several levels down from the library to a large pair of double doors engraved with the same symbols as the tapestries from the dining hall. The hinges lamented as we pushed them open to see an enormous corridor dimly lit like the rest of Drac—although the torchlight glowed a strange pale royal crimson, illuminating the entire catacombs in its particular hue. I noticed that down the many tunnels breaking off from the main chamber, the hue of torchlight became different, ranging from azure, viridescent, jaffa, and even gold. Standing beyond the doors, an engraved wall at the bottom of the stairway held the interpretation of what the colors meant.

Azure tombs were reserved for regular soldiers; indeed, more azure tunnels broke off from the main chamber. Viridescent chambers were reserved for officers, and jaffa were reserved for high-ranked officers, specifically captains and above. Gold signified special honors for war heroes, high-performing officers, royal family members, and emperors. Although I had not noticed a specific tunnel beforehand, the key to the colorations made mention of unlit tunnels reserved for traitors, deserters, and cowards.

"Mahala" was the woman's name on the grave. Yet her resting place held no record, just marked by a special identifier. It sounded like a puzzle piece Elior would comprise. And my suspicions were confirmed when I asked the emissary who Mahala was—he replied, "Elior's wife." I made it appear like the name did not mean anything to me, despite my knowledge of Elior being married at one time, long before the Great Collide.

The coven had been searching for what the symbol might look like through the archives of scrolls in the library but remained unsuccessful thus far. We learned the entire coven was not present during the massacre in the library. A few of them were in the catacombs, searching for unique markings.

"As you should be aware," the emissary stated, looking directly at Garvish and Bikarma. "Not all coven members are Lurkers. Some are obedient because they are not given any other choice. How does it feel to know you slayed five innocent humans to get what you want?"

The emissary left us in the catacombs and climbed back up the stairway toward the library. I could see his remarks burdened the boys and sense their downcastness. I pulled both close to me, with my embrace surprising them.

"Do not let our enemy make you doubt your decision," I state calmly. "We do not know whether he is lying or speaking truthfully to manipulate your minds. Keep trusting your instincts."

Garvish and Bikarma sighed heavily, and soon we were met by two others wandering around in the catacombs.

"We will escort you to wherever you desire," one of the coven members respectfully bowed to us. "There are many locked doors throughout, and we will assist you when you need to enter the chambers."

The coven member appeared humorously plump. Her cheeks bulged like she had packed food on either side of her jaw, yet the rest of her face appeared chiseled like an athlete. Her belly protruded outward like dough shoved through a funnel, flopping all over the place as she waddled from side to side. A short, older gentleman joined her. His stone beard looked frayed and long, but he did not wear a royal crimson robe like the other.

"You are not wearing a robe," I pointed out.

"He is not coven," the woman replied. "He came as a prisoner who did not join. He is a fortunate one."

"How do you mean?" I asked.

"For one, they did not take my tongue or my sight," he said, sniffing harshly through his nostrils and then shooting mucus from his mouth. "They claimed my participation in the uprising was pathetic enough."

"You took part in an uprising?" Garvish asked.

"Yes," the short man boasted. "I was the only one."

Amara, Amaterasu, and I did our best not to snicker while the boys burst out with deep belly laughter. It became contagious, and I could no longer hold it in. The other two ladies followed soon after. The stature-challenged man did not react or appear phased by our ridicule.

"What is your name?" I asked, wiping tears from my eyes.

"Sandulf Collins," the man said, shoving a cigar in his mouth and lighting it with the lantern he carried.

We all went silent.

"Sandulf Collins?" Garvish gawked. "The famous explorer?"

"He is," the coven woman concurred. "What of it? Do you all not have a task to complete?"

I made mention before of Sandulf Collins, who survived several expeditions into the Unlight. He is known for being the first to discover Gloom Gnawers and Lurkers. That was ages ago, and he looked like he had seen many. I could scarcely believe it, as his hands appeared fraught with arthritis, and time had desolated his features. He hobbled a bit, trying to keep up even with the waddling woman before us.

We walked the catacombs' main corridor, doing our best to decide where to begin our search. Collins suggested a few places, but the coven woman corrected him, saying they had already searched the places he suggested. He suddenly held a humble demeanor about him, apologizing to her as if his memory was not what it once used to be. I shall say he could not fool me. Collins was hiding something.

"Where were you planning to search next?" I asked. "Perhaps we can start there."

The coven woman brought us to a gold-lit tunnel. I observed Collins. I could hear the melody of his heartbeat. He did not react, not a single tell—not a twitch, scratch, or a clearing of the throat.

"Let us try another tunnel," I said, keeping Collins in the corner of my eye. "I do not have a good feeling about this one. If Elior is the one who hid the artifact, then he would not put it in such an obvious place."

The melody of Collins' heartbeat heightened just a bit. We went to another tunnel, lit up viridescent. Again, Collins made no reaction.

"Not this one either," I said.

By now, Amara and Amaterasu were picking up on my odd conduct. Amara caught my eye, and she then glanced at Collins. Her eyebrow raised, and a slight smirk appeared. Amaterasu came in behind me, and I whispered to her without the coven woman or Collins noticing. We came to another tunnel lit up with azure. Again, no reaction. I turned to the coven woman.

"What about the tunnels that are not lit up? How many are there?"

"There are six," she replied.

"Have you searched them?" I asked.

"We have."

I insisted she take us to them, and we stood at the entrances one by one. At the fifth unlit tunnel, Collin's heart began to race.

"I feel good about this one," I said. "I would like us to start here."

"What makes you want this tunnel before all the rest?" the coven woman asked, incredulously suspicious.

"Well," I answered. "Darkness hides many secrets. Elior holds the power of light, which illuminates what is hidden. This is the fifth tunnel, and as I have studied Inquisitive Psychological Premonition & Secret Arts at Langdon University, knowing the meaning of numbers is handy. For example, the number one symbolizes strength or unity. The number two symbolizes the depiction of opposites, such as light and dark, cold and hot, masculine and feminine. The number three symbolizes the divinity of life (so to speak), focusing on the mind, body, and spirit—and how such entities assimilate to coexist. The number four symbolizes a rooted perspective or holding onto the present, such as dedicating oneself to a season of life. The number six symbolizes intuition, unlocked potential, and clairvoyance—a MKR could be such an example."

"What of the number five?" The coven woman asked, keeping her suspicion. "Why the fifth tunnel?"

"Because the number five symbolizes freedom, adventure, and sensuality. Is that not what being married is supposed to be—that you live a lifetime devoted to the unconditional surrender to love itself?"

Both Garvish and Bikarma's jaws fell agape. I realized my education was not precisely wasted as they had once tantalized. Perhaps I could have determined the puzzle Elior left behind, even without Collins. Yet receiving a concurrence from his heartbeat that allowed me to draw my conclusion made the moment sweeter.

"I never thought that would come in handy," I heard Garvish say, his wide eyes glued to me. Amara and Amaterasu smiled, knowing it was not just my intuition; no one else needed to know that. And they seemed to enjoy seeing the young men at a loss for words as much as I did.

The coven woman unlocked the gate blocking our path, and we continued down the fifth tunnel, as dark and gloomy as any place I had witnessed in the Unlight. There were many unwrapped dry bones—signifying their shame—laying stacked in carved openings, whole bodies of men and women long decayed and most likely forgotten. These were the resting places for Eastguard's proclaimed cowards, deserters, and traitors. I became instantly drawn to sympathize with them—no grace for redemption nor ability to tell their tales of woe so that they might be understood. Instead, they appeared discarded like scraps of garbage. We saw bodies thrown atop one another in haste in several places. The stench remained foul and displayed a deeper lack of respect for those who once held breath at least.

We each carried lanterns, scanning the tombs to search for unusual markings. Collins' heart did not beat faster at all. I began to think I had read him wrong, that perhaps he was trying to catch his breath.

"How old are you?" I asked Collins.

"Why do you need to know?" He replied gruffly. "It does not seem relevant to our task?"

"I am a curious sort," I assured. "I remember reading much about your adventures. And I am curious where you have been for so many years. You have been proclaimed to be dead."

"Dead," the short old man laughed. "Lost. Forgotten. Abandoned. But no, not dead. At one-hundred and four, I still feel eighty or so."

"What befell you to come here?" Amaterasu inquired, joining my inquisitiveness.

"I would rather not speak of it while roaming around here," Collins admitted. "But for the past twenty years or so, I have been chipping away in the mines of Vlok after a failed attempt to reach the Isle of Secrets. I was so indebted to the investors who financed the entire operation; they sold me to Eastguard, and into the mines I went."

"Who were these investors?" I asked. "And what is the Isle of Secrets?"

"Eh, no one knows for sure what it holds," Collins sneered. "It is just some big landmass to the southwest of this place. A group of investors in Westmain, politicians mostly, have had their eyes on it for years. They thought I would be the proper explorer to discover what is there."

"How were you held responsible for the failure of the venture?" I sustained my consistent questioning. "I do not know of an explorer responsible for when an expedition goes wrong."

"They did not see it that way," Collins nervously chuckled. "I could thank them somewhat—Vlok fed me well and gave me great exercise. It might be the reason I am still kicking."

"So, then, what was the reason for your uprising?" I tried not to chuckle.

"They tried giving me latrine duties," Collins gritted. "I shall die before I have to deal with anyone else's shite again. My father, head of the 'Poop Patrol' in Langdon, wanted me to take over the family business. But I could not stomach cleaning the streets of excrement for the rest of my life. I wanted to see the world."

"Is that when Elior found you?"

"Elior," the old man dropped his tone as his mind drifted to reminisce. "My explorations would not have been the success they were without him. Despite everything I know about him, I still have many more questions like you. But my curiosity wanes of late, seeing that my bones shall likely meet the grave soon. Or so this coven woman keeps reminding me."

"This tunnel looks like it goes on forever," Garvish's complaint interrupted our pleasantries. "We could be walking for hours."

"Where does this tunnel lead?" Amaterasu asked the coven woman. "Does it end soon?"

"I do not believe so," she replied. "Up ahead, there is an opening leading out into the labyrinth. We should turn back to search down another tunnel."

"No," I replied, suddenly having a surge of instincts. I kept an eye on Collins, whose heart began to thump and even gave a tell by scratching his head when I continued my thought. "Elior is clever. Mahala's tomb is not in the records for being buried in the catacombs because she is not in the catacombs—she is in the labyrinth."

"How do you know that?" The coven woman demanded. "You cannot possibly know that."

"I bet there is a part of the labyrinth we can reach through this tunnel," I ignored her. "That is how she is so well hidden."

"You have a knack for puzzles," Collins could not help himself.

"I am not going into the labyrinth," the coven woman stated. "Lurkers are in there, and perhaps even worse things."

"You do not seem like one of the coven," Bikarma told her. "You do not act like one of them."

"All right," she confessed. "I am not really a coven member. My name is Barbra Brice. I was the librarian here until the 'emissary' showed up about three months ago. I wear this silly thing so they will not hurt me."

"What about you?" I asked Collins. "Why do not you wear a robe?"

"Never wanted to…besides…they do not have one in my size," he sarcastically replied. "The two of us have been down here, never knowing when they will continue feeding us."

Barbra proceeded to tell us of the strange occurrences that befell Drac. The emissary had brought the headmaster with him. The previous headmaster and several monks who did not comply with the headmaster were banished to the labyrinth. He gathered the most recent bodies brought to Drac, raised them into Lurkers, and set them free to hunt down the banished monks. He said that at least they were given a sporting chance. She promised to do all they required of her, including searching for the markings we were now seeking.

I quietly spoke with Amaterasu, coming to understand that about that time, she had visited with no one greeting her and could not find a soul in the city. When she received Lasair's summons, she realized the dilemma in Drac would have to wait. I figured for approximately a little less than two months, the monks were exposed to Cthulhu's hold through the emissary, coming to worship the creature, which meant Drac's monks were not of the Cthulhu cult, yet the emissary had come to revive it. The emissary said Drac would continue its intended purpose for Eastguard. However, I deduced the reason Drac was chosen—an endless supply of dead to become Lurkers, and Kalab sought to rebuild the worship and following of his snare.

"Lurkers have never stopped us before," I assured Barbra. "I believe Mahala's tomb is through this passageway, and it shall lead us to it."

I could feel my mind race back to the first time we ventured into the Unlight as I stepped through the opening in the tunnel. Yet the labyrinth was different. The passageway led us above ground, and we were now met by a misty fog that nipped the fingers and other exposed flesh. My hands remained warm, of course, but I could tell Collins, Garvish, and Bikarma were clenching and stretching their hands to keep their blood flowing—even silently blowing into their hands occasionally. Amara and Amaterasu did not appear to mind the briskness, and strangely neither did Barbra.

"Barbra," I said.

"Miss Brice, if you do not mind, dear. At heart, I am still a librarian and still hold to the principles of my profession."

"Very well," I reluctantly complied. "Miss Brice. What do you know of the labyrinth? Have you traveled through it before?"

"Through it, no," she answered. "I doubt anyone has ever successfully made it through. I saw the entrance once upon a time when I arrived years ago. But that is the extent of my knowledge."

I noticed the boys putting on gloves, even lending an extra pair to Collins. Miss Brice's hands remained uncovered. I was not the only one taking notice of her. Amara and Amaterasu sent me glances that communicated they knew something did not feel right with the woman. And as I pondered her words from before, the rhythm felt rehearsed to me.

We continued down the narrow corridor of the labyrinth, and I could barely see the stars in the sky above us. It gave me an idea, an escape plan—seeming like we would need one, feeling the makings of a trap closing around us. I reached into my pocket and activated my Magic Bean beacon to signal the Gullywhumper. When I felt Easton's thoughts, I echoed my message to him. The ship stayed above us, running silently and cloaked from sight. Gradually, we stepped out into a courtyard with a hefty spherical area with a towering copper statue depicting an ancient warrior slaying an enormous serpent with his bare hands. The statue stood precisely in the center.

The walls were covered in tangled vines that stretched out along the ground. I burned the vines from the walls while we searched for unique markings. There were none. We also noticed no other pathways leading out. The only way out remained where we had come from. I turned my attention to the statue once none of us found a single marking.

Admittedly, I became distracted by my suspicions of Miss Brice that I almost missed the clue. The eyes of the statue (the man) were not staring at the serpent. Instead, they were peering past it, toward a wall section on the courtyard's far side. Garvish and Bikarma followed me over, with Collins moving leisurely behind them. Amara and Amaterasu did not budge but kept their eyes on Miss Brice, who still loitered in front of the entrance.

"Be on your guard," I whispered to Garvish and Bikarma. "I do not trust Miss Brice. She is not what she appears to be."

"More than likely, she is a Necromean," Garvish whispered back.

"How do you know that?"

"She smells awful," he said. "A lot like the headmaster did. I got a whiff of him, so I did not sit near him. She holds a very similar stench."

I became more proud of Garvish's instincts, and I do not doubt that Bikarma held the same. They make a great team that perhaps loves the thrill of danger a little too much. I turned my attention toward the wall where the statue's eyes peered and ran my fingers along the rock surface, feeling a slight draft coming from the other side. I could even see a slight engraved marking that appeared like the hands of an SHC, pointing downward. I followed the wall to the ground, running my fingers through the dirt. I felt something metal wrapped around my finger—a necklace chain. I brought it up from the soil, along with a locket attached. I opened the rusty piece and saw an engraving.

Dusk in bone shall never be alone.

I knew not what it meant, but I felt I should speak the words allowed to the boys to see what they thought. When I did, there came a vast crack in the wall section. However, instead of crumbling, the wall faded into nothing, revealing a hidden chamber no taller than me.

I stepped inside but could see no sign of a corpse or bones. It scarcely looked like a tomb at all. The chamber held toys and baskets like a child's playroom, with a small wooden box on the top of a bookcase. I opened it to find two objects—a small notebook with a burned design on the front that held the appearance of Cthulhu. The other object I pulled out was a glowing viridescent oculus that, when I held it, whispered to my mind, "Ithir Agus Crainn," meaning "Soil and Trees." Then I heard the name spoken to me, "Uklallood." The whispers of its name became a melody, resounding like a lullaby, and pieced together repeatedly— "Uklallood. Ithir Agus Crainn."

"That artifact belongs to the emissary," I heard Miss Brice call out. "As promised, he has delivered the information you seek."

"Are you sure this is it?" I asked, stepping out of the chamber. I held up the oculus that began glowing even brighter. "It looks like just a shiny viridescent rock. Why does Kalab want it so badly?"

"The bargain was you keep the information, and the emissary gets the artifact," Miss Brice responded, her tone becoming firm.

"Are you not a prisoner here?" Amara remarked. "What is keeping us from keeping both?"

"He will not like it," Miss Brice focused on me, specifically my hand holding the oculus. "He must have what he seeks. It is the only way."

"You are a prisoner," I replied. "But you have accepted the bars that bind you. You are lost."

"How does it sit with you?" Bikarma pointed his buzzsaw rifle in the face of Collins.

"Did you think she was normal?" He asked. "Was it not apparent what she is? They are all the same! I have nothing to offer you to get me out of this alive. As I stand with you, they shall surely kill me now."

"Leave Mr. Collins alone," Amaterasu insisted. "Miss Brice, we are not above killing you. If you help us keep both, we can see you are handsomely rewarded for your troubles and remain alive to enjoy it."

"O' pretty girl," Miss Brice's voice suddenly became cackled and grim. "I would never go back to living when death has given me more than I could ever dream."

Miss Brice's robes fell from her body, exposing bare skin, covered in a dark cocoa muck, and pulsing out a sable gooey liquid from her pores. The lumps of fat that once were strewn over her belt raised up to portray hungry heads, even where her breasts would have been—their jaws agape and stretched unhinged, chomped at us like starving Suses. Her head leaned back ever so much as if the heads of her body had taken control. Her arms grew twice their length, as did her feet and legs, extending as a massive abomination in a collection of conjoined, bloodthirsty undead. She also became not the extent of our worries.

Lurkers growled and began climbing over the walls, which sent Bikarma and Garvish into a firing frenzy. Collins stayed close to the boys while Amara and Amaterasu fired on the abomination known as Miss Brice. The heads from her body stretched out in front, taking most of their sawblades, and to our shock, most of the blades did not sink into them. The skulls of the heads were like iron, resounding like metal on metal when hit. Amara shouted that we should aim for their necks, and we did so. I joined in firing at the Necromean, our sawblades cutting through the softer extended flesh, freeing the heads to fall. Yet, to our horror, another head popped out of the decapitations to take their place.

The abominable Miss Brice did not budge from the entrance to the courtyard. Her heads stretched outward like tentacles with enormous mouths snapping away at us. She would screech a blood-curdling cry every so often that awoke the Lurkers we had put down. We noticed that only the ones with their head still attached could rise again. So, Garvish and Bikarma doubled their efforts in slicing the heads off the Lurkers they dropped to keep them from reviving. The numbers of Lurkers were beginning to overwhelm us before Amaterasu desperately sent a shockwave into the wall furthest from Miss Brice. It shattered the rock face, and we all raced through the gap with Amaterasu laying down another shockwave that blasted the horde of Lurkers backward. I was the last through the gap, generating a flame cloud covering it as we escaped.

I did my best to send flames outward to keep Lurkers from hopping down on us from above. They were climbing the walls like insects, and the three of us MKRs did our best to keep them at bay. Garvish and Bikarma blasted our way through the Lurkers who landed in front of our position, and each taking turns taking point while the other reloaded. Yet I could sense ammunition was dwindling swiftly. Though I swiftly heard Easton's thoughts echo within my mind, I cried out to him to find us.

"Follow the flames," I desperately shouted.

It did not take long for the Gullywhumper to appear above us. I could hear Wild Willy calling to us, dropping several lines from above. There came the blood-curdling screech from Miss Brice, who leaped up and straddled the narrow pathways of the labyrinth we had run through, approaching promptly by hopping from one wall to another, using her extended heads to grip and push off to the next. While in midair, a cannonball slammed directly into her blubbery mass, exploding her into a mess of entrails. I could hear Meik's laughter coming from above. As they climbed the ropes, Garvish and Bikarma were already singing his praises. Collins clung to the back of Amaterasu as she climbed.

"You go first," Amara told me. "I do not need a rope."

I began hoisting myself up to reach the ship when I heard the Abominable Miss Brice scream again. I looked toward the entrails searching to find one another, slowly piecing themselves back together. Yet we had no time to waste trying to stick around and destroy her. Lurkers massed in the thousands at least, and knowing that Drac was lost, I cared more about reaching safety and studying the book we found.

Unfortunately, I have been doing just that for the past month after we returned to Havensire, leaving Drac to Kalab's control. Soon Amaterasu, Amara, and I will enter the Evergloom to free Elior from Cthulhu's grip. Hopefully, we find a way to destroy the creature, though its destruction is not my most significant concern.

I have taken the liberty to write down my findings from the little book we found in the labyrinth. From what I have gathered, in the way it was written, it appears to be an interview of sorts. The narrative describes a dialogue between two individuals. One is, perhaps, a student or a scholar looking for hidden knowledge of something they have stumbled upon. From what I can tell, the other is Elior, depicting his familiar features—eyes that change from gold, viridescent, and azure, along with his golden hair and heaven streaks in his beard.

The interviewer used strange words I had to research, words no longer in use to describe pigments—yellow meaning gold, green meaning viridescent, blue meaning azure, and white meaning heaven. These terms took almost an entire two weeks to decipher, but I have Havensire's library to thank for it. When I entered the massive collection of books in the new palace, a blanket of dust covered most of them, making me sure no one had entered the place for quite some time. The doors were heavily locked down, of course. It is a room full of books, after all. Any thief could walk away with practically billions of credits worth of artifacts. Indeed, I was tempted to sneak a couple out myself. But not even Bastian trusted me to be alone without the supervision of an armed guard. What an ally.

I thought of a name for the small book we recovered, as no title was on the cover—*The Evergloom King*. Some accommodating hints about the creature and its influence on the world are mentioned in the pages of its dialogue. It describes what is known as the Cthulhu Cult depicting some familiar embroidered shapes we encountered in Drac. Yes, the ones that were on the walls of the dining hall—Stusra, Olui, Pihojm, Eotaur, Brutaur, and Kelisk are all shadow entities that channel Cthulhu's power within the Evergloom, allowing the creature to reach out across the plain from the ethereal and into the physical realm, influencing the minds of those who receive its call. The shadow entities were mentioned as "clay reliefs" of the creature and are possibly located in the physical, ethereal, or the Evergloom itself.

The cult that the book mentioned continued to gain ground in many circles of power and influence throughout the course of history and obviously much longer before the Great Collide in accordance with the terms used for coloration. There is mention of another group, and I believe it is Elior, in the dialogue—an organization formed to oppose the Cthulhu Cult. *The Evergloom King* does not mention a name for the organization, but only their purpose in keeping Cthulhu from returning to the physical realm in its complete form. While focusing mainly on Cthulhu, Elior's dialogue touches on a man who remains in darkness and seeks to revive the creature fully. I can only assume he meant Kalab.

Events have unfolded beyond what I could ever fathom, so I have sent my writings to you, Nirnasha. By the time you read through my compiled thoughts of our ventures, Amara, Amaterasu, and I shall be well underway to meet with Lasair before entering the Evergloom. I wanted you to remain comforted in knowing all we have been through, and I shall never let go of your friendship or love. The curse of the gateway still weighs upon me, but it has not moved from my wrist. I hold firmly to hope I shall see you again, so I see that such things subdue this curse.

I have sent my writings to you, the book I mentioned, *The Evergloom King*, and the oculus. I believe it belongs to you. It must be the heart of your snare, your Leviathan. I believe Uklallood will be pleased to know it is in your possession.

You will also note that Wild Willy is the one who delivered these things to you. He did not ask permission to leave the Gullywhumper but told Meik of his intentions. For whatever reason, his heart has led him to this conclusion. It was surprising to all of us when he expressed to remain with you for as long as you are in service to Westmain. He has already signed on as your Skillhand Mate, as you are classified as a special interest operative. He would not take no for an answer and has the papers ready for you to sign. I hope you are well with my tidings. My love for you remains dearest to my heart. Keep well, and do not lose hope that we shall see one another again.

CESSATION

My name is Nirnasha Pericles. I am an MKR, more suitably known for wielding the power of Timber and Terra Firma. I wish to concur with the accuracy of the documentation, one known as Aagneya Nym, a fellow MKR who wields the power of Fire. She has written a historical manuscript that defines the occurrences of our explorations and the events that have befallen us from the time we graduated from Langdon University in Westmain. Though I may not be fully present as an eyewitness, I have no reason to doubt her words. I know her to be of noble character and a conscientious observationist—something I desire and strive to be moving forward. As this may seem like a cessation of her documentation, I would like to believe it is the commencement of another.

Her writings have convinced me it is necessary to continue recording the events that occur here, with myself, or any other events concerning the world as it is and MKRs. From the knowledge I have learned from *Gems of the Hidden Glade*, the mystical book given to us by Elior to train us in learning our abilities, I perceive the world as a turning point. Thus, I shall be adamant that MKRs be known for their sacrifice should there be anyone left to survive the coming shadows pressing in to invade this realm full of ignorant souls. I shall keep what Aagneya has sent me, near with me, at all times, as I am sure she is keeping our book of training safe and hidden away.

While I desire to fight alongside Aagneya, I know the reputation of MKRs must be upheld favorably. I remain obligated to my word and service to Westmain. I have accepted my responsibility and the presence of my now Skillhand Mate, Willy "Wild" Hancock. It is good to have a familiar face around despite how grueling it is to see him walk through the door with a new woman practically every night. Still, the walls are thick in Aagneya's residence. So, I shall say she made a solid investment.

My appetites lie elsewhere. It is an obsession. The viridescent oculus continues to glow, yet I do not hear the melody of my snare nor feel any power surge within. I believed that something extravagant would occur once I held it in my hands. Also, I have been waiting for my first assignment for over four months and have heard nothing from the Westmain government. I was exceptionally bored until Wild Willy appeared on my doorstep and presented me with what Aagneya sent me.

Uklallood has evaded my presence in the ethereal. Even though I call out to her, Lasair remains locked tight in her fortress. I know she can hear me, but I suppose this is a riddle I must solve on my own. The oculus travels with me to the ethereal but ceases to glow there. Returning to the physical realm the following day, it is glowing again. It makes me entertain the speculation that Uklallood is somewhere tangible—perhaps some type of power transported it here. I have always known that Uklallood is a tree that loves to hide, and I do not doubt it could hide in the physical plain and the ethereal. I remain significantly intrigued as I have dreamt of the tree most of my life, but it is only now that I have come to know its name.

But I could no longer stand it, pondering where to find my snare. I felt like my suspicion had to be correct. I requested an explorer mission to scout out a region of the Deadlands for signs of a new Mystic Silver deposit. I claimed that sometimes I could sense Mystic Silver under the ground, and sometimes it happened randomly, almost like a beacon guiding me to the metal. I claimed I was right the first time it happened and asked permission to see if I would be correct again. The Westmain agency was about to refuse before I reminded them that I had not received an assignment yet, and what good is an MKR just sitting around doing nothing when I could possibly gain the government some income? After a short deliberation, they allowed me to go on my mission, giving me a small squad of soldiers to help harvest the deposit should anything be found. There was one catch, a captain assigned to accompany us as a superintendent over me.

In a few days, we set out into the Deadlands, which struck me with a familiarity of my first travels with Aagneya and many others who never made it back. I wanted to ensure our party returned safely home, even if my suspicions about Ukallood went unconfirmed. I did not wholly prevaricate what I had said. I had a feeling in my gut, but unsure what it entailed—not a melody, but an actual instinct as I can only depict, thumping inside my intestines. At the same time, I also have a sensation that feels a bit like being intoxicated. And in the first few moments we set out, I could sense the oculus pulse as I held my hand around it in the outer pocket of my fit and flare frock. With each step I took, the sensation would grow stronger or weaker. The stronger rhythms let me know I moved in the right direction. I began thinking that Ukallood was playing a child's game with me.

A few hours passed, and we came to a small crevasse beneath a cliff. Next to it were several clumps of trees; one, in particular, I could sense was not a Dendro of the ordinary kind. The soldiers spotted an azure glow from the rockface and began to dart for it noisily. I had never seen Mystic Silver above the surface before.

"Why does your gaze not leave those trees?" The captain asked me.

"I do not believe they are just that," I answered. "Keep your men silent. We do not need to disturb sleeping Dendro."

The captain immediately hurried to his men, who he ordered to, in his words, "Shut your bloody mouths." A very undistinguished professional phrase, but it worked, nonetheless.

Wild Willy remained where he stood. I could feel him watching me as I made my way into the clump of trees. Surrounding one large, lusciously viridescent tree blooming with golden blossoms I knew had to be Ukallood. I looked back at the soldiers, who were still busy harvesting the Mystic Silver. It was not much, but it would take them at least an hour.

"I have something that belongs to you, friend," I told the tree. A small opening in the trunk appeared, and I placed the viridescent oculus within the opening. Something like an earthquake shook me to the ground. I peered up at where the tree once stood, now gone as if it had never existed. A surge of new melodies began to echo within me as I found my footing again.

"What are you doing over there?!" I heard the captain call to me.

"I had to relieve myself," I answered him when I stepped away from the clump of trees. "Are special operatives not allowed to do so? I enjoy a bit of privacy if you do not mind."

"You said those trees are Dendro," the captain said.

"They are," I replied. "Dendro like me, though—not you."

"In other words, do not pull your pecker out in front of them," Wild Willy teased. "You might lose it."

The captain gulped, and I had no reason to hold my laughter. At that point, I knew I would like to have Wild Willy along.

We returned to Langdon before nightfall and without incident. Upon my return, a messenger met me at the Dwelling Gates with orders from my superiors—finally, my first assignment. I was returning to Starvel. The message explained that I would receive further details upon my arrival. And I needed to depart immediately.

Stepping aboard an airship other than the Gullywhumper felt foreign to me, but I found it had other perks. Special operatives and anyone accompanying them were given lounge privileges with the officers. I continued reading Aagneya's documentation in our private room to help me recall our time together, solidifying memories of her in my mind. I read through the dialogue book she sent me, *The Evergloom King*, doing my best to familiarize myself with Cthulhu and its cult. She had summarized much of it to me already at the end of her writings, but I noticed more than her summary detailed.

The Cthulhu Cult is a plague upon the world, perhaps even going back thousands and thousands of years. With each new era came a new uprising, one pupil who would stand out from all the rest, even if they did not know the creature was pulling their strings. The cult took on many different names throughout history, many times without its members even realizing their call to revive it. I thought about my home kingdom, Nod, where much evil is justified to wage war against one another—north against south and south against the north. None are innocent in the bloodshed. While the kingdom's civil war remains deadlocked, neither side wishes to bring a truce. Soon, I would learn that Westmain is no different.

My mission in Starvel commissioned me to assist in the defense against the southern rebels, and suddenly I realized the only reason the government allowed Tailors to expand their dye styles was to receive a cut of the profits to continue paying for the stalemate. Southern rebels would commit small-scale attacks but soon dissipate into the immense trenches they dug outside Starvel. Wairships previously dropped EDOs from above but were having no success breaking through the deep-ground bunkers. They had forced the North to fight them on the ground. More so, Triune to the west had seceded from the north, now battling against forces out of Nium, who suffered such losses in the first onslaught, they required reinforcements from the city of Solice, a city far to the north of Westmain.

When I first set foot in Starvel with Aagneya and Elior, the city still had many buildings standing after the Eastguard wairships attacked. Now, all the walls were reduced to rubble, and the entire city lay in ruins. None of the populace remained, learning they were all relocated to Nium or Prag.

Westmain's northern army had reinforced their position with whatever they could, spreading their forces with superior firepower. Yet somehow, they appeared to be struggling, even losing the war. The rebels had gained hundreds of once-renowned Westmain soldier units turned rogue against them. These rogue units were highly capable snipers known as 'Mark Eyes.' I had to educate myself on military units, as I have never been enlisted. Military Infantry units are hardened and trained rigorously for combat. What many commanders may think of as a lack of intellect, an infantry soldier makes up for in sheer brawn. They are highly trained in firing buzzsaw rifles and are trained vigorously in close-quarter combat. Some military infantry become so good in their marksmanship when firing the buzzsaw rifle they are promoted to 'Mark Ranger(s)' and, better still, 'Mark Eye(s).'

Those who reach Mark Eye status are given a specified buzzsaw rifle with a long-range scope, a slightly larger air tank, and often a partner called a 'Spot Shot.' Spot Shots can be any infantry soldier of the Mark Eye's choosing should they not already be Mark Ranger. Mark Rangers are usually spread out into a variety of infantry platoons. In Aagneya's writings, she mentioned Garvish carried a new type of sniper weapon, which I am sure Westmain would love to get their hands on. But I am not about to give up that wonderful secret.

Westmain's defense in Starvel mainly consisted of 'Gunners' who were trained specifically for buzzsaw firing guns and wairship cannons. Seasoned Gunners can be recognized by the steam burns on their faces, hands, and arms. Most Gunners appear mountainous or sleekly defined in their muscle tone. Hearsay suggests that a seasoned Gunner's grip can pinch a pipe shut. Not only are they strong and hardened for heavy weapon combat, but they are well versed in mechanical repair. A Gunner must know how to fix any issues associated with the weapons they steward and fire, making them invaluable in combat and supporting infantry with cannon and sawblade fire barrages. However, like everyone else, Gunners do not see a sniper's sawblade.

Then there are the 'Engineers' who are also highly valued, especially aboard wairships. The maze of pipes below the deck of a wairship can be astounding and complicated. Each Engineer must memorize the blueprint layout of the pipes for their particular wairship before they may join the crew. Even a seasoned veteran Engineer who is transferring to a new wairship must memorize the layout of their new assignment before they can go aboard during a flight. Should an Engineer be assigned to a ground defense, they are put in charge of rebuilding and refortifying defenses. And the poor sods were the biggest target for sniper fire in Starvel.

I learned from the operations commander that he refused to try and repair buildings. They were using whatever they could to quickly refortify their positions and keep the Engineers covered, manning the materials and supplies received from Harvenger. I inquired about the rebels' position to the east. The commander assured me the mountains leading to Harvenger were untravellable, and Nium wairship patrols now cut off the rebel forces in Triune. If the rebels wanted to move into the north, they would need to push through Starvel, which also happened to be a significant resource for water sanitation exports. Thus, it became clear that I was brought in for one purpose—to rip the rebels from the ground.

Wild Willy and I were assigned the finest sleeping quarters they could provide. I sincerely say this yet stress the travesty—a dug-out room full of rubble, no doubt once a comfortable residence. The rain that poured down that night dripped through the middle and ran out the large opening that once held a door. Both of us had chosen a corner to huddle in for the night. I ensured Wild Willy had the driest place, knowing he needed sleep. My mind held too many thoughts of Aagneya, wishing she was sleeping beside me.

A few hours passed, and the company commander arrived to meet me, a cheeky Westmainian oval eye cocoa veil reaching a bit above my frame. From the beginning of our encounter, he made it clear that he was not fond of special operatives, but he expected us to do our duty quickly and then depart for our next assignment.

"I believe you are not informed," I replied. "My assignment is to see an end to the rebellion."

"What? Are you supposed to be some sort of secret weapon?" he scoffed.

"Something like that," I grinned.

The rain had not let up when morning came, and the skies remained darker than my sable skin. A heavy fog rolled in and became trapped within the valley below Starvel, which allowed the rebels to move without being seen. But I could feel their vibrations. I did not have the heart to tell Wild Willy how many were there, as they outnumbered us immensely.

I spoke with the relieved guard watch stationed in a burned-out tavern behind Starvel's rubble walls. About ten soldiers were resting when we entered. I approached two guards who clarified that the fog appeared regularly in the early morning and dissipated by midday.

"Once the fog rolls away, you should be able to see the remains of their Steam Tech," one guard told me.

"I was here a while back," I said. "I remember it to be somewhat clunky but still bothersome."

"Bothersome does not begin to define how things are now. That was before Keepers joined them," another said. "I have been stationed here for more than a decade. When the rebels began, we could wait them out, starve them even—Starvel stood as an impenetrable position for them. But now, I know they have Keepers."

"How do you know?"

"They have got new machines—some I have never seen before, built specifically for the purpose of tearing down walls. Much of the populace was caught in the onslaught in their last run. That is why we moved them out."

"We were able to push them back," said the first guard. "Only after they launched EDOs on our walls and laid waste to the city."

"Are there any Keepers assisting our forces?"

"Just Liam Slopes and Rori Plainspark. Both have their hands full assisting the Engineers, repairing cannons, and buzzsaw firing guns. They have no time to enchant better Steam Tech."

"Where are they?" I insisted.

"Just up the road at the mechanics' shop."

"More like a scrapyard," interjected another guard, making them all chuckle.

Wild Willy followed me as we made our way up the road. Soldiers were strewn about, with the dead slowly being picked up by medic teams while the others appeared as if they wished they were. The morale of the Westmain forces certainly needed a boost, and the first idea that came to mind was recovering the enemy's Steam Tech remains to learn about the Keepers in their command.

"You look as if you are planning something," Wild Willy said, his mouth chewing away at his Pumca, a mixture of mentha, cannabis, and malus pumila juices. Its uses come in handy to calm the nerves and are often chewed by soldiers who have 'war jolts.'

I heard much about being a soldier from Wild Willy in Langdon when he did not entertain a female companion. Though rare, he did not go out fraternizing some nights, and when he did not, we usually held good conversations in front of the fireplace. He explained that war jolts can vary between involuntary muscle spasms and sudden visions of experienced trauma. Many soldiers who have seen war can hold a high level of anxiety that can also trigger relentless night terrors.

"You go to war," he said one night, already moving into a drunken stupor. "Once you do, you can never truly leave it. It always follows you."

I can attest to his words. I certainly remembered everything I went through with Aagneya, Elior, and everyone else. We faced many horrors together. But I never experienced war jolts. I studied Musculoskeletal Therapies & Botany Biology at Langdon, which included being educated on how the physiology of flora can affect nerves in the body. Perhaps being a MKR kills that part of one's nervous system. I sometimes feel like witnessing dreadful and traumatic things is my second nature. Or is it more so that I have experienced death already and am not afraid to greet it again?

What also amazes me about being an MKR, besides the magic pulsing through my veins, is an MKR's ability to remember. I can still recall and visualize conversations as if they are performed right in front of me. I noticed this, too, in Aagneya's writings. Though she addressed her ability to remember conversations before she became an MKR, I highly doubt it did not cross her mind that such an ability became heightened. If she did not notice, I must be the only one who did. And I guess this ability is somewhat like war jolts, apart from the symptoms.

I would have to explore such thoughts later as we reached the mechanic shop where I was met by Liam Slopes, a young Westmainian sphere eye creme veil with dark cocoa eyes and straight sable hair pulled back behind his head into a messy bun. He appeared athletically built, with a chiseled jaw and an unwelcoming expression. I introduced myself as a special operative, which made him soften his scowl, and he called for Rori to join us. She held some unique features for a Westmainian sphere eye sable face. For one, her curly hair held a golden hue with a hint of royal crimson, and her eyes were bright azure. The other was that she had a metal appendage from her left elbow to her hand. She did not greet me with the scowl Liam had but remained surprisingly cheerful.

My Mystic Silver arm stayed hidden under my fit and flare frock sleeve, covered with a mystic midnight glove. I have learned not to shake with my right hand and extended my left instead to greet them. It is not that I am ashamed of what Elior replaced, nor am I ungrateful that he saved me. But there are three things my right arm now does that it did not do before. One, it is much stronger than my flesh arm. Two, it draws too much attention when it is uncovered. And three, it keeps me wondering how Elior enchanted it—as he had also taught Easton to create the Gullywhumper in all its glory. I genuinely desire to know how to enchant for myself, and I felt I could learn if I paid close attention.

"What can we do for a special operative?" Rori asked.

"I have a plan," I looked at Wild Willy with a slight grin. "First, I should tell you why I am here. My name is Nirnasha Pericles, and this is my Skillhand Mate, Wild Willy. Our first task is to recover Steam Tech wreckage from the enemy. I would like to know how skilled their Keepers are."

"Just how will we do that," Liam scoffed. "Want us to bring a team to pick up the pieces only for them all to be shot down by sniper fire?"

"I want you both to meet me up there at midday," I pointed to the northern watchtower that remained the only thing still standing, located toward the inner city and appeared to have a good view of the valley. "From there, the both of you will tell me which pieces you want me to recover for examination. That is all I ask of you."

They appeared baffled at my words but agreed not to be late. I began making my way to the watchtower with Wild Willy. We climbed the tall ladder, greeted by two guards standing watch. There could have been room for at least ten more of us, much more spacious than the quarters where we stayed, holding a seating area with a small table. Each guard took turns with spy spectacles to closely watch possible enemy movements. I relayed to them I was a special operative wanting to get an idea of the landscape, and the soldiers at the tavern told me the fog would clear up by midday.

"I can point out a few markers if you like once the fog fades," one offered.

"I would appreciate it," I replied. "The two Keepers you have here will also join us around that time. I would like them to answer some questions as we overlook the battlements."

"Very good, sir," both guards answered.

It was the first time I was addressed with such respect, and I turned my gaze to Wild Willy. He held a large grin on his face.

"Feels good to be thought of so highly, does it not?" he teased. "You think you are becoming a soldier now?"

"Not sure I have much of a choice," I admitted. "Until I fulfill my obligations to Westmain, I believe that is what they want me to be."

"Well then, be the kind of soldier you want to be, not what they want," Wild Willy patted my shoulder and sat across from me.

I knew he was right. Despite my obligations, I refused to become someone I did not respect. I did not become an MKR to receive renown or be ogled, although it seemed a little hypocritical that Wild Willy loved both. I said yes to Elior because I wanted my life to hold a higher meaning. I took the risk of becoming an MKR to know how to make the world better and, in some regard, put an end to useless conflicts. I was orphaned because of such things. My parents were lost just before I attended my first year at Langdon. I lost not only my parents but also my sister and brother. I have only told Aagneya this, but now it feels good just to write it down and say the words aloud.

I may be orphaned, but I am not alone.

Midday approached, and I heard footsteps climbing up the ladder. The two Keepers had kept their word and made it on time. I stood up, seeing the fog had almost faded. I took an extra pair of the guard's spy spectacles. I told Liam and Rori to choose three destroyed Steam Tech machines each, laying out in the valley, that they wished to inspect, something they thought would help us understand the abilities of the enemy's Keepers. Liam went first. Rori went second. I made a note, as did Wild Willy, of the pieces they had chosen. Before long, I heard more footsteps climbing up the ladder. It was the commander I had met that morning.

"What are you doing taking my Keepers away from their work?!" He demanded.

Wild Willy had placed his body intimidatingly between the commander and me. I paid no heed. I remained concentrated on the six pieces lying out in the open sun. I removed my fit and flare frock, which exposed my Mystic Silver arm. Everyone went silent, including the commander. I handed my fit and flare frock to one of the guards and proceeded to remove my gloves, not that I had to—I simply wanted quiet.

I reached out my hands to the pieces in the valley, and the soil beneath the wrecked machines lifted them in the forms of hands, wrapping tightly around them, and traveled quite swiftly to Westmain's position. The soil carried the machines back to the mechanic's shop, a spell that drained less than ten minutes of my time. I could still hear the melody of the soil well after, a soothing and revitalizing sound, a comfort I stood stronger now that Ukallood's heart was back where it belonged. As the melody concluded, I could hear it beat again, as if the Dusk Tree finally remembered to thank me.

The guard holding my fit and flare frock held it open for me when I turned to him. His eyes were still widespread, and I politely thanked him for his service.

"You are no longer in command," I glared into the commander's eyes as I put my gloves on. His pupils were agape, his jaw the same, like the others. "I am Nirnasha Pericles, MKR of Timber & Terra Firma, Special Operative to the Westmain High Counsel. This command belongs to me now, and you shall follow my orders from now on."

The ground came up to meet my feet as I stepped beyond the watchtower ladder, a firm pillar beneath me, and it held me up as Wild Willy joined me.

"Shall we go see what we have brought back?" I asked Liam and Rori, feeling a slight, cheeky grin arise. Both dubiously stepped out onto the pillar of soil. We slowly reached the bottom of the watchtower and marched off to the mechanics' shop. I could hear Wild Willy's chuckle increase as we stepped farther away.

SHOW YOUR SUPPORT FOR
SELF-PUBLISHING AUTHORS

Enjoying Secrets of Silver and Steam? Support this and more self-published works from this author by visiting Amazon.com, PublishersBrew.com/rhayes and click "leave a book review," or your favorite digital book platform where this volume is sold.

ACKNOWLEDGMENTS

A special thanks first and foremost to my Abba in heaven for giving me the creative mind and the inspiration to share this work. He is the light of my life and my greatest treasure. I acknowledge his sovereignty and His goodness, and give Him many thanks for my family, both through blood and through spirit.

I thank my mom for pushing me to be better at storytelling. I thank my dad for his support in the days of hardship we shared. I want to thank my brother who continues to be a monumental help in bringing my craft to life and has shared many days of hardship as we have laid loved ones to rest.

My heart goes out to the love of my life, my beautiful bride, Jennifer. Thank you for your support and keeping my confidence grounded. I thank Abba for you every day that you were created, and that you continue to cheer me on. Forever and always, I love you.

To my little girl, Avaleigh, you are precious to me. I also dedicate this work to you. May you enjoy each word and moment of the stories your daddy writes. And always remember how much I love you, and how grateful I am to your mom that she gifted you here to be with us.

I would also like to thank my mother-in-law, Wynne Eslick, who helped spark the inspiration for beginning this series as we casually conversed about Steampunk.

Finally, I would like to thank you reader, for supporting me and self-published authors like me who desire to craft stories from the heart of their imagination, and not for corporations just to turn a profit. Your support is worth more than you'll ever know, and it gives writers and artists like me the ability to pursue our passions in world building.

ABOUT THE AUTHOR

Born and raised in Chico, California, Ricky Hayes holds degrees in Journalism and Graphic Design, and has worked on the creative side of Web Development and Marketing for well over a decade. He is an award-winning poet and has branched out into self-publishing for numerous years, even before Amazon bought Create Space. He is the owner of Publisher's Brew, an aspiring author alliance established in 2022 for self-publishing authors but also maintains his passion for designing beautiful websites for clients.

In January of 2009, Ricky's mom passed away from ALS, which he believes marked his life to begin pursuing writing more passionately, as she remained his greatest encouragement until leaving this world behind.

Some of Ricky's favorite authors are Jules Verne, R. A. Salvatore, J.R.R. Tolkien, C.S. Lewis, Kenneth Grahame, and Paul Zindel.